FAMILY OF FEAR

In a small-town Vermont jail, young Todd Horgan helplessly paced his cell, accused of a rape and murder that only he knew he had not done.

In a Cape Cod cottage, his father, Andrew Horgan, learned the news, and flew to Vermont to find the son he had never known, the courage he had lost, and the love he thought he would never feel again.

In a New York penthouse, actress Julia Craven heard of Todd's trouble, and vowed to win her son's release, whatever the cost in money or cunning seduction.

In the next thirty-six hours, the dark side of human behavior would show itself in a peaceful Vermont town turned into a carnival of crime . . . a jail cell would become a chamber of horrors . . . and a family would fight the most desperate odds against greed, terror and rapacious evil. . . .

THE WAYS OF DARKNESS

"Intense suspense combined with keen perception of human nature . . . by the masterful author of *The Desperate Hours*."
—novelist Erskine Caldwell

"Riveting . . . Joseph Hayes makes it work!"
—*Indianapolis News*

D0907630

THE WAYS OF
DARKNESS

Joseph Hayes

AN ONYX BOOK

NEW AMERICAN LIBRARY

Copyright © 1985 by Joseph Hayes

Onyx is a trademark of New American Library

SIGNET, SIGNET CLASSIC, MENTOR, ONYX, PLUME, MERIDIAN
and NAL BOOKS are published by New American Library,
1633 Broadway, New York, New York 10019

First Onyx Printing, January, 1987

1 2 3 4 5 6 7 8 9

PRINTED IN THE UNITED STATES OF AMERICA

For Marrijane as always,
Wife, lover, comrade,
With love and gratitude

My task, which I am trying to achieve, is, by the power of the written word, to make you hear, make you feel—it is, before all, to make you see.

—JOSEPH CONRAD

AUTHOR'S NOTE

The individual characters who appear in this book are wholly fictional. No character bears any resemblance to any person, alive or dead, whom I have ever known. Any apparent resemblance of a character to any person alive or dead is entirely coincidental.

But the town of Shepperton exists—all over America. And so do its citizens, in other guises, with other accents, other names. There is a war going on, and whether they know it or not, they are its victims.

As we are.

THE INCIDENT

"Thunder?" He was not quite awake. "Thunder?"

"Yes, thunder. I heard it. Listen!"

Waking up completely now, the boy turned over in his sleeping bag and held his breath. He heard nothing. Only the deep primeval silence of the forest—which he loved more than any music he'd ever heard. "Not a cloud," he said. Plenty of stars, though. And a sliver of moon, very high, very distant, and incredibly beautiful tonight. A shudder of elation went through his body. "It's Indian summer—God wouldn't dare let the acid rain fall. You think He wants to get Himself impeached?" But his voice, and the words, were from another world, the one they'd left behind.

"Well," the girl said, "I do know thunder when I hear it. What else *could* it be? Oh, Todd, I'm freezing. It doesn't feel like Indian summer *here*." And when Todd laughed: "And if you don't believe in Him, what's God got to do with it?"

Whenever he was with her, he felt a strange exultancy, mind and body—something new, very fresh and strange to Todd Horgan.

"I never discuss theology on a camping trip. If you're freezing, all you have to do is invite company." And then he waited.

"Oh, Todd—again?" She laughed her childlike laugh, delighted yet hesitant. "Not so soon, please."

No underbrush in the clearing, and damn little on the ground, mostly sweet-fern. The trunks of the tall pines were very straight, very black. And through the open ceiling he

11

could see the moon-sliver. End of summer. Next week, probably one of those sudden Vermont snowfalls. Seven weeks into the new school year. New beginning. Because of her. The unfamiliarity and intensity of his emotions amazed him, as if he were on the brink of some incredible discovery.

Lynnette laughed. "After all that hiking?" she said.

"Does that mean yes?"

"Don't freeze them off on the way over."

Laughing too now, he unzipped his sleeping bag and stood up, the mountain air sharp and cold against his naked body, taking his breath, and then he took several strides past the campfire, joy pulsing, and he was with her again, her body scalding hot against his in her sleeping bag. Her breath was warm and fresh, fragrant as the pines, black eyes glittering with both anticipation and apprehension, as if she feared being hurt. They made love again, slowly and tenderly.

In the dim light he could see her head twisting from side to side, long black hair splaying across the whiteness of her face, and then—an aeon or two later—he heard the familiar whisper: "No . . . no . . . no . . . oh no . . ."

Afterward, as they lay close, he recalled the first time, only four weeks ago: *I guess I say no that way because I still think it's wrong.* Whispering, he asked: "Now do you see why I wanted to come here before winter? They close that road we took once the snow starts." He was staring upward. "The goddam world's another planet up there somewhere in the sky."

"Is it? Is it, Todd? I wish you were right."

And there it was again: that odd, plaintive note of sadness, hinting at something dark and secret that she would not, or could not, speak of—shadowing her mind, threatening. On campus she always appeared very self-confident—and poised and cheerful. Whenever he attempted to probe, he only stirred her quick Gallic temper. In the two months he'd known her he had learned that his asking questions caused some nameless pain, so he had stopped. Fine, plenty of time. He moved his body against hers, always astounded at the softness, the beauty. And said: "There's room in here for both of us—or do I have to freeze them off again?"

But feeling her body stiffen against his, he knew. *Separate sleeping bags,* she had said when she'd agreed to come. *I'm willing to cut classes on Monday if it's that important to you, but I won't sleep with you, that's all.* And her reason? *Because I've never slept with a man before.* Well, so be it. It made no sense. But it deepened the mystery: She was unlike any girl he'd known.

He'd wanted to laugh but he hadn't wanted to blow the whole thing, so he'd said he would borrow a sleeping bag from someone. And, because she'd hinted that she was afraid of bears, he'd brought his .357 Magnum which he usually took along only when camping in Canada or Alaska. But three hours ago, seeing it as they unpacked the trunk of his little Fiat X19, she had stepped back, eyes black and bright with terror: *No guns. No guns, Todd. I hate guns!* Astonished again, he had hidden the revolver in its holster under the seat of the car, which was now stashed off the gravel road about a mile due west, if he could trust his compass.

Remembering now the stricken expression on her face, he felt that familiar, overwhelming tenderness return: She was so damned frail, inside, as if anticipating hurt, flinching from some pain. What? Why? He kissed her on the forehead—oh, God, is this what love is?—and whispered: "I'll freeze 'em off again."

"I'm still cold," she said.

So he took time to build up the fire. It wasn't the most ideal campsite in the forest, this shelf of grass on a cliff top overlooking a ravine, with giant pines walling it on three sides.

The fourth side was open—Lynnette had cried, *It's beautiful! It's like being on a stage!*—and beyond an open space, the forest continued. In the dark he had not been able to see what lay at the foot of the cliff, but by flashing the torch down and over the area, he had spotted thick underbrush and what appeared to be ferns reaching the bottom edge of the cliff. Probably a stream, water of some sort anyway.

Wishing he'd chopped more wood earlier, he returned to his sleeping bag. *Joy*—that was the word. He'd never really known joy before. Should he have two or three more tokes before he tried to sleep? They'd shared two joints earlier while he charred the steaks. No wine, though, no alcohol of any sort. Another of Lynnette's contradictions: pot but no booze. Sex but no sleeping together. *Alcohol does terrible things to people—terrible.* And while they ate, he'd learned another fact that startled him: In Maine, where she lived, her family had never had a cookout or been on a picnic. It was about all he knew of her family, except that her parents were French-Canadians. *Canucks,* she had once said, *ignorant Canucks, and Catholic. I don't know what I am. Sometimes I don't really think there is a God, do you? If there was, He'd make sure people were punished for what they do, wouldn't He?*

He decided against any more weed, slid down into his bag, and zipped it up. Then he looked across at Lynnette. In the light of the low flaring flames, only her head was visible, black hair glistening, eyes closed, her lovely face in repose. An enigma. Bewildering. Was he imagining that she could love him? Neither of them had used the word.

It was too big a word. Did anyone ever love anyone else? Hell, he didn't even know what the goddam word meant. From what he'd seen, it was just one of the thousands of weird lies that people told themselves and each other in order to get from day to day, year to year.

There was no way for the fire to spread—he'd cleared the area of cones and needles—but he decided not to go to sleep till it had died down. The wilderness was being destroyed and poisoned and desecrated all over the country. And now the government itself was on the attack to destroy it—in the name of progress and, of course, profit. Greed.

All, all of a piece throughout . . . chase had a beast in view . . . wars brought nothing about . . . lovers were all untrue . . . 'tis well an old age is out . . . time to begin a new. . . . Always, it was always time to begin a new—but it never happened.

He felt himself drifting into sleep. The world would never change. He'd known that for years. But now he'd discovered that *he* could change . . . was changing . . . had changed.

He had no idea how long he had been sleeping when a sound wakened him.

What?

Voices. Voices whispering.

With enormous effort, nerves tightening, stomach going hollow, he stopped breathing. Was he still asleep? Dreaming? He forced himself not to open his eyes.

"Ve got orders—"

"Yeah, but—"

"Orders not to even *talk* to anybody—"

14

"Yeh, but look, look at her. D'ya think she's naked in there?"

"I shoulda known that's vhat vas on your mind."

Todd opened his eyes a slit. His whole body had gone rigid and cold. Over the floor of bare ground, faintly lighted by the glowing coals of the dying fire, he saw two pairs of boots. Knee-high, laced—hunting boots.

"Let's just see if she's naked."

Todd's eyes found the hatchet: red handle at an angle, blade exposed, its edge buried in a limb of dead pine.

But he could not move.

"Ralph?"

"I told you when ve come in the park—this ain't only a yob ve could lose." This one spoke in a low voice with a foreign accent—what kind? "Ve shoulda done our job like normal."

"We got it done." This voice was high-pitched, almost a squeak, and uncertain—no accent, just a dull flatness of a dim mind, slightly wheedling. "We delivered."

Still, Todd could not move, not only because he didn't know what to do but because his body had gone limp and weak.

"I'm varning you, Jesse," the accented voice said, "this could be trouble. Real trouble."

Was Lynnette awake? Was she listening?

Don't move, Lynne, don't move, please, please don't move—

"Jist a friendly visit," the other said, and one pair of boots moved, crunching, coming toward him. "Hey you—kid. Time t' rise 'n' shine. Y' got company."

The boots were planted less than a foot from his eyes. He found strength enough to stir. He rubbed his eyes as if coming awake. "Who're you?" he heard his voice ask. He unzipped the sleeping bag part of the way and sat up. The cold air struck his bare chest, rushed into his dry mouth. Totally alert now, he frowned up at the man and feigned drowsiness. "Hi. What do you want?"

The man was not tall, but he was huge: red-bearded, eyes squinting, face a mask of jovial excitement. He wore khaki pants and a camouflage hunting jacket and a billed red-flannel cap. "Jist a friendly visit. We seen your fire."

The other man took several steps from the far side of the

fire. This one was extremely tall, lean, broad-shouldered. He also wore hunting clothes, no cap. He seemed younger and he had a shock of pale hair, so blond that it looked almost white in the dimness. "Ve don't mean any harm, kid," he said. Was the accent German? Swedish?

"Hell no," the heavy man said, "jist a friendly visit—seein' we're the only ones out here in these woods."

"Well," Todd said, every nerve leaping now, wishing Lynne had allowed him to bring the .357 Magnum from the car, "well, it's a little late for a cocktail party, isn't it?"

"Flip on that flashlight, Ralph," the enormous bearded man said. "Le's see what kinda smartass we got here."

It was no flashlight. It was a powerful square searchlight that fixed Todd in its blinding beam and illuminated the whole area. "We're hunters," the tall younger one, Ralph, said from behind the glare. "Got a camp way over there by the lake. Run out of booze."

"Sorry," Todd's voice said, carefully casual, "no booze." Where had he put his hunting knife? "Sorry."

"Haul yer ass outa there, boy."

He had to decide. If either one moved toward Lynne's sleeping bag, he had somehow to be between, but how? *How?* He was helpless enough without having to stand up and face the two of them naked. Reaching for his jeans with one hand, he unzipped the bag all the way with the other and stood up.

The big man laughed. For such a heavy man—a solid block of beef who had to weigh three hundred pounds, maybe more—he had a peculiar high-pitched laugh that, more than the thin frigid air, sent a shiver down Todd's flesh. He pulled on the jeans. Jesse—if the other one was Ralph, this burly massive one was named Jesse—spoke. "Lookit tha, willya?" He took two strides toward Lynne's sleeping bag. "Hey, missie. Look what a puny prick sonny's got. Y'wanna see a real bong?"

Lynnette was awake. She was still lying on her side, only her head visible. Her dark eyes were fixed on Jesse—and they were shimmering with terror.

"Y'agree missie? Got a little-boy cock, don't he?"

Todd moved. He stepped around the huge solid hulk and stood above Lynnette. (Jesus, Lynne, it's my fault. I got you into this!) "We got any grass left?" He turned to face the dazzling light, ignoring Jesse, and lifted his voice slightly, hoping it would not quiver or break into a falsetto: "Ralph, if we give you what pot we've got, will you split?"

"How come you know my name?" the accented voice asked. "You *are* a smartass, ain't you?"

"Like hell!" Jesse's voice squeaked. "No deal. We didn't come up here for no dope."

No one spoke. No one moved.

Trying to think, Todd allowed the silence to stretch itself out.

"Your turn, missie," Jesse said. "You naked in there too?"

"Stay where you are, Lynne." Then into the light: "Well? It's a deal then. You take the grass. I forget your names."

"You don't give orders, sonny. You're too young and too little t' give orders to grown *men*. Ain't that so, Ralph?"

But Jesse was ignored. Todd, his whole body taut, blood scorching, guts twisting, forced himself not to speak.

Finally, the voice behind the light said, "It's a deal, kid."

Jesse erupted. "Like hell, like shit, like fuck it is!" His tone was a high shrill screech. "Screw the grass. We gonna have some of what you been havin', smartass. Missie, you climb up outa there. *Now.*"

Another pause—but shorter this time because Todd had reached a decision. It was a risky gamble: He could predict Jesse, but what about Ralph? Once *he* saw Lynnette—

"Okay, Lynne." He took three steps toward her. "Stand up."

A large bird flew over. Hawk or buzzard—in search of carrion? In the silence they could hear the flapping of its wings. He took advantage of the sound to turn around to face the two men.

"Todd—" Lynnette said.

"Get out and stand up," Todd said, his voice hard. Would she do as he told her? Trapped in that bag she'd be totally vulnerable.

His eyes were on Jesse. The big face was agape, his mouth a dark cave in the shaggy red beard. His eyes were intent—wide and glittering. Todd heard the sound of the zipper. He knew she was standing up because he saw Jesse's eyes narrow to ugly bright slits as his gaze moved up and down her body.

Todd heard Lynnette breathing behind him. He concentrated on Jesse. But in his mind he could see her body—was she trying to cover her breasts with her hands?—and he felt his groin tighten, his penis harden, that familiar shotaway empty sensation.

"Don't try t' hide nothin'," Jesse said, his high thin voice almost a whisper. Then, without turning his head, he asked, with mockery: "Change your mind, Ralph?"

Had he? That was the risk Todd had to take. He was tempted to glance but did not. No one had touched it; the hatchet had to be where he'd seen it a few minutes ago.

"Lynn," he said. He had to act now, before any one of the others moved. "Lynnette—"

"Yes?" He could hardly recognize her voice. "What, Todd?"

"Run!" he shouted, using all the voice he had left. "Into the woods, *run!*"

The abrupt bawling of his voice exploded and roared through the clearing and then echoed loudly among the trees as he moved, fast.

He stepped closer to Jesse, and with the help of the light, taking care to aim, standing on one leg, he lifted the other leg and kicked. His foot plunged with all his strength into Jesse's tumescent scrotum. There was a low grunt, the mountainous shoulders doubled forward, and the red-bearded face became a grotesque mask of disbelief and shock. And then from the dark cavern at the center of the beard a great animal howl of pain erupted, and the bearlike body collapsed to its knees, wobbling.

Todd heard himself bellowing *Run!* over and over as he leaped toward the fire, stooping to grab the handle of the hatchet from the firewood.

But as he whirled, crouched, with the hatchet in hand, the light lifted and he heard Ralph's voice cursing in a foreign language. Then he saw the source of the beam above his head. He struck upward with the hatchet. At the same instant, glass shattered and the light went out.

In the sudden dimness he was blinded, but the growling in a foreign language continued. Todd went into a low crouch as he heard Jesse's cries of pain turn into an outraged murderous snarl. He felt a blow on his left shoulder—the heavy light itself crashing downward—and caught a shadowy glimpse of Ralph's long legs close, very close. Gritting his teeth against the stabbing pain in his shoulder, he lashed out with the hatchet.

It struck solid flesh, and above his head there was a grunt, but the tall man did not go down. His eyes now adjusted to the semidarkness, Todd slashed again, and then again, finally straightening and backing away from the tall shape that, silent now, was coming at him slowly, limping but inexorable.

He began to swing the weapon in a series of horizontal arcs, holding Ralph off while he backed away. The hatchet made small swishing sounds in the air; above these he heard Lynnette, in the distance, screaming now.

Don't scream, Lynne, run, don't scream, they'll find you if you—

Where was Jesse?

Before he could glance around, he saw Ralph come to a halt, heard his voice, the accent more pronounced: "You crazy, kid? You try to kill me?"

"Yes!" Todd cried, feeling it, knowing: *"Yes!"*

"Now ve all in big trouble. *Big.*"

"I'll lay your goddamn skull open," Todd warned, the taste of blood on his tongue, the fury cold in him now, coupled with amazement at the sudden savage need to see blood. "I'll kill you both!"

But where was Jesse?

Still swinging the hatchet but no longer backing away from Ralph, he risked a glance.

Jesse was nowhere in view. Nowhere.

But he caught a quick glimpse—or perhaps he only imagined it—of a slim white shadow fleeing among the dark tree trunks.

"He vent after her," Ralph said. "He catch her, ve all, all in big—"

But Todd had moved. He was plunging toward the woods in the direction Lynnette had taken, dread and panic replacing the bloodlust, Ralph forgotten.

Then he felt the blow.

In the small of his back.

His momentum carried him forward a few steps as the pain exploded, and then, stumbling and falling and trying to roll so that he could use the hatchet, he realized he must have dropped it when the pain struck and he went down.

His mind blanked for an instant. Then, writhing but trying

to stand up from the floor of pine needles, he knew that Ralph had thrown the broken searchlight with deadly accuracy. He was crippled, unable to straighten up.

He heard a snarl as the tall man stooped above him. Todd attempted to roll to one side, but the tall man was too quick, too strong, too overpowering.

He felt hands of steel grasp one arm and one leg and then his body was being lifted. He caught a momentary glimpse of the man's face: narrow, fixed and grim, pale eyes glinting coldly. And then his small body was above the man's head, twisting helplessly, the pain forgotten, and he was being carried high above the ground, the tall man stalking in long strides past the fire, toward the edge of the cliff.

When he saw the empty darkness yawning beyond the grassy ledge, Todd made a desperate final effort to wriggle free. He failed.

And then he was free. For a long moment, a sensation of floating. No, it can't be like this, this is not happening, no! And then his body began to drop, to descend faster and faster, tumbling crazily in the thin cold air.

ONE

To hell with it.

The man was not in bed when the phone rang in his weathered shingle-walled house on the shore of Cape Cod Bay. He wakened from his normally restless, normally shallow sleep, on the couch in the living room, some book or other on the floor, lamp still burning.

The phone continued to ring.

He sat up, running a hand over his blunt-featured face and then through his gray-streaked dark hair. He was wearing the cords and sweat shirt he'd worn all day. Bad habits, stupid lonely habits—they accumulated over five years.

The house was cold. What time was it? And the phone was still ringing and to hell with it. In those same five years he'd become more and more accustomed to saying to hell with it, not only to ringing telephones but to everything. And everyone.

Regardless of which—not annoyed, not curious, just sleepily indifferent—he reached to answer. The surf was loud tonight, out beyond the moor of bayberry and blueberry, already browned by autumn, but he could hear the voice distinctly: a woman's, clipped, husky, no-nonsense Yankee, a stranger's: "Mr. Horgan?"

"Yes."

"Mr. Andrew Horgan?"

"Yes, it is."

"I'm terribly sorry to disturb you at this time of night. My name's Ann Merrill. I'm dean of students at Melville College. I'm afraid I have some rather bad news for you, Mr. Horgan.''

Utterly baffled by now, he asked, ''What is it, Miss Merrill?''

''Your son, Todd—I'm afraid something rather dreadful has happened. I don't have all the facts yet but—''

''Miss Merrill—''

''Yes?''

''Miss Merrill, before you go on . . . I'm sorry, there's been some mistake. I don't have a son. I don't have any children.''

''Is this Mr. Andrew Horgan, the photographer?''

''Yes, but—''

''I'm calling from the college office and I am looking at Todd Horgan's registration. Age nineteen, two home addresses: Southampton, Long Island, and New York City, a number on Fifth Avenue. But no phone numbers. Father: Andrew W. Horgan. No address. Profession: photographer and author.'' Then she paused and said: ''I took a chance and found your address in *Who's Who*.''

Stunned now, Andrew said: ''I'm sorry, Miss Merrill, but may I ask: Does this . . . this son of mine have a mother?''

''Yes. That part's as bewildering to me as—you'll excuse me—as your attitude. His mother was Julia Carpenter. Deceased.''

Julia. After all these years. Christ! ''Julia Carpenter is *not* deceased, Miss Merrill. Her name's Julia Craven now and she's starring in a play on Broadway. I was married to her years ago, but we had no children. I'm sorry.'' Why the hell did he keep apologizing? ''There's some mixup in the records.''

''I see.''

''I don't think you do. Nor do I.'' He was standing up now, his bare feet chilled on the carpet. ''I'm not trying to evade responsibility if that's what you think. And I've no idea how any of this happened, but I did not have a child when I was married to Julia. We've been divorced for more than nineteen years and—''

But he broke off. And Miss Merrill waited again. The line hummed and crackled over the miles between Cape Cod and wherever the hell Melville College was. They were both, he knew, sharing the same thought: age nineteen, nineteen years divorced.

Finally, the possible—but very unlikely, very damned

22

unlikely—import of the conversation reaching him, he said, "Perhaps you'd better tell me what's happened."

He heard the woman sigh, the sound suggesting relief. "I'll admit it's rather confused at the moment," she said, clearing her throat. "Todd went camping with a girl, another student, in a state forest about fifteen miles north of here. Something happened. The authorities in Shepperton—that's the name of the small town at the eastern edge of the forest—well, the police were not very informative when they telephoned to ask me to inform the parents of both students. Your son—Todd, that is—drove into Shepperton an hour ago to inform the police."

"Miss Merrill, excuse me—what state are we talking about?"

"Why, Vermont, Mr. Horgan. Shepperton, Vermont."

"What about the girl?"

"The girl—we've informed her parents in Maine—the girl, I'm afraid, is missing."

"What did the boy . . . what did Todd say?"

"I don't know what he told the police, but I do suspect they don't believe him. They plan to search the woods as soon as it's light."

"And where's . . . Todd now?"

"He was suffering from exhaustion and exposure and bruises, two of them quite severe, they told me. He apparently fell off a cliff. He was treated in the emergency room of the local hospital but . . . Mr. Horgan, I'm sorry. That's the most I can tell you. I think they have him in jail. I'm sorry. I am sincerely sorry."

What could he say? That it was not his business, that it was no concern of his, that he knew, whether she did or not, that this boy named Todd Horgan was not, could not, be his son?

"I hope I haven't upset your life too much, Mr. Horgan."

What was there to say to that? That in the last five years it had not been much of a life? An empty shell of a life, really, without flavor, without meaning. Instead, he said: "You know Todd Horgan. I don't. Do you think he could have harmed that girl?"

"No," she said promptly, "no, I *don't*. I do know him, yes, and I think the police are dead wrong even to suspect such a thing. Any more questions?"

Andrew felt his lips twisting into a smile. How long had it been since he'd even felt inclined to smile? "No more, thank you. But now I'll answer yours. Until this phone rang tonight, I didn't know I had a son. I'm still not sure but you've just made up my mind for me. I'll be in Shepperton, wherever the hell that is, some time this morning.''

"I've got to go," she cried. "I've got to get to him. He needs me!''

Julia, who always slept in the nude, had thrown on the first piece of clothing she had seen, the leather trenchcoat she'd worn home from the theater less than two hours ago; as she began to prowl the huge penthouse living room, it fell away from her body and she looked like an adolescent girl, distraught and disheveled. Then she stopped moving. "Why is he doing this to me? He knows I have a hit play. He's doing this to *spite* me!''

Amazed again—even after three years of marriage—Merle Elkin said, "Julia, he's your son, not mine, but—''

"You don't want me to go!" she accused. "Well, you're right—he's *not* your son and I'll do what I have to do!" She rushed toward him, pushing her blond hair away from her face. "Why the fuck didn't the college have our unlisted number?''

"Damned if I know. The woman I talked to, this Tracy Larkin—one helluva nice voice—works for some television station there and she put it all together because apparently she's a great fan of yours. She got the name of the show's press agent, and Max gave her the number here. If it hadn't been for Miss Feisty, we still wouldn't know anything had happened.''

"Well, I wish I *didn't* know." She stepped closer; tall, pale, intense, her lovely mobile face challenging. "Merle, tell me: What am I going to do?''

If he told her to go, she wouldn't. If he said not to go, she'd be packed in half an hour. Merle Elkin decided: "It's Monday now—theater's dark tonight. It's your only day off. You need the rest.''

"You don't want me to go!" She swooped down on the marble cocktail table and snatched up a cigarette from a jade container. "You don't like Todd. You never have." She lit the cigarette from the matching jade lighter. "You said this Tracy Someone told you the police suspect Todd of—''

Merle interrupted, playing his first card. "If I weren't in rehearsal with this damned musical, I'd go myself.''

"You?" One elbow cradled in the other palm, she blew smoke, regarding him with her greenish-blue eyes. "You, Merle? Why?"

"Because if they find the girl, if something terrible has happened to her and they charge Todd—the press already knows that Todd Horgan is the son of Julia Craven. If that's on TV in that hick town, the networks and wire services will pick it up. Max Grossman's worried about what it would look like if his mother simply stays in New York and goes on appearing in her show . . ."

He saw her brows, always a shade or two darker than her lustrous blond hair, form a straight line over her eyes; he saw her chin lift. And he waited.

Until he heard her say, "Poor Todd." Her tone was soft, gentle. "He's such a darling boy. Why does he always have to get involved in these childish goddammed escapades?"

Tightening the sash of his dressing gown, Merle decided to play another card. "Why don't you say to hell with it and go back to bed?"

Eyes widening, she made a straight cross to where he stood. "How can I do that? How?"

"By phoning your old friend, the famous shyster of shysters Gerald Usher Lewis, and asking him to go to Shepperton—to represent Todd, just in case."

Julia, frowning, turned away and then moved drifting along the mirrored room to the terrace doors. She was not really thinking. Because by now, he knew, she had already decided.

"Do you have Lewis's number in Boston?" Merle prompted, knowing she needed a cue in order to state the decision she had reached.

"Yes." She returned to him. "Oh, you bastard," she whispered as she kissed him on his bearded cheek. "You just don't know what it is to be a mother, do you?" And then she was striding toward the hall. "I do have Lewis's number and he'll come. He'll come if I ask him."

Merle lowered his body onto the deep soft sofa. Yes, Lewis would come. Did Julia imagine he didn't know of her affair with the great Gerald Usher Lewis when she was in Boston during the tryout of *Angel's Revenge*? It must have been a torrid two weeks if he was any judge. And he was a damned good judge. Julia couldn't pass up a chance for another such romantic interlude, regardless of circumstances.

Well, with Julia out of the city . . . there was that young featured dancer in his show who fancied himself another Travolta. He'd welcome some private sessions with his choreographer.

Whatever you think now, whatever you feel, Andy, I do love you. I always will. You're the only man I'll ever love.

Love. Which Julia had just turned into a dirty word.

He had been leaving then, grim and sick with nausea and hate and a rage that terrified him. Andrew was remembering the tired cliché words again now as he piloted his Maule M-7 in a northwesterly direction over Cape Cod Bay from the Provincetown field where he hangared it. Plymouth Light to port. And he was remembering, for the first time in years, what had preceded Julia's tearful words: himself entering the shabby two-room apartment in the old brownstone in Greenwich Village, opening the door, hearing sounds even before he saw them. Julia naked, flat on her back on the floor in front of the white fireplace, her long legs wrapped around the man's body, ankles clenched behind his broad back . . .

And afterward, while he packed, the excuses—cruelly ludicrous to him, reasonable to her: *It didn't mean anything. He's the casting director for Rollo Taggart himself. He promised me an understudy role.* And then the blame: *It's your fault— you're always away somewhere on assignment. Six months taking those awful pictures in Viet Nam. What was I supposed to do?* And then: *It couldn't have happened if our marriage was what it ought to be, could it?*

The Boston Light was in view now, the glittering city beyond. The one person he didn't want to remember tonight was Julia. Forgetting Julia had been relatively easy. By the time he had met Cassie eight years later, Julia was no longer a part of him.

Cassie: hair the rich color of honey framing a tanned and sun-brightened face, soft yet strong. Whenever he thought of Cassie, he thought of the sun and blue water and sand. His beach that had become theirs from the first day he'd discovered her there, standing at an easel, wearing a one-piece swimsuit the color of cinnamon and painting the bleached bones of one of the abandoned fishing vessels that dotted the curving stretch of sand. He had been fighting a hangover with another shot of scotch and a walk when he saw her. He had stood staring at her for some time, mesmerized—a strange overwhelming incredulity and enchantment that he had never even believed in before—and then he had walked to where she stood. She turned to look at him, carefully, brown eyes squinting, and then she said, *You're drunk, aren't you?* He had always been a little drunk in those days, although most people didn't know it. *Yep,* he said. She turned to the easel. *Well, sober up and I'll talk to you.* And he had. For the first two years of their marriage he had, even when drinking, remained sober.

He was over land now. At this hour of the morning the world below was a pattern of darkness with an immense complexity, yet a satisfying simplicity: the lighted streets of sleeping villages, the slow-motion of headlights on country roads, the dots of light from isolated farms. He was reminded of Saint Exupéry over France, over South America, the desert, over Arras from above; he was the only writer who even came close to capturing in words that sense of awe and poetic wonder that Andrew had consciously tried to convey in his photographs. Seeing the world this way, from above, only then could he recapture—fleetingly—that sense of adventure and excitement that had once been life.

Life with Cassie . . . less than two years after they were married he had begun to drink again—really to drink. He had not known why he drank, not then, although he gave reasons—pressure of work, deadlines—and Cassie had reached for other explanations: *You're not happy with me. Or you wouldn't need to drink the way you do! Are you still in love with Julia Craven?* He had examined his mind, coldly and soberly, between bouts. All he felt for Julia Craven was a sort of distant disgust. And as for Cassie, *she* had taught him what love could be.

Then why the hell *did* he drink?

He did not know. But when he had lost control of the plane at six thousand feet and been forced to crash-land in an Iowa wheat field while doing aerial photographs for his third book, he had made up his mind: He did not want to die. He wanted to live, with Cassie, forever if possible.

It was then that, grimly determined, he had entered the hospital outside Providence for a month's therapy, a month during which he had learned that he drank, not for reason but for *no* reason, simply because he was the victim of an addictive disease. The only cure, complex and difficult and requiring more willpower and honesty than he knew he had, was to recognize the disease, accept it, acknowledge that he suffered from it, and then determine that he would conquer it by not drinking. Not one ounce, ever again. He had emerged shaken but exultant. From that moment on he had thought of alcohol as cyanide. A man does not drink cyanide unless he wants to die. And he had wanted, then, to live.

The next five years were a time of such profound fulfillment and casual day-to-day joy that he had begun to feel guilty. Did any man, in a world full of pain and suffering, deserve such fortune?

Then, on an April morning he had wakened and she was not there. It had taken him a long, long moment to realize that she was not sleeping. There was no breath, her eyes were closed, and when he touched her face, her flesh had already cooled. He always remembered afterward how amazed he had been that, outside, gulls cawed, and across the moor the surf continued its familiar thunder.

Even then, at that time, he had not taken a single drink. Nor would he until such time as the emptiness inside became so unbearable that his own death, guaranteed by his nature and his physical susceptibility to alcohol, seemed the logical and reasonable way out.

In the five years since that time, he had reconciled himself. He had become an automaton, an unreal and burnt-out man, now approaching forty-five, whose sole pleasure was flying, alone, above a world that he could observe or experience only from a distance.

There was a slight turbulence over the foothills south of the White Mountains in New Hampshire but by veering west he was able to escape it. Distances in New England, compared to the rest of the country, always astonished him: No place was really very far from any other place, especially by air.

Dawn had come by the time he reached the Shepperton area, which—considering the bleak gray sky—was miraculously free of ground fog. He had radioed the Burlington Airport and learned of a private airstrip at the ski lodge called the Alpine Chalet.

There was no one in sight when he climbed out of the plane with his duffel bag and the Leica CL slung over his shoulder.

The only buildings were a tiny waiting-room structure, deserted, and a small hangar, closed tight.

But there was a rustic sign reading WELCOME TO ALPINE CHALET and an arrow pointing to a flagstone path leading into a grove of white birch trees. Pleasantly conscious of the crisp air and the fragrance of damp earth in the early morning, he arrived at the chalet, an enormous building with balconies and steeply pitched roofs which he had seen from the air. But its somewhat rustic exterior did not prepare him for the spacious elegance inside: a high-beamed room with great fieldstone fireplaces at each end; long, shining trestle tables; deep leather chairs and couches of every length. Maybe he should have worn gray flannels and a tweed jacket instead of whipcords, desert boots, turtleneck, and his old weather-beaten flight jacket. But *he who would travel happily must travel light*—Saint-Ex again.

When he'd phoned to inquire about landing privileges, he had not made a room reservation. One of the risks of arriving by air to take pictures in remote towns was that there were often no cars to rent, possibly no taxis. So he'd learned to evade commitments until he could get the lay of the land.

There was no one behind the curved and elaborately carved reception desk; nothing so plebeian as a bell to ring for service.

"Mr. Horgan?"

He turned. The voice was that of a young woman—small and slim, with short, vivid red hair, small-boned face and body, bright blue eyes. She was facing him with her head slightly tilted. "You *are* Andrew Horgan, aren't you? Todd's father?"

Not a hotel employee then—one of Todd's friends. "And your name?"

"Oh, I'm sorry. I'm Tracy Larkin. Ann Merrill—at Melville College in Haddam—she told me you were coming. So I assumed you'd stay here."

"How far from town are we?"

"Four miles."

"Can I rent a car?"

"In Shepperton?" She was smiling, a frank, amused, girlish smile, slightly teasing. "There are two taxis but only one driver and he's really too old to drive. And usually smashed."

"Hotel in town?"

"Only one, by the railroad tracks. Sort of flophouse residential. Mrs. Wharton's Guest Home is on the green—white columns, filled with precious antiques, including Mrs. Wharton. Colonial Motel's a mile out. How about Cottages on the Green? Cozy, no room service, telephones in cabins one through five only—"

"I'll take number five."

She laughed. He liked the sound: a low chuckle of genuine amusement. "C'mon, I'll drive you." She was already moving, quick and jaunty, toward the doors. "I'm not really a tour guide. I work for the local television station."

She was wearing a green shirt dress, a blue parka, and navy-blue loafers, and looked like a little girl. But as he followed her outside and down the flagstone steps to the parking area enclosed by huge timbers, he noticed her legs: slender but shapely, flowing to trim ankles—a woman's legs.

She led him to an ancient MG, green with a fraying canvas top, and as he opened the door for her, her eyes caught his, an expression of puzzlement turning to amusement. "Thank you," she said. He'd forgotten. It was, he understood, some form of rudeness these days for a male to hold a door for a female. He settled into the low bucket set beside her. To hell with it.

As they sped along the narrow twisting road between leafless trees, she explained that she was only doing her job, so no need to thank her; the police would not allow her to interview Todd, who was in the jail at the courthouse, but wasn't really "in jail" because he hadn't been charged with anything; she was a theater nut and had majored in drama—"I'm great with lights but I could never play anyone but myself"—so she had recognized the name Julia Carpenter and, "by hook and devious crook," she had reached Julia Craven's husband by phone but she was not sure what Miss Craven would decide to do.

To hell with Julia. "Any news about the girl?" Andrew asked.

"So much for Julia Craven," Tracy Larkin said. Her tone was puzzled. "No news yet. The police are probably searching the woods by now." And then, with a sidelong glance: "Why do you ask?"

"I was thinking of the girl's parents. It must be hell not to know . . ." He frowned, turning to stare at Tracy Larkin's delicate profile. "It's a natural question, isn't it?"

She was slow to reply. Then: "To some people." Then, as if asking, or prompting: "Most parents with a son in jail . . ."

She let the sentence hang unspoken, so he said, somewhat gruffly: "I don't know my son any better than I know the girl. But I do know where he is and I still think it must be more hellish for them right now, *not* knowing."

"True, Mr. Horgan, true." It was a whisper, as if she was thinking it over. And then, in a different, more businesslike voice: "How long since you've seen Todd's mother?"

"Is this an interview for your broadcast?"

"I do an editorial commentary after the news—human interest addenda. It isn't often that anything like this happens around here. You might say never. I'd like to cover all the angles. How do you feel about seeing her again after all these years?"

"I feel," he said, "that that's none of your business."

Tracy Larkin laughed again. It was a good sound—hearty, very much alive. "You're a crusty bastard, aren't you?" she said. "You want to get some breakfast?"

"If you'll drop me at the courthouse, I'd be very much obliged."

The "outskirts"—they passed the white Colonial Motel— were pretty close to downtown because Shepperton was a very typical New England small town, although not quite so small as he'd pictured it. The Congregational church was on one side of the green; its plain white front and slim tall spire were so photogenic that it—and the long green itself, with low storefronts along two sides, town hall, grange, huge old mansions, also white, the granite courthouse at one end, and Cottages on the Green Motel at the opposite end—all of it, including the circular frame gazebo or bandstand on the grass of the green itself, under high old trees, was such a cliché that no respectable photographer would think of taking its picture. But its quiet charm was undeniable—even to a crusty bastard like Andrew Horgan.

When the MG stopped at the curb in front of the high, wide steps of the courthouse, with bare lilac bushes on both sides, Tracy Larkin had one more thing to say: "Mr. Horgan, before you go in—"

He struggled out of the bucket seat. "Yes, Miss Larkin?"

"You may as well know. It's my opinion that the police think your son murdered Lynnette Durand."

* * *

Since taking office as State's Attorney, Blake Arnold had never had the opportunity to prosecute a major case, certainly not one that *could* turn into a capital offense situation.

The chief of police, Kyle Radford, had been a town constable when Blake had gone off to Deerfield and Williams and Yale Law, so when Chief Radford had phoned during the night to report what had happened, the two men had held a short but friendly conversation. Radford had explained that, because the incident had not occurred within the town limits, Sheriff Wayne Wheeler was officially in charge of the investigation. *And he can have it,* Radford had said on the phone. After that, Blake Arnold had not been able to sleep very soundly.

So, when he drove to the courthouse—damned if he'd get up this early for anything else, except possibly to go deer-hunting, and the season wouldn't open for another ten days—Blake did not go directly to the marble-floored rotunda and up the stairs to his own office, but to the offices of the Eden County sheriff on the ground floor.

Sheriff Wayne Wheeler—big and hearty and in his fifties with brush-cut gray hair above a square weathered face—was not one of Blake's favorite people. And when he got up from behind his desk, he stood six or seven inches taller than Blake, making him conscious of his short slight frame.

Wheeler answered Blake's first question in his gruff and confident voice: "Yessir, I interrogated the boy personally, with Chief Radford present, and I don't have any doubt we got a homicide on our hands. We read him his rights, even though he's not charged yet, and we got a tape. You like to hear it?"

"You sound as if you'd made up your mind, Sheriff," Blake said.

"It don't always take forever. I been in this business about's long as you been alive, Mr. Arnold. My gut tells me. I know these rich college kids in their fancy sports cars. Think they own the world. He killed her, hid the body, then drove in here yelling rape."

"Let's at least wait till we have the corpus delicti, if any."

"Ten to one we do, and once we get the autopsy report, we'll find she was pregnant."

"You even have a motive, don't you?"

"Wait and see."

"I suggest that's what we all do."

Wheeler grinned and grunted, lowering his thick body, which was going slightly soft, into his swivel chair.

"Before I listen to the tape," Blake said, "is there a bulletin out on the girl?"

"Won't do a damned bit of good, but there is. Five states missing-persons. Ontario and Quebec too. Men and dogs scouring the woods since dawn. So far, they located the campsite. You like some coffee?"

"No thanks. Find anything?"

"Among other things, a hatchet."

"Don't you take a hatchet when you go camping? Comes in handy for chopping firewood."

Wheeler uttered a sour, mirthless laugh. "Just the same, you won't mind if we have it run through the lab at state police barracks, will you? Fingerprints, bloodstains, standard procedure."

"I'll listen to the tape now. If *you* don't mind."

As he left the office, he heard the sheriff calling after him: "You think she found her own goddam way out of that forest? You think we're gonna find her *alive*?"

Blake didn't know. But after he'd listened to the tape alone in the interrogation room, which also served as the visitors' room, he stood up and went down the narrow stairs into the jail itself. Old Kopit, the night jailer, was still on duty. Crippled in one leg in a hunting accident years ago, Gardner Kopit was tall and spare, with a jutting chin and hooked nose. He was a man of few words, none of them ever cheerful. But Blake went through the routine: "You got somebody in here aching to talk to me?" and Kopit muttered, "Talk? He won't talk to nobody."

Blake followed the limping old man between two rows of cells, three on each side. The walls, the floors, even the bars in this area were painted a sickly battleship-gray. Kopit unlocked the last cell on the left, the only one occupied.

"Leave it open. I'll let myself out," Blake said.

"If you say so. Against regulations, though."

In the cell, Blake was as appalled as he invariably was: two narrow bunks on one wall, one above the other, a stainless steel commode and washbasin in one corner, no shelves, no desk or table—nothing. "My name's Blake Arnold," he told the only occupant of the cell. "I'm the state's attorney here."

"And I'm the guy who came here to report a crime and got thrown into the clink. What do you want?"

The boy had sandy hair about the same color as Blake's own, but shaggy and considerably longer, and a trim beard that was slightly darker in shade. His eyes were quietly hostile. He was also about Blake's height, five eight, but he was at least twenty pounds lighter and his lean boyish face had a healthy tan. He was wearing dirty jeans and a khaki-colored jail shirt. He must have been shirtless when he drove into town.

"Chief Radford told me on the phone during the night that you refused to make any phone calls. Have you changed your mind?"

"There's no one I want to call."

"Your parents?"

"Dead."

"Both?"

"Both."

"How do you feel? I understand you're scratched up and something about an injured collarbone and bruised spinal column."

"To hell with all that shit. What's happening? Have they found Lynnette? Is she alive?"

"We don't know yet. I thought you might be able to help me—"

"I told them everything I know. They taped it. They don't believe me. Sheriff Wheeler thinks I killed her. I don't give a shit what he thinks, or what you think—I told the truth." He came forward, close, and faced Blake head-on. His bluish-green eyes were bright and sharp, but no longer angry. There was a plea in them, and in his voice, too. "She didn't have any clothes on. She could die out there in the cold even if those two didn't—" He broke off and turned away, staring out the barred window, his body suddenly taut with fury. "Let me out of here! I'll find them. Somehow I'll find them! I'll *kill* the bastards."

"If she's in the woods, we'll find her." Blake heard the gentleness in his own voice. "The forest's a big place, Todd. It'll take time." Then he said, "By the way, how'd *you* manage to get out?"

34

Without turning, the boy said, "I had a compass and I knew where the car was." Then he added: "She didn't."

Blake took a single step. "Todd—those two men. You described them very clearly. What interests me is the truck. You said you saw a truck—"

"Yeh. When I came to—I was in a sort of marshy pond—I climbed up the cliff, and when I got to the top there was no one at the fire. I guess I was going a little bit crazy." He turned, his face a mask of misery. "All I could think of was that they'd taken her. And I was just about to take off in the direction I saw her run when I heard this sound. Way off. It was dark as hell. Then, from the same direction, I saw lights. Two lights. Like headlights. I found my field glasses and tried to get them focused. And then I heard the sound again and decided it was the engine of a truck. The lights moved around some and then sort of disappeared. But there were four red lights, very tiny, and I got my glasses focused and I saw the rear end of the truck. That's what it was—with a roof and panels. White, I think. Looked like Massachusetts plates. But it kept moving away and it was dark. . . ."

He shrugged his shoulders. "There wasn't anything I could do. All I could think of was getting out of there myself and getting some help." His chin lifted, his shoulders straightened, and his voice was hard. "And this is where I end up."

"What would a truck be doing there? Camping? In the tape you mentioned the men identified themselves as hunters. Season's almost two weeks off. Poachers?"

"I don't know the answer. I don't have any answers. All I know is what happened and what I saw. And nobody'll believe me." It was a challenge. "Nobody."

Did Blake believe him? He was not sure.

"Todd . . . if I were your lawyer, I'd be inclined to think you have a good case. But as prosecutor, I say you'll have to prove it. And that's why I'm not going to recommend your release—not yet, anyway. You'll just have to tough it out in here till we see what happened to your girl. Okay?"

The shrug again. "Do I have a choice?"

"Not now, no. Tell me, Todd—do you love the girl?"

"Damn right I do!" It was an angry snarl. "Till I met her, I didn't even *believe* in love!"

"I have a wife whom I love very much—so I know how you feel."

"*Nobody* knows how I feel." The boy sank down to the bunk. "It was my fault. I didn't kill her, I didn't hurt her, but it was my fault. Maybe I deserve what I'm getting."

Blake Arnold stepped to the barred door. "I'll see what's being done about trying to locate that truck. My office is upstairs. Tell Kopit if you think of anything else you might have forgotten in the excitement."

Blake left the cell and went up the stairs and directly to the Shepperton Town Police area. He could not help feeling a pang of disappointment. When he'd told Valerie, who was still in bed when he left the house, that it might be a big case, even murder, she had said, *Let's hope nobody's dead, but if anyone is, I know you'll handle it.* Now, though, he had the feeling that it would all blow over. If the boy was telling the truth, even if Lynnette Durand was dead, the police wouldn't have a shot in hell of locating those two men.

Chief Kyle Radford was behind his desk in his cluttered office. Feeling more comfortable at once, Blake asked, "How's Rachel these days?"

"This Indian summer's some relief," the withered old man said, "but Rachel, she's lived in New England all her life and she'll never get used to these winters."

"Valerie's the same," Blake said and sat down, remembering: *Winter in Washington'd be nothing like this. And there'd be the cherry blossoms to look forward to, and so many museums and galleries. Why don't you forget about running for the state congress and make a try for the big one?* "Any news?" he asked.

"The kid's been lying to us. His father is not only living, he's sitting out there waiting to visit his son. So I called Miss Ann Merrill again, over at the college in Haddam—she's the one I spoke to when we got the kid's address from his billfold last night. His mother's alive and well, too. Name's Julia Craven."

"The actress?"

"Seems so. I recollect seeing her in some movie once. Y'know what this means, don't you?"

"She's a star on Broadway now, I think."

"Means that once the news gets out, we're all gonna have just one helluva case on our hands. And I don't relish it one goddam bit. This town could become a tourist attraction. Just like it was when the leaves was turnin' a month ago. Worse'n winter when the ski nuts take over. Busloads of sightseers, reporters all over hell's half acre. And if that kid goes to trial here—''

A familiar voice spoke from the doorway: "Only our State's Attorney don't think we got a case. That right, Mr. Arnold?"

There was a throb of excitement beginning in Blake's chest and he was not sure whether he liked it or not. "Let's just hold him and wait and see—"

From the door Sheriff Wheeler spoke again: "Something I forgot to mention, Mr. Arnold. Like what we found in our routine search of the kid's sporty little foreign car. Would you believe a .357 Magnum? A Ruger Speed-Six."

"Had it been fired?" Blake asked. His mouth was dry.

"No. But it was registered in New York State, not Vermont."

That did it. Blake stood up. "We've got enough to hold him now. He admitted on the tape that the marijuana you found in his pocket was his. That's possession. Now, illegal transport of a lethal weapon—"

"Now," Wheeler said, "now you're talking like an officer of the court!"

"Also," Blake went on, trying not to betray the mounting ferment inside, "he's accused two John Does of attempted rape. He's a material witness."

"Now we're getting somewhere!" Wheeler said.

"And to give us more time, don't make the official arrest or file the formal charges until Judge Patton convenes court this morning at ten. That puts the preliminary hearing over till tomorrow, so he can't post bond before then." Blake moved to the door, stopped and turned. "And no more interrogation till the arrest—then make sure there's another officer present to corroborate that he was read his rights. No telling what smartass big-city lawyer Julia Craven might hire. I don't want this case fucked up by technicalities."

He went out and into the rotunda, empty now, with office doors and the main courtroom opening off it, and up the marble steps to his office. He phoned Valerie. After he'd told her the news, leaving out his interview with Todd Horgan, she said, very quietly: "Honey, it's the biggest break in a lifetime, isn't it?"

"Ay-uh, charges are pending, Mr. Horgan. Right now your son's what we call a material witness."

Having been kept waiting on a bench, Andrew was now standing at the counter speaking with Chief of Police Radford. "I'd still like to see him," he said.

"Officially, visiting hours are from two to four P.M. But you come a long ways, so I'll make an exception. Come 'round the counter, down this hall here. Now, you go right through that door that Miss Ray'll unlock for-you and down the stairs to the first room on the left. I'm not even going to search you, Mr. Horgan. I got a son of my own and *he's* got three—I know how a father feels."

After going through the thick door, opened by a dour, stocky woman in uniform, Andrew heard the heavy lock turn metallically behind him as he descended the staircase.

With his hand on the knob of the closed door, he hesitated. What was he doing here? Why had he come? Curiosity? No—more than that. Yet he felt weak, stomach empty, a hollow hunger gnawing. Well, he was into it now—he was here. He opened the door.

A barren room, dull gray, bleak, with no windows and a long narrow conference-type table down its length. Then he saw him: at the far end of the table, head down on folded arms, so that all Andrew could see was a thatch of blondish hair. He felt a stab of panic. What the *hell* was he doing here?

"I don't need a lawyer." The voice was muffled, lightly pitched, boyish. "I told the assholes. They don't listen."

"I'm not a lawyer," Andrew said quietly.

"I told them I wouldn't talk to any newspapers." Then he lifted his head. His face, somewhat obscured by a short beard, looked very young, very vulnerable; green eyes, Julia's eyes, curious and cautious, not quite defiant. "Who the hell are you?"

Andrew couldn't quite bring himself to say *I'm your father*—because, damn it, he wasn't totally convinced of that—so he said: "My name's Andrew Horgan."

There was a long silence. The boy's face did not change at first, even slightly. Then an ugly, mocking grin twisted the beard and the eyes narrowed. "No shit?"

"May I sit down?"

Todd pushed back his chair on the concrete floor and stood up—a slim figure, supple, not tall, suggesting youthful vigor. "Oh, hell yes, Pop. Come right into my parlor and set your ass down. I'm sorry they had to take down the Chagall and the Matisse—it makes the walls look so naked. That's the only other chair in the house. I'm only allowed one visitor at a time. But you should've seen this place a few hours ago. Uniforms everywhere, throwing questions. *Why'd you do it? Where'd you hide the body?* Sit down there now and *you* throw *your* questions. And remember, man, anything you ask may be held against you.'' He threw himself back onto the chair and grinned. ''Miss Ray told me the rules: no physical contact. You didn't have your heart set on giving me a fatherly hug, did you?''

Andrew lowered himself to the chair and looked down the length of the table. ''If I did, you're damned well making sure I don't, aren't you?''

The same grin—mirthless, mocking. ''What'll we talk about, Pop? Nietzsche? Camus? Existential angst? Or maybe Ansel Adams or Eddie Steichen? How come you haven't published a book in five years?''

Andrew considered his answer, then said: ''I could say the public doesn't buy books of photographs. The truth is, I haven't done any decent work in the last five years.'' He did not add *Since Cassie*. He was tempted to admit he was oddly touched that Todd knew his work. He did say: ''Maybe you do need a lawyer.''

''What the hell are you doing here? Who sent for you? Not Julia—''

Slightly startled at the boy's use of his mother's first name, Andrew shook his head. ''I haven't talked to your mother in twenty years. *You* sent for me.''

''Like fuck! I didn't send for anybody. I don't *need* anybody. I haven't done anything!''

''That may be true—''

''*May* be? It *is* true! I don't care what anybody thinks. I don't give a shit what *you* think, either.''

''You sent for me by putting my name and not your mother's on your college registration.''

Todd groaned. ''I had to put down someone. If I had put down Julia Craven, I'd have had every stagestruck student at Melville trying to seduce me, male and female.'' He visored one hand over his eyes and peered down the table. ''More to the goddam point, mister, is why you came.''

It was a good question. It was the basic question. ''I suppose I came because I didn't know you existed.''

A long silence. Todd did not move.

Then he said, "The world is ninety percent liars. Probably more. I never expected you to be anything else."

Slowly Andrew said, "I was in a hospital once for twenty-eight days. Long enough to learn many things. The most important one is, to really live, the best way is absolute honesty." He sat back. "I'm not lying to you, Todd."

The boy's sandy brows came together in a straight line over his eyes. "You knew she was pregnant—that's why you left her."

So. So that was what Julia had told him. And by the time he was old enough to ask, that was what Julia herself undoubtedly believed. And what was he to say now?

"True?" Todd asked—as if doubt had begun to flicker behind his eyes, which were dark now, probing. "True, mister?"

"The trouble with the truth," Andrew said, "is that sometimes when you tell it, it makes *you* the sonofabitch."

"Not," Todd said, "not any more the sonofabitch than I've always thought you were. So . . . you're saying *she* lied—is that it?"

"Julia doesn't exactly lie," Andrew said. "At least when I knew her. Not consciously."

"You punched her out, she had to be hospitalized, and you walked out on her—all lies?"

Andrew was trapped. Lies, yes, but he was damned if he was going to defend himself. He'd slapped her, hard, once, with an open palm, so he'd "punched her out." The police had had her examined in the emergency room of a hospital, one X ray, fifteen minutes, so she'd been "hospitalized." Lies, yes, but by the time she'd told them, they'd become truth to Julia. And by the time Todd had lived all those years believing them . . .

"She convinces herself first," Todd said, a knowing, accepting expression in his eyes, something close to pain. "If she believes something herself, it can't be a lie, can it?"

Abruptly then, in his mind, Andrew had a swift clear vision of Todd's childhood and adolescence: the slow, anguished realizations and the bitter rebellion. And no escape. No one to turn to, no other parent available . . .

"Todd," he said, "if you could get out of here right now, this minute, what would you do?"

When he heard the words echoing off the bare walls, he realized he was committing himself to act, to do *something*. Had he finally accepted the physical fact that this young man was his son?

"I'd find out what happened to Lynne."

"Now . . . how would you do that?"

"Christ, I don't know. I'd find those two bastards and if they wouldn't tell me, I'd kill them both!"

"I'd advise you not to talk about killing in here. Now maybe you'd better tell me what really happened."

Todd stood up with such violence that the chair fell backward behind him. "I'll tell you. I told them, they won't believe me, I'll tell *you*. Listen, I believe in the truth as much as you do, maybe more. I can't find any, anywhere, but I'll tell you the truth now, so you listen, you *listen*!"

Standing then, eyes burning green fire, but lowering his voice, he told the whole story from the time Lynnette was wakened by what she thought might be thunder to the time he had climbed back up the cliff and found no one at the campsite, heard the truck's engine and saw its lights, and then found his way back to the car in the dark and drove into town, almost insane with worry.

When he finished, his body was quivering all over. "And I don't know what happened to Lynnette." He whirled about and stepped to face the wall. "Did she get lost in the woods or did they find her and rape her, kill her?" He began to beat on the wall with his fists. "Or did they take her in the truck? I'm going to go crazy in here if something doesn't *happen*, if somebody doesn't *do* something!"

Andrew rose and strode the length of the table. He took the boy's shoulders in his hands and shook his body, which was still shuddering.

"You're not going to go crazy. You're going to go back to that cell—"

"And what?" Todd twisted out of Andrew's grasp and faced him with a fierce truculence. "And what? Tough it out, like Nixon? Or pray? I've got no one to pray to!"

"No, not pray. But not stop hoping, or trying."

Tears glistened in the boy's eyes, and in that instant Andrew saw him as a child, as he must have looked as a child, the time Andrew hadn't been there, the time Andrew had been cheated out of, the time Todd had needed him. "What

41

can I do?'' the boy-child asked, helpless now, begging.
''What?''

''You can begin by sitting down''—he stooped to put the
chair upright—''and by telling me exactly what those bastards
looked like, how they talked, what they said—every smallest
detail about them and that truck.''

Todd sat down in the chair, his flesh no longer quivering,
and Andrew half-sat on the table, one foot on the floor.

''Well,'' Todd began, ''one of them was named Ralph—''

''No. From the beginning. The moment you woke up and
saw their boots and heard them. Every word, every syllable
just the way you remember them. From the time Lynnette
woke up because she heard thunder . . .''

Tracy Larkin, on the wide granite terrace at the top of the
courthouse steps, was waiting.

Having prepared the copy for her morning newscast at the
station, she had returned to the courthouse with Russ Owens,
the cameraman she liked working with. Her hope was to get
some footage on Andrew Horgan emerging from the interview with his son or of Julia Craven in case she should come.
But she had just learned from Holly Ray, behind the desk at
the jail, that Lynnette Durand's parents had arrived from
Maine and that Mr. Durand was in Chief Radford's office.
The mother—a small countrywoman type with frail, slumping
shoulders and unkempt grayish hair—had black eyes that
might once have been beautiful but were dulled now by her
corrosive anxiety, if not grief. In her uncertain English, accented by Quebec-French, she had refused to answer Tracy's
questions and had turned away, hand covering her face, when
Russ had tried to photograph her with his shoulder-held camera. And Tracy had been reminded of what Andrew Horgan
had said on the way into town from the chalet: *I was thinking
of her parents. It must be hell not to know.* What a thing to
say, what a beautiful way to feel—at a time when his own
son was in danger of being charged with murder.

Now, outside, she was still thinking of Andrew Horgan: a
strange man, a strange intriguing man. His brown eyes, as
carefully polite as his almost courtly manner, seemed to
conceal some sadness, or loss, something less than pain, yet
something more. What?

Another Indian summer day, perhaps, but still chilly at this hour, and Tracy was wishing she had not traded her warm parka for the blue blazer she now wore. Russ said, "Town's restless today."

She looked down the green toward the bandstand at the far end. It was true. The atmosphere of the town had changed in some subtle way. Did more cars pass by the courthouse than usual at this hour or did she imagine it? And were there more people on the streets along the green? When had the phones begun to ring? Probably some had heard the news on the radio. And the sirens and blue-and-red lights flashing had certainly been heard and seen. But her morning spot would be the first to carry the complete story to date. Larry Tomlinson, on the scene in the forest a few minutes ago: *Nothing so far, Tracy. No body yet.*

Yet. The word reverberated in her mind—ominous, possibly tragic.

Then, behind her, the doors of the courthouse opened. She turned, aware that Russ, too, had swung about. Mr. and Mrs. Pierre Durand were emerging together, the woman taking her husband's arm and ducking her head away. Pierre Durand was taller than his wife, massive-shouldered, with a heavy-jawed weather-lined face, a shaggy black moustache beneath a great nose and above a clenched, jutting chin. He had, she saw at once, fierce eyes of polished ebony. Tracy caught Russ's eye and shook her head. Puzzled, he nevertheless did not set the camera purring. As Mrs. Durand passed, Tracy was relieved to see that some of the panic had faded from her face. Pierre Durand, wearing a shiny blue serge suit, pulled his crumpled felt hat down, uttering, *"Non, non, non."* When they reached the old brown pickup truck at the curb, Tracy said, "Now, Russ—okay."

The camera began to buzz and the Durands were in the truck when the courthouse doors swung open again. Andrew Horgan came out, duffel bag in hand, camera over his shoulder. He hesitated a second; then he saw Tracy and came down a few steps to face her, as Russ came up the steps with his camera to tape the scene.

At the same instant that she realized she, too, was now on camera and automatically assumed her professional role, she saw that Andrew Horgan's face had changed: There was a sharp glint in his eye and his body seemed tauter, shoulders tense and stiff.

43

"Mr. Horgan," she said, "you've just talked with your son, haven't you? How is he? How does he feel?"

"How would any nineteen-year-old feel," he growled, "when he's being held in jail under suspicion of a crime because he reported it? Miss Larkin, I need your help."

Startled, conscious of the film rolling, Tracy saw another change take place on Horgan's not-quite-handsome face: Slyness leapt into his gaze, as if an idea had just occurred to him. "Help?" she echoed brightly for the camera's benefit. "Well, Mr. Horgan, perhaps later. At the moment I—"

Andrew Horgan made a sharp slashing gesture with one hand, cutting her off, and his tone changed. "I have just learned that there were two other men at the scene when Lynnette Durand disappeared. They were driving a big white panel truck with a Massachusetts license plate. My son saw it through his binoculars."

"But, Mr. Horgan—"

The gesture again, sharper and more authoritative this time as he went on, eyes burning into hers: "Anyone who might have seen such a vehicle during the night or early-morning hours can reach me—not the police, *me*—at the Cottages on the Green Motel."

Tracy made one last attempt to get the story back on track: "Two men, Mr. Horgan? What were they doing in a state forest at midnight?"

"For one thing, they were trying to rape Lynnette Durand—"

And with that word the whole scene exploded. Tracy heard a deep snarl off to one side: "Rape my daughter?" She felt a huge hand on her shoulder, felt herself spinning about, losing her balance, and she caught sight of Mrs. Durand's panic-stricken face in the truck window at the foot of the steps. Then she saw the thick trunk of Mr. Durand's body, legs apart, planted, facing Andrew, who had not moved. Everything seemed to be happening with the unreal clarity of a nightmare. Russ had backed away, doing his job, and the professional part of her mind whispered silently, *Not too long a shot, Russ, stay in there close,* while another part of herself cried out, also silently, *For God's sake, Andrew, get the hell away from here.* It was then, trying to rise, that she heard: "You his father, you brought up that bastard, you—"

But the sentence was never finished. As Andrew opened his mouth to speak, a hand crashed against his face, open-palmed, and as the sound cracked like the report of a small-caliber pistol, she saw Andrew's head swivel with the blow, then heard: "You never punish him, mister. *I* punish him!" Then, choking with disbelief and revulsion, she saw the same hand swinging again, from the other side, the back of it smashing, with a harsher, more terrible sound, against the other side of Andrew's face. She saw blood appear between his lips, her eyes darting to Durand's big angular face—fixed and grim and ugly, black mustache quivering—as she felt her own outrage take over: *Andrew, do something, do anything, run!*

But he did not run. He dropped the duffel bag, taking the big man's coat lapels in both hands and bringing Durand's face close to his own—was Russ still filming?—and she heard him say, in a whisper that was low and intense but amazingly free of anger: "Listen, listen, *listen* to me! I know how you feel. But my son did not harm your girl. He loves her."

"Love?" Durand wrenched himself free, violently. "Love!" he spat the word again as if it sickened him, black eyes bright with disgust and hate. "I know what *he* means by—" but he did not finish. "Anything happen to my girl, I *kill* the bastard!"

And then, so fast that Tracy did not realize he had moved, Durand brought his fist up. It smashed the side of Andrew's face. There was a flat sound, as of wood against wood, the ugliest sound she had ever heard, and Andrew fell to one side before his body crumpled to the steps.

Choking down the nausea that erupted all through her, the taste of raw metal in her throat, she rushed to where he lay, to hell with the camera, and as she dropped to her knees on the steps, she heard the word *Kill, kill, kill,* repeated over and over and receding with Durand's heavy boots clumping down the stone steps.

TWO

Todd was probably better off in jail.

After watching himself on the TV screen—taking the double thwack and then the single blow that brought him down—all Andrew Horgan could think of was that Todd was probably a helluva lot safer in jail than he would be on the street.

When Tracy interrupted the newscast for a commercial, he rose from the maple-framed easy chair—all the furniture in the cottage reminded him of an Ethan Allen showroom—and went into the bathroom to shave.

He'd already decided to use a disposable razor because the electric would be too damned rough on his swollen jaw, which had turned a lovely shade of lavender. There was a loose tooth in back but the taste of blood was gone.

When he heard Tracy's pleasantly low-pitched voice again, he listened: "Now for the human side of the news and Tracy's commentary. The face you see on your screen now is that of Lynnette Durand, officially listed as missing." He stepped to the door. "Anyone having any knowledge of this young woman is asked to contact the nearest police agency immediately." Lynnette Durand was a dark vivid beauty of a girl with a curious trepidation behind her smile—and astonishingly young.

Tracy appeared again. Andrew was startled by his reaction: In her own particular and individual way Tracy Larkin was a beauty, too. Even doing her job, in spite of or because of the authority with which she spoke, she projected vitality and animation. On the screen her short red hair looked brighter and the blue of her eyes was incredible—why hadn't he noticed this before?

"I spoke a few moments before airtime with Donna Lehrman, Lynnette Durand's roommate, who has just arrived from Haddam. I asked her about Lynnette Durand's personality and her own views of the strange disappearance."

Donna Lehrman, wearing a man's plaid flannel shirt over a sweat shirt, was heavyset, with dark intelligent eyes, frizzled brown hair, and bluff manner. "Well . . . Lynne's usually cheerful, y'know—on top of it. But . . . she . . . sometimes she seems like there's something inside bugging her and she acts so cool and carefree to cover it up, sort of." Tracy's voice prompted: "Do you think Lynnette might have run away on her own?" The girl shook her head. "No way. Her father's a lumberjack or some such but Lynne hates the woods. She wouldn't have gone there with anybody else but Todd, I can tell you that."

On camera again now, alone, Tracy continued: "You heard Andrew Horgan's words a few moments ago. His son, Todd Horgan, claims that there were two other men at the scene, that they threatened to rape Lynnette Durand, and after a violent scuffle of some kind, they left in a closed truck, white, bearing a Massachusetts license plate, number unknown. In the interest of justice, anyone who has seen such a vehicle in the area or around the state forest is requested to contact this station or the police. . . . More news as it breaks, and be sure to tune in at six-thirty this evening when I'll be back with a detailed update on the biggest story to hit the Shepperton area in the three years that I, Tracy Larkin, have been bringing you the news. Until then—"

Andrew flipped off the set and returned to the bathroom to finish his shave and to shower. All of a sudden he felt tired. In spite of the certainty he'd felt when he left the jail, how the hell could he be sure that Todd was telling the truth? After all, what did he really know about this boy who was—yes, he acknowledged this much now—his son? He couldn't let himself be blinded by some inner, irrational necessity to believe that his own flesh and blood would not, could not, murder a girl whom he loved. What if *she* did not love *him* and—

He removed the towel from around his waist and stepped into the shower. The steam and the needles of heat did not revive his spirits.

Had Todd invented the whole story? Did such a truck really exist?

As he turned off the water, he heard the telephone ringing. He returned to the spacious old-fashioned bedroom and took up the phone.

"Hi," a voice said. "It's me."

Just like that. As if she'd known him all his life. As if he'd know at once who was calling.

Into his mind flashed the picture of her on the screen: full-lighted, pale skin lustrous, eyes direct and frank and blue, so damned blue. "Hello," he said.

"Breakfast now?"

"Sure," he heard himself say, naked body tingling. "Soft scrambled eggs. *Very* soft."

"Why didn't you hit him back?"

"I couldn't."

"I know. It was a foolish question." And then: "How do you feel? You want me to bring aspirin? An icebag? A dentist?"

"No. No, thank you, Tracy."

"Your voice sounds . . . different."

"I don't know why." But he did know, or was beginning to. He, too, had caught that low tone of tenderness in his own voice when he'd used her name for the first time.

"Meet you at Colby's. Just off the green on Hancock. Half an hour too long?"

"I'll survive."

"Until then, Andy." And a click.

Suddenly a half hour seemed a very long space of time.

He glanced down his body. It had happened. Out of nowhere a quivering sort of excitement, which he had all but forgotten, had returned to every muscle and nerve. He stared down at the erection with a slow but satisfying astonishment.

"Sonofa*bitch*," he heard himself whisper.

"Hello?"

"Mrs. Lucas?" He knew the thin voice. He could picture her small birdlike face.

"Yes. Who's this?"

"This is Bruce Southworth. Has Coach Lucas left for school yet?"

"No, Bruce, but he's having breakfast." She sounded the

48

way she always did—uptight, bugged by something, maybe everything. "Is it important?"

"S-s-sort of, yes, ma'am."

"Harry, it's your star sprinter, Bruce Southworth."

While he waited—he could talk freely because Mom had already left for work at the library—Bruce could hear a child's voice chirping away and he remembered: *It's little Cindy,* Harry had said. *She's the one I could never hurt.*

"Hello, Bruce," Harry said in his heavy bass voice. "What's up, kid?"

"Did you hear the news on TV?"

"I don't have time for that in the morning." Harry was always sort of gruff when people were listening. "Something about the school?"

"N-n-no. About us. You and me."

Harry cleared his throat—a warning. "What about the school, Bruce?"

Bruce lowered his own voice although there was no need to. "Y' remember that truck we saw last night? The white one with the Massachusetts p-p-plate that came charging around us in such a goddam hurry, clipped our fender and made you run off the r-r-road?"

"Can't this wait till we get to school?" Harry growled.

"That g-g-gal on TV made it seem kinda important. The police want anyone who s-s-s-saw the truck to report it."

"You know we . . . you know you can't do that, Bruce. You know why, too."

"I did get the license n-n-n-number after it hit us, remember? And you got so mad—"

"Brucie"—and then he lifted his voice and corrected himself—"Bruce, this will have to wait till I get to the gym. We'll talk in the locker-room office between first and second period. Meantime—"

"It's got something to do with k-k-k-kidnapping, Coach. Maybe a m-m-murder."

"Do as I say," Harry barked. "Don't talk about it until I see you at school!"

Click.

Bruce, again hating the way he stuttered when his heart started to race, put down the phone. The house felt empty and he was running late, so he picked up his books and went outside. Some mornings the mile into town seemed like fifty or sixty. Had he fucked it up again? But shit, no one had heard him. It was Harry who'd said *Brucie*. He never called him that except when they were alone together.

What was he going to do? He knew the story Harry had laid on his wife and that he'd told Mom—that lie about him and Coach Lucas and three others on the track team going up to Montreal to see a hockey match on Sunday afternoon.

But the road back from Montreal came down from the northwest, and the road he and Harry, just the two of them, had been on came down from the northeast past the forest— the road back from Lake Massawippi, just over the Canadian border, where they'd spent the day and evening in a fishing camp. It had been, as Harry said, a heavenly time, but now—

Oh Christ, he had to give this a good think. If Mom ever suspected what was really going on . . . Jesus, it'd kill her! He started to jog—maybe that'd clear his head.

Mom had always been so proud that he could get decent grades and be in line for an athletic scholarship to UVM. *If your father was alive he'd be so proud, and it makes all my work worthwhile.* She *had* worked, too, day after day in the public library. All those years working for him, working hard.

Oh Christ, he couldn't fuck that up, too. It wasn't his fault. He didn't want to be the way he was, any more than Harry did.

There was nothing he could do about that dude in jail. It wasn't his business. He didn't even know him. Tough shit.

He'd hit his stride now. The rest of the way to school'd be a breeze.

"Mr. Horgan, when a student registers here and I see that sad, distant look in his or her eye, I take a special interest. In his studies, Todd gets A's in any subject that interests him, squeaks by in the rest. A brilliant but undisciplined mind."

Andrew listened to the husky voice, the clipped words. Had he been wise to telephone Ann Merrill at the college? What did he really hope to learn? "What about his professors?"

"Some of them admire his independence; others can't stomach that bitter ironic streak. Myself—I think of cynicism such as his as a thwarted, frustrated idealism. Todd's a spoiled boy in rebellion, but a victim—"

"A victim?"

''Not only of his personal background but of our society—
money, fame, selfish greed. What I've come to call the
pragmatism of dishonesty.''

''Then . . . if he told you a bizarre and unlikely story that
would exonerate him—''

''*You* believe him, don't you?''

Did he? Amazed, he said, ''Yes, damn it, I think I do!''

''Good! You see, some of these young victims of dishonesty are so revolted that they make the Truth a kind of
quixotic ideal.''

Andrew heaved an audible sigh. ''I guess that does it.'' His
spirits lifted. ''Thank you, Miss Merrill.''

''And now what?''

He laughed, the sound strange in his own ears. ''Now I
think I'm going on a quixotic sort of quest myself.''

''Good luck then. Ring me here if I can help.''

Andrew lowered the phone and stood up from the bed,
glanced at his watch. Twenty minutes before he was to meet
Tracy. The pain in his jaw had moved in, to the bone, and
become a steady ache. A quixotic quest, but where the hell to
begin? He pulled on his flight jacket and was about to go out
the door when the phone rang.

''Mr. Horgan?''

''Yes.''

''I saw you on the TV. I'm in a b-booth and I'm in a hurry,
so l-l-listen, I g-g-got to talk fast. That truck, the white truck
w-w-with the Massachusetts plate—it run me and my friend
off the road last night. I didn't take down the n-number but I
remember it. 779 OKR. Got it? Sorry, I'm late for class. So
long.''

There was a click and Andrew stood holding a silent line.
Then he moved fast, going outside. There was sunlight, pale
but definite, and already the air had lost its cold sting.

He had just enough time to walk to the courthouse before
joining Tracy if he hurried.

''I tried to talk to Sheriff Wheeler. All he did was shake his
head. Says it was probably some fresh kid who saw your
newscast and got a kooky idea to pull a fast one. For kicks!''

Across the table from him in the booth, Tracy said, ''It
could be a hoax. We get nuts calling the station all the time.

"Goddammit," Andrew said, "it was *not* a hoax. Even if it was, it's their job to trace it down."

His brown eyes were alive and hot and she discovered that she wanted to put a palm softly along the purplish bulge on his left cheekbone. "It's been a long night, hasn't it, Andy? Is that what your friends call you—Andy?"

"Sure. But I don't have too many friends . . ."

Curious, tempted, she didn't ask why. "You said the voice sounded young and said something about being late for class—"

"And he stuttered. Or stammered. Whichever." Andy shook his head and grinned across at her in a lopsided way. "I've just about had my gutful of that sheriff. All he's looking for is proof that Todd killed that girl. Would you believe the sonofabitch asked me whether I wanted to sign a complaint against Pierre Durand? Said we had him on film. Assault and battery. *Christ!*"

The breakfast rush was almost over. In Shepperton, from early morning till after midnight, Colby's was *the* place. Not that it was that attractive: dark-paneled walls hung with Sunday painters' autumn scenes, a counter with stools separated from the so-called dining room, and a long bar out of view in the rear room.

Which gave her an idea: "Maybe what you need's a brandy to settle you down before you eat—"

Something came into his face then: a quiet kind of gravity as he frowned, a strange bemused composure. "I don't drink," he said. "I can't. I'm an alcoholic."

Startled, she spoke without thinking: "I've never heard anyone say that before."

He shrugged his heavy shoulders, and his shaggy dark brows lifted: "Why not? It's a simple medical fact like any other."

"Yes, but—"

"Like saying: I'm a diabetic. Or I have high blood pressure. Or a bum ticker."

It was a subject that repelled and fascinated her. Because: "My father was one, too, I think."

"Was?"

Her mind returned, in a vivid, hurtful flash, to a day in the snow, the two coffins being lowered into the two graves, side by side, with a solemn, slow, simultaneous inevitabilty, the old priest's reedy voice intoning, the snow falling, the mourners in a half circle, eyes turned inward, and herself alone, never more alone. . . .

She felt now a hand over hers on the tabletop, a muscled, gentle hand, without pressure. "If I stirred something"—she heard his voice—"I'm sorry."

"He was a poet of sorts, was Charlie Larkin. Loved Dylan Thomas, quoted Synge and Yeats by the yard. A poet of sorts, my father." Her body had stiffened, and all through her she felt that cruel emptiness and loss and anger that she had known in the cemetery at thirteen. "He killed himself and he killed my mother in a car accident on an icy street in Boston when I was very young." Even now her voice had not hardened: "And I'll never forgive him. Hard as I've tried, I just can't."

When her eyes met Andy's now, what she saw there was pain—in *his* eyes, for *her*. For a second she panicked, tempted to stand up and run. She didn't *want* his damned compassion! How had he tricked her into—

"Tracy Larkin!" A harsh impersonal male voice called from the counter. "Tracy! Telephone!"

Relieved, she withdrew her hand and stood up in such a rush that the glasses and china clinked and clattered on the table.

Then she was moving, swift and certain again, herself again, toward the barroom in the rear.

What was happening? She hadn't talked about her father for years—no, not years, *ever*, with *any*one!

From the telephone booth she could look down the length of the bar. The room was empty. She spoke into the phone.

"Tracy, you sure stirred up a hornet's nest this morning."

"Good," she said, irritated at once, and for no reason, by Steve's tone and the old, stale cliché: "So? I stirred up a hornet's nest. Did I also set the town on its ear, or bite off more than I can chew, or—"

"Hey, Trace, slow down. That's what I mean: You're getting too involved. You're losing your journalistic detachment for some reason, right?"

"You're the boss," she said. "Tell me."

"Phone's been ringing off the hook. That girl's been sighted everywhere from here to Montpelier, to Boston to New York City."

"What was she wearing?"

"Wearing?"

"Lynnette Durand was stark naked."

"How'd you get into this mood? I heard the phone ring during the night, but I went back to sleep and when I woke up, you weren't in the house."

"That'll teach you not to hire a girl to do the news and then take her into your bed. What's doing, Steve?"

"Well—God, I hate it when you get into this mood—well, the most serious is: Sheriff Wheeler called the station. Says they're doing their job and he doesn't need or want your help."

"He's already told Andy that."

"Andy?"

"Andrew Horgan. The boy's father. Did you interrupt my breakfast to tell me this?"

"No, I didn't. I called to tell you that a Max Grossman telephoned from New York—he's Julia Craven's press agent—to say that she's on her way here—"

"Hang out the banners! Roll out the drums!"

"She's coming on a private plane with none other than Gerald Usher Lewis."

"Lock up your daughters—"

"Mr. Grossman didn't know what time—"

"Relax, Steve. If I don't get the grand entrance, I'll get some tape on her before air time. Anything else?"

"Tracy, for God's sake, what's got you so uptight?"

"Anything else?"

"Yes, damn it, there is. I love you."

What could she say? What she always said? The ritualistic *I love you, too*? She couldn't. Not this morning.

But why? Why, *why*?

Because she didn't love him. Or anyone. And never would. Because she was twenty-five and going nowhere, no compass, no focus, no—

Then she saw Pierre Durand. He was sitting at the bar, staring into the mirror behind the bottles, his huge shoulders slumped, head down between them. Waiting for the bar to open.

Had Andy's compassion for the man sprung, at least in part, from some quick recognition of their shared weakness?

She returned to the dining room. Yes, weakness. Not disease, no phony excuses, self-indulgent refusal to pass up the next drink, and the next, and—

At the table, where Andy was eating, she said: "Massa-chusetts—what's the license number?"

"Aren't you going to have breakfast?" Andy asked.

"Sure." Still standing, she picked up a slice of toast, placed the fried egg on it with a fork. "I have my own spies in the courthouse. What's the plate number?"

"Double seven, nine, OKR," Andy said.

She nodded, placing a slice of ham on top of the egg. "I'll find out whose name's on the truck registration." She put the other slice of toast on top of the ham. "The rest is up to you."

And then she was walking toward the door, wishing she had coffee to go with the sandwich and again wondering why the sweet hell she was feeling and acting this way.

Then she halted, turned on her heel, returned to the booth. "I forgot to mention—your ex-wife, in person, is on her way."

She didn't stay to see his expression. She didn't *want* to see his expression.

"Let's just say: for old time's sake, Julia. Nostalgia."

He was replying, aloud, over the steady satisfying thrum of the plane's engine, to Julia's question: *Tell me, Lewis, why are you doing this?* But the inner voice, amused and con-temptuous, by which Gerald Usher Lewis lived, mocked his answer. He was flying Julia to Vermont because he had no exciting and challenging case at the moment, because he was bored, because the house on Beacon Hill was a luxurious, empty mausoleum, and very much because there could be a great deal of money involved. Also, he could use Julia, or someone like Julia, at this particular time.

"And how's your wife?" Julia asked, sounding as if she cared, sounding like the actress she was. "What's her name—Jessica?"

"Cynthia." He squirmed in the seat. He'd had to take the single-engine prop Citabria because of the size of the field in Shepperton, but he preferred the Lear jet because the pilot seat better accommodated his bulky body. "She's very busy, always—the Boston social-cultural whirl." Busy when she was up on the uppers and not busy at all when she was down on the downers—which she could always seduce some doctor into prescribing.

"And you have a daughter, don't you? She must be in her teens by now."

"A son." He pulled on the throttle to slow down and took a cigar from his breast pocket. "Seymour's sixteen, in Groton—a bright kid." Bright, but a sneering little prick, who last month called his father an asshole to his face. "And your current husband?" he asked, as if he didn't know. "Dancer, isn't he?"

"Choreographer. Merle's involved with some dancer in the new show he's rehearsing. I'm not sure which sex this time."

He lit the cigar and did not ask about Todd. No point; he'd rather get the facts and then make up his own mind. Earlier she'd said, *He was certain to get into real trouble, sooner or later,* and almost in the same breath, *He's such a dear child, utterly incapable of harming anyone.* Julia was one of those people—their number being legion—who are perfectly capable of holding two diametrically opposed concepts in the mind without so much as suspecting any contradiction. Such people amused him really; they were so easy to handle. Julia had not mentioned the two weeks they'd spent together at the Ritz-Carlton. He himself wasn't ready to use that memory yet.

So he said; "I told you when you came aboard that I'd talked to the sheriff at Shepperton." From whom he'd gotten the impression that they didn't know what the hell to do till they knew what had really happened to the girl. "I *didn't* mention that they told me Todd's father was there." And when she didn't rise to the bait, he jiggled the line in the water: "A man named Horgan. You led me to think your son was Rollo Taggart's son."

"Did I? I don't know why I would have done that. . . ."

But Lewis did: It had fitted her purpose at some point. Julia, he knew, created the truth as she went along.

"Poor Rollo," Julia said. "He was old enough to be my father, of course, but he *was* kind. When he died, I really thought I'd never get over it."

But she had, of course. Was it that *National Enquirer* rag that had hinted that Rollo Taggart had taken his own life? Lewis doubted that there was anything she couldn't "get over"—by moving on to something, or someone, else.

Julia was staring out at the clouds. She was a remarkably beautiful woman: features near-perfect, blond hair dazzling, chin set at a slightly arrogant cant. Always a challenge. To any man.

"I didn't even know you were married before Rollo—"

"Andy left me when he learned I was pregnant. And the very next day—at an audition in the old Morosco Theater—I met Rollo. I was scheduled to audition for him but I couldn't. I couldn't because Andy had broken my jaw the day before—when I told him I was pregnant. I was in the hospital for a week."

"After the audition, of course—"

"Oh, stop trying to trip me. Rollo took me to his suite at the Waldorf."

"Where he seduced you," Lewis prompted.

"Where I fell hopelessly in love with him." It was hard for Lewis to imagine Julia hopelessly in love. "I don't know why I'm telling you this," she said.

And when she did not go on, he asked, "And Rollo didn't mind that you were pregnant?"

"He *loved* it." She turned her head to fix her direct, ingenuous gaze on him, her green eyes childlike in their innocence. "He arranged everything. Todd was born in Vegas. I was divorced as soon as I was out of the hospital, and Rollo and I were married the same day."

"A Las Vegas package deal."

"Oh, stop it. You sound just like Todd."

So . . . her son knew the whole story—or her distorted and romanticized version of it. "How much of this does Andrew Horgan know?"

"Only what he reads in the papers, I suppose. He knows that he deserted me when I needed him most. He fucking well knows *that*!"

And what did Gerald Usher Lewis know? He smiled to himself. What he knew now was that he'd been had. Somehow Julia was hoping that her first husband, first of three, would be in Shepperton today. "You must have loved this Horgan bastard very much."

"No one's ever made love to me the way he did. He was the first, and not anyone since ever has."

"Present company excepted?"

Julia laughed. Her tremulous, throaty laugh was famous: sincere, childlike, contagious. The bitch. She'd used him. She'd manipulated the great manipulator. She'd not only turned what might be a routine legal case into something more, while obtaining the best defense counsel the kid could have, but she'd provided herself with a private plane, with pilot, to take her to a romantic reunion with her first husband. He remembered what she'd said during those two weeks at the Ritz: *I'm only alive when I'm on stage or in bed.*

Well, he'd make her pay. In his own way. It wasn't too bad a bargain. He was at loose ends and there was a certain satisfaction in having a woman that every male who saw her on stage or screen lusted to bed down. He'd get his. Gerald Usher Lewis always did.

"Take off your clothes."

"Here?"

"You heard me. Strip down, lady."

"But I—"

"Do it!"

Then abruptly, he pushed the wheel forward. The nose of the plane went down. He move one foot and then the other. The plane rocked as it plunged. Then he gunned it. He heard her scream over the roar of the engine. The earth below—a pattern of rolling hills and woods and stone fences—tilted crazily and he stuttered the engine, still diving. The stall-warning indicator began to beep.

He risked a glance. She had begun to undress, her hands frantic. Her eyes were wide and wild. The terror in them caused his prick to harden.

When she was naked, he leveled off and turned to her. She was no longer Julia Craven, the haughty star, the self-composed celebrity. She was a terrified, vulnerable, defenseless woman, very naked—and at his mercy.

"Don't hurt me," she said. "Please don't hurt me."

But he knew that was not what she meant. He knew she meant the opposite. She wanted to be punished.

They were all bitches and they all wanted to be punished.

THREE

There's something about a small town . . .

That's what Andrew was thinking as he sat in the booth, sipping his fifth big mug of coffee, waiting for Tracy to return. Those tired clichés about small towns were probably true. If you were brought up in one, you never forgot it; and if you weren't, you wished you had been. He himself had grown up on the south side of Chicago, but now observing the quiet comings and goings this morning, the nods and greetings and chitchat and banter, he had begun to feel an odd kinship with the town. He'd become aware of some glances and whispers with eyes averted—what was it Tracy had said on the way in from the airstrip? *Everybody knows all, tells all in a small town.*

"Mr. Horgan?"

He looked up. Two kids stood there, a boy and a girl about Todd's age. He recognized the girl: Donna Lehrman, Lynnette's roommate, heavyset, frizzle-haired; she had been interviewed by Tracy earlier in the morning. But it was the boy who had spoken.

Andrew started to stand, but the boy said, "No, please." His voice had a rough texture and the accent of New York City. "We don't want to bother you. We saw you here by yourself, so we—"

"Please sit down," Andrew said. "You've come from Melville?"

"Yes, sir. I'm Norman Shatsky—Todd's roommate." Rather chubby, bushy black hair, intelligent eyes behind thick horn-rimmed spectacles, an attitude of grave concern. "Look, Mr. Horgan, we came over to see whether there was any way we could help."

Andrew turned his attention to the girl. "I'm curious about Lynnette Durand."

Lighting a cigarette, Donna said, "That picture of her on TV—Norm brought that over. It's the one beside Todd's bed. Did you see it?" And when Andrew nodded: "Behind that All-American cheerleader crap, there's something sad about Lynne. Y' know?" And when he nodded again: "Well, whatever that is, that's what Todd sees—"

"Yeh," Norman interrupted. "He's the last of the romantics extant." He shook his head. "He's a goddam *idiot* romantic if you want to know. And that leads to things, that's all."

"Such as?"

Norman ran a hand angrily through his hair. "Such as getting bombed out on booze—or booze and pot and juices inside that maybe are worse—"

"So bombed out that . . . what?"

"He's got at *least* three reckless driving charges against him, at *least* one drunk-driving that I know of. One assault and battery that we won't *talk* about."

"I think we should," Andrew said, very tense now. "I think we better."

Norman glanced at Donna, who looked away and blew smoke. So Norman went on: "Some guy, some townie over in Haddam, made a pass at Lynnette. Not just a casual, *verbal* pass—a real obscene physical grab-ass pass in a bar one night. Until that night I didn't know Todd had a temper. Man, it's violent. It's wild. He goes ape. I didn't know he had *fists* till that happened."

Norman sat back and stared into space, while Andrew felt a slow panic move into his mind.

Norman leaned over the table to say: "They won't let me see him. How's he *taking* all this? He hasn't gone into one of his glooms, has he?"

"He's damned miserable. And angry as hell. Does he have serious depressions, Norman?"

"I keep forgetting you don't know him——"

"Does he?"

"Yes, sir, he does. Sometimes he cuts classes two or three days in a row."

"Drinking?" Andrew asked, knowing.

"That adds to it, but mostly just a weird kind of existential despair. Scares the shit out of me."

Andrew knew it well. From experience. He had also learned, through his own research and in that month in the hospital, that there was more than a possibility that alcoholism was a genetic disease. And then, after Donna and Norman had gone—"We're at the Colonial Motel if you need us"—Andrew had a new experience: an overwhelming desire, like an ache, to save his son before it was too late. To use his own painfully earned knowledge to spare his son the anguish he had suffered.

But doubts had wormed into his mind now. Depressions, booze, a violent temper, at least one violent act, maybe others. Still, would Todd have invented the truck? And what about that phone call from the kid who'd seen it? Some friend of Todd's? No, damn it, he'd given the plate number. . . .

As he was about to sit down again, he saw the chief of police, Kyle Radford, approaching from the counter, coffee mug in hand. What now?

"Town's gettin' crowded," Chief Radford said in his abrupt, thin voice. "Sightseers, morbid curiosity, human nature. Lots of these kids up from the college, too. Any excuse to cut classes, or is there that many down there fond of your son?"

"Both, probably," Andrew said, still standing, waiting. Still confused as hell.

Chief Radford was not wearing his cap. His head was a bald pate with a fringe of gray around it. "Y' mind if I sit down?"

"You have some news for me?" Andrew asked, sitting across from the small man whose face resembled a shrunken leather mask, its expression unreadable.

"Ay-uh, you might say that. First off, your son Todd's got a police record. Y' know that?"

"I just learned it."

"Second, blood test came in from the hospital. Your son's

blood. Showed traces of what's legally called a controlled substance." He stood up. "Fancy name, but meaning drugs." He tilted his head. "All Sheriff Wheeler needs. He's on his way in from the scene to file the charges personal. Court's already convened today so there'll be a first hearing tomorrow morning."

"Thanks," Andrew said, and started toward the door.

"You're the one he gets it from then." And when Andrew halted to turn: "That quick temper. Your son comes by it natural, don't he?"

Andrew did not reply. He paid his check at the counter and went outside and walked along the storefronts toward the green.

"Hey, Flagg, wait for baby!" Tracy's voice, behind him, lifted.

He turned and watched her approach: a small woman, girlishly slim, hair brilliant in the sun, step brisk, almost frisky. He felt the hollowness return to his midsection and a tightening farther down and remembered that moment on the telephone after his shower. . . .

"That's the last line of an old World War One play we did in college," she said. "Where are you going?"

"Damned if I know. I have to think."

"Well, you can do that on the plane. My car's behind the courthouse."

He had forgotten the silken clarity, the translucent skin of youth, almost luminous—

"Where are we going?"

She brushed past him—a fresh fragrance, the scent of wildflowers: He'd never noticed it before. "Lowell, Lowell, Massachusetts."

He fell into step. Not tall himself, he seemed to tower over her. "You have the name of the company?"

As they turned onto the street bordering the green, he caught sight of the lumbering figure of Pierre Durand climbing the courthouse steps.

"Wylie Trucking, Inc." Tracy said. "Address, phone, the works." She slid her arm through his and looked up into his face, smiling, as they walked. "And now you can tell me the first names that your son heard those two use last night."

* * *

The search is still on, Mr. Durand. Even got a helicopter out there now.

Pierre Durand, coming outside again, stood somewhat unsteadily at the top of the courthouse steps. Sheriff Wheeler himself had just now told him the latest: *Todd Horgan's officially under arrest now. Misdemeanors only, so far, but enough to hold him till we know what happened to . . . I mean, till we learn where your daughter is, Mr. Durand.*

Pierre peered down the length of green. It looked hazy. Everything looked hazy. But he was *not* drunk. *You better get hold of yourself Mr. Durand. Hate to see Chief Radford have to haul you in for public intoxication.*

Him? They'd arrest *him*? Just like the motherfuckers—arrest *him* instead of doing their real job. *Merde!* Real criminals always walked off free but a law-abiding citizen—

He went, carefully, down the bank of steps to the street.

Way it works, way whole world works, always has. Poor man. Couldn't afford no expensive lawyer. Couldn't hardly afford to send his daughter to college. Even *with* the scholarship. Smart girl, Lynnette—*smart*.

Lynnette, baby, where are you? It was like a moan inside. What's happened to you?

It was too much, too much—how much can a man take?

Walking, making every effort to keep his huge body stiff so nobody'd get the wrong idea, this early in the morning, hot already, goddam blue serge, hot as hell, walking, he saw an open-topped car angle into a parking slot along the curb. Filled with kids. College kids. Getting out. Girls in shorts. Bare legs. Young. Smooth. Bare . . .

College girls. Way college girls dress today. Half naked— T-shirts, tits bobbing—showing it all, asking for it, begging for it.

Whores. Bitches. Look at them dancing around, showing off, laughing, joking, not caring. Look at the *whores*!

He wouldn't look. They couldn't make him look. That's what they wanted.

Off to his right a street led to the Catholic church. Where Thérèse had gone. To mass. To confession maybe—

Let her confess. Let her tell the priest *her* part in this. Nagging him out of his mind: *Lynnette deserves college. It won't cost much. You're making good money again now that the paper mill's back in operation.*

63

Let Thérèse, her mother, confess that it was *her* fault this thing had happened.

If Lynnette had stayed home where she belonged, up there in Baileyville, if she'd listened to *him*, hadn't been so *réfractaire*, so goddam hell-bent to get away—

He reached the white sign: MRS. WHARTON'S GUEST HOME. A mansion. White columns. Shutters. Big lawn. Jesus—why'd he let Thérèse convince him? *You don't want people to think we're poor dumb Canucks, do you? You don't want to shame Lynnette, do you?*

Instead of going up the walk to the wide veranda, he went around, past bay windows, to the rear. Where the brown pickup was parked. Sweating again. Indian summer, sure as hell. And getting hotter. He unlocked the door. The rifle was still in its sling. He took it down and slid it into its case, glancing around. Nobody's business but his.

With the rifle case in hand, he locked up again—didn't want anyone getting to his stash of booze.

That rifle was his most valuable possession. Weatherby Vanguard Thirty-Ought-Six, with Mauser action, Weaver scope. He was returning to the front of the house. *Merde*, with that gun he could pick off a deer at two, three hundred yards, or moose, or a black bear, no sweat.

He went up the steps, across the veranda, and into the hall—where a man felt he had to walk on tiptoe, Christ-sake—and as he climbed the curving stairway, he was trying to think ahead.

Court hearing at ten tomorrow morning. Well, if they didn't punish the boy for what he done, old Pierre Durand had his own way to see justice done.

"Wylie Trucking, good morning. This is Sandy. Can I help you?"

"Hello. Can I talk to Jesse?"

"Jesse Kull? I'm sorry, miss, it's his day off today."

"Oh shit. How 'bout Ralph?"

"Ralph? We don't have any Ralph working here, miss."

"Sure. Y'know. Sure, the Ralph who works with Jesse—"

"Oh—Rolf. Of course, sure. Sorry. Monday's Rolf's day off, too."

"Rolf—funny name, ain't it?"

"Not for a Swede. Not if your last name's Arneson, I

guess. Listen. It's Monday morning. I'm busy. If you want to leave a message, I'll connect you to the garage."

"No, no message. Y' been very helpful. Thanks a million, Sandy."

Tracy replaced the phone on the hook and came out of the telephone booth in the lobby of the Alpine Chalet. Her mother had always told her she had a whiny voice. Which was why she'd worked on it in college to bring it down to a pleasant, deeper sound. But a whine came in handy sometimes. Busy little Sandy must have thought she sounded like just the kind of female barfly who'd be chasing a big handsome Swede like Rolf Arneson.

Without glancing in any direction, she hurried out to run through the birch grove toward the landing strip, where Andy was doing what he'd called his preflight checkup.

"Another Indian summer day."

At the barred window, Todd turned his head to look over his shoulder. Chief of Police Radford, hard and lean and withered-looking, was standing in the door. "I told you, son, you don't have t' stay in the cell. Move around, watch TV."

"I saw all the TV I want to see," Todd said, not moving. And then he asked the elderly man in the gray uniform the same question he'd been asking for a century or two now: "Have they found her? Are they *trying*?"

"Subside, son, subside and *you* answer me this: Why'd you take a Ruger Speed-Six on an overnight camping trip?"

"I wish to God I hadn't left it in the car!"

Chief Radford moved into the cell, eyes cautious but not unfriendly. "Son, a man can't blame you for being in this mood, but if you mean—"

"I mean I wish I'd shot their balls off, both of them." He whirled around. "What are you getting at? You think I brought it along to kill Lynnette?"

"Y' know, to put it straight out, you're not the easiest person in the world to be nice to."

"Not in a goddam cell like this! What's the deal here— punish the bastard *before* he's proved guilty? Where do you find *that* in the Constitution?" He stepped closer. "You and Sheriff Wheeler think you've got a murder case, don't you? Just what you need to shake the dust out of your skulls around here, isn't it?"

"Not me, son." He moved to sit down on the lower bunk. "Day's hardly begun an' I'm tired already. The girl's father pestering us every fifteen minutes—"

"The man's going crazy with grief! He's her *father*. You saw the TV news, didn't you? What he did to my father."

"No, but I heard. I also heard your father stood and took it. . . ." He turned it into a question, then waited.

"So? I thought that was pretty terrific! I thought that took guts!"

"Ay-uh, mebbe. Or mebbe your old man feels kinda guilty—"

"And maybe he should!" Todd pivoted about to stare through the bars: a parking area, police cars, and beyond, a narrow tree-lined street.

"Did you get any shuteye?" Radford asked.

"No." Todd, frowning, turned to study the man. He tasted bitter contrition on his tongue—a familiar taste. "I don't have to sleep," he said. "But thanks." He didn't say that, exhausted, he had drifted off once around dawn, only to be brought upright and sweating and shaking all over at the sound of Lynnette's terrified screams, the memory of her slim white shadow ghostlike among the tree trunks.

Hatred overwhelmed him. Again the savage need, the craving and necessity for revenge raged through him and for a second he was certain that his throat and chest would explode.

Through a haze he saw Radford stand up. "You and the girl—you was smoking pot last night, weren't you?"

Damned if he'd lie. "So?" he said.

"Scrambles up the brain, that stuff. Possibility is, mebbe your girl decided to lay down and sleep, wait for sunlight . . ." The old man moved to the door. "By the way, they found a big square sorta searchlight out there. Busted." He turned in the doorway. "Just like you said. Nurse who treated you last night—she says it certainly could have caused that bruise on your back."

When the chief had gone, Todd sat down on the bunk. He discovered that there were tears in his eyes, and in a moment his chest was heaving and he was sobbing, trying to stifle the sound but unable to control the pictures in his mind. Even if she had got away, what was she feeling now? What was she going through in there alone? She hated the woods. What had he done to her? He loved her. How could he have done this to her?

* * *

Thou shalt know the truth and the truth shall set you free.

Well, now Tracy knew a bit more of the truth—enough to feel certain they were not on what Steve would most certainly have called a wild-goose chase.

Once she had seen the photographic equipment on the rear seats of the little plane, she had realized who Andrew was. His blunt-featured face appeared fixed but troubled as he gazed ahead, one hand carelessly on the wheel. She probably should have apologized for the strange mood that had come over her when she'd learned that Julia Craven was on her way. What was Andrew Horgan to her? Just another man, physically attractive, nothing more. Oh hell yes, more—he was an admitted alcoholic. *Never again, I swear. That was the last drop ever.* How many times had she heard that? Your last drop, Charlie Larkin, was the one that killed you. So much for that.

Keeping her tone particularly casual over the low thunder of the engine, she said, "I'm pretty ignorant but I know who you are now."

"Then maybe you ought to tell me," Andrew said. "I've been thinking all morning that I'm damned if *I* know who I am—or even what I'm doing."

She decided to ignore that. "Steve has one of your books—with aerial shots of the Rockies. Very dramatic." Dramatic, hell—those photographs were breathtaking, awesome. But for some damned reason she had to say: "Steve is Stephen Savage. He owns the TV station I work for and he's the man I'm living with."

No response. Not a nod or glance. Nothing.

She was tempted to add something about not being committed to Steve either, or to anyone. You want to make a *complete* ass out of yourself, Tracy? "Steve won't approve of my running off like this, but I'm hoping to get a better story with you."

"You want a story and I want the truth," Andrew said.

"You still don't believe your son completely, do you?"

"Right now I'm operating on the premise that my son really hates lies as much as I do, so wouldn't tell them to save his neck. What do *you* think?"

It was a flat, low-voiced demand and she felt the anguish as if it were her own.

He cares. This man really cares. "I don't *think*," she said. "I know now. A man named Jesse Kull and another named Rolf—not Ralph—Arneson are employed by Wylie Trucking."

She could feel his eyes on her. There was a change in the sound outside the cabin and she realized the plane had picked up speed.

Sometimes I think, her father had often said, *sometimes, daughter, I honestly believe that there are only two kinds of people in the world: those who care and those who don't give a damn for anyone or anything but themselves.*

"Well," Andrew said, "we do both want the same thing, don't we?"

"I knew someone who used to say *Justice is truth in action.*" Dear old, sweet old drunken Charlie Larkin. "Years later I learned he was quoting Disraeli."

"Maybe," Andrew said, "maybe justice is something we have to invent, and believe in, in order to go on. Punishment. Expiation. The prison cell, the hangman's noose. Some moral accountant with a heavenly computer in the sky keeping the record book—everlasting bliss or eternal hellfire. The human animal does seem to have a sort of universal longing to believe that somehow, some way, justice will be done. Maybe that's what makes him human."

It was more words at one time than she had heard him speak before. Slightly startled and with a slow suffusion of pleasure and excitement, she asked, "And what do *you* believe, Andrew Horgan, pilot, photographer, and closet philosopher?"

"None of it," he said very quietly. "If I believe anything, I guess it's that there's no such thing as justice, here or hereafter, no divine order whether we want it or not, and I can't invent a god to believe in just because I need one."

The utter bleakness of his tone reached her depths and she felt a slight shiver go through her body. And, again, she thought of her father.

Now, almost trembling, she asked, "Are all alcoholics alike?"

"In many ways, yes." He knew at once what she meant—he would know, of *course!*—and to whom she was referring. In a tone so gentle that it was almost tender, he added, "He was sick, Tracy. Not a vice, not a weakness—a sickness like any other."

"Excuses!" Her furious voice crackled in the small cabin. "He drank to kill pain. He drank because he was an idealist and the world thinks idealists are fools! Because he was a poet who had to write shitty prose for a shitty newspaper. Because he was loved or wasn't loved! Because, because, because! Don't give me that crap! He drank because he was a selfish, self-indulgent bastard, and he *robbed* me—he killed himself in his own way and he took my mother along with him. Am I supposed to forgive him for that, too?"

"I hope you'll be able to forgive him someday, Tracy. For your sake. If you want to become a woman."

"I am a woman, damn you!" She realized she was crying, tears scalding in her eyes. She never cried, hadn't cried since she was thirteen years old. She realized that she was shouting, too: "Did you ever forgive Julia Craven?"

He was staring at her now. "For what?"

"For whatever she did to you to take the life out of you!"

"Is that what you think?"

"I think you still love her. I think you don't want to see her because you still love her!"

Andrew didn't speak for a long moment. But she saw a slow, bewildered smile on his wide lips. "Now you remind *me* of someone."

His lopsided face hung misty in her gaze but she refused to turn away. "Who?" she challenged.

The smile faded. Slowly. "Someone who's also dead."

She waited. Her throat was clogged, her voice gone. This . . . this had not occurred to her. What did he mean? Who?

He faced forward again. The clouds puffed against the windshield, distorting the light on his face. She had stopped breathing.

"Her name was Cassie. She was my wife for seven years."

Her impulse was to reach for him. "I didn't know," she said—a choked, cracked whisper. "I'm sorry. I had no way of . . ." She hesitated. "Then *she's* the one who—"

"No!" *He* was angry now, hands gripping the wheel, the muscles in his jaw quivering. "She didn't take life from me. She gave it to me!"

And then she had to ask, had to: "How . . . how'd she die?"

The anger in his voice was gone. What replaced it was worse. "She had a blood clot floating around in her bloodstream. She didn't know. One night we made love and went to sleep. She didn't wake up."

"Oh, Andy"—and this time she did reach. She placed a hand over his on the wheel. The wheel went forward. There was a slight downward movement of the plane's nose. He corrected it. She realized that the only other time their flesh had touched, he had placed *his* hand over *hers*. She had no words.

"That was over five years ago and I wish to hell I knew why I was telling *you*."

"Don't be angry," she whispered.

"It happened. Things just happen. Chance. Accident. Justice? There are no reasons, no meanings. . . ."

Again her father's face flickered in her mind: her last view of him, eyes shut, features composed, just before the lid of the coffin closed over him, the only peace he'd ever known.

"Andy," she said.

"Is your seat belt fastened? We're approaching Lawrence. There's no field at Lowell. We may have to walk the fifteen miles between."

"Andy . . . I know something about loneliness, too—"

"And . . . Stephen Savage?"

"I live with him. I didn't say that . . . what were your words? . . . I didn't say that he gave me life." Then she added: "And I've *never* talked like this before. Not with anyone. Ever."

"Oh, yes, Mr. Wylie, he's right here. Hold on."

When he heard it ring, even though it was midmorning, Rolf Arneson's first thought had been: They've tracked us down. But hearing Christine use Mr. Wylie's name, he felt his gut simmer down. "Rolf, it's your boss." He stood up from the bed, wearing only a T-shirt, and went into the living room in five or six long strides—a tall, lean young man in his late thirties, known as the Big Swede by the regulars in the Smugglers Cove, where Christine tended bar.

"Mr. Vylie?"

"You didn't report in when you got back from your delivery last night." Mr. Wylie's voice, usually friendly, even jovial, sounded funny—kind of grim. "You know the rule, Rolf."

"Jesse and me, ve was both so beat—"

"Don't give me any shit. Beat? It's the easiest run you'll ever have. You got orders: Report to me, I don't care what time of night. I have my orders, too. I have to report, too."

"You nefer told me that, Mr. Vylie."

"Lots of things I don't tell you. Lots of things it's better you don't know. Better for you."

Lots of things Rolf had put together, too. But he said, "Von't happen again, Mr. Vylie."

Then, as Rolf saw Christine through the kitchen door, standing at the stove but listening—and staring at the gash on his leg just above the knee—he heard Mr. Wylie's tone change: "Everything go without a hitch?"

"On target," he said, using the Green Beret lingo that seemed to impress everybody. "Vithout encountering any enemy resistance vhatefer, sir."

"Nothing happened? *Nothing?*"

Rolf's hand tightened on the phone. "Vhat do you mean, Mr. Vylie?"

"I mean I got a map in front of me. I mean I've had a call from the police in a place called Shepperton, Vermont. Inquiring whether Wylie Trucking had any vehicles in that area last night. And about an hour ago Sandy had one from some gal with a squeaky voice asking for either you or Jesse Kull. Only she didn't know your first name was Rolf, not Ralph. Squeaky-voice dame—that ring any bells?"

"Ve don't talk to nobody on the run. Mr. Vylie."

"Well, maybe I'm just jittery, but it does make a man wonder. Any connection, Rolf? Anything happen up there, anything at all?"

Rolf could feel his grip on the phone sending pain into his shoulder, and his scrotum had begun to shrivel up. "No sveat, Mr. Vylie. Some drunk on the road, vouldn't let us pass, vas all. He vas in the wrong but you told us not to stop for anything so I yust drove on, but not speeding, like you said. No traffic laws broken. Ve yust got the hell outa there."

A long silence. Outside the picture window in the small suburban cottage, Rolf could hear a mother calling her kid. Christine was standing in the kitchen door, pushing her long light hair back from her forehead, no longer staring at the hatchet wound but at his face. He didn't seem able to take a deep breath.

"Listen, Rolf," Mr. Wylie said at last. "Listen. I know

71

you're not the dumb Swede you act like. That's all I'll say on the phone. Except this: If there's more to this than you're telling me, you'd better meet me somewhere we can talk. Not my office. It's not just the government, Rolf—it's the people paying us to do the job. They're a helluva lot more dangerous than the government. *Now* . . . do you want to meet me somewhere?''

Rolf considered. He couldn't tell him about picking up the kid and throwing him off the cliff. Or why they were in there. Or about dumping the stuff in the lake instead of in the old quarry six or seven miles away, like usual. Above all, he couldn't mention what Jesse had—

"I told you the whole story, Mr. Vylie," he said.

He heard a long drawn-out sigh. "That's it, then. We didn't have this conversation. Forget it. Forget every goddam word of it, hear?"

After Mr. Wylie had hung up without saying goodbye, Rolf continued to hold the phone. That Jesse, that dumb-ass redneck Jesse Kull—

Jesus.

Then Christine spoke: "I knew when you came in this morning, *something* happened."

"Nothing happened." He discovered the phone in his hand. He slammed it down. "You heard me. Nothing at all."

"Bullshit." She came into the room, the negligee open top and bottom, her long legs exposed when she sat down on the sofa and crossed them. "This is Chrissie, remember? Not your ex-wife. This is Chrissie Linquist, who's been around all the curves and pays her half of the rent. Give."

He went into the bedroom. Fast. Too fast. "Fuck off."

While he was pulling on his clothes, his day-off clothes, he was trying to keep his mind blank.

But Christine followed and stood in the door. "You weren't sloshed when you came in this morning—"

"Me and Jesse,'ve had a few."

"Liar. You usually do but you were in a hurry. A big hurry."

"I got to get over to Jesse's."

"Now you're in a hurry again." Her voice was the one she used behind the bar when she wanted a customer to stop making a pass—half-teasing, but gritty. "You don't have to rape *me*, Rolf."

"I didn't *rape* anybody."

"Like hell. You woke me up, tore off my pajamas—you threw me back on the bed and you held me like I was fighting you, and you raped me like I was some kind of stranger." She moved to block the doorway as he stepped toward it. "I'm not complaining. The pajamas're right there on the floor." She held up her hands and turned them. "Look at my wrists. I hurt other places, too. You can be a rough fucker when you want to."

"I didn't mean to hurt you. I'm sorry, Chris."

Her face twisted into a grin. "I'm not asking you to be sorry. One dumb Swede plays house with another dumb Swede, she expects something dumb. But what?"

The sense of urgency went out of him: What good would it do to warn Jesse? He gave up. It had happened. Feeling a slow cold fear begin deep in his gut, he said, "I didn't rape anybody. Jesse did."

Christine's face went blank, and white, and her blue eyes seemed to pull back into her head. "Jesse?"

"I tried to stop him. I ran after him but I couldn't find him in the woods. Then I heard her screaming again. By the time I found them, it vas all over."

"Jesse? That big ox. Jesus, if Jesse raped anybody, he must've broken every bone in her body."

"That's vhat I mean. By the time I got to them, it vas too late."

73

FOUR

"Mr. Wylie, two people in reception to see you, Mr. Wylie."

When he heard Sandy's voice on the PA, Earl Wylie wiped his hands with paper toweling at the sink and then went through the wide double doors from the garage into the office area. Earl Wylie wished he didn't stiffen and feel his insides start to empty out whenever Sandy called him to the front office. He wished he could control the pictures that flashed through his mind: two FBI men waiting, with warrants, with handcuffs maybe, and questions. Questions he didn't dare answer because what would happen to him if he did answer would be a hell of a lot worse than anything the police or the courts could do. So much worse that his mind flinched from the thought.

By the time he reached the reception area, recalling what his wife, Paula, always said—that she wished the waiting room looked less like a doctor's or dentist's—he had himself in control. The two who were there now were not seated on the imitation-leather couch or on the plastic-covered chairs: a man in his forties with a camera slung over his shoulder and a red-headed girl wearing a blue blazer and a green dress. Not cops. Well, at least he could breathe normally again.

For fifteen years Paula had been telling him that now that he was boss of his own business, he should try to be more polite. So when he introduced himself he nodded his heavy balding head and tried to smile pleasantly. "What can I do for you?"

"Sorry to bother you, Mr. Wylie," the man said—average

74

height, average build, but trim, gray-laced dark hair, brown eyes maybe six inches below the level of Earl's. "My name's Andrew Horgan. And this is my daughter, Tracy." Earl nodded again. "We've been visiting my son at his college in Vermont."

"About fifteen miles south of Shepperton," the girl said, and tilted her head as if she were waiting.

Shepperton. Again. He felt the tightening return to his chest and along the heavy soft flesh of his tall body. "Well?"

"My son," Horgan said, "was driving with his sister shortly after midnight last night when one of your trucks ran their car off the road."

"Outside of Shepperton," the girl said.

He felt both pairs of eyes on him now, riveted, prying, waiting again. He hoped his own eyes reflected his bewilderment, not the acid dread that was beginning to pollute his blood. He shook his head. "Not one of my trucks. Some mistake here." But was there? And what *kind* of mistake? "Yesterday was Sunday and we don't operate trucks on Sunday." He tried the smile again. "Sunday is the day we rest."

"I memorized the license number," the girl said. "Massachusetts 779 OKR."

"Well, miss, I'm not a man to call a pretty young lady a liar. That number's one of ours"—he prided himself on knowing every detail of the business—"but maybe, in the excitement and all, you didn't get the number right in your mind." So this was the reason the Shepperton police had called. "One little digit could make a difference, you know." But would it explain the call from the woman with the squeaky voice? "Anyone can make a mistake in a situation like that. Was your brother hurt?"

It was the father who answered. "There were no injuries but the police are charging my son with reckless driving and failure to have his vehicle under control."

No sweat, Mr. Vylie. Some drunk on the road, vouldn't let us pass, vas all. Earl Wylie felt a vast warm sense of relief rise through his body, expanding. "Listen, Mr. Horgan, I can sympathize, honest. If you don't believe me, you're welcome to examine our records. We log every truck coming and going, time of departure, destination, manifest, time of return. Come on back to my office."

But they did not move. Either of them.

Then the girl said: "One of the men had a red beard, darker than my hair, but red."

Jesse Kull. Oh Christ, the girl had seen more than the truck! Earl Wylie forced himself to shake his head. "Don't sound like anyone in my employ—"

"Weight maybe three hundred pounds," the man prompted, "or heavier," and Earl Wylie saw a glint in the brown eyes, a glint he didn't like.

The sense of relief was gone now. It had turned into something else. Something like fear. Or worse. "I don't know anyone weighs three hundred pounds." Paula's words sounded in his mind: *Honey flows slower but it gets more done than vinegar.* "Listen, Mr. Horgan, I got two kids myself. I really am sorry your son's in trouble with the police. Maybe he had too much to drink, y'know? Kids do that. But, like I said, there's some kinda simple little mistake here. And like I said, too, you're welcome to look at the logs. What more can I do?"

Instead of answering, the man said, "The truck's parked outside in your lot. There's a dent in the right front fender. With red paint in the dent." And then he added, "My son drives a maroon-colored car."

That did it. All the dread and confusion and frustration of the morning exploded into anger. "Listen, you—I don't even know who you are. You got no right barging into my place of business, asking questions, calling me a liar. I'm an honest businessman and I got a good reputation—ask anyone who knows me!"

But the man just stood there. Didn't even blink.

"So if you two don't haul-ass out of here, I'm gonna call the police and have you arrested for trespassing on private property."

It was the girl who spoke then: "Go ahead, Mr. Wylie. Phone the police."

At once he regretted his words. She'd called his bluff. But how did she know he didn't dare bring the police into this? How *much* did she know?

He forced a change into his tone: "Listen, folks, I don't want trouble any more'n you do." He was thinking of Paula. He was thinking of Rusty, who'd made it into Boston College. He was thinking of Wendy, first in her senior class at St. Agnes Academy. "Look," he said, "we're reasonable people, ain't we?" He said *ain't* only when he was excited like this, only when he was really in a stew. "My truck didn't have nothing to do with it, but I'll pay for any damages to your car, give you my check right now, write it off." He heaved a deep breath. "Man can't be more fair than that, can he?" It was almost a plea. "Put the whole thing behind us."

"It won't get my son out of jail," the man said, and stepped to the outside door. "Come along, Tracy."

He watched them go.

Jesus, oh sweet Jesus Christ. Rolf Arneson was a liar, Jesse Kull was an imbecile—he should never have trusted them with a load like that. Oh sweet mother of God, it was coming apart, all of it!

He went into the office area and faced Sandy, who was seated at a typewriter behind the sliding glass window. "You heard that girl's voice? She's not the one who called earlier and asked for Kull and Arneson, is she?"

"I told you, Mr. Wylie. A tiny, whiny, squeaky voice. Sounded like some hooker from the Smugglers Cove."

He nodded and walked down the hall to his private office. His body, when he lowered it into his swivel chair, was slack, no blood, sapped.

His mind refused to concentrate. He pictured the big new house in the country. Because Paula, raised on a farm, had always wanted to live out of town. He thought of the balances in the bank, healthy for the first time in their life, and of the stocks they owned. Earl Wylie, an investor in the stock market—that still didn't seem possible.

If the daughter, Tracy, was in the car with her brother, how could she have seen Jesse Kull's beard in the dark? And how could she know he weighed three hundred pounds?

Oh God, it was happening. He should've known it would. He should've known that sooner or later . . .

Well, he had no choice now. He'd rather cut off his right hand at the wrist than do what he had to do. He took his private address book out of the drawer. On the page with *V* at the top, the area code and number—with no name, but with two words, to remind him: EMERGENCIES ONLY. Precautions, always precautions and thin ice—it was no way to live. And too late for precautions now. What he had always feared, from the beginning, from the first time Nick Verini and the two thugs with him walked into his office—everything he'd feared was about to happen. And all because one of his drivers got in a hurry and ran some drunken college kid and his sister off the road.

Hollow inside, he reached for the private telephone, the one he'd had installed six years ago. He dialed. Nick Verini's unlisted number in Boston.

It was all coming down now, all of it, unless Nick Verini could think of some way to . . .

"He's in deep," Andrew said. "Whatever it is, he's in over his head."

Tracy did not reply.

"Do you think we gave ourselves away?"

When again she did not answer, but sat staring out at the streets of Lowell as he drove the old Chevy—the one he'd been able to borrow at the Lawrence Airport because they tried to accommodate private pilots, especially those who refueled—he glanced at her. Her face, the lift of her chin, the way she sat, the glisten of sun on her hair—everything added to his feverish excitement. Even the compassion he felt for Earl Wylie could not reach that intoxicating sense of triumph. The man had reminded him of some big helpless animal trapped in his own cave, and terrified. But the man was his enemy and he damn well couldn't afford pity now.

He drove in silence, but faster than the casual traffic on the highway leading back to the Lawrence Airport.

Finally she spoke: "What now—back to Shepperton?"

"Back to Wylie Trucking as soon as I get my other gear from the plane. I had no idea we'd hit paydirt so soon."

"You're going to take more pictures?"

"I've already got the truck, the license plate, the building. I'm going to get a shot of everyone who goes in and comes out."

"What time is it?" She glanced at her wrist. "Oh *God*! I'll never make it."

"Julia will just have to arrive without fanfare. Sorry."

She faced him. "You don't sound sorry in the least. Aren't you eager to see her again?"

"I'm eager," he said, "to get Todd out of that damned cell. I know how a person feels in a place like that."

"Oh? You've spent time in a jail?"

"Three nights and two days." His mind recoiled from the memory, but since she'd asked—and since, for some damned mysterious reason, he *wanted* to tell her—he said, "Twenty years ago. The last time I saw Julia. Greenwich Village, New York City. The golden days of youth. I came home from an assignment in Nam and found her entertaining a gentleman caller. You're old enough to know that term, aren't you?"

"Oh, I may have read it in some dusty old Victorian romance when I was a child. Please go on. I'll work my way through your prehistoric euphemisms."

Christ, what kind of girl is this, after all? "I threw him down a flight of stairs in an old brownstone. It could have killed him but it didn't."

"Oh? And what did you do to Julia?"

"I packed my things and when she started screaming that she loved me, I slapped her, once, across the side of the face with the palm of my hand."

"And she had you arrested?"

"The neighbors downstairs had called the cops and when they came she told them I'd beaten hell out of her."

"And then you wished you had—"

"No. By then I just plain didn't give a damn. But I know what it's like to be in a cell—and it's not the way it looks in the movies. They can't show you what it's really like inside a man's mind."

He'd said enough. He'd said too much.

"Did she press charges?"

"No. But she didn't put up the bond, either. By the time I got to a friend who could, she'd cleared out. And cleaned out the joint bank account. It took me a year to repay my friend for the bail and fine. By that time she was married to a man named Rollo Taggart—and her career was made."

"You see," Tracy said. She sounded pleased—downright triumphant. "You see, you're human after all. *You* can't forgive, either, can you?"

In the airport parking lot, he went around the rear of the car to find her standing, head to one side, eyes inscrutable. "I guess," he said, "I guess I won't know whether I forgive her or not until I see her, will I?"

"Well, you won't see her when she lands." She started off, toward the airport building.

"How are you going to get back?"

A few yards away she stopped, turning, lifting one hand to shade her eyes. "You don't get rid of me that easily. I'm going to phone Steve and catch hell and then I'm coming back here to wait for you."

Steve. He'd been amazed earlier, absolutely floored, when she'd made sure he knew she was living with somebody, but now what he felt was closer to resentment, possibly even jealousy. And damned if he liked the feeling. "I'll wait if you're not here," he said, another part of his mind oddly gladdened.

He was about to head for the hangars when he saw her move. Toward him. What now?

When she was close, closer than she'd been before, she held her head very straight, no tilting, eyes sober, even somber. "Why'd you tell Mr. Wylie I was your daughter?"

"I don't know. It just seemed to make sense at the time. We went in there without deciding exactly how we'd—"

"I'm *not* your daughter, Andy," she said firmly.

"Well," he heard himself growl, "you're young enough to be."

"Like hell." But her tone was no longer crisp. And her eyes had mellowed into a deep clear blue. "Daughter indeed," she whispered as she took a step, and now she was very close. "I don't feel like your daughter."

Then, without otherwise moving, she kissed him on the lips—a gentle pressure, silken and soft, and he caught the clean scent of her breath and skin.

There was a teasing delight in her eyes as she moved away, not looking back, her step jaunty, buoyant with youth.

Even after she'd disappeared through the doors, he didn't move at once. Then the intoxicating urgency returned. And his doubts were gone, too: Todd was not lying! Christ, it'd been years since he'd felt like this!

And how long since he'd kissed anyone, or been kissed, on the lips?

"But Todd—oh, darling, this is *ghastly*!"

"Look, Mom, no windows."

Todd was seated, after the usual ritual kiss, at one end of the long table in the visitors' room—where, maybe three aeons ago, he had been interrogated. "You should see my cell," he said. "It's the one Galileo slept in. His formula's still carved on the wall: E equals MC squared."

Julia, still standing at the other end of the table, made a gesture. "Disgusting. It's terrible. Revolting!" She shook her head, once, as if this time some scene designer had been too realistic, had gone too far. And then she came along the table toward him in a rush, breathless. "I didn't even check into the hotel. Darling, I'm going to get you out of this dreadful *dungeon*!"

"How?" The knot in his stomach, which had given him hell for hours, tightened. It was smaller now, rigid—worse than the steady throbbing in his spine and the pain in his shoulder. "I'm what they call a material witness—which means, I think, that they can hold me without bond. Till they decide whether I really did witness my own crime."

Julia was smiling. "Well, I'm relieved you can still joke—"

"Maybe you could seduce the jailer while I dig a tunnel."

She took off the belted leather trench coat, and he could see her designer jeans tucked into knee-high boots with spike heels. "Oh Todd, you poor child." She perched herself on the table's edge, legs dangling, green eyes bright with what might be, just possibly *could* be, genuine concern. "Have you looked at yourself in a mirror?"

"Mirrors are verboten. Like knives and razor blades and cheeseburgers. But I'm well-showered—first thing they do. Strip you down, make sure you've got nothing shoved up your ass." He heard his own voice: light, amused, detached. "Then they dehumanize you. That's important. Kafka had it right. Reduce him to nothing, a cipher, a zero. He wouldn't be here if he didn't deserve it, would he?"

"Is there anything I can do? Anything?"

That did it. "I thought you'd never ask." The tight knot burst. "You're goddam right there is!" He stood up. "You can tell me what's happening out there. Where's Lynnette? You can tell me whether Lynnette is dead or alive!"

Julia was frowning. "They don't know yet. But I saw two planes in the distance as I flew in, and a helicopter. And here—Christ, there must've been a hundred people waiting for me around the courthouse steps. Someday I'm going to smash one of those fucking TV cameras. How the hell did I get into this?''

He turned away. To face a bare wall. Another one. He was beginning to shake all over. Again. He placed his forehead against the wall.

"Now, Todd, none of that. You know what Dr. Saul said about those depressions . . .''

Sure he knew: very common among the young today, and very dangerous. Suicide rate of youth absolutely appalling. And screw you, Dr. Saul.

"Todd darling, there *is* something I have to ask you. . . .''

He didn't turn. "Feel free. This is the interrogation room—''

"I can't understand why the college informed your father and not me.''

He had been expecting this—or should have. He turned to face her. There were times, such as now, when Julia looked so wounded and vulnerable—vanity? ego? Both—but real, genuine, nonetheless painful. He decided to tell only part of the truth, but an important part: "I guess I just wanted to make it at Melville on my own.''

Julia seemed to consider this. Could she accept it, understand?

Then—as he might have anticipated but invariably didn't— she simply evaded. "What's he like—your father?''

It took him a second or two to reassemble his thoughts. The focus had shifted. As usual. From himself to her. But something drove him, that mysterious, nameless something, to say: "He didn't strike me as the kind of man who'd walk away and disappear just because he found out his wife was pregnant. *Or* that he'd break her jaw and put her in the hospital.''

There was a lengthy silence. Somewhere in the building a heavy door clanked shut with a metallic, mechanical sound.

Julia stood up and stepped away from the table. Her eyes were clouded, and hurt. "He's been telling you his lies, has he?'' She moved without purpose, one hand lifting to pat her glistening blond hair. "This was his chance, wasn't it? That's why he came.''

"To see me, *yes*. I've always wanted to meet him—''

"Yes. Well. That's only natural, I suppose.'' She wandered away. "I'm curious, too." Then she stopped and frowned across the distance between them, as if wondering whether she should say: "Andy's the only man I ever loved. Can you believe that?"

"Why not?"

"I've depended on others. I've been grateful. And slept with—oh God, how many? But . . ." She shook her head, as if she were lost.

"Mother," Todd said.

"Yes?"

"Why the hell did I have to get thrown into the slammer before we could *talk* to each other?"

It had been the wrong thing to say. He was an absolute master when it came to the wrong thing to say. He saw her retreat—first her eyes, then her feelings, then her whole body.

She began to move again. "Oh, Todd, you've always had the queerest way of looking at things. Now listen, this is important. I've hired a lawyer. The best in the business. His name's Gerald Usher Lewis—everyone calls him Lewis. He's tough and he's clever and he's got a bagful of tricks—"

Angered in spite of himself, Todd said, "I haven't done anything." And then, with contempt: "I don't *need* a bagful of tricks."

"Don't *need* a lawyer? Look at you. Look where we *are!* This is no time for your childish idealism and romantic—" She rushed at him. "I've hired him, that's all, at great expense."

"Cheap lawyers with bagsful of tricks don't come cheap, do they?" he said. "I've heard of Gerald Usher Lewis—who hasn't? College linebacker, wasn't he? Owns some heavyweight fighter, made sure the operators of some call-girl ring didn't go to prison—or was it white slavery?"

"Todd, you stop this. Lewis is in town here now, out there somewhere, doing what, I don't know—he calls it reconnoitering the territory. I want you, please, Todd, to do exactly what he tells you to do. Don't use your mind—use his. He'll get you off!"

Another silence. He stared at her: She had no idea what she'd said—not the slightest idea.

It was the same; everything was the same as it had always

been, a kind of climax, a kind of perfect goddam paradigm of his whole goddam life!

"You think I'm guilty, don't you?" His own voice reverberated strangely in his ears. "You honest-to-God think I've committed some—oh God, oh *Christ*!"

"Todd, stop this. I'm not blaming you—"

"Blaming me? Blaming me for *what*?"

"All I want you to know is that, whatever, I'll stand by you. Regardless."

"Regardless? Regardless of *what*?"

But then he gave up. Inside, something caved in. Hopeless, hopeless. He sat down at the table.

What the hell did he expect?

The only time I'm really alive is when I'm on stage with the lights burning down—she'd been quoted once in an interview. Well, he'd known that for years.

He lowered his head onto his folded arms on the table.

He heard: "I don't understand. Why is everybody always expecting me to behave in a certain way? I don't know what people want. I can't read minds. . . ."

No, Mother, not minds, but lines of dialogue, stage directions typed in a script.

"Mother, will you do me a favor?"

"Anything, Todd." He heard her footsteps on the bare concrete floor. "I'll do anything for you." He felt her hand on his head. And then, inevitably: "You're my son."

"Will you go register at your hotel now?" Her hand withdrew from his head. This, also, was the wrong thing to say, possibly the worst. Too late, he realized: The one thing Julia Craven could not bear was rejection.

"Todd, what I don't understand, have *never* understood" —her voice had changed, had sharpened—"whenever I'm in a hit play, you find *some* way to ruin it!"

"I'm sorry, Mother." The past again, all those years: sorry, sorry, sorry, sorry . . .

"Well, of course if you don't *want* me . . ."

He lifted his head. Their eyes met. Hopeless. She picked up her coat and stepped to the open door.

Where she stopped and turned. "They'll have to let you close the door when you talk to your lawyer. That's your constitutional right!"

When he was alone—tempted to laugh, *wanting* to laugh— the awful sense of abandonment returned. A dark wave en- gulfing him, he couldn't breathe; he was going under; he was helpless and alone. No one really cared. No one gave a damn. No one. Anywhere.

It must be something in the blood, Tracy was thinking. Some mysterious father-son thing. Primal maybe.

She took the bag of sandwiches from the man behind the counter and paid the girl at the cash register, sorry to leave the delicious, mouth-watering smells. She went out and climbed into the Chevy at the curb.

Driving the strange bleak-looking street on the outskirts of Lowell, she let her mind return to Andy and why he was here. *Was* it something in the blood or something in the soul? Not love, certainly—his son was a stranger. Guilt, perhaps— guilt regardless of the fact that he didn't know of his son's existence? Well, whatever or whichever or neither one, he was doing what he felt he had to do and she loved him for it.

How can I leave him, Tracy? Someday you'll know what love is. Yes, Mother, you loved—and what happened to you? Where are you now?

The road dipped down off the interstate and ran along a narrow canal on her right, a stagnant channel of scummy water. On her left, after several hundred yards, the low concrete building of Wylie Trucking Company appeared. And across the canal on her right, she looked up at the bleak wall of an abandoned woolen mill: some of the grimy windows cracked, others smashed out, the rest dark and opaque. Al- though she could not see the tripod or camera, she could see the one window on the third floor from which the glass had been completely removed. She'd taken out the pane herself on Andy's orders while he worked on his equipment.

Without hesitating at the NO TRESPASSING sign, she made a right turn into an opening in the high, rusted chain-link fence. Vaguely she remembered reading of the textile mills all over New England closing in the '30s, years and years before she was born. Damn the man, he'd made her more and more conscious of her twenty-five years. Compared to what? His forty-five. *Damn* him!

She eased the car over the short ramshackle bridge spanning the canal and parked it behind the building, out of view of the parking area of Wylie Trucking, which had been almost empty two hours ago but was now crowded with trucks.

It was dim inside the mill. Eerie, with shadows and a musty stench and—what terrified her and set her heart pounding—the sound of small flapping wings. Bats. She went carefully up the two steep flights of narrow wooden stairs that she and Andy had climbed in their search for an observation post. And again the feeling returned: What a strange place to be. What a strange, unlikely thing to be doing.

Unlikely, yes. Strange, yes. But *doing* something. Involved. *Alive*, mind focused, every nerve quivering, blood throbbing.

The room Andy had chosen must once have been the third-floor supervisor's office. Bare of furniture now, except for a set of rusted file drawers, a metal desk, and one rickety wooden chair, it was an enclosure, really, with windows along one wall overlooking the canal; the other three walls were head-high partitions, half-glassed, with a full view of the vast workroom that stretched like a dark, decaying cave. Her footsteps stirred dust and echoed off into the stale, mote-filled air over the long rows of bare worktables.

Andy was still at the window, hunched forward on the chair. His back to her, field glasses at his eyes, he did not turn. Her impulse was to kiss him. Again. "Pastrami and potato salad and pickles," she said. "The iceman cometh."

"A lot of trucks have come in," he said. "The drivers go in and punch out their time, I guess, then leave. But that's all, period. Wylie hasn't come out."

She perched herself on the steel desk, which she'd dusted off earlier, and took the food from the paper bag. "But no red beard," she said, "no blond Viking?"

Without standing up or lowering the glasses, he extended a hand. "I know I'm right, damn it. Wylie had to send for them after what we told him!"

She placed a half-sandwich in his hand and said, "Unless he goes to *them* after he closes shop."

"Then we'll follow him."

She got down and set his coffee on the windowsill within reach, careful not to touch the tripod holding the camera, and then she did kiss him. On the top of his dark, gray-streaked hair—which was not as crinkly-crisp as it looked, but rather fine and smelled of hair, not hair spray. And then, because she'd been reminded, she thought of Steve. *Bigger story, hell, Tracy. Julia Craven in this one-horse town—that's our story!* After Steve had said that, and more, when she'd phoned him from the airport waiting room earlier, she'd returned to the car where Andy was waiting. Both had been aware that when she'd left him five or ten minutes before, she'd kissed him on the lips—a kiss she damned well didn't understand herself!—so neither had spoken at first. Then, on the highway leading back to Lowell, he'd pulled the car onto the gravel shoulder, stopped it with an angry squeal of brakes, and this time *he'd* kissed *her*. An almost desperate kiss, which she had returned just as intensely and which neither had referred to, by so much as a syllable or gesture, since.

Possibly reacting to her silly excuse for a kiss just now, Andy said, "You want me to apologize for saying you were my daughter, don't you?" He bit into his sandwich and chewed. "All right, damn it, I apologize."

"Maybe," she said, "maybe I want you to stop *thinking* of me as your daughter."

"Maybe I already— Hold it!"

He had straightened in the chair, both hands on the glasses now.

"What?"

"Maybe nothing. Damned strange, though."

She slid off the desk. "*What*, for God's sake?"

"A red Ferrari just pulled in." He stood up and handed her the binoculars. "What the hell business would a car like that have in . . ." He stood behind the camera and began to adjust the telephoto lens.

She lifted the glasses, swung them till she caught a flash of red, returned the focus to hold the red, her finger working the knob to clear her vision. Beside her, the camera was now clicking, over and over. She saw a dark young man—thirty? younger? older?—climb out of the sleek red car with windshield and windows so dark that they looked opaque. He was small—short, compact, slender, wearing a white turtleneck sweater and tight black trousers. He moved with an easy self-confidence, a not-quite-swaggering arrogance, as he started toward the building, removing his dark sunglasses. She could not make out his features but he had a short black beard and a mane of stylishly long hair, also very black, which glistened in the sun.

He went up the two steps of the entrance and disappeared inside.

"I couldn't see his face clearly," she said. "Could you?"

"With this lens I can get a closeup of a wart on an ear. But the Ferrari's license plates are at the wrong angle. Guy's probably selling brake fluid, or antifreeze."

"If he is, he's selling a lot of it. Do you know what a spanking-new Ferrari Mondial costs?"

"No, but I'm sure Steve does."

Steve? How the devil did *he* get into this? She sat down on the chair and kept the binoculars. "Have some potato salad," she said. "I'll be the spy."

He moved from the tripod but said nothing. In a moment she could feel his eyes on her, studying her from behind.

So she said, "I really shocked you when I told you I was living with Steve, didn't I?"

"None of my business, is it?"

"I don't know." It was very quiet in the old building, not so much as a bat fluttering. When he didn't reply, she said, "You were no more shocked than I was when you told me you'd thrown someone down the stairs and might have killed him. That doesn't jibe with you somehow."

"What would *you* do if you found Steve making love to someone else?"

She hesitated, but only briefly. "I'd turn around and walk away."

"Would you?" His voice sounded pleased. "Well, that's what I've been wondering about—"

"What?"

"Whether you love him."

She waited a long time then. Nothing moved on the parking lot across the canal. Finally, having framed the words in her mind first, she said, "I don't *want* to love anybody that way. Ever."

But before he could answer that, she lifted one hand and leaned forward.

A white-on-black Ford Bronco had turned into Wylie Trucking. Two men. She caught a brief glimpse of a red beard as the vehicle came to a halt.

"I think—" she said, and then she yelled: "Get on the camera, for God's sake!"

The driver stepped down and out: very tall, very lean, shock of straw-colored hair. She was not breathing. She heard the snapping of the camera. Snick, snick . . . snick.

She moved the glasses. The other man, who had slid out on the far side, appeared from behind the car.

He was not big; he was huge. Not tall, but so massive that she felt a shudder pass down her body. Her palms were damp. She watched as, moving slowly, bearlike, he joined the tall man. For an instant his enormous head faced full-front, tilted up. Snick . . . snick-snick. A hole opened in his red beard, brilliant in the sun. Whatever he said, the other man shook his head and threw a long arm over the bear's shoulders as they walked.

She heard Andy continue to click the camera until both men disappeared through the door. Then he stopped.

"Jackpot," he said. It was a whisper. "Bingo."

Facing young Nick Verini across his own familiar desk in his own fimiliar office, Earl Wylie was doing his best to hold himself together.

"Cops come in different colors, different shades, Earl. And different sexes, like father and daughter. Me, if I'd been here, I could've told. I got a nose for them fuckers."

Nick appeared to be in his thirties somewhere: thick black hair, too long for Earl Wylie's tastes, narrow face, short black beard. His dark eyes glittered with more questions than his wide, full-lipped mouth was asking.

"Where's the two drivers now?"

"Out in the garage." Earl heard a high-pitched tone in his voice that was *not* familiar. "Waiting."

Nick Verini nodded. "That's where I'll talk to 'em. You said all the trucks were in—what's taking everybody so long to clear out?"

"Took them by surprise, I guess. Whole hour before regular quitting time, office staff. You want some coffee, Mr. Verini?"

Nick stood up. "Any other kind of coffee but espresso is black piss." Then he stepped to the door and opened it. He moved as if he were charged up inside. Two girls passed down the hall, one humming, one giggling. Nick Verini's eyes narrowed, watching the girls. Then he returned to the desk. "Time's wastin', Earl."

Just then Sandy's voice called from the front of the building: "Have a nice one, Mr. Wylie." It was her way, every afternoon, of telling him that she was leaving and locking the door.

"Everyone's gone, Mr. Verini," Earl said. And what now, what? He stood up. His legs were a little wobbly. "This way."

Nick smiled. "I know the way," he said, in that easy, smooth voice, without a trace of any accent.

He went out and Earl followed. The way Nick moved, it reminded Earl of some small animal in the woods: lean and little and quick—and alert, always wary, like his eyes.

Except for one chassis up on a lift and the unmarked truck with the license plate 779 OKR, which he'd ordered washed down, inside and out, and kept out of sight, the large garage was empty. His own footsteps did not sound, but Nick's heels clicked sharply on the concrete. He was wearing wing-tip cowboy boots, real lizard with high heels. Christ, what a wacko.

When they reached the two men standing at the far end by the workbench, neither Jesse Kull nor Rolf Arneson spoke or so much as glanced at Earl. Their eyes were on Nick. After Earl introduced the drivers by name, he was careful, as he'd been instructed, not to use Nick's name at all.

"You kept me waiting," Nick said. He was very polite. "I drive all the way from Boston and *you* keep *me* waiting. . . ."

He let it hang there. Jesse opened his mouth but before he could get a sound out, Rolf said: "Ve vas at the Smugglers Cove—that's a yoint vhere ve hang out, sir. Jesse's vife had to phone there. It's our day off."

Nick was looking at Rolf—looking him up and down, as if sizing him up. "Don't ever keep me waiting again," he said, still polite, his voice like smooth silk.

"Yessir." The big Swede's pale-blue eyes looked eager to please. How much did he know, or suspect?

"Something happened last night," Nick said. "You shut up, big man. Let redbeard tell me. Well, redbeard?"

Jesse Kull ran a thick hand over his bald pate, which was

90

freckled and glistening with sweat. "Well, we was on our way back. The road was dark and it's narrow up there and we come around a bend and there was this car, a maroon station wagon, maybe a Plymouth or Dodge, kinda dark red. It was goin' slow. We was on it before . . ." He stopped and one big paw reached up to pull at his beard. "I wasn't driving."

Nick's eyes went to Rolf. "In a hurry, big man? In some kinda hurry?"

"Nosir, not speeding, nosir. Mr. Vylie varned us never to—"

Nick made a sharp downward gesture, hand stiff. "Shove it," he said. "You were speeding. Did you hit the car?"

"Yust a sidesvipe. I used my horn, yust a—"

The gesture again. Then: "Who was in the wagon?"

"I couldn't see. I vas trying to stay on the road."

Nick's eyes, very dark now, darted to Jesse Kull. Nick didn't need to say anything.

"Two men," Jesse Kull said. "It was dark. I couldn't see—but two men's heads."

"Not a girl? Not a girl with hair the color of your beard?"

"No girl."

"Did the wagon go off the road?"

"Maybe," Rolf said. "I couldn't be sure in the rearview. Ve couldn't stop. Mr. Vylie said never to stop, except for red lights, not even a cup of coffee—"

Earl heard Nick Verini, standing beside him, take a deep breath—more like a sigh. Then he spat on the floor. Without moving, he said: "You're a coupla lyin' motherfuckers."

Jesse Kull's bald head was wet now, his eyes wide, with a frantic look in them. The big Swede's face looked as if someone a lot bigger had hit him full-blast in the stomach and he was trying not to bend over. And Earl himself knew then that, whatever was coming, it had to do with something a helluva lot heavier than one of his trucks sideswiping a car on a country road. He wanted to sit down. No, he wanted to get the hell out of here.

"Now," Nick Verini said at last, "now I'm gonna give you a lesson, all three of you fuckers. I'm gonna give you a lesson in the facts of life. So you listen, all three of you, you listen." He had begun to move, slinking, his voice sharp-edged and flinty. "Number one: You know that what you got

in that truck is not mud. It's not fertilizer or garbage or shit.
You know where you pick it up and you know where to
deliver it.'' He had moved away. "You got your orders. You
know how goddam much you're being *paid*.'' He stopped and
stared at them, then let his gaze drift to include Earl. "Maybe
none of you really savvy what a big operation this is. Maybe
you ain't got brains to really dig what could happen to you if
you get too nosy or if you get picked up by the fuzz.'' He
came closer. "You want me to explain? It's like this. You
can get in your car, right in your own driveway some nice
morning, and boom, no car, no Jesse, or no Rolf, or no Earl.
Poof. Just a lotta noise, a lotta flame, a lotta smoke.'' He was
not moving now. "Or . . . like this: You can be in some bar
having a coupla beers and the door opens. It's a holdup. You
get in the way—just sitting there you're in the way—so blast.
Shotgun maybe. No head. Routine. Happens all the time.
Right place, wrong time.'' He was standing with his legs
apart, fists on his hips. "Or you could be driving on some
interstate, just breezing along, some sniper on an overpass
. . .'' He tilted his head to one side. "These things happen.
They just happen. You beginning to get the drift? Cement
block, bottom a some river. Old cars junked, big claw comes
down, crush, crush—who knows there's a body inside? Old
mine shafts, Pennsylvania, Kentucky, West Virginia—bodies
down there rotting in lye. Dust to dust . . . Bodies fall outa
planes all the time. Over the bush up in Maine, Michigan,
Canada—wolves, vultures,' bears. Or Florida, over the
Everglades—alligators. Or the Caribbean—sharks. Happens
all the time. Not even a funeral. Nothing—*just plain nothing*.
You know what *nothing* is?''

There was a long silence. Earl's whole body had gone
limp, gut twisting.

Then Nick's voice became a tolerant, fatherly purr: "I'm
only trying to make you face the possibilities, that's all. I'm
only trying to make you see the *consequences*. What we got
is a big operation. All over the country. Millions of dollars.
Millions.'' Then he shouted: "And we're not going to see it
fucked up by any two-bit shits, not for *any* goddam reason!''

No one spoke. No one moved. Earl couldn't take his eyes
from Nick's face. He had known; he had known from the
beginning, in a way. But now, spelled out like this, in

words—his mind reeled; he felt a billowing black cloud of incredulity settle over him. The only word that occurred to him was *inevitable*. He'd always known. He was so sick now, physically sick, that he was afraid he was going to throw up.

But Nick ignored him and stepped toward the others. His tone was low again, a cold whisper: "Now, which one of you lying motherfuckers is going to tell me what really happened up there last night?"

"It's not a capital case, at least not yet. So I can't help wondering why the suspect's mother brought in the big guns."

Across the small polished table in the cocktail lounge of the Alpine Chalet, Blake Arnold saw Gerald Usher Lewis lean back in his leather chair and heard him laugh. The man's face was familiar from newspaper stories over the years: big and hard-fleshed, heavy, like his barrel-chested body. His gray eyes remained detached and unamused, even when he laughed. "You're also wondering"—his voice low and lazy and relaxed—"why I invited you for a drink."

True enough. But Blake, wary as well as a trifle awed in a ridiculous, boyish way, said, "Maybe to size up the offensive team—just in case it turns *into* a capital case."

Now Lewis was grinning, eyes appraising, as he drew on his cigar. "I'm here to see my client's rights don't get trampled on up here in the boondocks."

Although aware that he was being needled now—part of the famed lawyer's courtroom technique—Blake nevertheless felt a spasm of vexation in his throat. "We do have strange folkways up here in the wilds." He was thinking of Valerie now—she'd once called his attention to it: "For instance, in our peculiar twang, you'll notice that the word *lawyer* comes out sounding like *liar*."

Gerald Usher Lewis laughed again and drained his glass. "Another scotch?"

"No, thanks, this is my second. And I never drink this early. You've talked to your client. The court records are open to you. What can I tell you?"

Gerald Usher Lewis tilted his big balding head to one side and blew smoke. "I've very little on the girl as yet."

It was Blake's turn to smile. "I see. I understand that one

of your best defenses is to try the victim. If the victim's not a saint, the killer, or rapist, had cause—"

"Rape? Murder? They do have the body then."

"What body?"

Lewis's grin widened. "It could be interesting, couldn't it? You and me. We'd both like nothing better than a first-degree murder indictment, wouldn't we? Julia Craven's a famous woman. And I'm queer for large sums of money. And you, I understand, have political ambitions." It was not a question.

Astonished but not yet angry, Blake took a final swallow and set down his glass. "You've done your homework, haven't you?"

Blandly, almost lazily, Lewis said: "It was done for me before I arrived."

Blake stood up. "We'll go to trial, Mr. Lewis, only when we know the state has a case and only if the *facts* warrant an indictment. Judge Patton will decide on that tomorrow morning at ten. Thanks for the drinks. See you in court."

He turned and went into the lobby and through it. We'll go to trial, Mr. Lewis, only if I think the state can win!

He went out the door and onto the flagstone veranda. The sun was gone and the day had turned gray. As he stepped down into the parking area, Blake discovered that he was breathless. To score one against Gerald Usher Lewis himself! Well, he knew now that he could handle him. The challenge itself was a pleasure. Also, damn it, he'd taken a fierce dislike to the arrogant sonofabitch!

Driving slowly toward town in the ten-year-old Mercedes sedan, which Valerie's father had left them in his will, he turned on the headlights even though it was not quite dusk. If the girl was dead, there was nothing he could do about that—so why not hope that, *if* she was dead *anyway,* the kid was lying about the truck and the two attackers? Nothing Jesuitical about that; nothing unethical or immoral about hoping . . .

Unable to enjoy the landscape rolling by in the fading light below, Tracy had begun to give in to her doubts.

But she could not reach—was she sure she wanted to?—the excitement and hope and anger that she sensed running through Andrew Horgan. On the way to the airport, he'd said: *The sheriff can't ignore this!* And on takeoff. *This is it, Tracy—we've got the sonsofbitches. We've got them!*

The throb in his voice, the hard, bright vitality in his eyes, then and now, added to her reluctance, but she said, "We know, I'm not saying *we* don't know. I'm saying I've watched the police in action—it's a different mentality, Andy."

"We've even got a close shot of the fender with the dent and the red paint in it! I'll find the damn car. It's in Shepperton someplace. Or I'll find that kid with the stammer if I have to enroll in Shepperton High School in the morning."

Leaving the mill, she had first begun to fight her uncertainty: *We don't really know what they did, do we?* He had turned a furious face to her: *I know that tall one threw my son off a cliff. He didn't know there was a marsh down below. He didn't give a damn whether he killed him or not!*

Remembering now, Tracy decided to let him have the satisfaction of hoping, even if he was in for disappointment, or worse, when they reached Shepperton. After all, she had witnessed the transformation of a man in a few short hours: He was vitally alive now, juices flowing. A different man.

So she said, "Just after takeoff you said we're in for a change in the weather. How do you know?"

"I said I thought Indian summer was over because of the clouds, and the change in the light. If you're going to take photographs from a plane, you damn well better know what the clouds tell you!"

In her mind, though, she could not resist her misgivings. She'd covered several trials: The testimony of the defendant was, *ipso facto*, suspect even under oath. And except for his word, even if the truck had been in the area, how place it in the forest?

She looked out the window and down. The woods were thicker now. On the winding ribbons of roads, there were fewer cars. The country was more rugged, houses farther apart, fewer firms. The abstract beauty of the scene touched a chord in her.

"Do you have a favorite author?" she asked, on impulse.

"Author?"

"Out of all, *all* the others. Not a great one necessarily. Not Tolstoi or Proust or Joyce or, God help us, Herman the whale—just a personal inside favorite."

"Saint-Ex," he said without hesitation.

"What?"

"Antoine de Saint-Exupéry. I doubt anyone reads him these days."

She was too startled, too incredulous to speak. A flush of warmth flowed through her. She continued to look down at the world passing by beneath.

"Who's *your* favorite?" Andy's voice asked.

She said, "My father read *The Little Prince* to me when I was a child. Later, in high school, I discovered *Wind, Sand and Stars*, the others, *Night Flight*—it's been Saint-Ex ever since." Trembling now, actually quivering all over, she found herself struggling to hold on to the moment. "Just a coincidence, I guess."

"I guess," Andy said. And then he added, "Maybe."

Below, now, there was Shepperton itself: the sprawling cluster of rooftops, the steeples of the churches in the glowing but fading sunlight, the streets angling out from the green, crisscrossing others, the courthouse . . .

"Where are we going?" she heard herself cry. "We're not going *down*!" She faced him. "Andy, where are we going?"

"Out to the scene of the so-called crime," he said.

"But I can't. Drop me off at the Chalet. Oh, Andy, damn it, I go on the air at six-thirty. And I have to develop the pictures and write my copy, Andy, please!"

"Let's assume they killed her." It was as if he hadn't heard her. "Let's assume there's a body. Somewhere. Let's examine that idea. There are a lot of places it could be."

It. The word must have struck him as it struck her because he stopped talking and eased the wheel forward and the nose of the plane began to dip slowly.

"They've been searching since dawn," she said. "Steve said they hadn't found it by the time I talked to him, but maybe by now—"

"Let's also assume," Andy said, "that they haven't. That's one place, the woods. There are others. It's a long road between here and Lowell. They could have hidden . . . her body anywhere. Maybe they had the body in the truck when they ran the kid's car off the road. Maybe that's why they were in such a hurry, couldn't stop—"

"Then what are we doing here?"

"Because," Andy said, "because we can't search the road—that's more than a hundred miles. They may also have disposed of it in Lowell. That's four places, Tracy: the woods, the road, Lowell, and one other."

"Where?"

"There must be ponds or lakes in the forest?"

"Dozens. All sizes."

"And how long," he asked, "how long does it take a dead body to surface after it's thrown into the water?"

"Hours. Days." And then the meaning struck her. "I don't know," she said in a small voice.

"Probably depends on temperature, lots of things . . . Well, it's a long shot, Tracy, a very long shot."

The plane was skimming over the tops of the pines, more slowly now but so close that she felt she could reach down and touch the tips of them. His excitement finally reached her, a prickling sensation in her nerve endings.

"The police planes may have missed something," she said. "Or the body might not have surfaced before they stopped searching. . . ."

The plane banked, and in a few seconds it was leveling off to fly above a narrow sand-colored strip of gravel road, walled on both sides by very tall trees, which ran diagonally from southeast to northwest through the forest.

"If there are any searchers still in here," he said, "we should be able to see them, probably at the campsite—"

"If they're not," Tracy said, "we'll find it. We'll find a low cliff with a marshy stream at the bottom—"

"We've got at least an hour before dark," Andy said.

Inondazione.

One small crack in the dam, a fault so tiny that it cannot be seen, and then it begins, the dam crumbles, the water gushes, and everything is destroyed. Flood.

This was the image that had been haunting Vincent Verini's mind through the cocktail hour while Francesca and Monsignor Kimbrough discussed the family: Angelo—oh, what a fine young man, what a joy for a mother to say that he was doing so well, taking so much of the load off his father's back, and married, what little charmers his twins were. . . . Excellent, excellent—and Dominic? Well, Nickie was young, he was just having a hard time finding himself, no, not yet married but he was taking more and more responsibility, wasn't that true, Vince? "Yes, Francie, yes—he's doing a job for me now." But . . . but should he have sent Angelo up to Vermont instead?

I've got my shit in a row now, Poppa—don't sweat it! Nickie, Nickie—Vincent Verini felt a weariness in his tall body. Two years of college and talking like a bum, talking like Bogart, or Cagney—worse, like he was trying to live up to some childish idea of what he was, instead of concentrating on his job. And that goddamn little car. And those cowboy boots—it was beneath him to dress like he did. And those fancy guns; an automatic for God's sake, and that foreign rifle. Long hair, beard—would the kid ever get it straight who he was? The son of Vincent Verini himself, that's who he was. If he was anyone else, just another *soldato,* not Vincent Verini's own flesh and blood . . . Well, he hadn't given up on Nickie. Yet. You can't give up on your own family—that is a matter of honor.

Leo Kimbrough, who always wore his Roman collar when he came for cocktails or dinner to the Verini house, had an Irish face that, after two drinks, turned into a red and beaming mask of joviality. "As Nickie's confessor," he said now, "I have warned him repeatedly that anger is one of the cardinal sins. My advice to you would be: relax, it takes longer for some to grow up, as we know."

"He's thirty-three years old," Vincent Verini said quietly. "Jesus was crucified at that age."

The monsignor smiled. He was a youngish man himself, one of the new breed who seemed to enjoy blasphemy. "He'll surprise you yet, sir."

"*Figliuolo mio,*" Verini said. "Say a mass that it'll happen soon."

And then Kimbrough was pouring himself another drink, which meant that he was staying on. So Vincent Verini, who did not drink anything but wine, and only with meals, allowed his mind to return to the decision that he had to make. Soon. Except in the old days, when he himself was young and hotheaded, like Nickie, he had never decided whether a man should be eliminated without careful, cool consideration of the risk in allowing that man to live.

The monsignor was saying then, as he did on every visit, that the way they had restored this beautiful old house in the country was nothing short of a miracle . . . while Vincent

Verini again went over the facts as Nickie had described them over the phone two hours ago. Did the boy really have it in him to put the lid on things up there? Nickie's anger went to the bone. It seethed and simmered and then erupted like a volcano. But more: that sex thing, whatever it was. Like the time in Portland when he'd raped that girl just because he had a chance—almost screwing up everything he'd been sent there to do. *Unstable*—that was the word in the letter when he'd been expelled from college. *Emotionally unstable*. A weakness, and Vincent Verini, at sixty-three, having seen where weakness leads, had nothing but contempt for it. But not for Nickie, not for the boy himself. He loved Nickie even more than he loved Angelo, somehow, much as he could depend on Angelo.

Well, the die was cast now: Maybe this would be Nickie's last chance. Meanwhile, he himself had to act or not act—

"Vince, Father Kimbrough is leaving." Vincent Verini followed them into the hall. Michael, the elderly butler, aristocratic Irish himself, was already holding the monsignor's black raincoat. Francie was moving toward the kitchen door in the rear to oversee dinner. Poor Francie: at sixty, still a passionate hot-blooded woman, while the years had sapped her husband's sexual powers. A mood of sadness passed over him as he took the envelope containing the check from his inside pocket, placed it on top of the wrapped box of Cuban cigars, and handed them to Leo.

"You are always so generous," the cherubic-faced man said, shaking hands. "I'll say that mass. I can see you're troubled. Goodbye, sir. And God bless you."

When he went out, Vincent Verini did not follow. Plenty of security out there in the dark, real muscle all over the three hundred acres, and no trouble between the families, but he was too old and too content with his life to take chances.

Alone, he turned and began to climb the wide, curving stairway. He realized that he had made his decision. To survive himself, he had no choice.

Going into his study and closing the soundproof, bullet-proof door behind him, he recalled with wry amusement that a newspaper poll a few years ago had revealed that 67 percent of the American people thought that the most efficiently run business organization in the country was the one into which he had been born. Well, the other 33 percent, whatever their choices, had been wrong.

He sat behind the carved mahogany desk and picked up the phone that in his mind he referred to as the hot line. Dialing, he recalled his selling speech: *It's a problem more and more corporations such as yours face today. We use small, little-known companies, respectable, drivers with clean records, not criminals. The overall operation, sir, is nationwide and we have not had a single mishap or exposure. You have my word.* The word of Vincent Verini himself—a man of honor. An honor that he was not going to have besmirched.

Silence. It was the only way. *Morte. Silenzio assoluto.*

FIVE

"Good evening—Tracy Larkin, Channel Seven Newswatch, with the local evening news.

"What you're looking at on your screen now is a still photo from the air, showing the body of a female, nude, floating on the surface of Echo Lake in the Franklin State Forest.

"The body was sighted from his private plane by the well-known photographer Andrew Horgan, who is the father of Todd Horgan, nineteen, who late last night reported the disappearance of Lynnette Durand, also nineteen, a fellow student at Melville College in Haddam. Todd Horgan is in the Eden County jail on charges of drug possession and illegal possession of a firearm and is being held for questioning. A police search for Miss Durand has been carried on all day in the forest and in Vermont and adjoining states.

"The cause of death has not been determined. An autopsy will be conducted at Shepperton Hospital, and as yet, the body has not been officially identified.

"Meanwhile, Todd Horgan has identified these photographs of two men he claims attacked him and Miss Durand at his campsite during the night. An investigation has revealed that these two men reside in Lowell, Massachusetts, and are employed by Wylie Trucking Company of that city. The name of the bearded man on the right of your screen is Jesse Kull, and the one on the left—"

All for a piece of tail. It filled Nick with disgust. He flicked off the TV. Those two. Seeing their pictures on the

101

screen, he could smell that stink of fear they gave off in Wylie's garage two, three hours ago. Those two dumb creeps, for a piece of ass that you could buy anywhere, or get for free most places today, they had to fuck up the works. And in a state forest! Jesus. *All ve vanted to do vas bag us a deer before the season started. Ve vas on our vay to the main road vhen ve seen the light from their campfire*—the tall one, the bastard. Maybe it was the mountain man who actually offed the girl but it was the tall one he hated. *We got rid of the body,* the sweating red-bearded prick had squeaked.

Like hell, like fuck you did, dummy!

Now it was up to him. Nick Verini, the kid himself. All the way up from Lowell on I93 and I89—fuck the fuzz; the Ferrari had a police-radar detector—he'd had a kind of fever in his mind, heating up the closer he got to Shepperton. Trouble? Danger? Leave it to Nick. Good soldier Nick. The best! Now he was here, on the scene—in charge. On his own. This was the part of his life that made him know he was alive.

And he had to say this: This Alpine Chalet was some all-right place for the sticks. *Di lusso.* Big sitting room, stone fireplaces in this room and the two bedrooms, all the comforts of home. And then some.

Get the lay of it and report back here. To me, to me only. Later, Poppa, later—not till Nickie gets the whole picture.

So now he made a phone call. Before leaving Lowell, he'd asked for a rundown on the name of the man Wylie had given him, Andrew Horgan, and now he had it, the complete poop; he had it in his own private computer, his mind that Poppa didn't think he had. So he told the voice at the computer center in Revere to do the same now on a Tracy Larkin, works for the TV station, Shepperton, Vermont, in her twenties, red hair. Get on it! It wouldn't take long, way that those computers work.

That face, those goddam blue eyes, just the kind, cool and ladylike, that turned him on.

"I never took no sauna before," Georgie was saying as he came into the room. "Hot? My balls'll never be the same!"

Georgie was wearing a white terry robe with the lodge's initials on it: AC. It didn't reach down to his knees. Another big one, another tall fucker. He was barefoot and toweling his hair—white-blond hair, thick, not long. But ugly? Jeez, was that an ugly excuse for a face!

"Forget your balls," Nick said, still not standing up. "We got work to do." Dummy—another dummy to work with. Georgie had been sent in after Nick had talked to his father from Lowell. He'd been waiting for Nick in Manchester. Tall and dumb—goes together every time. Except for his father, of course. Except for Vincent Verini himself. Tall and lean and dignified. There was the smartest man he ever knew.

"Do we eat?" Georgie asked.

Time to cut him down to size. "You eat when I say so. You piss when I say so. You fart when I say so." Nick stood up. Jesus, the soldier had to be six foot four, maybe five. All muscle, and with that face—he didn't scare Nick. "Got me, Georgie? Capeesh, Georgie?"

"Yeh. Sure. Don't get edgy." As Nick went toward his bedroom, Georgie said, "Y' see them girls coming through town, boss? Must have a college here. All that fresh tush—"

"Georgie," Nick said, in a fine, silky whisper that he knew would stop the blond shithead. It did. "No tush, no juice, no pills, no boo, no *nothing* till we clear here. That's the way I operate. Got me?"

"Got you." That was better. Much better. Georgie knew who Nick was. Who his father was. "What you got in mind, Nick?"

Nick didn't move; he knew that there was more power in standing still and speaking quietly. "I got somethin' in mind but I just decided to do it myself. Can you drive a Ferrari?"

"I just parked it, didn't I? While you signed us in—"

"That ain't driving, Georgie-boy." A hot anger was mixing in with his contempt. "You get a dent in that car, so much as a nick on the paint, Georgie-boy, and I'll zip you myself. Personal. Capeesh?"

"Jeez, boss—"

"Get dressed. Something that fits in here. You got any plaid flannel shirts?" And when Georgie, dumb Georgie, shook his head: "There's a ski shop downstairs. Buy whatever they suggest. You're a tourist. You're a sightseer. You're nothing, a nobody. Stay that way."

Looking baffled, frowning, Georgie began to whine: "You musta wanted me up here for some cocksuckin' reason."

"It just come to me, Georgie."

"Yeh?"

"How'd you like to spend a night in jail?"

"I spent a few."

"Matter-a-fact, I got two jobs for you. One, to drive the Ferrari. I wanta know how you handle the gears. Drop me when, where I tell you. Follow me in the Ferrari, and hang back. Pick me up when I'm finished. Capeesh?"

"A piece of cake, man."

"Number Two: After that, get yourself busted. Might need a job done inside. Like that one in Springfield, remember?"

"I hope they got better food up here." He was opening another stick of gum and shoving it into his maw. "That's it?"

"Chew that crud while you get dressed. But spit it out before you go down'n buy them new threads."

Still frowning, the big yellow-haired clown went into his bedroom and closed the door. Why didn't Poppa ever let him choose for himself?

And now, he knew, he'd waited long enough. He had to report. He took up the phone again, and at once his heart began to go haywire.

Reluctantly he pushed the buttons, preparing himself for the litany: He should have called earlier . . . was he covering all the angles? . . . did he want his older brother Angelo to come? . . . whatever he did, or ordered done, it had to look accidental. . . .

The phone at the other end was buzzing. By now his heart was working like a jackhammer and he could feel sweat in his armpits and around his sack.

If you live to be a hundred, kid . . . Why did he have to remember that now? Old uncle Bernardo, drunk at Angelo's wedding: . . . *you'll never be the man your father is.*

He spoke to Michael, the old Irish butler, who answered; then he waited. *He* had to do the talking this time. He had, at least, to *suggest* what Vincent Verini could do at *his* end. *Remember this, son: It costs money but you can always buy ninety percent of the cops and ninety-nine percent of the lawyers.* Well, it was time to start buying—but should he suggest that to Vincent Verini himself?

As for Nick, he already knew what *he* had to do, here, but he was telling no one, not even his father. What he had to do was get that red-haired TV slut off the case, her and her photographer pal who told Earl Wylie he was her father. Lying bastard. Anything Nick Verini hated, it was a liar.

He heard the phone being lifted, and, beginning to shake in his gut, he braced himself for the sound of his father's cool, thin, confident voice.

Andrew was not only amazed but appalled at the carnival atmosphere around the green.

Since leaving Colby's—where he had watched Tracy's telecast from the bar, washing down peanuts with Perrier and wondering whether Todd would be allowed to see it—he had been sitting on one of the few unoccupied wooden benches. On all sides people had gathered. On the small bandstand a couple of kids were strumming guitars, and there was a blare of rock music from the radio of a car parked on the street. The sound of voices and laughter came from all sides, fresh and cheerful in the cool evening air. Very strange. Could Todd hear them? Very discouraging, as human nature too often is.

Todd.

Visiting hours are over, Mr. Horgan. The uniformed woman named Holly Ray, behind the counter, had been fat and pleasant in the morning, but fat and coldly severe at the end of day. *It's after six o'clock.*

He had damned well known what time it was because he and Tracy had raced in from the airstrip, had developed the film together in the darkroom of Barney's Camera Shop off the green—Tracy seemed to know everybody in town—and then they had taken her copies to the television station on a hilltop a mile west of town. She'd insisted he take the MG: *I can use the station's van to get back to town. Do it all the time.* She had kissed him quickly when she got out.

No, Mr. Horgan, Holly Ray had said, *we cannot make an exception. We did that this morning, remember.*

He had then asked to see Chief Radford but was told that Sheriff Wheeler was in charge of his son's case, so he went across to the rotunda to the Sheriff's Office. *Something important, Mr. Horgan? Something confidential or something I should know about?*

Acting on angry impulse then, he had taken the photographs from the manila envelope and tossed one 8 × 10 black-and-white to the desk—one of the several he'd taken from the plane over the lake. He watched the uniformed officer's beefy hands pick up the print, eyes narrowing in his broad angular face, and then, with a certain stab of satisfaction, he saw Wheeler stand up, so fast that the chair rolled away behind him and clattered against the metal file cabinet.

Then their eyes met.

If this turns out to be Lynnette Durand's body, your son's gonna be charged with murder. You know that?

He had nodded, but persisted. *I also know that I don't want anyone else telling me. May I go in?*

I don't give a damn what you do or what you think, I've got work to do. Then, into the intercom: *Miss Ray, let Mr. Horgan see his son for five minutes only. Then get Chief Radford over here and see if you can locate the State's Attorney and the coroner.*

On the park bench now, Andrew became aware of a change taking place around him. The car radio no longer blasted; the laughter had faded away; the voices seemed hushed. He could hear only one guitar now, its melody soft and lonely on the night air.

Then he realized what must have happened. Somehow, in its own way, the news that Lynnette Durand was actually dead had reached the crowd, and now they knew where the police cars had been going.

He stood up.

Death. Its mystery, its awesome finality, always incredible, even when expected.

He cut across the grass to the street and turned toward the motel cottages. No wind yet, but the air was chilled. Cars were leaving now. Passersby, mostly college kids, averted their eyes as they passed him under the yellow streetlights.

Inevitably then he thought of Cassie. The gulls cawing outside the still house on the beach, and the quiet lovely statue on the bed . . .

He thought of his own goodbye, in the plane, scattering her beloved ashes over Cape Cod Bay, which she had loved as much as he.

He saw a white sign, dimly lighted, in front of a pillared white house: MRS. WHARTON'S GUEST HOME. Only one light in a window on the second floor—had the devastating news reached

Pierre and Thérèse Durand? Only they could *really* know its overwhelming finality. And no word of comfort would be sufficient now. Nothing, no one, could reach the vast emptiness. He knew.

An hour ago, in the visitors' room of the jail, he had felt a bewildering hunger rising through him as he waited for Todd to appear—something new to him, a yearning to be in the same room with his son again, the boy who was still a stranger to him.

When Todd came in, his sandy-bearded face a noncommittal mask, there was no greeting except *What's happening?*

Andrew had placed the four photographs on the long table: two full-length shots and one closeup of each man. And Todd had not hesitated. *This one chased Lynnette into the woods. This one threw me off the cliff.*

Just like that.

Then, excited, and thinking probably that this was all, Todd had regarded him with an odd expression on his young face. *You said you spent a month in the hospital a few years ago. Why?*

The abrupt and unexpected shift of focus to himself had startled him at first, but served to delay the moment he dreaded. *Treatment for alcoholism,* he had said.

Did it work?

I haven't had a drink for ten years. Or wanted one.

That's terrific. Todd had said it in a low whisper, his bluish-green eyes bright with genuine approval, even admiration. How very damned odd that the boy should be thinking of *him*. Even now. *That took guts, didn't it? Real balls. That's really terrific.*

But time was passing. Tracy was waiting for Todd's confirmation before she could use the photographs on the air.

Todd, I've another picture you have to see. He placed it on the table.

He discovered then that, guts or not, he could not bring himself to look into his son's face while Todd stared at the photograph.

The little lake's about half a mile from the cliff, he heard himself say. He'd flown very low and dangerously slow, trusting he wouldn't stall, after Tracy had spotted the pale object on the surface. The photograph revealed only the facedown body, black hair splayed on the water.

I guess I knew, he heard Todd say. Nothing more, nothing else.

When Todd did lift his eyes finally, he was standing very straight, slim body stiff, eyes closed. Andrew had been tempted to reach, to put out a hand, but . . .

You've had a busy day, haven't you? Todd's voice was even and low, without a tremor. *You're the only one who's been doing anything.*

When, throat locked, he could not answer—in the presence of death, only silence—he saw Todd move, blindly, to the door. *Would you mind if I went back to my cell?* Then, at the open door, Todd turned to face him. *Thanks,* he said. *Thanks for everything.*

And then, as if he could think of nothing else to say, Todd extended his hand. Andrew stepped to him and shook his hand.

It had been the first time their flesh had actually touched.

Going up the stairs from the jail, he had remembered what Todd's roommate had said: *Mostly just a weird kind of existential despair. Scares the shit out of me.* What now? What kind of despair now that he knew the girl was really dead?

Andrew had reached the end of the green. Across the street he could see, through a curious blur in his eyes, the lighted sign, COTTAGES ON THE GREEN, and the semicircle of small white cabins beyond. Overwhelmed by the depth and complexity and intensity of the emotions that seemed to be always quivering in his blood now, Andrew crossed the street and went up the flagstone steps. There he halted, and turned.

The green, framed in rows of lights, was all but deserted. The actuality of death had reached the town—not the possibility but the grim and terrible reality.

Then, moving slowly along the curb, a low-slung sports car glimmered red in the yellowish glow of the streetlamps. It crawled past, not turning down the long street running along the green, and continued, picking up speed once it had passed the cottages. There were two shadows in the car now, not one, almost but not quite invisible behind the darkly tinted glass.

Should he have given the sheriff the photo of its driver, which he had, in closeup, in the manila envelope? What would it prove? What could it establish?

As he moved toward his cottage, Andrew remembered what Wheeler had said after he had given him the photos and the two names, just before he left the courthouse: *Jesse Kull and Rolf Arneson—well, I can have the names run through the computer, National Crime Information Center. But these pictures, they won't help much. Only, let me tell you, that truck's been spotted sixty places between here and Timbuktu since that Larkin girl mentioned it on the air this morning. Way I see it, all you got to link that truck, any truck, to this whole thing is the defendant's word and an anonymous phone call that only you heard.*

Andrew had said: *My son, who is not a defendant, has just identified those two as the men he saw at the campsite last night.*

I said we'll run a check, okay? Only hold on a sec. Only reason my men didn't find the body is: It must've surfaced after I called off the search at four-thirty.

By then Andrew's anger and frustration were so acute that he couldn't resist saying: *That was a brilliant stroke, Sheriff. With two more hours of light left. Brilliant!*

Sheriff Wayne Wheeler had grinned his patronizing, mocking grin. *Your son'll be a defendant officially tomorrow morning at ten o'clock. And most likely for homicide. She didn't go for no midnight swim, you know.*

About to unlock the door of Cottage Five, he discovered a small buff-colored envelope tucked in the frame. Inside, he turned on the light and opened the envelope, which had the suggestion of a steeply pitched roof over the words ALPINE CHALET engraved on it. The same design and words were at the top of the sheet of paper inside. And scrawled below: *I'm here, Andy. And very lonely. please come. Please. I couldn't get you by phone so I'm having this delivered by hand.*

He did not have to read the signature. He recognized Julia's childish scribble. And then he saw the word just above her name: *Love.*

What Thérèse Durand needed most was someone to share her grief with her.

No, not anyone. Not Pierre.

Thank God, oh, thank You, God, that he's still asleep.

She was sitting in the chair by the window. Staring at the yellow lights, and the brown grass, and the white gazebo.

And then down again, at her hands, small-boned but gnarled, raw. Awkward. She wished she had a rosary. She had nothing to do with her hands.

Her mind was jumping all over the place. Every time she tried to hold on to a thought, another one crowded it away.

Pierre don't know. That's the thought that kept coming back. After he come in earlier, staggering and looking at her in that way, like he wasn't seeing her, he'd finished the bottle. . . .

Such a pretty table—dark, smooth, mahogany maybe—with the rings on it already from Pierre's glasses and the bottle . . .

Oh, thank You, dear God, for letting him sleep now. So he didn't have to see the TV downstairs in the old parlor . . . sliding doors . . . oh, what a beautiful house, that white stairway going up in a curve and all those big framed pictures on the wall, proud-looking people in their old-fashioned clothes . . .

Lynnette, Lynnette, oh Lynnette, *ma belle enfant, cherie,* was it my fault, what did I do, where did I go wrong?

Pray. That's what she'd said maybe they ought to do just before Pierre sprawled across the bed. *Pray? You pray, Thérèse. I got my booze, you got your prayer. Same thing, Terry, same thing . . .*

Terry. How many years had it been since he'd—

A knock on the door?

Oh God, they'll wake him!

She felt herself moving fast, careful not to stumble.

It was the chief of police. What was his name?

She closed the door behind her and stood out in the hallway. She whispered: "Yes, *yes?*"

His little face. Lined and dry. Like a nut. Police cap in hand, bald head. Identify the body . . . hospital . . . one of you . . . anything can do? No. Send nurse, medicine? No. Like to see priest, Father Whiting? Priest, yes, oh, *yes,* someone to talk to. Daughter at peace . . . God's will . . . Thank you . . . thank you . . .

She was alone again. Had she thanked the man?

She went into the room.

Pierre asleep. *Tant mieux.* Tenderness swelled through her. Such a fine, tall, upright man he'd been. Neat moustache then, handsome. And gentle. Yes, once, *aimable.*

She returned to the chair.

And she hadn't cried, not yet anyway. On the way, yes, and in the courthouse, some, but not since she knew, really knew . . .

God, how can You do this to me? Why?

Such thoughts frightened her.

How long before the priest would come?

But she couldn't really talk to anyone, really tell what she—

Don't punish her again, Pierre, please

How's she gonna learn? She won't learn—

Not with your belt—she's too old, Pierre—

Oh, Papa, I won't, I don't—Papa, all the other girls—

Now, how's that feel? Teach you . . . no loose bitches my family!

The memory was too much. Too much to bear.

But God never gives us more than we can . . .

Oh, God, if You love us, how can You allow so much evil in the world?

Thérèse Durand was weeping at last.

"Tracy, you're trying to make this thing bigger than it is," Steve said.

"In my book, one human being dead is big enough. Ask Mr. and Mrs. Durand if you won't believe me. But this *is* bigger. In some way."

"Maybe we'd better go into my office."

"You're the boss," she said, following his tall, slender figure down the short hall running between the three tiny offices and the studio, which was dark now behind the sound-proof plate glass—meaning that the seven o'clock old movie was running.

In his office Steve closed the door, put out his cigarette, and lifted his dirty bucks to the desk top. "Trace, you ought to know I'd never pull rank."

Tracy stretched out full-length on the sofa. "Lay on, Macduff."

"Let's try to keep this strictly business, right? I've been on the phone for more than an hour—networks, other stations all over New England want to use our tape. And three papers, including the New York *Daily News*, want copies of those photographs."

"Welcome to them. We need all the help we can get, *right*?"

"Help? What the hell is this, a crusade? You've antago-
nized the local police, too. Sheriff Wheeler says you're doing
police work—"

"Somebody has to."

Steve Savage's youthful voice sounded as reasonable as his
calm gray eyes looked. "You know as well as I do: If we
antagonize the police, we're cutting ourselves off from the
source of the only hard news there is in this area, right?"

"Right, Steve." She closed her eyes. She was tired, after
all, but so keyed-up that it didn't matter. "Say it, please, say
it."

"You don't have enough respect for the word *alleged*,
Trace. As in: Those two men were *alleged* to have been in the
area, *alleged* to have had a minor accident on the road, so
forth, so on, right?"

For some reason his easygoing voice and the word *right*,
more than the reprimand, worked on her nerves tonight. And
she was hungry again.

"You know, don't you, Trace, that you practically accused
those two of being implicated in the Lynnette Durand case—"

"They are."

"Oh, Trace, come on. There are legal implicatons here.
An anonymous tip on the telephone . . . Tracy, be reasonable."

She stood up then. "Also, I didn't get an interview with
Julia Craven when she arrived—"

"Or Gerald Usher Lewis. He's a celebrity too. Also, do
you know how many complaints we've had already about
showing that photo of the dead girl on the air?"

"It's gruesome all right. Let them know it."

"Gruesome? Tracy, these are churchgoers—religious, respectable people. That was a naked body."

Tracy leaped to her feet. Was she going to laugh? "You
mean it wasn't gruesome *enough?* Only obscene." She was
moving in a short space. "*Mea culpa, mea culpa, mea max-
ima culpa*—that's what my pop used to say when he was in
his cups and couldn't take much more!" She faced him over
the cluttered desk. "All right, I'll see if I can get an interview
on tape before the eleven o'clock sign-off. Anything else,
Mr. Savage?"

"Yes." Steve's gray eyes, never intense, but now very
sincere, were fixed on hers. "I missed you today, Trace."

She felt a sharp twinge of guilt. "I missed you, too,

Steve,'' she heard herself say. Another twinge, sharper this time because this had never been quite the truth and it was definitely not the truth tonight. She stepped behind the desk to kiss the top of his brown head. It smelled of hair spray and it was slightly stiff. Not like Andy's.

Steve got to his feet then. He seemed taller today, so much taller than Andy, and much more handsome. So, the sense of disloyalty hurtful, she kissed him on the lips. But quickly, fleetingly, and then she was going out the door, hating herself.

The weather was changing. As Andy had said it would. Andy again. A feeling of moisture in the air and it had cooled even more. She took the van, which was parked next to Steve's black Volvo, and as she drove down the hill she turned on the headlights.

At Barney's Camera Shop, on Oak Street a half-block off the green, she picked up the envelope with the duplicates that Barney had promised to leave for her in the straw basket hanging on the door. Good old sleepy-eyed Barney—four kids and a pretty wife and wandering hands, especially in the darkroom.

She phoned the Alpine Chalet from a booth on the corner of the green, only to be told that Mr. Lewis would hold a press conference after the hearing in the morning and that Miss Craven was not taking any calls. She left a message—in her mind writing off the possibility of an interview in time for the sign-off. This morning, the thought of actually speaking with Julia Craven had roused a girlish, not to say childish, excitement in her. Now . . .

She dialed the Cottages on the Green and asked Mrs. Stillwell for Cottage Five. ''He just came in half an hour ago, Tracy,'' Mrs. Stillwell said.

When she heard his voice, she said, ''No pastrami at Colby's, sorry. Are you hungry?''

''When?'' he asked.

''Twenty minutes?''

''I'll be there, Tracy.''

''You gave the pictures to the police, right?'' And then she giggled.

''Before you went on the air,'' Andy said. ''Is that funny?''

''No, Andy—that's *right*. Just *right*!''

Driving the van along the deserted green toward the court-house, she saw a sheriff's car, blue and red lights flashing, move slowly along the far side, followed by an ambulance, its light a steady blue—going in the direction of the hospital. The body had been recovered.

Above the tall, white columns of Mrs. Wharton's Guest Home, there was a single lighted window on the second floor. Were the parents at the window now? Watching the two-car cortege, knowing . . .

Did the scrutiny reflect an awe or reverence for human life, shock at violent death? Or only dull curiosity?

As he crossed between tables toward a booth for two at a side window—faces turning, a lowering of voices, no impolite whispers—Andy was wondering.

He sat and ordered a Perrier, ignoring the menu, looking out the window at a dark vacant lot, a few barren wintry trees between Colby's and the store beyond: STODDARD HARDWARE. EST. 1910. He'd never reached any conclusion in his mind as to the basic nature of the human animal. It had once seemed so vital to decide. But . . . in the years since Cassie's death, he'd lost interest in the question itself. If life was as accidental and transitory as that, what difference did it make? To hell with it.

He thanked the girl and sipped the lively but tasteless liquid.

Love. Since reading the word on Julia's message—or plea, or summons—he hadn't been able to get her out of his mind. Curiosity? Cowardice? However she had used the word, he had no intention of seeing her tonight. At the hearing tomorrow—well, that was inevitable. And soon enough. Until then . . . to hell with that, too.

Tracy was late. For all he knew, she was habitually late. He knew damned little about her really. And even less as to how he felt about her. Nevertheless, he glanced at the entrance again.

Then, at his shoulder but behind him, a male voice said, "Y' want company, Mr. Horgan?"

He turned—and recognized the young man at once. He had his photograph in the envelope on the seat beside him. Several photographs, in fact: a long shot, a closeup, and several of the red Ferrari parked at Wylie Trucking in Lowell. The short, trim young man with a neat black beard had a highball glass in his hand and he was grinning. Andrew's blood was beginning to pump faster.

"Buy you a drink, Mr. Horgan?" He slipped into the seat opposite. "That's right, you don't, do you? Not for ten years. I forgot."

Startled, Andrew said: "You also forgot to introduce yourself."

"Yeh, I did. Name's Doe." He was wearing the same white turtleneck, blue blazer over it now. *"That's* Italian, ain't it?"

Andrew kept his eyes on the openly mocking dark ones opposite him. "Giovanni Doe," he said. "How's the Ferrari running, Gino?"

The grin flickered, but only momentarily. "You're what they call observant—comes with your business, I guess. All eyes."

Andrew felt a constriction in his throat, around his chest. "If you have something to say to me, say it—I have a guest coming."

"Cute redhead. I seen her on TV."

"Say it."

The mane of glistening black hair shook. "Nice plane y' got parked out there at the Chalet—"

"Say it, I said."

"That house on Cape Cod—y' miss it?"

"I was there this morning."

"Yeh, I know." The skin on his forehead and above the dark line of beard was very smooth, dark tan but somehow unhealthy-looking. "What if I told you it burned down?"

"Are you threatening me, Gino?"

"Threaten? What'd I say could threaten you, Mr. Horgan? Lotsa houses, they burn down all the time on the Cape."

"A house is a thing." But his mind flinched from picturing it—*had* it burned? "I like it, yes, as houses go. It's hard to scare a man who doesn't give a damn about *things.*"

"People, then. You give a damn about people? Your own health, say. Both kneecaps working fine, are they? Eyes give you any trouble? Eyes important, your line of work."

Anger was relaxing the tightness somehow. "My mind's just fine, too," he said.

"Y' mean"—and the other man leaned closer—"y' mean y' don't give a shit whether you live or die?"

115

Andrew considered that a moment. Not for this bastard's sake, but for his own. Yesterday, he might have answered himself differently. Now he thought of Todd, he thought of Tracy, he remembered the day—and then he lied, relishing it: "Gino, you also can't scare a man who doesn't give a damn whether he lives or dies. Sorry."

"Wife dead and like that—that what you mean? Cassie, that her name? Kid you ain't seen in . . . how many years?"

"Kid I *never* saw until today, Gino. Sorry."

"How 'bout Julia Carpenter?"

"I don't know any Julia Carpenter."

That, for some reason, did it. The dark eyes, glittering with pleasure till now, went black and sharpened. He set the glass down with a thud on the cloth. "Y' know who I mean. What're you, some kinda wise-ass? You know who I mean."

Andrew saw the thick lips twisting, saw the thin shoulders hunching forward, the eyes going flat. Startled, he realized that he was facing a furious young man who was fighting to control his rage. And it had happened just like that. "I know who you mean, Gino," he said. "I haven't seen Julia Craven in twenty years and she means nothing to me. Anyone else? My parents are both dead."

"Ain't nobody untouchable, Mr. Wise-ass."

"Name's Horgan," Andrew said, "*Mister* Horgan." And then he added, politely: "Mister Doe."

"Y' think we're playin' some kinda game here? I got news for you, man." He leaned forward again. There was a film of moisture on his forehead and when his lips moved, they revealed brilliant white teeth. "I got big news, so listen."

"I'm all ears, Gino."

"You're all mouth and—" But he seemed to get hold of himself, with difficulty. He ran a hand through his hair. "Beautiful woman, your ex. Big star. Some night she comes outa the stage door, crowd all 'round, she feels a kinda wet something on her face all of a sudden. It starts to burn—she starts to scream. Pretty soon everybody's screaming. And Julia Craven's face, it just burns away. No face left."

He sat back and his eyes were calm and glistening again. With satisfaction.

It took Andrew a second or two before he could say: "I'll tell her to be careful."

The lips curved into a grin again. "Y' don't want that to happen, though, do you?"

"Nothing I've done has anything to do with Julia Craven. I told you: I haven't seen her in twenty years. She knows nothing about—"

"About what . . . *Mister* Horgan?"

Andrew spoke slowly and carefully: "About what *I* know."

"Which is?"

This time it was Andrew who leaned forward. "Which is that you wouldn't be here and you wouldn't be trying to throw a scare into me if all we're talking about is a college girl being raped and murdered."

Gino Doe—whatever his name was—took a long time to absorb that. No grin now. And his eyes had gone flat and dull again.

Finally, though, he spoke, but in a whisper, after casting a glance over the restaurant: "There's a friend of mine outside. Outside the window. This window."

Andrew's first impulse was to look through the glass, but he forced himself not to turn his head, or even to glance. He knew he would see only trees and shrubs. His body felt stiff and unreal.

"With a rifle. *My* rifle." His lips, framed in moustache and beard, were thick and sensuous, moving: "A Steyr AUG. Kraut gun. Austria. Y' know anything about guns, man?"

"Only," Andrew said, "only that in the hands of certain kinds of animals, they kill people."

A crooked smile. "All the time, man, all the time. You got the idea. And right this fuckin' second it's trained on your left ear." And when Andrew said nothing: "Called a bull-pup. Automatic rifle. But with class. Makes an M-16 look like shit." His eyes betrayed an inner excitement. "Night scope, not just a red spotting scope, dawn and dusk, a *night* vision scope—sees in the dark!" His tone was more excited, more satisfied. "On target at five hundred meters. Y'know how many yards that is?"

Wondering whether he had a voice, Andrew said: "Four football fields, end to end."

Grin more crooked, eyes narrow and shimmering. "Customized electronic trigger. And quiet. All anyone hears is a little fart sound. Target, he don't hear nothing."

"Target's apt to bleed, though. People eating dinner just might notice if a man falls over bleeding."

"All I got to do is lift this glass"—his lips were moving slowly—"lift it and finish this drink. I do that, man, you get a bullet through your thick skull. Capeesh?"

The strength seeped from Andrew's body and his mind threatened to blank out.

"So . . . so just sit up there straight, *Mister* Horgan, sir, please. Sit and listen. That's a nice wise-ass shit. Not so tough now, are you? Listen to what you're gonna do and also what you're *not* gonna do. . . ."

SIX

"Miss Larkin, the sheriff says he'll see you now. But that he's very busy."

Mind clenched, knowing that Andy was waiting in Colby's, Tracy had decided to wait it out, cooling her heels until he gave in. Which he had done, she knew, because she had sent in word that she wanted to apologize.

"Thank you, Mrs. Powell," she said to the tall, spare woman who was on night duty.

And when she had crossed the rotunda to the sheriff's department and arrived at his open office door, Wheeler did not look up from the desk. "Apology?" he said.

"If I've caused you any trouble, Sheriff." She was despising herself again. "Or embarrassment."

"Trouble?" Wheeler's voice was heavy with irony. "Embarrassment?" He looked up at her then, his grin transparently insincere. "About what? Taking pictures and putting them on the air and out to the public before the authorities even know they exist?"

"Mr. Horgan gave you those photos *before* I went on the air—"

"Suppressing evidence, obstruction of justice. Miss Larkin, I got grounds to charge you *and* Andrew Horgan."

Tracy had begun to tremble inside. She wasn't sure whether it was fear or anger. So she said nothing.

"Police work is not your job, missie." He stood up. "That's what they call fair warning. Do you read me?"

"What the sweet hell are the police doing?" Tracy asked, unable to stop herself.

"We are not releasing any additional information at this time. You can quote me verbatim. Doing so might affect the investigation. Period."

"What information?" Tracy stepped to the desk. "What investigation?"

Wheeler slammed his fist, knuckles down, on the desk. The sound exploded in the small office. "Listen, little girl—you're worse than Pierre Durand. He's been in and out of here all day, getting drunker and drunker, acting like a crazy man—"

"He *is* crazy," Tracy said. "With grief."

"What I *ought* to do is charge that Canuck with drunk and disorderly, throw him in the cell with that kid, and let nature take its course. No jury'd convict him and this damn thing'd be over!"

The shock in Tracy's every nerve and fiber would not let her speak. She turned away. Her body was cold, her face on fire. Was it possible she'd heard what he'd said? Was it even *possible*?

"You quote me, missie, I'll sue."

Then her anger reached her throat. She tasted it and her very cold body went very quiet. She reached into the envelope and riffled through the photos, then extracted two: one full-length shot, one tight closeup. Shots she had not used on the air because she and Andy had decided there was as yet no tie-in. Which was the only reason she was here. Apology, hell!

"I can't waste any more time, Miss Larkin," Wheeler growled. Then he stared at the two pictures she'd tossed, face up, onto the desk. "Who's that?"

"I don't know. Why don't *you* find out?"

"Why the hell should I?"

"Because, Sheriff," she said, "because I think you're into something *more* than a murder case and you don't know it." She tossed a third 8 × 10 to the desk. "That's the car he drives. Why don't you run *his* picture through your computers and see what you come up with?"

"Why? We got a rundown on the other two your friend Horgan gave me a while ago. Clean. No criminal record. Tell him. Just a couple of truck drivers trying to make an honest living.''

''This man's involved and I'll bet you *he* has a record!''

The police officer's face regained its mocking tolerant expression, almost pitying. ''What you got to go on this time, missie? Another stuttering kid on the telephone?'' He came around the desk to tower over her. ''From now on this courthouse is officially closed to the press. Mrs. Powell will type up anything we think the press has a right to know. Do you read me, missie?''

She did not reply but went out and through the dim rotunda to the front doors. So much for freedom of the press.

Outside, she went down the steps to the green. As she walked along its edge, past the familiar stores and under the shadows of the peaceful, high trees, a sense of strangeness took over. A feeling of unreality. Not much more than half of an ordinary day and night had passed since she'd met Andy in the lobby of the Alpine Chalet, yet the town seemed to have changed. Or she had.

''Well, thanks all the same, Mrs. Lucas, b-b-but I don't need a ride. I'm almost h-home.''

''Get in the car, Bruce,'' Lesley Lucas said. Several other cars passed, headlights stabbing, going toward town. ''You're getting home late, Bruce.''

He was beside her on the seat—not tall, not so tall as Harry, athletic enough but not the same macho type she always associated with Harry's track teams. ''I've been studying. In the l-l-library.''

She recalled something about a scholarship. And that Bruce's mother had been a librarian for as long as she could remember. ''Coincidence,'' she said. ''I was on my way to the library myself when I—'' She broke off. She hated her own voice. Thin, precise. *The voice of a bird*, Harry had said, more than once. *But a pretty bird, Les*. She had been on her way to the monthly library board meeting, and when she got into the three-year-old Plymouth wagon in the driveway, she'd noticed first that it had been washed, which was a trifle strange, and then, behind the wheel, she'd noticed that the front left fender was brighter than the right one and the hood—a different shade of maroon. And that's when she'd remembered that odd conversation on the telephone at breakfast between Harry and Bruce—which Harry had shrugged off when he came back to the table: *Oh, just a little trouble with a truck on the road. No harm done. On our way home from Montreal last night. Nothing to get whipped up about.*

"N-not many more days like this," Bruce said. His voice had a tentative note in it, a waiting, apprehensive kind of note. "My mother always s-s-says: Weather changes f-fast in Vermont. Summer one d-d-day, first snow the next."

Driving to the library, less than fifteen minutes ago, she had also remembered the local news broadcast at six-thirty—that pretty red-haired woman reporting the discovery of a body in the lake and then: *In an incident that may or not be related and which has not been reported to the police, there was a near-collision on Route 57 north of Shepperton when a white panel truck with Massachusetts plate 779 OKR forced another vehicle, identification not available, off the road. There was contact between the two vehicles because traces of maroon-colored paint were left on the fender of the truck. Police, presumably, are continuing to investigate.*

It had been then, remembering and puzzled, as she was about to make a turn into the library parking lot, that Lesley had changed her mind. She had thought of returning to the house and confronting Harry, but Cindy would still be up and awake, and if she was wrong, if her suspicions, by then knife-edged and painful, were wrong, if she was only what Harry always called her—*insecure, your own worst enemy, a congenital nag, Lesley*—well, she was not going to put poor little Cindy, only five, through one of those dreadful scenes if the child could be spared.

"Bruce," she said now, gulping air, "Bruce, you and Coach Lucas didn't go to Montreal to see a hockey match yesterday, did you?" And quickly: "Don't lie, Bruce. Harry's already told me."

As she had done on her way out of town, she pictured the map in her mind: Route 57 ran northeast, along the edge of the forest, not northwest toward Montreal.

"Well, Bruce?"

"This is where I l-l-l-live, Mrs. Lucas."

She swung the wheel and stopped the car on the gravel shoulder without turning onto the rutted dirt driveway, which curved back to a small shadowy farmhouse with lights in the windows. "Well, Bruce?" she said again.

"If Coach Lucas t-t-told you, then you know."

"He didn't tell me where you did go."

Bruce's voice, in the dimness, sounded bleak and miserable over the sound of the motor: "It's a l-l-lake just over the border. A cabin. A f-f-fishcamp."

The stutter was getting worse; she felt a pang of satisfaction and no qualms whatever for having tricked him. None. "And how long has this been going on?"

"Just since the t-t-t-t-t-term started—"

And then she had to ask the question that had been tormenting her for months, years: "Were the girls students?"

"The g-g-g-girls?"

"Don't lie to me, Bruce, don't." Her heart was fluttering. Her small hands were gripping the wheel. "Were they students? Your age, I mean, not Harry's, not women." She tried to control the high-pitched agitation in her voice: "Were they *children*? Tell me." She closed her eyes: the way they dressed, the way they danced, the way they crossed their legs in the front row in class. "I know the little bitches!"

She heard the door of the car open. Then she heard his voice: "Mrs. Lucas, it was just Coach and m-m-me. Honest."

But then panic flashed through her. He couldn't leave. "Bruce!" She opened her eyes. His face was at the window. "Then why would Harry lie?"

"Search me," he said. In the dashboard light his boyish handsome face looked relieved. "No reason to l-l-lie."

"But he did! And about the accident. And the fender. And . . . three other boys with you—"

"I d-d-d-d-d-don't know, ma'am."

But now she remembered something else. "Do your friends call you Brucie?"

"Brucie?" He straightened and stood back from the car so that she could no longer see his face. "Yeh. I guess s-s-some d-d-do."

Brucie, Harry had said on the phone, and then: *Bruce, this will have to wait till I get to the gym.*

She was going to be sick.

"Tell your mother hello." Was that her voice? Did she say that?

"I will. Thanks for the l-l-l-l-l-lift, Mrs.—"

She was driving. Along a narrow dark road. Alone. And the suspicion had taken root in her mind.

But she couldn't accept it. It was too horrible, too hideous, too . . . too incredible, to—

She didn't accept it, but she was sick nevertheless. She was so sick that she had to pull off onto the shoulder again, open the door just in time, and then, her thin body heaving, to vomit onto the gravel.

"New England boiled dinner is Mrs. Colby's specialty, Andy. You don't have to eat it, but don't let Mr. Colby see your face—you look positively nauseous!"

And that was the way he felt, too. He had been debating whether to tell her or not. Could he convey the overwhelming consuming fear that had taken over since the nameless young man had left the table? No man likes to admit, even to himself, that he is weak enough to feel terror. But terror it was, not a shaking panic but a steel-hard shaft driven deep in him now, so deep that even Tracy's quick and open kiss when she had come into the restaurant—*Getting to be a habit, isn't it?*—even her own strange mood had not really reached him.

"You may as well tell me, Andy." Her blue eyes were intent and questioning. "What's happened?" And then another thought clouded them. "Have you seen Julia?"

It was a woman's question. It reminded him of Cassie's foolish fears. And it kindled something tender and nostalgic in him—without touching the hard-packed dread.

So he decided. "I had an uninvited visitor while I was waiting. The owner of the Ferrari."

"Here?"

"Right where you're sitting." No need to mention the possibility of the rifle in the vacant lot outside the window. "His name's Gino. Gino Doe."

A faint but troubled smile faltered across her face. "I gave his photograph to the sheriff a few minutes ago. It's in a bottom drawer by now." She continued to eat. "Tell me."

His jaw aching, the helplessness inside turning to hopelessness as he spoke, he told her. The threats: his plane, his house on the Cape, Julia's face. And then, remembering the words, Todd. *Dangerous places, them jails. Tell that kid of yours to be careful in there. Him out of the way, some accident maybe, whole thing'd blow itself out, wouldn't it?*

Tracy had stopped eating. "The bottom line," she said.

"Tell me, Andy—what does the sonofabitch want you to do?"

"Not just me, Tracy. Us. You and me—"

"He's demanding we close our eyes and lay off," she said. And when Andrew nodded: "Which means," Tracy said, "that we're getting too close."

He reached for her hand on the table. "Goddammit, Tracy, you weren't here. You don't know."

Tracy's glance aside told him that a head or two had turned at the harsh urgency in his voice. And to hell with them.

"He really got to you, didn't he?"

"If you want me to say I'm scared, I'll say it. Not just for myself. You . . . you're in this too, Tracy."

That redhead—she don't know what can happen to her, too. Like all sorts of things happen to females every day.

"I can imagine," she said. "We grow up knowing—"

"It's not just him. We know that now." Her hand felt frail and delicate in his grasp, so he relaxed his grip and placed his palm over it. "I've been sitting here trying to dope it out. It's a hell of a lot bigger than us, darling."

"Don't be ashamed of being afraid. Don't pull that masculinity crap on me." And then in a different tone: "Did you mean what you just said? I won't hold you to it—"

"What?"

"Darling."

"I meant it."

"Let's get the hell out of here." She was already moving. "I need air."

He stood up and reached into his pocket, placed a twenty-dollar bill on the table, and followed her to the door and outside. There was even more of a chill in the night air now, a sharpness.

As they moved toward the green, she said, "Verbal threats are legally a form of assault."

"What do you want me to do? Bring charges and put *him* in jail? In jail with Todd?"

She took his arm. "Poor Andy. Poor dear Andy."

The accumulated frustration and anger and impotence dragged his steps. "Tracy, it's crazy. It's all crazy. When I told him the police had pictures of those two drivers and the truck and license, he didn't even blink." *Mr. Horgan, the cops, they don't have a prayer against us and most of 'em know it. We got friends, man, friends in high places, the highest.* "He's not afraid of the police."

"The hell he isn't," Tracy said. "If someone somewhere wasn't afraid that if Kull and Arneson tell what they know, something's going to be exposed, why the sweet hell would he be doing all this?"

Around the green now, in addition to cars parked bumper-to-bumper, there were two vans with network symbols on their sides. And while many of the benches were again occupied, there was no carnival atmosphere. They turned together away from the courthouse and toward the other end, toward the Cottages on the Green.

"What I didn't tell you, Tracy, is that he also said that if we play ball, he'll see that Todd never even goes to trial."

"You believe that?"

"I told him he couldn't pull that off." *You're full of shit* is what he'd actually said. And it had been then that the rage had erupted again, low and intense, a snarl: *Listen, wise-ass bastard, listen, we can do anything. We call the shots, capeesh? We can send the kid to prison or we can send him home on probation with a fine for possession of weed. You choose.* Andrew's face was clenched and pain was climbing his left jaw.

He felt her tighten her arm, bringing his against her body. "Maybe we *don't* have any choice," she said.

"All I *should* care about is seeing that Todd isn't tried and convicted for something someone else did."

"And *is* that all you care about?"

"Honestly, Tracy, I don't *know.*"

"You ready to cave in and follow orders?"

"I don't know, I said. Damn it, I don't *know!* The sonofabitch is dangerous, make no mistake, but I'm convinced now: He's only a cog." Then he heard his own choked, angry voice: "Any way we turn, it could be the wrong way now!"

She increased the pressure of her arm and he could feel the soft fullness of her breast through her clothing. They crossed the street toward the lighted sign and then they were moving along the flagstone walk past the cottages.

"I'd hate to believe what you're suggesting," Tracy said.

"I hate to believe it myself." As she released his arm, he unlocked the door. "I'm not sure yet that I—"

He heard the phone ringing inside. He swung the door open, flicked on the light, and crossed to the night table by the bed.

"Andy?"

He recognized her voice at once. Had he been unconsciously expecting it? "Yes, Julia—"

"Andy, didn't you get my message?" Her voice had changed, the tone deeper, the words more precise. "I had it hand-delivered by one of the bellmen. If that ski bum didn't—"

"I received your note, Julia, but I've been on the go. . . ."

He saw Tracy moving from the door, slowly, toward the window.

The silence on the phone stretched itself out. A familiar silence in spite of the years: Julia had never been able to bear the feeling that she was being ignored.

"Andy, I'm going absolutely berserk out here by myself. Have you had dinner? I'll order from room service. What are you drinking these days?"

"Sorry, Julia—"

Tracy was not looking out the window. "I think you should go," she said. She was staring at him, face thoughtful, eyes guarded, as she moved to the door.

"Is there someone there, Andy?"

"Hold on, Julia," he said into the phone, and then to Tracy: "Where are you going?"

"It doesn't matter, does it? If we've given up, it doesn't matter." And then: "Oh, for God's sake, Andy, no choice. You'll have to see her sooner or later. What are you afraid of?" She opened the door. "I'll take the van. The MG coughs at night. Goose it." She went out and closed the door.

"Andy, are you there?"

Julia could never bear, also, to be kept waiting, and she was always terrified of being alone. It was all coming back to him. "I'm here, Julia." He'd often wondered what he'd feel, if anything, and now all he felt was irritation.

Some night she comes outa the stage door . . . crowd . . . wet something on her face . . . just burns away . . . no face left.

Could he tell Julia?

"Well, Andy? You used to make up your mind much faster than this."

He had to tell her. Tracy was right: no choice. He had to

warn her. "I'll watch you eat," he said, "but in the dining room."

He heard her laugh. That, too, sounded different: lower-pitched, less spontaneous. "What're you afraid of, Andy? I won't seduce you."

"That's true, Julia." An old familiar anger sounded in his tone. "You sure as hell won't."

He replaced the phone and stood staring at the closed door. *Was* he afraid? Of what? Of what he might begin to feel?

Before he could answer the question in his mind, and as he took off the flight jacket and stepped toward the closet to take down the tweed, the phone jangled again.

And to hell with it—

But when it continued until he had the jacket on and the knob of the door in his hand, he uttered a curse—too damned much was happening too damned fast!—and crossed to pick up the phone again, barking his name into it.

It was not Julia. Or Tracy. A man's voice that he did not recognize at first: "Is that you, Andy?"

"Yes."

"Andy, it's Bud Florsheim. Your neighbor on the Cape. I had one helluva time tracking you down, but I heard on the CBS news that you were there—"

"What's up, Bud?"

"God, I hate to be the one to tell you, but the fire department didn't know where—"

"What's happened?" But he knew, he really knew. He was only waiting for the words.

"I got some bad news, friend. I was walking my dog on the beach and I saw the flames and I ran like hell to my house, but by the time the fire department got there, with the wind and all, it was too late to save it. . . ."

"What have you found out, Sheriff?"

"Oh God. I thought I was shut of you for the night. How'd you get in here again, missie?" Glaring, Wheeler stabbed at the intercom and barked, "Mrs. Powell!"

"I came in the back door."

He sat back. "I don't owe you an explanation but I'll give it to you anyways. Getting to a record, if any, from a name, that's easy. From a photograph only, that takes facilities *this* facility don't have. Do you read me, missie?"

"Stop calling me *missie*!" She took a single step. "You haven't done a damned thing since I left here a while ago."

Chief Radford appeared in the open doorway. "Passing by, couldn't help hearing. Facilities? What sort of facilities we talking about?"

Tracy took two steps and picked up the three photographs. She turned to Radford. "This man's in town. That's the red Ferrari he drives, and less than an hour ago he assaulted a friend of mine in Colby's Bar and Grill."

"Tell your friend to come in," Wheeler growled, "identify this picture and file charges."

Chief Radford interrupted. "Assault?" He stepped in and took the photographs from her hand. "Physical assault? I got extra men patrolling the streets tonight. But no report of any—"

"Not physical," Tracy said, trying to control her temper. "Verbal threats."

Wheeler stood up, towering over the other two. "We got serious things on our minds around here tonight, damn it to hell. I told you your press privileges have been revoked."

"He's in town, Chief," Tracy said. "And I'm betting you'll find out he's involved with organized crime some way. It's your town, Chief."

Radford, without taking a step, accepted the challenge. "Sheriff, all due respect, all that, but Tracy's right: This time the crime, if there is one, is in my jurisdiction." He turned to Tracy. "Now. What makes this individual so important to you?"

"She's trying to tie him into—"

"Excuse me, Sheriff," Kyle Radford said, "I was asking Miss Larkin."

Tracy's mind had wandered: By now Andy would be on the road to the Chalet in her green MG—

"Tracy?"

"All I want to know is who this man is and what his criminal record is—how really dangerous he is."

"Dangerous?" Wheeler echoed. "We don't have any reason to even—"

This time Radford ignored him. "I saw that red car, too, Tracy. Thought it might be some college kid. Assault's a misdemeanor in this state, physical contact not necessary." He moved, short and vigorous, to the door. "Come with me,

Tracy, over to my office." He was on his way. As she followed, he said crisply: "I'll find out which is the closest facility that can do the job, and then I'll send an officer there with this photo. God knows where. It'll take time."

"But it'll be *done*," Tracy said. "Thank you, Chief."

In the dim, empty rotunda they heard Wheeler's voice call: "Your funeral, Chief. Only I was trained not to waste taxpayers' money."

Ignoring it, Radford said, "You'll be home through the night, will you? That's the old Savage place out on Brookfield Road, isn't it?"

Home? Steve? "I haven't looked that far ahead. Thanks, Chief." Then she went out the rear door and into the parking area behind the courthouse to get into the van.

The night air had sharpened even more and the sky had darkened above the treetops. She was remembering something she'd read, in her stagestruck days in college: *The reason I don't enjoy doing movies is that there's no immediate response. To do my best, I need the feeling of an audience responding, listening to me, loving me. . . .*

Was Andy with her now? Responding? Listening? Discovering, perhaps, that he was still in love?

The electric shock of sheer, naked, undeniable jealousy that was shooting through her was as incredible as everything else she'd been feeling all day.

Love. She was the one who had told herself, and others, including Steve but not yet Andrew Horgan, that she could never feel, that she wanted *never* to feel, the possessiveness, the slavery of that kind of love.

But she didn't want to think about that now—herself, or Steve, or Andy, or Julia Craven. She stopped the van under a streetlight and, with the motor running, separated the black-and-white 8 × 10's. Then she turned, not toward the Brookfield Road leading to Steve's house—*was* it her home and *would* she be there during the night?—but toward the new subdivision on the east edge of town where she knew Blake Arnold lived.

Another exercise in futility? Damn, damn, damn!

When Blake Arnold came to the door of his pleasant split-level suburban-type house on the pleasant curving street in Laurel Heights, she shook her head at his invitation to come in and handed him the 9 × 12 manila envelope. "You

130

probably didn't see my newscast. The Viking and the mountain man are the ones who murdered Lynnette Durand. No, I *can't* prove it! The young one with the black beard's in on it, too, but I don't know how. He goes with the fancy car and he's in town. I'll call you later—''

"Tracy, hey! Come in and have a drink and calm down."

"I'll phone you."

Calm down. It was good advice. But how, pray, how?

A drink. Is that what Andy was doing? Having a drink with Julia? What was the phrase—cutting up old touches? One of Charlie Larkin's phrases.

She was driving the van—automatically, by habit—along the familiar night-hushed streets and then onto Brookfield Road, moving now between outthrusts of low bluffs with shrubs and small trees struggling to survive on them, and then into the clear, with meadows lined by stone fences on one side, on the other a field of gray stones in a haphazard pattern where they'd erupted over a hundred spring thaws and had not been cleared.

She could not see the lights, but less than a mile ahead stood the old house that had belonged to Steve's parents before they died: an old but still handsome Victorian structure, now gray with time and weather, the lawn gone to hell long ago, but great verandas that gave it a sad sort of seedy grandeur.

Oh, Steve, we were getting along so well. We were really finding our stride till this thing. . . .

There was a brief flicker before her eyes, instantaneous, a quick glittering, so quick that she was not sure she'd seen anything at all, and then she felt the thing, whatever it was, around her neck, under her chin, cutting into her throat. Instinctively she tried to turn her head, but could not. A hot thin line of razor-sharp pain sliced her throat. She caught a whiff of someone's breath at her ear. "Keep driving, slut." A voice, a whisper, "Don't slow down. Don't touch the horn. Try to turn your head, it comes off in your lap, capeesh?"

No matter which way he turned, or what he did, it was the end of the road for Rolf Arneson and he knew it.

Silenzio, y'know that word? Silence. Either one a you two gets loaded, or decide to spill your guts to your wife, or even your priest—forget it. So cut off your tongue. Right now. Silenzio!

By now, this many hours later, this many drinks later, Rolf's whole tall body was sick—gut shot away, chest shaking, like there was a big bird in there trying to get out. His mind was busting with the absolute certainty that his life had come to an end. Not last night when he blew his cool and threw the kid off the cliff, or even a few minutes later, when he stood looking down on the girl's dead naked body, but this afternoon in Earl Wylie's garage . . .

Take a vacation. You'll get paid. Go fishing, hunting, get drunk. Only stay the fuck away from here.

He'd tried to drink himself into a stupor but all that happened was his mind kept working, clear and hard. At first all he could think of was running, just getting the hell *out*. Anywhere but Lowell; anywhere but here. Florida, California, Canada, Mexico. But, having stood and listened to that cocky little bastard in Wylie's garage, he'd known: There was no place to run. They were everywhere. Not the police—*them*. And now he was one of them. *Silenzio*. He'd heard of the vow of silence.

He looked at his face in the mirror behind the bar. It stared back at him, dazed, eyes so pale the blue blurred into the white. Someone else's face. Not his. In the mirror he could see the booths along the wall behind him. Monday night was always slow. The Smugglers Cove was quiet now. Three guys still wearing their hard hats, a young couple that looked like a pickup, a hooker and a dude in a three-piece suit who looked like he didn't belong. Average night, kind of night he usually enjoyed. If only he could shake off this feeling, even in his balls, that something evil and awful was going to happen, had to happen. And that there was nothing he could do to stop it. Kismet—where'd he heard that word? Somewhere . . .

He heard Jesse's high-pitched laugh from the other end of the bar. Where he was talking to the dyed blonde. A regular. Not a hooker, just a housewife in the neighborhood. A real lush.

Jesse laughing it up. What'd *he* have to laugh about, stupid bastard? All his fault. Taking the rifle on the haul . . . turning into the state forest . . . wasting four, five hours trying to get a deer—*Outa season, so what? Who's gonna be in there*

t' arrest us?—instead of taking the load to the regular place . . .
old quarry they'd been using for more than a year now . . .
and Jesse'd been the one spotted the light from the fire, too
. . . just when they'd finished unloading.

And it was Jesse who'd done it to the girl . . . his idea to
get rid of the body in the lake . . . with the load . . . shaking
in his boots then, almost crying . . .

Jesse Kull. He was the reason they were in this fix, and
who was doing the laughing?

Rolf tossed down the rest of his drink, not even tasting it,
and clinked his fingernail against his glass. Christine, who
was fooling around at the cash register, turned her head and
then came down to him—no hurry, tall and easy, one gor-
geous woman, too much class for this dump.

She was shaking her head, looking him over. "Why don't
you go home, honey? I don't get off till one-thirty and you're
stinking."

Her face floated in front of him, half-smiling, kind. Her
boobs, outlined in the tight pink sweater, looked plush, lus-
cious. "One more, Chrissie. Then I go."

She took his glass, shaking her long pale hair, which all of
a sudden he wanted to plunge his hands into. "I thought,"
she said, "I thought for sure once you saw the seven o'clock
news, you'd take yourself off the hook. No more news on till
eleven. That's an hour and a half. Go home and take it
easy."

Take it easy. He doubted he'd ever be able to take it easy
again. *You kill her for cunt? You risked this whole operation
for pussy? I can't believe it! That's murder one, man, and
you're in deep shit. Both of you. Both, capeesh? You, too,
tall man.*

Admiring the back of Chrissie's body as she poured tonic
over his vodka, he still couldn't believe it. Any of it. Hell, he
and Chrissie had it made. Now—hell, it was on TV. NBC
news. The bastard kid was in jail. He just couldn't believe
any of this was happening and if he got loaded enough,
maybe . . .

When Christine set the drink in front of him, he saw Jesse
shambling down, swaying like a drunken bear, to stand beside him, glass in hand. Face and scalp covered with sweat,
glistening, and his mouth grinning in the red beard. The
dumb bastard, he didn't know what he was into and now he

was too bombed out even to give a damn. Jesse always stood up at a bar; it was too much of a struggle to get his hulk up onto a stool. "Harriet's gonna be pissed," he said in his high, squeaky voice. "I didn't even get home for supper. You have supper, Rolf?"

All of a sudden he hated Jesse. Maybe he'd hated him since it happened and didn't know it. Now he really loathed the red-bearded bastard.

Christine, who had not turned away, leaned across the bar. "Jesse still won't tell me how he gets it on with Harriet." It was her teasing tone, her flirting, mocking, sort of bawdy tone that pleased him and made him sore at the same time and yet always turned him on a little when he was in the Cove, with customers eyeing her. She leaned closer now, and whispered: "How can you get close enough to get it in, Jesse?"

And Jesse laughed his cackling, good-natured drunken laugh. "Harriet, she don't have time anyway. Now they got soaps on TV at night, she's too wrung out to do nothin' but snore when we hit the sack." And then he laughed and drained his glass.

But Rolf knew. *I'm tired a being sucked off,* Jesse'd said, less than a week ago in the truck. *Someday I'm gonna get a real piece again before I die.*

Well, he'd done it. And now look at him.

Rolf had picked up his glass and lifted it to his mouth when all hell broke loose, and everything happened so fast, he couldn't sort it all out, he was drunk but—

The two outside doors burst open, first the front and then, almost the same instant, the one on the side street. A clatter and then a wooden slam and then a deep harsh voice yelling: "Don't nobody move, it's a stickup!"

There was a woman's stifled scream from behind and then the second man swung his gun toward a booth, it was a shotgun, Christ, they both had shotguns, and one was on Chrissie, she was staring at the face of the one with the gun on her, but they didn't have faces, neither one, ski masks, round holes and a slit in black wool, and the one holding the shotgun on Chrissie was saying, in a rush, everything in a breathless rush, like he was scared too: "Put the bills on the bar, bitch," and she didn't even glance at him, just hurried to the cash register, the drawer slamming open, tiny bell, which sounded loud, that was the only noise except the two men breathing, and then the one bellowing, "Cash and wallets on the bar, *everybody,* fast!" And the shotguns both moving, sweeping over the room, no words, no screams, and then it came to him: *You can be in some bar . . . holdup . . . get in the way . . .*

So he knew, just like that. This was it. He knew but he wasn't even surprised. He just knew and he had to move, *shotgun maybe,* so he didn't glance at the storage-room door, he just got it in his mind, and the door to the alley out back, if he could dive down to the floor, get behind the bar, but before he could move, there was an explosion, deafening, glass shattering, whole building shaking, earthquake, volcano, where was she, where was Chrissie, she was still standing up but her head was gone, only red blood, blood everywhere, a scream behind him, Chrissie's body crumpling, no head, another blast, Jesse, Jesse holding his stomach, hands turning red, eyes surprised, wide, and then a pain along his own arm, the pellets, but he was able to drop off the stool, only his leg gave way, buckling, the one the kid'd slashed with the hatchet, and then he was down, rolling over fast, Jesse beside him, eyes open, glassy, and then he was down on his back on the floor and staring into the black hole of the barrel, close, closer, the mask beyond, and he knew, but it did no good, knowing, too late, too late—

SEVEN

"Julia, for God's sake, will you listen to me? I've come here to tell you something important."

"You look so grim, darling. So serious. Has it been that bad, so terrible for you over the years?"

Ever since he had entered Julia's suite, Andrew had had the odd impression that, instead of participating, he was observing. *Oh, Andy,* she had said breathlessly, *I can't believe it!* Even the setting seemed to be a room on the stage or in a movie: spacious elegance with a rustic touch, low fire in the fieldstone fireplace, muted lights. *How do I look, darling?* She looked just fine: low-cut dinner gown, the color of rust adding luster to her excited blue-green eyes and a glow to her bare shoulders. *Tell me the truth, Andy. Have I changed?* Relieved that he felt no physical or sexual quickening in his body, he'd said, and honestly: *You don't look twenty years older, Julia.* And then she studied him intensely. *Well, you do look fit. And I love those gray streaks. Why, you've become almost handsome.*

After which she'd explained that the dining room downstairs stopped serving at nine, so she had already ordered dinner from room service. *Oh, stop scowling. It wasn't my idea. What do you drink these days?* And, remembering that, one way or the other, Julia had always had her way, he told her that he'd joined the Perrier brigade.

I don't believe it! But she'd poured him a club soda and herself a gin with a splash of bitters and had then sat down on the love seat facing his over the cocktail table, a highly

136

polished timber slab. *Beautiful woman, your ex. Some night she comes outa the stage door—*

"Tell me, darling," Julia said now. "*Has* it been just awful for you?"

For an instant he realized that she longed, really ached inside, to hear him say that he'd been miserably lonely, but he said: "Five of those years were the greatest I ever knew."

She frowned then, wounded again, and said, "I'm so glad." Her tone had become brittle. "But I don't want to hear about it."

So he said: "You haven't mentioned Todd."

At once she stood up. "What is there to say?" She began to move, aimless, glass in hand. "I'm doing all I can. What more can I do? Why do people always expect me to do things differently?"

It was a familiar tune. But it had nothing to do with him. "Julia, I came here for one reason. I have to tell you—"

"You didn't come to see *me*, did you? You weren't even *curious*. You didn't return my calls—"

"Julia, come back here, sit down, and for once in your life, *listen*!"

She studied him from across the room, eyes brilliant with defiance, but again hurt and offended. "Andy, you have changed."

He stood up. "In twenty years, if you don't change, you might as well be dead."

She was frowning again. But with a wary, angry hostility in her gaze. "You sound so goddamned *sure* of yourself!"

"I'm sure of one thing, Julia—"

"You sound just the way you did that day when you beat me up!"

"I struck you, Julia. Once. That's not a beating." But even now the old anger and resentment would not return. "I didn't come here to talk about the past," he said.

"Then why?" She came toward him, fast. "Why the fuck did you come?"

"To tell you that you're in danger."

She halted. Her mobile face went through a series of changes: startlement, mistrust, shock, then a flash of utter disbelief—and after that, a slow, unavoidable realization that she could not deny. "Danger?"

"I can't explain any more because I don't know. Someone

burned down my house on Cape Cod. That same person, or persons—it's not just one—threatened you."

Her tone was a whisper now: "Why should anyone—"

"Not to kill you, Julia—but to disfigure you for life."

Again her delicate face trembled through a series of expressions, before her mind accepted. She moved a few steps to sink down onto the love seat. She was not acting now. She lifted her face and there was an almost childish appeal in her stunned eyes. "Why? Why *me*, Andy?"

He moved to sit beside her. "Todd stumbled on to something when the girl was killed. I don't know what. Yet. To keep me from finding out, they'll do anything."

"Then why the fuck don't you stop trying to find out?"

"Because if I do, Todd will be indicted for murder tomorrow, and possibly convicted later."

She leaped to her feet and her tone took on a screeching sound as she wheeled on him.

"You never gave a fuck before! All those goddam years!"

"You never told me, Julia! And you told *him* I walked out when I learned you were pregnant."

"Well, I *was* already pregnant that day!"

It was the sort of irrational logic that he had never been able to follow, or deal with, so he ignored her words and let her stride away in triumph.

He rose to his feet. "That's the message, Julia. I don't feel like dinner, thanks."

Staring wide-eyed with panic as he stepped to the door, she almost shouted: "You can't leave me now! What am I going to do?"

"There were others threatened as well, Julia. Talk to your lawyer friend. I'm sure he'll be able to hire someone."

"Andy, darling, please." She was coming toward him, one hand reaching behind her body. "Why can't you stay? We'll skip dinner. We'll forget all of it, everything, the way we used to do—"

Then, even as he heard the sound of a zipper, she stopped walking only seven or eight feet away and the dress was falling from her body.

She was standing staring at him, confident and childishly delighted and challenging, totally nude. Her body had changed little; if anything, it was softer, more rounded, more womanly. She placed both hands behind her back. She placed her feet together. Her eyes bored into his.

And he realized that this was exactly what she had planned for later in the evening, after dinner. . . .

"Andy, no one's ever made love to me the way you did."

She came toward him in a rush and would have kissed him on the mouth, but he turned his head slightly and felt her lips warm and moist against his cheek, her breasts against his body, and then she was stepping back, her eyes probing his, taking on a girlish mischievousness. "You didn't kiss me when you came in. Do you think I don't know why?"

Seeing the vulnerability in her eyes, as nakedly exposed as her body, he realized that he had no need to punish her. *I guess I won't know whether I forgive her till I see her, will I?* He'd said that to Tracy.

"Sorry, Julia." He was thinking of Tracy now. "I'm not in love with you."

"What difference does that make? We're here, we're alone—what's love got to do with it?"

He was opening the door. "Everything," he said.

And then he heard her voice behind him, harsh and wild: "You bastard, oh, you loathsome sonofabitch, don't you dare! Who are you to walk out on me again?" But he was in the corridor, closing the door without glancing back. "It's your fault, not mine, *your* fault Todd's where he is right this second!"

He was passing the elevators. He could hear her voice screeching hysterically. Fortunately he could not make out the words as he went down the wide stairway.

Although logs flamed in the fireplaces, enormous stone caves at both ends, the high-beamed lodge room was almost deserted as he crossed it to go out.

It was raining. A fine cold drizzle. As he was about to step into Tracy's green MG, he saw a wet glitter of red beyond. Six or seven cars away, the Ferrari was angled into a parking slot. He felt a furious eruption in his chest. He had to fight down an angry, reckless impulse—irrational, savage—to attack the car itself, smash it with a stone, trash it completely.

Instead, he settled into the low seat of the MG and started the engine, gunned it violently, and in a few moments he was on the twisting road back to town, the road that Tracy referred to as North 57.

Where was Tracy now? Now that he knew that he loved her.

He'd realized that when he'd stood staring at Julia's naked, soft, desirable body—and had felt no desire.

Even when she heard Pierre stirring on the bed, even as she felt the dread coming back into her nerves, Thérèse Durand could not get her daughter's face out of her mind. The way it had looked there in the basement of the hospital. So pale, so still. Unreal. Like she'd never been alive.

"What time's it?" He always asked that, first thing.

"I don't know," she said. "It's night, though."

"Where's the bottle?" He turned on the floor lamp. "It was right there." His voice was thick, but he was always sober when he woke up. "On the table."

"It was empty," she heard herself say, beginning to tremble inside. "You drank it all."

"Mensonge," he growled, sitting slack on the edge of the bed now.

She did not lie. She had stopped lying about the drink years ago. "I put the bottle in the wastebasket."

He kicked over the basket and the bottle rolled out onto the carpet. He stared at it, not at her, when he said, "I got plenty more in the truck." He stood up, his huge body steady, strong. "Gotta take a piss."

He went out the door, but instead of going down the hall, he clumped down the stairway, such a lovely stairway, and then she heard the front door open and shut. She only hoped Mrs. Wharton wouldn't see him. But she was relieved to be alone again. She was vaguely hungry—how long since she'd even thought of eating? Before they'd gone to the hospital. How many hours ago? What a kind man Dr. Nichols was, so tall and straight and dignified, so soft-spoken, like he really, really cared. How could such a man do the things he had to do? To Lynnette's body. *Horreur. Quelle horreur.*

You dare not quarrel with God's ways, Father Whiting had warned, when he'd come to call because that nice chief of police had asked him to. They'd sat in the parlor downstairs, just the two of them. Father Whiting was also a caring man. *If we poor mortals are humble, when we can accept His will, then we find peace even in the midst of chaos and grief.* But

140

. . . but an innocent child like Lynnette . . . if God was fair and just . . . a girl who loved life so much . . .

After Father Whiting had given her his blessing in Latin and had gone, she'd climbed the wide stairs again. Pierre was somewhere then. Some bar. She didn't care.

And it had been then, hard as she'd fought it, tight as her mind had clenched against it, that she'd remembered: Lynnette wearing her new swimsuit last summer—how beautiful, how young and alive!—and wearing it because Pierre had insisted. *Let's see what you wear when you go out to the lake with all them boys.* And then his terrible scowl when he saw it on her. With Lynnette's dark eyes knowing, hating, that awful fear in them. *You might's well be naked.* Herself helpless. And scared. And Lynnette quivering all over, eyes wide and wild and angry. *Go out in the hall, whore, and look at yourself in the mirror. That's the way they see you. You might's well be naked. That's how you let them see you!*

Now, hearing the front door open and close again downstairs, his step on the stairway, she admitted something to herself that she knew was sinful, knew she should never feel, knew she had denied feeling for years: She hated him. Husband or not, sacred vows or not, she hated him.

When he came into the room, he was carrying another bottle of liquor. He went to the bed and got down on his knees and looked under it. When he straightened, he was holding his rifle-case. He tossed it to the bed. That old hunting rifle that he put so much store in.

She couldn't speak.

Seeing what she was staring at, he said: "I told you comin': court lets him off, he answers to me."

The clot in her throat broke. "Oh, Pierre, Pierre, *mon cheri*, it was God's will. Please, leave it to God!"

"I don't leave nothin' to nobody. What'd God ever do for me?"

"Don't blaspheme, too." She was hearing her words: They seemed to come without her knowing or willing them. "Please don't talk that way. At a time like this. Don't talk about *more* deaths."

"You gonna defy me too? Like your daughter always done—"

"I'll call the police. They'll put you in jail!"

His black eyes narrowed. "You do that. I'd like that." He

grunted a kind of laugh that wasn't a laugh. "Put me in there with him, I'll get it over with *rapidement*."

Fury, fast and scalding, burst in her head, as if something had ruptured there, and instantly the hot poison was in every pore. "I know why you hate him so!" Voice shrill, voice loud. "I know, Pierre, I *know*!"

Black bushy brows together, he snorted: "He turned our daughter into a whore, that's what he done. *Prostituée!* You know what camping means. Fucking, that's what. *Fucking*, that's what they were doing!"

"And you—you were jealous!"

He stood very still. His eyes didn't blink. But they looked stunned. The rage in her went cold. She opened her mouth to speak—what had she done, what had she said?—but before her lips could move, she felt the blow along the side of her face.

Then she was half on the bed, half on the floor, trying to scramble away. She saw his face, massive and ugly and ferocious, close to hers, a stranger's face. She tasted blood in her mouth and felt his hard hands tight on her arms, felt herself being lifted, her feet off the floor, felt her stiff body being shaken, heard him swearing, all the words she hated, all in a jumble, his breath sour and stinking, close to her face. Her body went limp then, her head flopping now, side to side, up and down, the bones in her arms crushed, pain everywhere, her mind snapping open and shut, going dim, then exploding, and then she felt her body being lifted higher, limp and helpless, and she wanted to die, quick now, to die. But then her body was free, for an instant, in the air, and she felt the bed under her and knew, with an instant's regret, that she was not going to die.

Would she ever, ever be warm again?

The heat and steam in the shower stall had just begun to penetrate the cold of her flesh—the chill was in the marrow of her bones by now—when Tracy heard Steve's voice. She turned off the shower to listen. "What I don't understand is, if he forced you to strip in the van, why didn't he rape you?"

She placed her forehead against the wet tile, closing her eyes, and answered: "Do we have to go over this again? When he took the wire from around my neck, he took my clothes and the keys to the van to make sure I stayed there.

Hawley Mill Road, where it dead-ends at the old mill. While he got away.'' Her body had begun to quiver again, but her teeth, thank God, had stopped chattering. "He said it himself: It was just to show me what *could* happen."

"Well, it's hard to believe. But I guess no woman wants to admit she's been raped."

"Steve, *listen!*" She turned and placed her open palms on the glass door. "Steve, I told you: I was *not* raped."

"Then I don't see why you don't go to the police. The ragout's hot whenever you're ready to eat."

Beginning to shiver, she turned on the shower again, adjusting the water temperature. Her body, after the long cold walk in the freezing rain, was demanding heat. The needles of scalding water stopped the shivering at once.

When she'd come into the house—Steve's house, not theirs—Steve had been shocked and overwhelmingly solicitous, his eyes raking her naked body even as he threw a blanket over it and helped her to the sofa in the living room. And then the brandy and the questions: Did she know who the man was? Had she seen his face? What did he *do* to her? What was that red line around her neck? Why didn't she stop a car on the road instead of walking? Why didn't she go into one of the houses along the way? Why wouldn't she let him call the police? When she was calm enough, body huddled and convulsive, teeth sounding in the words, she had answered. No, she had not seen his face but she knew who he was, she'd recognized the sound of the Ferrari engine. It had been parked there waiting. He'd done nothing to her except talk and make her take off all her clothes. The red line was blood—the sonofabitch had threatened to cut off her head. She had hidden from all cars while she walked because it could have been him coming back, or she might really have been raped by someone else, since she was naked. And she didn't stop for help in one of the four houses because two of them were dark and he'd warned her not to bring in the police, and that's the first thing anyone would do. And she was damned, she was double-goddammed if she'd walked all that way to have *him* do that now. The sonofabitch had *warned* her—couldn't Steve understand that?

But now, turning to allow the water to deluge her back, she was not so sure. Was she giving in, letting the sonofabitch win? Was she doing the wrong thing? Was this how *they* always won? She turned again, tilting her head back, and felt the heat scalding into the raw ridge of burning under her chin.

There was another reason, even more important than his threat—*you go to the cops, this'll happen again, for real next time*—more important even than that. She'd had it clear in her mind several times while she walked, exposed, alert, in terror, hearing every car motor, every crackling sound in the dark woods. She'd had it clear several times then, but now it would not come into focus again.

So she turned off the shower, toweled down, and put on Steve's heavy terry robe—how great to have her body covered again—and went barefoot down the worn old carpet on the stairs and past the Victorian drawing room and down the center hall.

In the big old-fashioned kitchen, Steve turned from the stove, wineglass in hand, and said, "I liked you better the other way."

She sat down, tasting anger, wondering why, and stared at the stew on the plate he placed before her, wanting to thank him, wondering why she didn't. The delicious aroma was overpowering. Steve prided himself on his cooking. Then she began to eat, discovering that her mouth was dry.

Taking his seat at the other end of the table, tilting his chair back as he sipped his wine, Steve said, "I ate about an hour ago. When I gave up on your ever coming home, right?"

It was then that she said, between bites, "Thanks, Steve. Just what I need."

His handsome boyish face smiled. "Whether you were actually raped or not, I honestly do think we'd better report what happened, Trace."

"Stephen," she heard herself say, the wine warm and good in her, "if you really do think I was raped, why don't you want to go out and find the sonofabitch and kill him?"

The smile faded. His blue eyes appeared to be considering this. "Would you like it if I turned savage on you? Would that prove I love you, Trace?"

She didn't answer. A vague memory flickered in her mind— something about finding Steve having sex with another woman. What would she do? . . . she'd walk away . . . proving she didn't love him. . . .

"When you're finished eating," Steve said, "I'll carry you upstairs and show you how much I love you."

And then, as if something had exploded inside, it all came together. Her mind cleared. She put down her fork. "That's what you've been thinking about ever since I came home, isn't it? The way you looked at me. Your questions." She stood up, tugging at the knot of the nubby sash that held the robe together, tightening it. "It turned you on, didn't it? The idea of my stripping down in the van, walking naked along the road—it made you horny just thinking of my being raped! That's why you won't believe me. Christ, no wonder so few rapes are reported!"

She started from the room—trembling again, chilled again— and he leaped up to block her way at the door.

"Trace, you've got me wrong. You know I always want you."

"Especially now, especially tonight! Well, the reason I wouldn't report what happened, even if I *had* been raped, is that that'd play into their hands. If the police arrested the sonofabitch, they'd put him in jail with Todd Horgan. And what'd happen to Todd Horgan then? They'd kill him somehow, some accident, and that'd close the book on the whole thing. Just what they want: no more questions, investigation. And the two who really killed that girl will get off free and no one will ever know why they were there in the forest last night! Now get out of my way. I'm going to phone Andy Horgan."

But Steve did not move. A change came over his face. He shook his head once and then said, "They won't get off, Trace, and they won't be punished." His tone was very low. "It came through the ticker just before I left the station. Those two, Jesse Kull and Rolf Arneson—they're dead. I believe you now, Tracy. There *is* some sort of conspiracy. I was waiting to tell you, but—" He stepped away from the door. "They had their heads blown off in some blue-collar bar in Lowell, Massachusetts. I believe you, Tracy! And if you won't talk to the police, what about Blake Arnold? He'd advise you."

"Not until I've talked to Andy—"

"I see. I think I'm beginning to see."

A vague disturbance, which she could not define, had been building in her all day.

Almost everyone in Shepperton and the surrounding area

had tuned in on the news through the day and evening, and Valerie Arnold was no exception. In spite of the tragic elements, it was all very exciting, and of course, being the wife of the State's Attorney, she had a particular, not to say personal, interest. So when she heard the ten o'clock news out of Burlington on the TV in the living room, she flipped off the set and went up the half-flight of steps and stopped in the door of Blake's tiny study, which all their neighbors called a den.

When he'd told her over dinner about his meeting with the great Gerald Usher Lewis—*Just when I'd started to think we might be stuck in this town forever, to score a big one against the champ; you were right this morning, Val, this is it!* —Blake had been excited as any schoolboy, a quality she found particularly appealing. But now it was she who had information for *him*.

He looked up from his desk, taking off his reading glasses. And she told him, taking delight in being able to participate.

When she'd finished—"The police in Lowell have no suspects and the newscaster said they think it was just a routine robbery"—Blake did not speak but sat very still, frowning down at the legal-size typescript he had been reading. "Something troubling you, honey?" she asked.

"Just the opposite," he said, grinning up at her. "Accidents happen. This removes the only other possible suspects."

"But you told me earlier"—she took several steps toward the desk—"you *said* Todd Horgan had described two men and you showed me those photographs that Tracy Larkin dropped off, the same ones I saw on her newscast—"

"Happenstance," he said. "Happenstance and accident— fate playing right into our hands!"

"Then you think the boy really is guilty?"

Blake was smiling. "He's not guilty till a court decides," he said, mildly—a reproof, and a familiar one.

"I'm always forgetting that quaint mythology, aren't I?" She took a cigarette from the pocket of her housecoat. "Even if a person actually kills someone, in *fact*, he's innocent if his lawyer can convince a judge or jury that he didn't." She lit the cigarette.

"I didn't make up the rules, Val," he reminded her for at least the millionth time. "And I thought you'd stopped smoking."

"I did. I often do."

"It's not a quaint mythology. It's the adversary procedure, the basis of the whole system. And it works. Where would we be without law?"

"That," she said, elbow in one hand, cigarette in the other, "that is the non sequitur lawyers always use. To keep from questioning how we might do better if we'd reexamine the premise."

Blake stood up. "It's what I believe."

"It's what they programmed you to believe in law school, honey." She moved to the couch to sit; it had been a habit since she'd realized years ago how self-conscious Blake was about her being taller than his five foot eight. "Don't mind my skepticism—that's what *I* was programmed with in dear old Bennington. Do you mind if I read that?"

"This? This is a transcript of Todd Horgan's interrogation."

"I thought as much. Do you mind?"

"Yes, I do mind, damn it. Val, this is confidential material, property of the court." He was sliding the typescript into his briefcase. "Ethics, honey. Legal ethics."

"You don't want to know what *I* think—isn't that it? Your mind's made up because it's your job to prosecute."

"I've got enough to convict. Even against that wily scumbag, Gerald Usher Lewis."

She was about to ask why, if that were true, he objected, but the telephone rang.

Scowling now, he picked it up and spoke his name into it. And then, while Blake sat down and swiveled his chair so that she could not see his face, she heard: *"Yes,* Mr. Hyatt. And how are you, sir?"

The change in his tone, from businesslike reserve to hearty joviality, stirred a resentment in her that she recognized as foolish, irrational, but which she couldn't somehow suppress, so she stood and left the room, carefully closing the door, hearing: "Well, it's a genuine pleasure to hear *your* voice, too, Mr. Hyatt. This is indeed a surprise. How's everything in Washington?"

Valerie went to the bedroom to change into a nightgown and robe. She was not fond of herself when these moods struck. Usually she could joke, make her points with playful mockery. But then, usually, she was not so involved in any of Blake's cases. Somehow, possibly because it concerned life and death, and/or because it was taking place here in town, or maybe only because of the tragedy of it all—whatever, she was oddly confused, perturbed. Oh, she was so sick of this town! And of this small new split-level house cheek-by-jowl with other small new split-level houses almost exactly like it. And all that she'd come to detest in the so-called justice system in her ten years of marriage. Life itself and death itself, all turned into an intricate game that any *child* could play if he learned the rules and was willing to play by them, blindly.

She was fluffing her brownish hair at the mirror when Blake's reflection appeared in it.

His thinning sandy hair was tousled, his tie askew, and his gray eyes were darkly bright with a kind of stunned elation.

"Blake, what is it?" She stood and turned.

He was grinning. "Honey, don't pack your bags yet, but we're on our way to Washington!"

"Washington? When was the election?"

"No joke, Val. Clifford Hyatt, the kingmaker himself, wants me to run for Congress." Incredulity and joy crackled in his voice. "Not Vermont Attorney General—the big one!"

His jubilation was infectious. She felt a breathless exhilaration taking over. He took her into his arms, her face against his. "I don't believe it. I can't *believe* it, Val!"

"There's a bottle of champagne in the fridge," she whispered.

"Let's have a party!" he almost shouted, and then they were moving toward the small but efficient kitchen, not quite running down the half-flight of stairs.

Blake was opening the bottle and she was taking down glasses when he said, "Mr. Hyatt agrees with you, Val. He doesn't think I have a case."

She set the two glasses on the cabinet top. Then, carefully, she said, "I guess everybody's heard about it, even in Washington." She heard the cork-sound and watched him pour. "And, as you always say, everybody has an opinion."

"It's not an opinion, really. He just thinks I shouldn't risk going up against Gerald Usher Lewis unless I've an airtight case. Bad politics. Not good for my image if I should lose."

She took a slow sip. "I thought you said Mr. Lewis was gung ho to go to court—"

"He is. I told Mr. Hyatt we were in pretty deep but he said

148

there's always a way out without dropping charges. That wouldn't look good, either. People expect *someone* to be punished.'' He drained his glass. ''And he's right. That part is up to me. Some plea-bargain arrangement—scare the kid into pleading guilty to a lesser charge. Involuntary manslaughter maybe. Mr. Hyatt says to just get it over with. He doesn't want a public trial.''

''Why not? What's *his* stake in this, one way or the other?''

Blake poured another glass, the wine fueling his high spirits now. ''How do I know? Maybe Lewis got to him. Maybe it's *his* idea. Maybe Lewis knows Hyatt and he used him, rather than put it up to me himself. How do I know and what do I care?''

Softly, she asked, ''Don't you care, Blake?'' And then: ''*I* care.''

Now he was frowning again. ''Ten minutes ago *you* thought Todd Horgan was innocent.''

''Ten minutes ago you thought he was *guilty*!''

Abruptly, Blake was angry. Furious. His face reddened. His eyes narrowed. ''For the last time, Val, it's not your business. You want to get away from here, don't you? Damn it to hell, I'm doing this for you!''

She placed her half-empty glass on the table. ''I don't want you to do anything for me. I want you to do what you believe is right.''

''Now *that* . . . *that* is horseshit.''

''Only in legal circles,'' she said.

''This *is* a legal matter. If the kid killed the girl and I can't *prove* it in court, why should I take it to trial?''

''*Fifteen* minutes ago you were convinced you *could* prove it! That was when *going* to trial would help you get to Washington. Now . . .'' She let the sentence hang and turned away. ''I still want to know why Mr. Clifford Hyatt, the man who makes and breaks governors and senators, wanted to convince you to sweep this whole thing under the rug. Which quid for what quo?'' She stared at his flushed face. ''Oh, for God's sake, Blake, grow up!''

''You're the one who'd better grow up! Why should I ask questions when—''

''You should ask questions because, damnation, that's your job! Tracy Larkin asked on the news: What were those two

149

men doing in the forest last night? And I'm asking: Why were they killed tonight? Can *you* prove they didn't kill the girl? Have you even *tried* to find out?" She stood and knocked her glass off the table in one swift angry gesture. "There's your case, Mister Prosecutor. You can't quash one you never had but only wished you did!"

As she left the room—blood pumping, disgust mingling with fury, tall body stiff—she heard Blake's voice, muffled, behind her: "Jesus Christ. Jesus Christ almighty . . ."

"You've got a case, Tracy, even if he didn't assault you sexually."

Chief Radford had listened to everything she had to say, not prompting, the door of his office carefully closed. Now he said very quietly, "No criminal assault, but battery."

"You believe me then, you believe he didn't actually—"

"Why shouldn't I, Tracy? Try to settle down, girl. Now. That ring around your neck is evidence enough, but you'd have to sign a complaint, of course—"

"No!" She twisted in the chair. "No, no, no!"

Radford stood up behind his desk. "Kidnap. That's stronger—"

"Please. Chief, you promised." The panic was threatening to erupt. "You promised this would be off the record!"

"Tracy, you can't give me something like this, then tie my hands." He moved, small and alert, around the desk to look down on her. "I want whoever did this off the streets. Can you identify him? Did you see his face?"

"I don't want him in jail with Todd Horgan!"

Radford nodded his head, as if he'd already guessed. "It'd be possible to make arrangements. Separate cell. Gardner Kopit's on duty. He'd—"

But she was shaking her head. Why had she come? Why had she imagined . . .? "No, no. I can't take that chance."

Radford reached to his desk and picked up the photograph she'd given the sheriff earlier. "This is the man, isn't it?"

She stared at the face. A shudder passed through her. Sickening swift hate flooded her mind. "I know it is, yes, but I can't swear. The sonofabitch never let me see his face!"

She'd come here because she needed someone, she'd needed Andrew, but when she'd tried to phone him, Mrs. Stillwell had said, *He hasn't come back yet, Tracy. Do you want me to*

THE WAYS OF DARKNESS

have him call you? No, no, no! So she'd taken Steve's black Volvo and driven to the courthouse, passing the cottages—Number Five was still dark—her mind and body suffused with a hot, furious jealousy that astonished her: She knew where he was, who he was with, she knew.

"Well, I know who this bum is now." Radford tossed the photograph to the desk. "Had it officially checked out in Montpelier. Name's Dominic, called Nick, Verini. Age thirty-two. Son of Vincent Verini, who's what you media people call a *reputed* or *alleged* mob boss. Son Dominic's never had a legitimate job in his life. Seventeen arrests, everything from fraud and larceny to assault with intent to kill, and including rape. But only two convictions. He's spent a grand total of less than seven months in jail. That's the kind of slime we got in our town now. Right now he's registered at the Alpine Chalet under the name Joshua Enright." Radford lowered his voice: "And unless you bring charges, that's where he'll spend the night."

"How can I sign a complaint if I can't identify him?" She heard her own voice: forlorn, desolate. "And . . . and what about Todd Horgan?"

"I told you—"

Shaking her head, she got to her feet, feeling faint but the anger giving her strength. "You must know by now what happened to Jesse Kull and Rolf Arneson."

"Ay-uh, I know."

"You don't think that was coincidence, do you? *Now* there's no way to prove they killed Lynnette Durand, and if Todd Horgan was dead too . . ."

Chief Radford moved to sit behind his desk again. "Ay-uh, you're right as rain, Tracy." His small, lined face looked gray, eyes dim and distant. "I been goin' over all the pictures—truck, license plate, faces . . ." Suddenly he seemed old, old and tired "There's nothing anyone can really do."

"Why?" she asked, taking a step. "Why—if the police know, if you know?"

"They've got devious ways, girl. They buy the best lawyers, politicians. They own businesses, legitimate corporations as well as whorehouses, nightclubs, gambling joints. They go to church, contribute to presidential campaigns, plant spies. If anyone crosses them, they terrorize. If they can't terrorize, they kill. Human life means nothing. Oh, Tracy, we all know this. They've been exposed over and over—''

"Then why can't we *do* something? If the police know, the government knows, the people know—''

He shook his head from side to side, staring down on his hands—small, tight fists on the desk. "Everybody's too busy, I guess, cocktail parties, football, watching TV, church, making money—especially making money." He lifted his head to look into her eyes. "Nobody really gives a damn, I guess. Nobody gives a damn till it happens to them."

Tracy remembered her father: Charlie Larkin, the rebel who cared, who drank himself to death because he cared too much and could do nothing.

On impulse she moved around the end of the desk and placed one hand on Radford's shoulder. "If they knew, out there, what was happening here, to us, now—would they care then?"

Before he could speak, the telephone buzzed on his desk. She took her hand from his shoulder then, but did not move away.

"Radford speaking . . . Yes, Blake? . . . No, sorry. Dr. Nichols hasn't sent over the autopsy report yet. You know, don't you—it'll only be a preliminary finding, probable cause of death. . . . Oh, you'll have it in plenty a time for the hearing, don't fret. . . . Ay-uh, well, Nat Nichols is the only pathologist in fifty miles—hospital duties as well as county coroner. Busy man. And, Blake, you know about his wife, don't you? . . . You can almost always reach him at the hospital. . . . Welcome, Blake. G'night."

He replaced the phone and, after a second's hesitation, leaned down to open the bottom drawer of his desk.

His tone was more normal now, crisp and curt again: "Took this off a young punk, druggie, passing through two, three years ago." He placed a blue-black revolver on the desk top. "It's a Smith and Wesson Nineteen. Lightweight, small enough for a woman to handle if she has to. Ever use one of these?"

She was staring at it. It had a short barrel and a walnut handle. "I never shot a gun in my life."

"Holds six shots. You got to make every one count and the first one's the most important." His eyes were boring into her. "I been debatin' whether to give it to you. Seeing that red mark on your neck about convinced me."

She stepped around the desk, still staring, not reaching. Throat locked, she felt the sharp burning line of pain under her chin.

"Self-defense only—"

"I . . . I don't think . . . I couldn't *kill* anyone."

He stood up, all business again. "Never know. Never know till you have to. Here, I'll show you how it works."

"Dr. Nichols, I'm sorry. I wouldn't bother you but it's Blake Arnold on the phone. He says it's very important. I didn't want to ring the room."

"Thank you, nurse."

"I'll stay with her."

Ashamed of himself, as he always was when he left her lying there, ashamed of his own ability to move, to live, he glanced once at his wife on the bed—what was left of his wife—and left the room when she did not open her eyes. When her eyes were open they begged him, please, to let her die. Yet morning and evening—and during the day whenever he could in good conscience escape from the pathology lab in the basement—he sat by the bed, knowing and waiting and wishing that, by some miracle, he could trade places with her.

He took the call at the nurses' station, growling into the phone without preliminaries or greeting: "No, Blake, I haven't done the job on the girl yet. But you'll have the report by seven in the morning."

"Haven't you . . . don't you have even a preliminary . . . ? Well, it's very important, Doctor."

"I've done only a most superficial examination of the decedent's body. All I can tell you is that she did not drown. And I can safely say, I think, that she did not die by asphyxiation due to strangulation. Also, no evidence of severe blows to the head—"

"Doctor, that's not what I . . ." Blake Arnold had had a few drinks. Maybe more than a few. Well, he'd have his usual three himself, later, to get to sleep. "Can you give me anything . . . anything positive? Surely you must have some idea if you . . ."

He damn well did have some idea, but his job, by law, was

to establish the manner, cause, and circumstances of death, and he'd learned not to go out on limbs. The girl had probably been sexually assaulted, and brutally, and his own guess was that he'd find fractured bones everywhere, possibly puncturing the lungs. But he asked, "How much does your defendant weigh?"

"Weigh? Don't know exac'ly." The voice sounded far away. "Maybe a hundred forty, maybe fifty. Why?"

"Blake, I'm not going to be put in the position of making guesses. When I've done the full PM, I'll get it to you. Now, why don't you have another one for me and go to bed? It's after eleven. Good night."

"But, Dr. Nichols, there's no doubt in your mind that it's homicide?"

"No doubt whatever. Good night."

Nichols put down the phone and returned to Mariah's room with that ugly ambivalence of reluctance and eagerness that he had somehow come to live with. Along with shame, and guilt.

When he was seated and the nurse had left the room, he regarded his wife's face again: gray and haggard and wasted, but composed now, between the bouts of agony and moaning, when no amount of medication could reach the pain. In those more and more frequent times the desperation in her eyes riddled him with such a sense of impotence that his mind swelled with rage. *Please let me go, please, Nat.* But Dr. Foster Martin, who was in charge of the case and had the godlike final word, was one of those who passionately believed that life must be extended as long as there were means to do so. He'd had conversations with him, ranging from bitter pleas to furious clashes of shouting and threats. Yet he had never replaced the doctor with another. Was it possible that he himself simply could not bear to let her go?

Nevertheless, he had been tempted over and over to take the only action really open to him. The support system was a complex marvel of modern science, but to disconnect it was a simple matter, very simple, and tempting. But he also knew that now that we have developed the miraculous means of prolonging life, we have created a trap: We are now forced by law to use them, or else to be legally guilty of a crime. Possibly murder . . .

Murder. He remembered Lynnette Durand's parents when

they had identified the corpse: the mother, no tears, staring and silent; the father, towering and stiff, running a hand over his shaggy black moustache, whispering to his wife in French that Nat had been able to translate: *Look what he did to our girl.*

He resumed his nightly vigil. Plenty of time before morning to face the task he'd been putting off. He could do it before he went home or he could do it in the morning and then type out the official report on his old typewriter in the lab. The nights were always endless.

Even though the clock on the wall over the counter in Colby's read 11:27, Andrew still could not face the prospect of being alone in the cottage. Where the hell was Tracy?

Driving into town earlier, he had felt an enormous weight lifted: He was really leaving Julia behind now, and forever. It was over, at last.

Nibbling at the cold roast beef sandwich that the bartender had prepared for him and which he had taken into the dim, deserted front room of Colby's, he discovered that, hungry as hell, he could not eat. Rock music blasted from the bar— college kids dancing it up, laughing and drinking. He sipped the coffee, Tracy's face hovering vividly in his mind. Where the hell could she be?

Using the local directory, he had phoned from a booth and Stephen Savage had answered. *No, she's not here, Mister Horgan. Don't ask me where she's gone. I thought she was with you.* The voice, impatient and irritated and youthful as hell, suggested a concern that, afterward, Andrew wished he had explored. *She tried to phone you before she left.*

So then, remembering the name *Tower Road* and the route he'd taken back into town after dropping her off at the station for her newscast, he'd driven out of town. At the dead end of Tower Road, the small concrete-block building was dark except for the red light blinking atop its ghostly tower. From the hill he could see flashes of lightning over the bluffs and ridges in the distance, but it had stopped raining.

Where else could he look?

Now, in Colby's, draining his mug, he remembered: *Cute little redhead, I seen her on TV.* Behind him was the booth where he'd sat with the young dark-bearded bastard, whose name he still did not know.

The fear, which had, by degrees, turned into a deep and pervasive dread, exploded into panic.

He went out the unlocked front door.

He was walking now, fast, toward the courthouse.

If that bastard touched Tracy—

He climbed the high flight of stone steps three at a time.

A rawboned woman he had not seen before was behind the counter. No, Chief Radford was not in. Sherff Wheeler? He was taking a nap and could not be disturbed.

"A nap?" he heard himself snarling. "Is that all he has to do? Have you seen Tracy Larkin this evening?"

"She was in two times. Early, around eight, and again to talk to Chief Radford about . . . oh, ten-thirty or so." And then, as relief seeped through him, he went out, thinking of Todd below, in his cell.

Moving with less urgency now, he walked to where he'd parked the MG along the curb of the green—recalling his own experience in New York twenty years ago. He'd never forget that sick, half-angry, empty feeling: Here I am and nobody gives a damn, nobody. He got into the car. To drive along the length of green between the rows of streetlamps.

If we've given up, it doesn't matter, does it?

No, Tracy no. He was going to see it through. Out of love. And . . . and because there has to be some kind of justice. If not, then we let the jungle, and the jungle animals, take over completely.

He parked Tracy's little car, locked it, and walked, with reluctance, toward Cottage Five. Like the others, it was dark. He turned the key in the door—only to discover it was locked from inside. Stiffening, alert at once, he was trying to decide what to do when he heard his name: "Andy?"

Tracy's voice. Tracy. Here.

And then he heard himself say, "Yes, Tracy. It's all right. Unlock the door."

He heard the bolt slide and then he saw the door swing open. He stepped in and reached for the switch.

"Don't turn on the light. Please." So, instead, he closed the door and slammed the bolt into place. "Mrs. Stillwell let me in." Her voice was different. Low. Shaky. She was a shadow huddled in the big chair. Unmoving now. "I had to . . . oh, Andy, don't be angry."

156

"Angry?" He stepped toward the chair. "I've been look-ing all over town. What's happened?"

"What could happen in a nice, peaceful little town like this?" But the mockery was in her words, not in her tone. "Or in a nice peaceful large town like Lowell, Massachusetts. Oh, Andy, darling"—and now she was standing, moving toward him—"I'll tell you later, not now. Andy, hold me. Help me. I'm scared, too. I'm really scared. Please hold me."

Against his, her body was quivering head to toe, and her face, cool and soft against his cheek, was damp with tears.

Merle was too gentle and Lewis was too rough, much too rough. What was he trying to prove? Julia, even now, was unable to get Andy out of her mind. Damn him!

Alone in the bed, she was also unable to go back to sleep because of Lewis's voice on the phone in the sitting room. Goddam it, this was no time of night to conduct business! Why hadn't he told the desk downstairs that he wouldn't accept calls through the night? And why had she stayed here in his suite instead of returning to her own? If there was anything she hated, it was sleeping with someone. Oh, screw-ing, sure, but sleeping in the same bed, all night—how could she get the rest she needed to face tomorrow? And perform-ance tomorrow evening. . . .

She stood up. She could no longer hear his voice. She made up her mind. She'd had it. She was going back to her own blessedly empty suite.

In the sitting room Lewis was sprawled in a huge chair, white terrycloth robe open, feet on the cocktail table, smoking a cigar. "Man phoned to offer me a cigar. A lot of cigars. Cuban." He scarcely glanced at her naked body. "A decent steak, a sauna, good fuck, a cigar—all a man needs now is a shower. You have yours?"

She hated him. Just like that. He was a gorilla. He walked like a gorilla; he screwed like a gorilla. "I'll take mine in my room," she said.

But it was as if she had not spoken. "Did you ever talk to someone and then have an aftertaste?" Lewis asked. "Like the sweet-sour smell of lime. Bitter almonds. Mr. Vincent Verini, the man himself. That name ring any bells?"

"Listen to me when I talk to you!"

His broad, beefy face twisted into another grin. "Relax, Julia. Mix us both another drink. The night's still young."

"Mix you, own goddam drink!"

She returned to the bedroom. She began to dress.

And heard his voice: "You're paying me for my advice, Julia. Which is, simmer down." She heard ice tinkle against glass. "I'm the bearer of glad tidings. I can close out the case and we can be on our merry way by noon."

"How? Who's Vincent Verini?"

He appeared in the door as she zipped up her gown. "A gentleman, Julia. A genuine fourteen-karat gentleman of Sicilian descent. Who has just phoned to call in his marker. When a man like Vincent Verini calls in a marker, that's it. Well, I owe him one."

"What does he want?"

"He wants the case closed. Tight. Once and for all. And now."

"What's he got to do with Todd?"

He took a sip of his drink. "That's the sort of question you don't ask Vincent Verini."

"What are you going to do? Bribe the judge?"

"Only as a last resort. For all I know, he's already in Verini's pocket. All I can tell you is that I'll strike a deal with the State's Attorney. And then we'll get the judge to approve it. You stand to save a bundle. I don't collect my fees in bed, you know."

She was seething. "You bastard, you goddam filthy bastard!"

"Now, Julia, now." He took another swallow and his tone hardened: "The truth is you provide something I need and I sure as hell provide something you need, lady. And legal fees are separate."

She glanced around the room. Had she left anything? Inside she'd begun to tremble. "And Todd? What about Todd?"

"I'll do the best I can, Julia. I haven't had time to research minimum sentences in Vermont, but—"

"Sentence?"

"I'll try for probation. Or suspended. But we may have to settle for a year or two."

"A year or two? In prison?"

Lewis shrugged. "Less, if he's a good boy. Less if he doesn't talk to the guards the way he talked to me this afternoon."

She sank down to sit on the bed. "Oh God, oh God. You just don't know Todd. He'll *die*."

Lewis's tone was light and cheerful again. "You should have raised him better, my dear. It's against the law to get girls pregnant and then strangle them, or drown them. Has been, even before Theodore Dreiser." He was smiling to himself as he poured another drink. "He won't die unless he hangs himself in his cell. *That* could be arranged, too. You're lucky it wasn't."

Then Julia remembered Andy's words—*To tell you that you're in danger . . . not to kill you, Julia, but to disfigure you for life*—and she said, "I don't understand any of it. Is that how she died, that girl? Choking? Drowning?"

He stepped toward her. "We won't know that till we see the autopsy report." He extended the glass. "Which will give the cause of death as anything they want it to be."

"Who's *they?*"

He grinned again. The ape. The *baboon!* "That's another question you don't ask," he said. "Here, finish the drink. I'll tell you what you have to explain to your son tomorrow, and why."

She leaped to her feet, reaching, knocking the glass out of his hand, seeing his startled face briefly, hearing the glass shatter against the fireplace, before she discovered that she was running, holding up her long skirt, hoping she wouldn't fall in the sitting-room foyer, running along the empty corridor.

Why were they doing this to her? Why was everyone trying to confuse her, torment her, make her suffer? What had she ever done to deserve this?

"How you doin', lover boy?"

Andrew recognized the voice. And now he had a name to go with it because Tracy had told him before she went to sleep. But he did not answer until he had maneuvered himself into the bathroom with the telephone cord under the closed door. He did not turn on the light. Then he spoke in a whisper, hoping the ringing had not wakened Tracy. "What do you want, Mr. Verini?"

"So. You know my name."

"Yes, I know quite a lot about you now."

"Getting in deeper 'n' deeper, baby. Didn't listen, did you?

Like the Surgeon General says on the cigarettes—could be dangerous to your health.''

''I asked you a question: What the hell do you want?''

''Sorry t' hear about your house, Pop. Accidents will happen.''

''Say it!''

''Redhead sleepin'? That why you're whispering?'' Then a sound, a sort of sneer, or audible leer: ''Y' gettin' any, Pop?''

''She told me about your joy ride.''

''All of it?''

''All of it.''

''Then why ain't I in the slammer for rape?''

''Because you didn't rape her.''

''You believe that?''

''Damn right I do.''

A snicker then, a whinnying sound. ''Shows you what *could* happen. Anybody, anytime.''

''Like what happened to Jesse Kull and Rolf Arneson?''

Silence then. Andrew was clutching the phone so hard that he felt pain climb up his arm. But he waited. He took a cruel pleasure in waiting.

Finally the voice spoke: ''Deeper 'n' deeper, baby. But you're learning, too.''

''I'm learning.'' Andrew still whispered, but each word was hard and sharp and distinct. ''I'm learning that I'm more like you than I thought. Now *you* listen. *You* learn. If any harm comes to my son or to Tracy Larkin, I'm going to kill you—''

''Hey, man—''

''Shut up and listen, I said! No matter what it takes, whether you're arrested or not, wherever you are, no matter how many thugs are protecting you. No matter where, even in prison, or how long it takes, if it takes the rest of my life. I'll find you and I'll kill you. Me. Me, personally. Do you understand that? Capeesh, you bastard? *Capeesh?*''

The silence was long enough to send a jolt of satisfaction through his clenched and rigid body. Again he waited.

''Cool it, man. That's my message. All you and yours gotta do is cool it. Tell that kid of yours to do what his lawyer tells him and he'll be out of jail by noon, case closed. That's my message, man.''

"What're you afraid of, Nick? What're you and your father afraid we'll find out?"

"We're not afraid of anything!" Fury in the snarl—a shaky wild note, alarm. "We're on top of it! Everything!" And then, as if able to get his voice forcibly under control, in a lower, level tone: "You ain't got a chance, lover boy. Take my advice this time. If you don't want your kid to go up for life—that's twenty-five years even if he's a good boy in the joint—and if you want that redhead in one piece, so's you'll even *want* to screw her, you'll take my advice this time." And then another change of tone, amiable, the friendly enemy now. "Just make sure the kid does whatever his mouthpiece tells him, that's all. Everything'll blow away. Back to square one. Go back to bed, Pop. Screw the slut, way I did!"

Andrew lowered the phone into its cradle, slowly, but did not move. Was Tracy still sleeping?

Deeper and deeper—true. But also wider and wider. What was Gerald Usher Lewis going to advise? And *why*? Did Nick and his father own *him* too? Or know they could buy him?

He edged the door open and, in the near-darkness, entered the bedroom and replaced the phone on the table beside the bed. He could not see her clearly—a dim paleness on the pillow—but he heard her voice.

"What did the sonofabitch want?"

"Just what he wanted before. Only more so." He returned to the maple wing chair by the window, where he'd spent the time after he'd finally been able to persuade her to sleep. "But he's the one who's scared now." He looked out the window. Nothing unusual. He smiled at himself. not a red Ferrari in sight. "He's scared and that could mean he's even more dangerous."

"He told you he raped me, didn't he?"

Andrew resumed his seat. "I have a feeling he wishes he had."

"Then . . . you still believe me?"

"Why shouldn't I believe you, Tracy?"

"And it doesn't excite you? The idea of someone else—"

"Look," he said, "I don't know what happened between you and Steve Savage, but if I thought Nick Verini had raped you, I wouldn't be here. I'd be out there looking for him with this gun Chief Radford gave you."

"To kill him?" Her voice was only a murmur. "I heard

161

you, Andy. I heard what you told him. What you'd do if he did anything to me . . .''

He did not answer. In spite of the havoc inside, he was not sure now, although he had been when he said it, that he could actually kill someone. Even Nick Verini.

''Andy . . . were you telling him that you're in love with me?''

''Something like that.'' And then: ''Yes. That's what I'm saying, Tracy. To him and to you.''

''Then why are you sitting way over there when I'm way over here?''

EIGHT

"Are they dead?"

"Both of them, Mr. Wylie, and Rolf's girl friend. She works there . . . worked there, behind the bar." As many times as he'd heard Sandy's voice on the phone, it was almost unrecognizable now. "I've been putting off calling you ever since I heard it on the eleven o'clock news. It was some kind of robbery."

. . . It's a holdup . . . so blast . . . shotgun maybe . . . no head.

Earl Wylie, who had been sitting up alone because he couldn't sleep, felt a spasm in his stomach. "Thanks, Sandy." Slowly he put down the hall phone, cold sweat on his palms, in his armpits, in his crotch. Then panic struck, a blast of numbing wind, but not in the hall—inside, inside his heavy, still, fifty-four-year-old body.

The gun. He had an old .22 automatic in the drawer, upstairs, in the bed table.

He started toward the stairway. His foot was on the bottom step when he stopped and looked up.

Paula, wearing a nightgown, stood at the top of the stairs. "I picked up the extension," she said. "It's after midnight." And then she was coming down, still slim as a girl, graying brown hair falling to her shoulders. "Oh, Earl. I'm so sorry. Two of your men—do I know them, sweetheart?"

He was shaking his head. "Paula, is my gun still in the—"

"Gun? Gun? Earl, what—"

163

"I may be next," he said. He heard a wild, shaky note in his voice. *"We* could be next."

"Earl, you stop this. I don't want Wendy to hear. Now you stop it." She passed by him swiftly. "Let's go into the parlor where we can talk."

"It's my fault," he heard himself say, still stunned, cold, following her into the large dim room. "I may as well've pulled the trigger." His own voice echoed strangely in his ears.

Paula turned on a lamp and then slid the doors together. The parlor doors. The kind she'd wanted in the new house because in the farmhouse where she'd grown up . . . "Now, Earl, you sit down. I want to know why you imagine—"

"I don't imagine anything. I just don't know *what* they might—"

"Who? Earl, I'm warning you. Make sense. I have a right to know. Tell me. Why do you need a gun?"

"Because there's no telling, there's no *knowing*. They're scared now and—"

"Who's they? What are *they* scared of?"

"I can't tell you that. If you knew, you'd be in danger, too." Then he felt something collapse inside, the blood seemed to leave him, and he sat down heavily on the old-fashioned divan in front of the red brick fireplace. "I guess maybe I always knew it'd come to this." How had he ever let himself get involved with that scum? Sick with disgust and loathing, he looked up and into her face, her still-beautiful and girlish face. "Paula, I'm not my own man. I sold out. They own me."

She did not move. "Oh, Earl, no one owns anyone. Not in today's world."

"They bought me like I was a piece of machinery. Like I wasn't even a human being."

"Earl, I've known something was distressing you ever since you came home from the garage. Whatever it is, I'm your wife. I demand to know. Now."

So he told her. He tried, while the quaking got worse inside, to start from the beginning and then—struggling to recall, struggling not to spare himself—he told her everything he knew. He admitted that he did not have it all straight, especially what had really happened up in Shepperton, Vermont. "I only know what Rolf and Jesse told Nick and me in the garage this afternoon. God, I still can't believe it. I can't take it in." And then, almost as if he was pleading with her to understand: "I told myself it was good business, Paula. I told myself, hell, businesses all over the country was doing the same." And it was true, too—they'd own the whole country someday, or control it anyway. "I'm sick of living scared," he said. "Like some animal in the woods."

When he went to the window to look out at the dark trees, picturing the acres beyond, he heard Paula, behind him: "If that's how we got all this, I don't want it."

"Do you mean that?"

"Earl, I'm not blaming you." Her voice came closer. "You did it for me—for Rusty and Wendy, too. But I don't want to lose *you,* Earl. You're the one who matters. To me. I won't lose you the way—" But she stopped.

He turned. "What are we going to do?"

"We're going to move away."

He shook his head. "They're everywhere, Paula."

"We'll sell the business, this house—"

"Paula, listen, you can't *hide* from them—"

"Sell later. First, we'll move somewhere."

"There's nowhere to move, nowhere to go—"

"*Or* you can go to the police."

"I can't. Do you think *they'd* protect us? What can they do? What are they doing anywhere else?" He strode to where she stood. "The government knows about these people, knows what they're doing, getting away with, all over the country, all over the goddam world! Sometimes I think the government's in on it with them!"

Paula smiled a faint, half-pleased smile. "You're angry."

"I'm angry because it's happened to me. To us. I'm angry because I was so greedy I *let* it happen. I'm angry at myself, Earl Wylie, churchgoer, taxpayer, upright citizen!"

"I like you this way, Earl. I love you."

That did it. How long had it been since either of them had used the word? A crazy recklessness went through him. "Did you mean what you said—about moving away?"

"Tonight. Rusty can get here from college in an hour. Wendy's upstairs—"

"Paula, we can't—"

"Go get one of your trucks. We can have it packed by

165

daybreak, everything we want. I'll drive my car and Rusty can drive yours. Do you still know how to handle a truck?''

"Where the hell will we go?"

"Someplace where they won't find us. West. North and west. British Columbia. Saskatchewan—''

"Paula, we'll have to change our names—''

"A rose is a rose—''

"The kids—''

"They're smart kids. It's an adventure—''

"College?''

"Good colleges all over Canada.''

"The kids'll have to know why—''

"Then tell them. Tell them what a sweet, greedy fool you are. Tell them you made a terrible mistake. Tell them what you told me—the truth. They can live with it if I can. They don't want to be orphans any more than I want to be a widow.''

"Paula, it's a helluva time to say it, but by God I *do* love you!''

"Well, that's enough. That's enough, isn't it? That and the truth—we'll make it!''

"Just the same, I'm going to get that gun.''

"What are you thinking of?''

"I thought you were asleep,'' Andrew said.

"Tell me. Please.''

"I was thinking how beautiful you look. Lying there.'' His mind had also been filled with a kind of wonder. After five years of being alone, how was it that now he was lying in this strange bed, with the rain drumming outside, the light from the streetlamps, faint and yellow, filtering through the drops on the windows, the changing, moving pattern of rainshadow on her body beside his on the bed? Lying curled on her side, one arm under the pillow, her face against its whiteness—her whole body seemed to glimmer with some mysterious promise of youth that he had forgotten long ago. "Your body seems to have a light of its own.''

"Doesn't hers?''

Startled, he asked, "Whose?''

"When you were with her, is that what you told her? Well, she may need such . . . balm for her vanity. I don't, thank you.''

And then he recalled Cassie. It had taken almost a year, after he'd come home from the hospital, completely sober at last, before he'd been able to dispel Cassie's haunting fears that he might still love Julia.

"I didn't even have dinner with her," he told Tracy gently. He didn't add that dinner was not what Julia had in mind—because Tracy must have known that.

"Is that true?" She twisted about and sat up, the bed shaking. "I'm sorry I asked that, Andy. I know you don't lie. It's the one thing I really know about you." And then, sitting stiff and still: "Cassie then? Were you thinking of her?"

"I was. Earlier. I was thinking that now even her paintings are gone."

"Gone?"

He realized that he had not told her. "My house burned. They torched it. Nick Verini all but admitted it on the phone a while ago."

"Oh, Andy!" She came against him, her body stretching out on the bed, its heat warming his. "I'm sorry, darling." She was holding him. "I'm so selfish, so *damned* selfish. Why didn't you tell me right away? I know why. When you came in here, I was a mess, wasn't I? Such a tangle, such a crazy muddle. And you knew. You understood. I guess I was in a state of shock. And scared, really scared. I still am." She was holding him more tightly, clinging to him, trembling. "Oh, Andy, you were so kind, so gentle."

He felt her hair on his shoulder. He reached his arm along her slender back, his hand in the hollow at the center of her waistline. Then he felt a dampness on his upper arm, where her face lay. "Go ahead," he whispered. "Cry, Tracy. Don't hold back—"

"I never cry," she said.

"Your loss," he said. "One of the things I learned ten years ago. I've cried often since."

She let go then. He held her while she wept, her flesh quivering as she sobbed.

When, in a few minutes, she was quiet again, he still did not speak, but waited.

"Andy . . ."

"I'm here."

"Isn't it awful? I was never able to tell Pop I forgave him. I was never able *to* forgive him—in time to say it. He never meant to hurt anyone. He cared. He cared more than anyone I've ever known. That's why he . . .'' Her voice drifted off. Her body had stopped quivering. "It's too late now.'' A whisper. "Why is it always too late?''

He thought of Charlie Larkin, a man he'd never known. And of Cassie, whom he'd known well, and loved. And in that moment, for the first time, but without a jolt—quietly, deeply—he let her go. Cassie was gone. And her paintings. And the house . . .

A door closed softly in his mind.

"Andy.'' Her voice was muffled.

"Yes, Tracy?''

"Thanks. Thanks for being you. For being here . . . for teaching me the difference between a boy and a man . . . and between having sex and really making love.''

He allowed a long moment to pass, while he found his voice. Then: "I'm the one to thank you, Tracy.''

"For what?''

"For bringing me back into the world.''

"The way Cassie did?''

"Yes.''

"That's the most beautiful thing anyone ever said to me.''

Hate was a feeling that Kyle Radford didn't like, particularly in himself. But in the course of the day he'd really come to hate Wayne Wheeler.

Kid just lays there in his bunk, eyes closed, the sheriff had just said. *Kopit tells me he didn't eat a damn bite for supper. Guilt, I'd call it.* But he was wrong. That thin red line around Tracy's throat was what had finally convinced Kyle. That thin red line.

So the chief decided to go over to Colby's for a cup of coffee. The rotunda of the courthouse had a strange empty feeling at night. On the steps outside he saw a single zigzag of lightning over the roofs of the town hall and the grange.

Winter comes sudden. That's what Rachel had said when he'd gone home for supper. Ay-uh, very true: two or three days of Indian summer, just to fool you, and then *wham*, rain and sleet and then snow. It was raining again now. Winter was coming in dark and brutal, just the same way something else was settling over his town—something even worse.

As he approached the restaurant, he saw Pierre Durand—no

mistaking that big bearlike walk—coming out of the side door on Liberty Street and shambling away into the darkness. Poor man—probably didn't even know where he was going. By morning one of the cars on patrol would probably find him passed out on the green and have to haul him in, throw him into a cell. He made a mental note to alert Gardner Kopit: separate cells if Pierre Durand gets himself arrested. Keep him away from Todd Horgan.

Entering the front door and passing through the dim dining area, hearing the blare and thump of music in the rear room, he was glad he'd changed into his civvies; this way, he could sit and have his coffee without attracting notice.

He was climbing out of his raincoat and slapping the rain off his hat as he made his way to the bar, feeling the arthritis pain in every joint already.

Behind the bar, Claude Aiken, tall and cadaverous and sour as ever, poured coffee as soon as he saw him. "Quiet night," he said.

Kyle Radford turned to look around. The place was packed, the blast from the jukebox was deafening, and the tiny dance floor was alive with young bodies writhing, wriggling, jerking spasmodically. "Ay-uh, quietest night I ever seen in here, Claude."

He nodded to the three or four regulars sitting, bleary-eyed and stony-faced, at the bar and then he caught sight of a stranger—not one of the college kids, only not much older: big and blond, broad-shouldered, tweed jacket, plaid flannel shirt, yellow knit tie, all new. An ugly drunk—look at those eyes. Mean. He didn't look like a reporter. Probably just someone from away, as the folks here said. Ski bum maybe. With snow predicted and hunting season about to open, the town'd soon be crawling with strangers again.

As he was moving away from the bar, he heard Claude say, "Another of the same, Georgie? Coming up." Georgie— his mind registered the name. There was something about Georgie that didn't sit just right with Kyle Radford.

The only table unoccupied was in a corner, so he threaded his way between tables, college kids mostly, and sat down alone and took a long swallow from the big mug. You could always depend on Colby's coffee.

At the table closest to him, he recognized a face: the girl who'd appeared on the morning newscast, Lynnette Durand's

169

best friend. Big girl, purple sweater, tight, big bosom, hair a mess. Across from her sat a boy with bushy black hair, solemn dark eyes behind thick black-rimmed glasses. The third person was a woman of about fifty—one of those thick, big-featured faces, not exactly masculine, but blunt. No frills, but a woolen tweed hat to match her suit. He'd size her up as one of those teachers from the college. And when the music stopped and he heard her voice—very deep and businesslike: "Well, *I'm* going to talk to him, Norman, and that's all there is to it"—he recalled having heard it before. But where? When?

"No visiting hours till two in the afternoon, Miss Merrill," the girl said. "And the hearing's at ten in the morning."

Merrill. Now it came to him. Ann Merrill—he'd spoken to her on the phone last night, once they'd examined the kid's ID.

The boy named Norman said, "It'd be just like him, if he's in one of his moods, to march in there and tell the judge he did it."

Ann Merrill's face looked up then. The tall blond ski bum from the bar was standing at the table, grinning down on them. "Music starts, who wants t'dance with Georgie?"

"Not I," Ann Merrill said. "Thank you."

When the girl shook her head of dark frizzled hair, Georgie drew back the only empty chair and sat down. Now Radford could not see his face, only his wide shoulders and powerful back. "Buy youse a drink?"

Drunk, Kyle decided. Though Georgie's voice was not slurred. Trouble, he concluded.

"Had my eye on you three." He swiveled his head to look at the girl. "Especially you, doll."

Well, Kyle Radford had his eye on Georgie, waiting. Let him hang himself.

"Purple's my favorite color. I go for that sweater, doll. An' what's inside."

"Listen, mister," Norman said, his voice just shrill enough to give away how scared he was.

"You say something?" Georgie asked, being polite. "Y' got something t' say to me? Like maybe she's yours? Like maybe you got it all wrapped up—"

Then Ann Merrill spoke: "Look here, whoever you are, we're having a private discussion and you're—"

The music started again. Georgie leaped to his feet and stepped behind Donna's chair. "Time t' shake it, baby."

Then, pale mean eyes on Norman over Donna's head, Georgie dropped his left hand and cupped it over Donna's left breast. She gasped and stiffened in her chair.

Glaring, Norman was still trying to decide what to do when Kyle Radford stood up and took two steps forward. He drew his badge from the pocket of his windbreaker and shot his hand, opening it.

When Georgie glanced down at the badge, Radford said, "Chief of police. Now these folks here don't want any trouble and neither do I."

Georgie lifted his eyes to meet Radford's. At an angle from above. Suddenly Kyle felt very small.

But he said, "Do you want to leave of your own free will, Georgie?"

Instead of replying, Georgie turned his gaze, almost lazily, to Norman, whose face had gone white, eyes large and inflamed, anger fighting fear. "Let go of her," Norman said.

"I don't take orders from Jew boys," Georgie said.

Then, before Kyle realized what was happening, Norman rushed at Georgie, muttering; and Georgie, in an action so abrupt that Kyle could hardly see it, released the girl's breast with his left and let go with his right—a level, straight punch, pistonlike. Kyle heard the sound, like wood against wood, and saw Norman take several stuttering steps backward before he fell, arms spread.

All hell broke loose then. Ann Merrill screamed. Donna stood up, knocking over her chair. Gasps and cries on all sides. Kyle saw Claude moving from behind the bar toward the jukebox. And in that second or two, he was afraid he'd waited too long.

But as Georgie took his first long step to follow Norman, who was struggling to sit up, blood around his mouth, Radford made his move. Taking his .38 from the shoulder holster under his windbreaker, crouching, he made it around the table fast, in time to plant himself in front of the tall man, gun in hand.

The music stopped.

Georgie was staring at the gun. In the silence Kyle heard himself say: "You're under arrest. Public nuisance, inebriation, disturbing the peace, indecent assault on the body of a

171

female, aggravated battery. And anything else I can think of while we walk across the street. Do you want me to read you your rights?''

''Fuck you,'' Georgie said.

Outside the windows lightning quivered, silver and bright through the drawn curtains. Then a low roll of thunder in the distance.

After they'd made love again, the strangeness gone, the intimacy even more exciting and satisfying than the first time, Tracy had drifted off to sleep in his arms. But he hadn't been able to sleep—or didn't dare to.

The incredible strangeness of it all had not left him: Tracy's hot pulsing body against his, the gun within reach, the door locked and bolted, a chair braced against it under the knob, the fear, the joy, the dread, the odd elation—all at the same time.

Each sound outside constricted his nerves. At least twice he had heard the low purring of the Ferrari's engine, the sound unmistakable, passing by, receding, not stopping.

Now he became conscious of another sound: the drone of a plane in the night sky. He could picture what the town would look like from up there; how ordered and peaceful and beautiful.

But now he was not up there. He was down below, here, under one of those dark rooftops. Inside one of those buildings.

No longer observing.

Living.

Then, as the drone died away, he found himself listening again for the sound of the Ferrari's motor. If he heard it stop, then what?

Nick Verini had parked the car along the curb of a side street where it ended at the green. The Ferrari was half-hidden by high shrubs. But he could still see the black Volvo and the green MG. And the windows of Cottage Five.

He was cold to the bone.

But taking no chances.

And every time he thought of those two inside, he recalled the slut's body in the seat of the van. Helpless. Writhing against the pain of the wire.

Naked.

Even thinking about it gave him a hard-on. He decided to jack off. Just to pass the time.

Turning out the lights in the pathology lab, Dr. Nathaniel Nichols took the elevator to the third floor to say goodnight to Mariah.

She did not know that he was there. She was no longer a part of the living world. Again, inevitably, he was tempted to perform the one single, simple act that would end it for her. But, again, he did not.

Driving out of the darkened, sleeping town, glistening from the earlier rainfall, he passed Dr. Foster Martin's big new house on Longmeadow Hill—elegant half-timbered Tudor, surrounded by an estate, hedged and manicured. Cars in the circular driveway. Foster Martin required four cars, including a Mercedes and a Porsche, for his family of three. The man who, for what he called moral reasons, refused to release Mariah from her torture, had become rich on the suffering and tragedies and pain of others. To Nat Nichols there was something vaguely obscene in this. In spite of the insurance he'd carried for years, the expenses of Mariah's sickness had eaten up the savings of a lifetime, so that his will, bequeathing everything equally to the three kids, was meaningless. His own father had been a country GP who had never refused to make a house call, summer or winter. Turning off onto Indian Hill Road, Nat Nichols was aware that his own feelings were as anachronistic as the old covered bridge he was passing through now.

Approaching home, he heard music echoing in his mind. As usual. Mariah could play anything: Chopin, Mozart, Stravinsky, but also the songs from Broadway shows they'd seen, or movies, and most particularly the family favorite, "They Call the Wind Maria." At parties, years and years ago, she had played honky-tonk, blues and boogie-woogie and jazz, her slim body moving on the bench, abandoned, happy. The memory was both pleasant and painful.

His old Colonial house, once a brilliant white, black shutters framing every window, was very close to the road, meadows on both sides, woods behind. As he pulled his old green Buick around to the rear, he had to fight memories: children's voices, laughter, the crack sound that a baseball bat makes, splashes and shouts from the pond. Where had it all gone? Now, it was as if it had never been. He always wished he'd taped those sounds, the way he'd recorded Mariah's piano playing, but he was not sure he could have brought himself to play the tapes now, even if he had.

He went in through the kitchen, as usual, turning on lights as he moved through the dining room. The thousands of meals eaten there, the discussions, the family quarrels, the teasing and laughter . . .

At the foot of the stairs, which disappeared steeply up a narrow well, he took off his wet coat and hat and turned on a lamp in the corner of the nook that had always been his own: bookcases, a small bar, a worn wing chair with footstool, a cobbler's bench stacked with books and magazines. There he had once spent hours, at the heart of the action yet within his own private retreat.

He poured himself his first whiskey—of the three that, each night, he hoped would allow him to sleep for at least three or four hours.

Then he went into the music room. He probably should phone Blake Arnold to tell him the autopsy on the Durand girl had only confirmed his earlier findings, but it was too late now. He had typed out the official form himself and it would be delivered to the courthouse first thing in the morning. He took another swallow of whiskey and turned on the hi-fi. Each night before going up to bed, he changed cassettes, choosing what he would listen to the following night. He returned to his chair in the nook, took a sip of his drink, and, hearing the music begin—Tchaikovsky's *Romeo and Juliet*—he took off his shoes, lifted his long, lean legs to the stool, and sat back. He could always picture Mariah at the piano while he listened—alive and vital, that faint abstracted smile that had always amused and pleased him.

His glass was almost to his lips when the music broke off. Startled, he stiffened.

A voice replaced the music, a voice he'd never heard before.

"Cool it, Doc," the voice said. "There's no one in the house. Relax and listen."

He sat up straight.

"Let me tell you all about your family."

He leaped up and went rushing toward the music room.

"Your son Daniel. Age thirty-seven. Married. Computer expert. Wife's name Lisa, same age."

The music room was dim. Empty. The voice came from the player.

"Nine-seven-five Irving Way, Palo Alto, California."

Stricken, he stood very still, listening.

"A nice house, Doctor, a very nice expensive house, fancy neighborhood."

He couldn't move.

"One son, named Aidan, age nine, fond of bicycles. Dangerous toys, bicycles. I was almost killed on one when I was a kid—by a truck."

Was it a joke, some weird practical joke?

"One daughter, Susan, thirteen. Nice age."

Or had he fallen asleep? Was he dreaming?

"Six years younger than Lynnette Durand—who was *not* raped. Hear me, Doctor? Lynnette Durand was *not* raped. Capeesh? Not raped any more than your granddaughter has been raped. Yet."

Weak now, horror and anger and a devastating sense of helplessness sapping his strength, he edged toward the piano and sank to the bench.

"Any more than your *daughter* has been raped, Doctor. Marylou Nichols, single, age thirty-three. One-twenty-four East Seventy-first Street, Manhattan, New York City."

He was tempted to stand up, smash the machine.

"Teaches music, Hunter College. Rides the subway often. Stands on edge of platform sometimes. People fall under those trains all the time, Doctor."

He lowered his forehead to the closed lid over the piano keys. Was this really happening?

"Other son, Gregory, age thirty. Juneau, Alaska. Import-export business. Hobbies: cross-country skiing and hunting. Dangerous sport, hunting. Accidents all the time."

He lifted his head, eyes closed, listening, unable not to listen.

"Wife, Diana. Also never been raped. Yet."

He stood up.

"Just the way Lynnette Durand was never raped. *Never*. You beginning to get the idea now, Doctor?"

He stood up, still weak, head spinning.

"Official report: Lynnette Durand was not raped, she was

pregnant, she died of strangulation, she was *choked* to death, and her body was thrown in the lake *because* she was pregnant. You *better* get my meaning, Doc. *Think*. Think about it, man. And about that wife of yours—all anybody has to do is pull the plug. Think about it, Doc.''

Click. Then a brief whirring before the strains of Tchaikovsky, melodic and aching with love, returned.

Then another click and the voice again. ''Maybe not soon, maybe tomorrow—accidents happen, man. You never know when . . . or where . . . or how. But they happen.''

He realized that he had stopped breathing.

''Will happen, too, Doc. All of it. If you turn this tape over to the cops. If you don't write that report real careful.'' The voice softened into sadness. ''*Anything* can happen, Doc. Anything. Ain't it a fuckin' shame?''

Click.

Music filled the house again. And Nat Nichols drained his glass and turned off the player.

Frustration and rage flooded his mind. And hate. Something he had not known for many years. If ever.

He thought of the boy in the jail cell—what was his name? To go back to the hospital, destroy the PM form, type out another—he'd be sending that boy to prison.

But if he didn't . . .

Dr. Nathaniel Nichols uttered a savage cry that reverberated through the still, empty house, where such a sound had never echoed before.

When it died away, leaving him drained and spent and very, very tired, he heard thunder rumbling in the distance, over the hills.

NINE

"Blake . . . you said you had other charges against the Horgan boy, didn't you?"

"Misdemeanors. Nothing much. Why aren't you sleeping?"

Valerie rolled over in the bed. "I couldn't. I've been wondering, why couldn't you use those?"

"Because that wouldn't close out the Durand case."

"That's what's been bothering me. Why should a man like Clifford Hyatt in Washington want to close out a case *here*?"

He turned to lie facing her, very close. "Look, Val, let's forget it till morning. I can't sleep, either. Maybe we could put each other to sleep—"

But she twisted away and sat up on the edge of the bed. "Not tonight. Please." She stood up. "Why do you always think sex solves everything?" She grabbed her robe and left the room on bare feet. Despising herself again. The house was cool, and although it was no longer raining, she heard a faint rumble of thunder in the distance as she went down the half-flight of stairs.

In the living room she found a cigarette without turning on the light—hoping he would follow and hoping he wouldn't.

But he did. "Todd Horgan's been under psychiatric care, Val. In New York City. Right *now* he's in a state of deep depression."

"I'd be depressed, too. Wouldn't you?"

"Perhaps he flew into a rage, a jealous rage—"

"Blake, you've been lying up there trying to build a case against him. Why?"

177

"It's my job."

"I thought your job was to see that justice is done." The end of her cigarette glowed in the dim room. "You have to have a strong enough case against him to convince him that if he won't confess, he'll be convicted and go to prison for years and years, isn't that it?"

"Honey, I'm trying to be patient." He went to the picture window to look out over the street, his back stiff. "Honest."

"Aren't you interested in what I've been thinking?"

"Not tonight, no—"

"Well, I'm going to tell you anyway. Hasn't it even occurred to you that organized crime might have a part in this?"

His shadow turned from the window. "Are you suggesting Hyatt himself—"

"I read the papers, Blake. And the news magazines. The mob is into everything. Not only underworld stuff, but legitimate businesses. Hotels and banks, factories, insurance companies, even chains of hospitals. Everything. It's probably the biggest business organization in the whole country."

He started toward the stairs. "I've got one helluva day in front of me—"

Very softly she said, "I think you don't *want* to believe it. Nor do I. Maybe that's what allows it to go on." When he halted on the stairs, she stubbed out her cigarette and asked, "Why don't you call Dr. Nichols again? He said he'd do the PM exam sometime during the night, didn't he?"

"At this hour?"

"You said he keeps strange hours. If he's not home, maybe he's at the hospital." She stood up. "Of course if you really don't want to know . . ."

"I'll do it from my study."

Oh, Valerie, you are a hag and a nag and a shrew. Worse. She lit another cigarette, then sat down again, waiting. Before going to bed Blake had said: *The coroner asked me how much Todd Horgan weighed. What would that have to do with it?* She'd had no answer then and she had none now. But it troubled Blake. Well, he *should* be troubled!

She heard his voice from above before he appeared: "You won't like this!" His tone vibrated with triumph. "Honey, it's over. It's sewed up." Then he was standing before her, legs spread. "He answered right away, so he wasn't sleeping.

But he sure as the devil didn't sound like himself. The official report will read: *Death by asphyxiation*. And *not* by drowning. Manual strangulation.''

She stubbed out the cigarette. "Well," she said, "that's what you want, isn't it?"

"That's our case!''

She stood up then and strolled to the window. "I suppose the police didn't look for fingerprints on her throat—after all those hours in the lake. . . .''

A teasing tone came into his voice: "Val, you read too many mysteries.''

She hadn't read a mystery novel since college. The street out front was still damp from the off-and-on rains of the evening. "Two or three years, you said. That's an eternity to a kid his age. And if he's innocent . . .''

"He's not innocent until he's declared innocent in court.''

Lightning flashed again, followed by a reverberating crash of thunder.

"May I use your word, Blake? Horseshit.''

"Hear that? Andy, do you hear that?''

He heard it. "It's only thunder, Tracy.''

His voice was drowsy because he'd been sleeping, after all—or half-sleeping, like an animal in the jungle.

"Thunder," Tracy said. She was kneeling on the bed. "What was it you told me? That the first thing Todd remembered was the girl asking him if he heard thunder?''

"And he said he hadn't. It was a clear night. Tracy—''

"It was, too. A beautiful night. No rain, no thunder! Oh, darling''—she leaped up—"we've got to move!''

He could make out her white body; she was scrambling into her jeans.

"Tracy, what are you doing?''

"Get up. Get dressed. I'll explain later." She was pulling on a T-shirt. "Do you have a flashlight?''

He was standing up now and fumbling himself into his clothes in the near-darkness. "On the table.''

"Bring it." She was drawing her poncho over her head. "Hurry! Will it work underwater?''

"It'll work anywhere." Dressed now, he picked up the gun and the flashlight. "Tracy, calm down. Where are we going?''

"No more questions. We don't have time. *I'm* going swimming."

He stepped to where she stood, flipped on the flashlight, and held it on her face. And growled: "You're not going swimming on a night like this!"

Her face was luminous, eyes brilliant with excitement. "Any bets, darling?" As she tilted her head, he caught sight of the ugly slitlike scar, a thin necklace of red against the lovely white flesh of her neck.

He tasted acid.

"Any bets?" she cried again as she went out the door.

Todd was lying on his back in the lower bunk, eyes closed, listening to the thunder.

He was not sleeping, but he was not really awake. Detached. A lotus-eater. *There is no joy but calm.* You said it, Lord Alfred.

Lynnette was dead.

The really strange thing now was that everything seemed to have lost all meaning or significance. Whatever was going to happen would happen. So be it. Even the recognition of his own despair was not really disturbing. No outrage now, no bitterness, no anger. As if his whole being had lapsed into a state of bleak acceptance.

She was dead.

Well, he'd known for years that the world was inhabited by selfish savages. Civilization was a cruel joke, a scam. Phony. Civilization was mad, insane at the core.

She was gone. Forever.

Even the pain in his spine and shoulder had become only a distant, impersonal discomfort. He supposed he had simply resigned himself, at last, to things as they are: reality. His fate was no longer in his hands—if it ever had been. Free will: another myth.

It no longer mattered. Nothing mattered but that one horrendous, incredible fact—which his mind could not comprehend: She was dead.

Trust me, kid. We don't even have a cause-of-death report yet. But whatever it says, we can handle it. Gerald Usher Lewis—just the asshole Todd had thought he'd turn out to be. How many hours ago now? *Damn it, I can't help you if you won't talk to me, Todd!* Asshole—had he used that word? He couldn't remember and what did it matter?

That was long ago. Before he knew . . .

And some time during the afternoon, Blake Arnold, the prosecutor again: *You recognize this truck, Mr. Horgan? Your father took this picture.*

The faces of the men—he'd wanted to kill them. Then. Now they were dead, too. So be it. . . .

"What you in for, Horgan?"

The calm was broken now—again—by the voice of the weirdo stretched out on the bunk above, out of view.

He decided to ignore it. *What are you in for?* Not *What are they accusing you of?* Sweet justice.

When old man Kopit had clanked open the steel-barred door a while ago, he'd sounded downright cheerful in his own dour way: *Ready for company, boy? Drunk as hell and don't want to be alone, he says. Always willin' to oblige our guests. Meet your roommate, George Bone.*

Todd had opened his eyes in time to see a tall man, about thirty, blond hair, climbing drunkenly up to the bunk above. Smashed as he was, he did it as if it was not a new experience. Then Todd had closed his eyes again, assuming at first that George Bone was sleeping it off, but hearing a sound which he finally had recognized as the chewing of gum.

"Hey, down there, you—I asked a question."

"Murder," Todd said.

"No shit?"

Todd closed his eyes again. *Sometimes I think you're right.* Lynnette's voice. In his mind. *If there really was a God, He'd make sure people were punished for what they do, wouldn't he?* The memory was visual, too: her face in quick, changing flashes—joy, that haunted look, her smile, that shadow in her black eyes. Now he'd never know, never understand how or why. Somehow he accepted even that.

"Heads up, comin' down." George Bone was standing on the concrete floor before Todd opened his eyes, towering over him, long legs spread. "No shit—murder one? Wow."

"Wow," Todd heard himself say, and saw the tall man frown.

"Me—just drunk and disorderly. Soon's they set bail, I jump it. All over the fuckin' country. Cops see my printout, they climb the wall."

Then silence again. Except for a cannonade of thunder somewhere over the hills.

"Y' better shave that beard before you hit the slammer. Even if they let you keep it, man, them cons 'll be up your ass before y' get outa the de-louse shower. Mincemeat in a week, sweet-lookin' kid like you." He did not move away. His body was no longer weaving and his voice was no longer blurred. He'd sobered up damn fast. "Two weeks in there and, man, you'll be lookin' for a way to take the rope-cure."

When Todd did not reply, George Bone turned and strolled to the window, stared out through the bars. Lightning glared beyond his head. "I seen it once. Down in Springfield, Mass. Old guy. Hung himself in the same cell. I woke up and there he was. Used his own pants. Tore 'em into strips to make a kinda rope . . ."

They had been passing alongside the courthouse, the jail windows on the ground floor dim behind their pattern of bars, when Tracy had told him where to drive: *Out route 57, north to the forest and Echo Lake.*

To take a swim? he'd asked.

And that's when she'd explained, excitement rippling in her voice: *Drums, metal drums filled with something or other, rolling down a hill on a quiet night with no clouds, no rain—and a half-mile away. That's what it would sound like, wouldn't it? Thunder! Well, wouldn't it?*

Why the hell hadn't he thought of it? And sooner? They were well out of town now, having passed the entrance to the Alpine Chalet. "I feel like an idiot. But I also know what you're thinking, Tracy." His eyes were fixed on the narrow pavement, glistening wet and deserted in the headlight beams. "If that something or other is what it might be, you're damn well not going swimming to make sure we're right."

She was sitting on her feet, only her head visible above the poncho. "You giving me orders already?" she asked, but her tone was not really teasing, light but with a challenge in it.

"Damn right I am! If what they're dumping is toxic—even nuclear for all we know—you could get sick as hell or worse."

"I know how to swim. I won't take it into my lungs or my stomach. You think I'm crazy?"

"Just a little, yes. Lungs, hell, Tracy—even your skin. How do we know what'd happen? Maybe years from now—"

"We have to be sure, don't we?"

"Some other way. Get a sample—"

"I want to know exactly what's in that water. I'll bet on it, though—drums or steel barrels on the bottom!" Her body was quiet, but her voice was brisk with exhilaration. "I'm counting on that flashlight."

"Tracy, get this straight. If you intend to jump out and dive in, I'm going to turn around right now." And then, gripping the wheel, lowering his voice: " 'Years from now,' I said. I care about what could happen to you years from now, Tracy." And then he added, "Even if you don't."

She moved then. She reached over and placed the back of her hand against his cheek. Her tone was soft: "Do you, darling?" And then she was sitting up straight and twisting about. "Steve usually has a Thermos in the car. What a coffee freak." She knelt on the bucket-seat, leaning over the back of it, turning on the flashlight. "Or we could use my blue jeans—soak them good and hurry back before they dry. There has to be a lab at the college." Then she yelped. "Bonanza!" Settling again, she shook the Thermos at her ear. "Andy, just think. What if we're right? I *know* we're right—nothing else fits. But what if they're doing this all over the country? And what about the water table in the ground? And the streams running off. People will be *drinking* that water! Oh, the cold-hearted, ruthless *bastards*!"

But Andrew's mind was on something else: time. How many hours until the arraignment? The clock on the dash read 2:42. How the hell could they get a water sample, have it tested, and learn the results in time to introduce them in court at ten o'clock? And suppose the drums hadn't leaked, or rusted through? Suppose the lake water was not yet contaminated? Even if it was, would that be proof, legal proof? Would a judge even *listen*?"

It was then that he saw headlights in the rearview mirror. From behind. The first car they'd seen on the road . . .

But obscured in the glare of its own beams, the car was not identifiable.

Except that the lights were set low and wide, and the roof of the car was also very low, like the roof of a sports car . . .

He decided to say nothing.

His muscles had hardened and his throat had locked. He was gripping the wheel. But Tracy was silent now.

So far, so good, Nick. By noon tomorrow it should be all over. I'm handling things from here. You keep the lid on up there. Good night, son.

Good night, Poppa. I'm on top of this one. That's what he'd said on the phone, and by Christ, he was, too! Nick Verini's like his old man. Knows how to operate. In command. A threat here, a bribe there, muscle, maybe waste some clown if he had to. Power—*that* was the name of the game! *Trust me, Poppa.* He hadn't told the old man about the coroner; he was saving that till after the hearing. Then he'd tell Vincent Verini in person once he was back in Boston: how he'd used the computer bank in Revere and then how he'd scared the old man shitless, knowing the names and ages and all the rest about the old man's kids.

Only those two . . . Those two up there ahead in the black Volvo—where the sweet Jesus did they think they were going this time of night? Hadn't figured on him, had they? Hadn't figured he'd be parked, lights out, balls freezing off, just in case, taking no chances . . .

Christ, these roads up here! Fucking roller coaster. And curves? Jesus, every hundred yards another one, and slabs of stone jutting out sometimes. Well, he had the wheels for it. Best in the world, only car worthy of Nick Verini. Ferrari Mondial, seventy thousand plus custom touches, worth every nickel. Listen to that power cooking in there. Made his whole body sort of throb with pleasure just feeling it under him. Going slow like this, hanging back, he loved that too, like he was some sort of jungle cat, straining to go, pounce, kill.

Times now, though, these roads, the taillights of the Volvo wasn't even in sight after it went around a bend. But where could it turn off? Woods on both sides.

More lightning, more thunder—fuck it. House here and there, all dark. People sleeping. Not knowing. That was the best part: people not knowing. Suckers. Ass-brains. Marks. An electric charge shot through him—a jolt, a shock, like joy. Everything jibing, everything under control. *His* control. Covering all bases. *Like that time in Springfield, Georgie. Only this time y' wait for my signal. This horn. You hear that? Two longs and three shorts like this, outside on the* street. Ferrari horn don't sound like no other. You hear that, that's when—zip the bugger.

Maybe the big ugly dimwit got it, maybe he didn't. *A confession'd close out the case*, Vincent Verini had said on the phone. Well, no reason to waste the kid if he was wise enough to go along. But if not . . .

And then, rounding another blind curve and again seeing the lights of the car ahead, he felt a familiar, almost sickening ache settle into his bones. No matter what he did, how hard he tried, busted his ass trying, Poppa'd never think it was right. Or enough.

Tyger! Tyger! burning bright . . .

Her eyes never leaving the round rearview mirror outside the window, the poem's words flowing through her mind—*In the forests of the night*—Tracy was again struggling with terror, something she had never really known until that time, only a few hours ago, when she had sat, rigid and not breathing, in the front seat of the van, that hated whisper at her ear, the wire cutting into her neck. *Do just what I say now, slut, you won't get blood all over them nice clothes. Which you can start takin' off right now.*

A few miles back, when the driver of the car behind had made no effort to pass, she had realized whose it was. *Garrote—y' heard of that. Used to execute people that way once, the old country.*

"Did Chief Radford show you how to use that gun he gave you?" Andy asked.

Grateful to have something to do, she picked up the gun from the console where Andy'd put it, within reach of them both. *It's very simple, Tracy. Double-action. All you have to do is take aim and pull the trigger.*

"It's ready to fire." Her voice was threatening to rise, to shrill. "Six bullets." It felt heavy in her hand.

"You hold on to it till we get there. Did you ever fire a gun?"

"No. Have you?"

"Not yet," he said.

Turn here, Red. Hawley Mill Road. We go to the end, I fuck you till your eyes pop out. Then I cut off your pretty head with this goddam wire an' leave what's left of you for the animals to find when they smell the blood. She was trying not

185

to shake, but her stomach now was as empty and sick as it had been then.

What immortal hand or eye could frame thy fearful symmetry?

She heard her voice, amazingly composed: "The forest entrance is about a mile ahead. What do we do?"

"We can't turn in if he can see us do it."

"There's a chance. Pretty soon, maybe half a mile, you'll see a sharp curve, around a bluff on the right. If you could take the curve fast enough, and speed up all of a sudden, and then swing in left into the road and turn off the lights . . ."

"Tracy, are you sure you want to go through with this? Maybe tomorrow—"

"Tomorrow'll be too late," she said. "That's the curve ahead. See the stone jutting out on the right?" She returned her gaze to the mirror. "That far back, he won't be able to see us for a few seconds . . .

Just cool it, that's all. You fuck off and maybe I won't have to do it to you. Maybe you'll live a while.

"Now!" she shouted. "Fast! And be ready to swing left about ten yards past the bluff. And then turn off the lights till he gets past!"

He should have raped her when he had the chance.

Christ, had he been tempted! He should've raped her and killed her instead of trying to throw a scare into her. If he had, he wouldn't be out here in the middle of nowhere, way past midnight, tailing a goddam black Volvo up hills, around bends. . . . Christ, this was weird country! He hated it. He hated everywhere but a city.

Now the car was out of sight again. But he liked it that he could check the impulse to gun it and shoot ahead. Liked it that he could just ease down on the gas pedal instead. Self-control. Discipline. Reason he hadn't raped her.

As he took the Ferrari into the curve, he realized: the redhead cunt was again doing what he told her. That's what they were both doing—splitting, getting out, running. To save her ass. Heading north. Canada, sure as shit. Doing what *he'd* told them to do! The realization sent another charge through him. Power—better than all the booze and drugs in the whole goddam world! And someday, when he was in Vincent Verini's shoes—

There were no lights on the road ahead. A flat straight stretch, black and wet.

He trounced on the fuel-feed and shifted, fast. The engine responded instantly, growling into a bellow. His body was thrown back in the seat as the car shot forward. Wouldn't be safe to open it up all the way, but if that prick thought he could . . .

A jagged slash of lightning stabbed through the sky, briefly illuminating the empty road beyond his headlights, but he heard no thunder; the engine was too loud.

Another curve. The Ferrari took it, low and clean.

More empty road ahead.

Christ, had they turned off?

Where? Woods on both sides, no house, no driveways.

Then he saw a sign. Blank. On the left side of the road, facing away.

He braked sharply, then eased the car along the left lane, pressed the release to lower the window, braked, and looked back over his shoulder.

FOREST ENTRANCE
200 FEET

He'd passed it.

And he knew.

Fury surged into his mouth, bitter, the taste of metal.

He tried a U-turn. The goddam road was too narrow, even for the Ferrari. He had to reverse once before he was heading back. Fast.

Had they spotted him and turned off to get away? Into the goddam woods? Jesus!

Was there a road through the forest to the other side?

Or . . . or was this where they'd been heading all along?

Oh Jesus, if he caught them now, he'd waste them both. Bam. Bam. Both of them!

No, he'd zip the bastard, one shot, then he'd do what he'd wanted to do earlier. Rape her first, then . . .

Nobody double-crosses Nick Verini like that!

He was choking on bile as he swung the wheel and turned right between two low, half-hidden posts and onto an even narrower road, unpaved, gravel, brown, not too rough.

Trees on both sides. Black trees. Blackness everywhere.

Kind of place he hated. Spooky. Wild. Kind of place that'd scare him if he was the kind to get scared. Like being in a cave with strange animals, or other creatures . . .

Nickie, you can't afford to boil over the way you do. Between your hot blood and that pecker of yours . . . You ever going to grow up, son?

Fuck you too, Poppa. This is my show. Fuck you and them and the whole goddam world.

"Tell me when to slow down," Andrew said.

He was driving as fast as he thought safe on the forest road, faster. The cold fear that he'd been trying to deny all evening took over completely now. If Nick Verini realized where they were heading, would he guess their motive? Or had their ruse worked? Once he'd made the turn, Andrew had stopped and snapped off the lights. Then, after the Ferrari had charged past on the highway, thundering as it picked up speed, he'd driven on, still very slow, no lights, using the flashes of lightning to stay on the road, until the black Volvo was deep in the steep-sided ravine formed by towering black pines. Only then had he flipped on the headlights and allowed himself this precarious speed.

The lake was some distance from the highway; he recalled this from flying over when they'd discovered the body, but distances from the air are deceptive.

"You all right?" he asked without taking his eyes from the pitted gravel surface ahead. He remembered her kneeling on the seat while they waited inside the entrance, knees braced apart, the revolver in both hands, directed through the rear window. "Tracy?"

"I'm too scared to talk."

Silence then. Darkness on all sides, only the narrow beams probing . . .

Blackness in the rearview mirror. If they could be off the road by the time Nick Verini realized . . .

"Any sign to the lake?" he asked.

"I can't remember. Isn't that terrible? I hope to *God* there's no sign!"

But there was. Not large, a single piece of stained wood suspended from the crossarm of a post: ECHO LAKE and an arrow pointing.

He had slowed somewhat but he made the turn too fast and

the rear wheels slid, sputtering on the gravel. He took a quick look ahead: the narrow lane, framed in bushes and trees, dipped down in a slope and then, after twenty or thirty yards, fanned out to form a small parking area.

He flipped off the headlights again, and very slowly, careful to downshift and not to apply the brakes because of the taillight, he eased the Volvo down and then across the flat space toward a low barrier—a long single log, barkless, gleaming once in another flare of lightning. It was suspended between two short timber posts. When the front bumper was almost touching the barricade, he killed the motor and released the clutch to stop the car completely without using the brake.

From the seat he could see the shadowy ridges of hills beyond a glimmer of water: the far side of the lake. And then, in a sharp burst of lightning, he saw that there was no growth, trees or bushes, visible beyond the barrier. Thunder reverberated over the mountains on all sides.

"They chose well," Tracy said, "the bastards."

Somewhere, out in the distance, from one of those hills, Todd had seen the glitter of red taillights over here, and the frame of the white truck parked, heading out. . . .

And then, in the vast silence he heard another sound, from behind and some distance away, but definite and definable: not thunder now but the deep thrumming roar of the little red Ferrari's powerful engine.

Would it continue on the road, or would it stop?

TEN

ECHO LAKE. Nick saw the sign just in time.

In time to tromp on the clutch and the brake pedal, so hard, so fast that the stop on the gravel was only an instantaneous jolt before he shifted and shot the car forward, turning into the narrow lane. Should he kill the lights?

It's got to be all over up there before anybody gets nosy about where those fools dumped the load. Too late, Poppa, too late now. *Accidents only, Nick.* Too late. Only one way to handle it now. My way.

Under the low headlights, the rutted gravel sloped down—like he was going into a black cave—so, working the clutch, he let the car roll forward and down, very slow, very slow. . . .

His mind was clear now. And a familiar excitement began to take over. The part of his job that really gave him a charge.

Not because of the danger—what could they do to him?—but because it would be his pleasure, his *soddisfazione*, to do what *he* had to do. To them.

Handling the wheel with his left, he reached to take the automatic out of its custom-made holster fitted to the space between his seat and the console. The neat little Beretta 76. *Not a man's gun, Nickie.* Like shit! Light, power to spare. Ten rounds. Ask the turks he'd used it on—they didn't think it was a toy. They didn't think at all anymore, period. He slipped it into the pocket of his blazer.

More thunder, but no lightning this time. Who needed it?

In the twin light shafts beyond the low hood, he saw the roadway level off into a flat space of gravel with a dead-end barrier—it looked like a log.

190

Only then did he see the Volvo. Off to his right. Dark. Backed into the woods, at an angle, between the tree trunks, only its front wheels on the gravel. And heading out.

He braked.

Had they seen him? Heard him?

Were they in the car?

No, he didn't want them to be in the car, sitting ducks. It'd be too easy that way.

Too easy for them, too.

There was only one hitch: what the fuck to do with the car and the bodies after?

But that was later, later. He was working on a high now. It was always like this when it came to the showdown: mind diamond-clear, body floating, blood like air in his veins, thin, light. *This was it!*

He moved then. You always have to move. That's the first rule of the game. Move first, and not what they expect.

He gunned the motor, headed straight, gravel spluttering under the wheels, braked sharply within inches of the log. He caught a quick glimpse of the far side of the lake as he threw the shift into reverse and backed up, stopped, then eased the Ferrari forward at an angle, until the passenger door was only a few inches from the nose of the Volvo. Then he braked again and switched off the motor but not the lights.

Your move, motherfucker.

From behind the black car—he'd had to decide fast—Andrew was watching through the rear window, through the empty interior and the windshield.

The bastard meant business. The two cars were almost at a right angle to each other and the Volvo was blocked. Behind him there were not more than three feet between his back and the trunks of the pine trees at the edge of the woods. The blue-black gun, which Tracy had handed him before going downhill to the lake, was directed at the ground, loose but ready. *Tracy,* he'd said, *Tracy, please—don't come back up here unless you hear me call you. And for God's sake don't use the flashlight unless you absolutely have to.* She had kissed him then, quickly, and had disappeared into the shrubs between the tree trunks. Then he'd heard her rustling through the dry brush, going downhill to the water.

Now he could hear nothing. Anywhere. Nothing moved. Anywhere. And even with no wind, the cold cut through his jacket and stung on his face. He was tempted not to wait. Surprise—maybe that was the key element. Step up onto the bumper, steady the automatic in both hands over the roof, pull the trigger. He couldn't miss the dark window of the Ferrari, get it over with before the bastard got out of the car. Before *he* could use that rifle he'd bragged about in Colby's. Then do it now, fast! *Do* it! The bastard might even be able to see down the hill from inside the car. What if he had that rifle out the window on the far side and pointed down the hill? Those damned headlights! With those shooting out over the lake, Tracy'd be an easy target.

So he decided, amazed at the cool, almost detached calmness that had taken over his mind. Crouching low, he slid along the passenger side of the Volvo toward the right front fender.

Was the bastard already out of the car?

One headlight was close, very close, so, using two hands, he aimed the revolver and fired. The light went out and he heard the tinkling of glass, then moved his aim to the other headlight.

Kneeling on a narrow ledge of stone on the bank at the foot of the hill, Tracy heard the shot while she was filling the Thermos, one hand under the icy water.

Her heart knotted. Her blood stopped. Hearing the report echoing in the distance, she lifted the bottle, hand stiff, inserted the cork, and then threw herself full length into the ferns growing along the bank.

Was he firing down at her?

Or at Andy?

Then she realized that the light above had dimmed somehow. And narrowed. Why?

She heard two more shots, in quick succession, and the light above went out altogether. She flattened herself into the marshy bed of ferns, beginning to shake all over.

Silence. Only that double echo coming back from the hills.

Darkness.

Utter darkness.

And then she knew: Andy had done the firing. Not Nick Verini.

What should she do? Was she safe here now?

Or would she be safer underwater? If she could testify that she had actually seen those drums . . .

And unless this was the regular disposal site, if they'd been placed here only last night, small chance they'd rusted through.

But if they hadn't, what would the sample in the Thermos prove?

Nick had begun to open his door but changed his mind. He had the Beretta in hand now, safety catch in firing position.

Hearing the first shot, he'd felt a quick elation. He'd thought the fucker was trying to fire through the windshield. But when he saw the single narrow shaft of light in front instead of two, a wild fury ripped through him. His headlights—the fucker was shooting out his headlights! So he'd reached, fast, and turned off the remaining one. At that moment, there had been two more shots. And sudden darkness.

Had the automatic shield come down over the second headlight in time, or had one of those two shots taken it out? Or . . . maybe the slug had gone through the guard after it was down. Three slugs, close range, just to knock out two lights, maybe one. Amateur asshole. Gun sounded like a .38. Maybe a .45. Probably a revolver. Six slugs, three already wasted. Maybe he could get the wise-ass to use the rest of his ammo. After that, the rest'd be easy: Zip the fucker up here, fast, before he could reload in the dark, then find the redhead, do it this time, not threaten, rip off her clothes, all of them, oh Jesus, what a body. . . .

No longer crouched down by the right fender of the Volvo, Andy was moving now, shoulders low, along the passenger side to the rear of the black car. Rage and hate, a primal ferocity that he had never felt before, was driving him, body and mind. He knew what he was going to do now, had to do, *wanted* to do!

He'd been so sure of the first shot that he'd missed with the second, so he'd braced his arm, but not fast enough. Because even as he squeezed the trigger again, he saw the light vanish and the red shield jut out to come down over the glass. But he'd fired again, fast. And now he couldn't see whether the bullet had penetrated.

But he knew, anyway, that the bastard was sitting in there behind that black windshield. He was still in the car. And if that third bullet had not pierced the shield, he still had one good headlight left. To turn on whenever *he* chose to do so.

Stepping up onto the rear bumper, lifting his body, which seemed weightless, and exposing his head and shoulders, Andrew placed the gun on the roof, both arms extended, both hands, cold with sweat, steadying the gun.

Now, eyes adjusting, he could make out the low sleek shadow of the Ferrari.

He waited. In the next flare of lightning, the dark opaque window would be clear. All he'd have to do was adjust his aim and pull the trigger.

And then he remembered. Too late.

Automatic rifle . . . nightscope . . . sees in the dark!

How the hell could he have forgotten?

And quiet. All anyone hears is a little fart sound.

He cursed himself savagely. The bastard didn't need light.

And he'd wasted three of his six bullets.

Nick, cold now and getting jumpy, was tempted to reach for the rifle in the back, to fling open the door, leap out, start firing.

But at what?

In which direction?

Where?

The fucker could be anywhere out there in the dark, anywhere.

And he sure as hell had a gun.

He knew where the cunt was, though. One of them had to be down by the water. Was she in there swimming around? On a night like this. Naked maybe.

Ve'd already dumped the load vhen Jesse seen their fire, the big Swede had said. And the one named Jesse Kull had whined: *So that's why we dumped the body in there, too.* Deer hunting, Christ-sake! *It got so late we decided to get rid of the cans.* Well, those two'd got what was coming to them. Now these two'd get theirs.

If they didn't—and now, tonight—he could hear Poppa's voice, so thin and sharp with contempt that he'd never be able to stand it. But there was still no panic in him, only that running, lightheaded excitement that he loved.

But what a bitch of a place to be. Like in a dream. And dark, Jesus, it was dark! And the tinted glass was against him; it hid him but they *knew* where he was, and he couldn't see out either window except when the lightning lit things up.

What the shit should he do? He'd never been able to sit in one place very long. Even church.

But one thing sure: He was safe. Unless they had a bazooka or some such. He twisted around to take the bull-pup AUG out of its case in back. Awkward thing maybe, but everything you could ask for in a firearm. But he doubted even *it* could blast through the glass. Nick Verini didn't drive around nowhere, in *any* car, that didn't have proofglass, windshield and all sides.

No thunder, no lightning. And silence. Complete silence.

What did it mean?

She couldn't go on lying here, wondering, imagining. . . .

She sat up, twisting about to place the Thermos, heavy now in her cold hand, on the ledge. Her fingers were no longer so stiff. That water was colder than the air.

Sorry, Andy. You do what you have to do; I'll do what I have to do.

But she dreaded it. After taking the flashlight from its pocket, she lifted the poncho over her head. Was the T-shirt too loose, the jeans too tight for swimming? She kicked off her loafers.

Then, already shuddering, she rolled her body over the gritty stone ledge and lowered it slowly—no sound, no splash, gritting her teeth—into the icy water.

With the revolver braced along the roof of the Volvo, Andrew was waiting for the lightning that wouldn't flash, now that he needed it.

His arms and fingers were aching. And he was cold to the marrow. But not so cold as Tracy. Had she gone in? Somehow he knew she had. Well, she was right: It was the only way to make sure. But what if the frigid water triggered shock, even cramps? What if—

Thunder rumbled again. But no lightning.

He was waiting to kill another human being. Self-defense,

whether he could ever prove it legally or not—self-defense and Tracy's defense. And he had no space in him for moral hesitation. If he hesitated—*while* he hesitated—that bastard was sitting in there trying to figure out how to kill *him*. No hesitation there, no civilized scruples. Not *whether* to kill, but *how*.

And if he let him, he had no doubt, none, about what would happen to Tracy.

Blue lightning shimmered and shuddered, filling the sky.

CRAACK!
At first Nick thought it was a clap of thunder. But then he heard the thunder, low and far away and rumbling. So he knew.

A quick shot of elation went through him. The fucker was firing at him from inside the other car.

He leaned across the console and passenger seat to place his right palm against the side window. He ran it over the glass. Which was smooth as ever. Not so much as a nick.

But the fucker was really out for blood.

He actually tried to kill Nick Verini!

And all he had was two slugs left in the revolver. When he used those, he'd have to reload.

Nick sat back and touched the control to lower the left window all the way, and yelled: "You ain't careful, lover boy, you gonna hurt somebody!"

He saw the flash clearly this time, quick and blue-bright, at the same second that he heard the *CRAACK*. From the top of the Volvo. He was tempted to use the rifle but he was enjoying it too much.

"Gonna kill me, lover boy?" he shouted. "You ain't got it in you!"

No answer.

Not a sound.

He touched the pocket to make sure the Beretta was where he wanted it, and then he took up the AUG.

And yelled: "I already killed her, lover boy. Like I told you, you didn't even hear it, did you?"

Then he waited.

But there was no sound now. Well, let the fucker sweat.

All he had to do was sit tight. Safe. Like in a fort. He wasn't going to blow this one. But, Jesus, he'd never been so *cold*.

* * *

Coming up for air, chest bursting, Tracy could see nothing. Hear nothing. What was going on up there?

She was tempted to call Andy's name. She listened.

There was no sound. None whatever.

No way to check her position. So she took another deep breath, careful not to gulp, and forced her body down again, below the surface.

The flashlight beam stabbed through the dark water, probing, penetrating only a yard or so before blurring. It revealed nothing. Again.

Could she be wrong? Assumptions? Hope?

She was using every muscle, legs and arms, fighting the stiffness, the cold. And fighting to stay down. Her jaws were locked, eyes stinging but not blinded. If they were in here, they had to be against the bank at the bottom of the hill. But . . .

Could the light, moving underwater, be seen from above? What was it Andy had told her about a nightscope? Down here she would probably not even be able to hear a shot if—

Then she saw them.

She swam closer to make sure.

No hallucination! No wish fulfillment! There they were, at all angles, metal barrels, some already half-submerged in mud.

She didn't have enough breath left. She couldn't take time to count—more than a dozen at a guess—so she flipped off the light and kicked her way to the surface, all doubt gone, invigorated by the certainty.

As air struck her face, pierced her lungs, cold but not so cold as the water. She started to swim on the surface in the direction of the bank at the foot of the hill.

She hoped. . . .

Because now she'd begun to fear that her whole body might go into shock if she stayed in the ice-cold water much longer.

Andrew had decided to move.

He'd had to choke down the temptation to shout Tracy's name.

Could the bastard have shot down the hill from the Ferrari? Or from alongside it?

197

A bitter, terrible fury was driving him. He found his way, keeping low, shoulder brushing along the driver's side of the Volvo, trying not to think, just doing, not thinking, doing. He'd been stupid, wasted two more shots, stupid. No punk like Nick Verini would be driving around without bulletproof glass. There had to be a way to get the bastard out of that car, so he could use the last bullet. . . .

He opened the door, and using the wheel to lift himself in, he sank into the driver's seat.

A sharp perpendicular zigzag light stabbed the sky and was gone. But in that instant he looked toward the drop-off. And realized: The bastard could not possibly have sighted and shot down the hill from the Ferrari.

Tracy, for God's sake, stay down there. Stay out of sight!

He buckled the seat belt around his body.

His mind was acting very strange. . . .

Perhaps what he intended now was irrational, too. But he couldn't wait till the bastard did get out of the car to go to the edge. Or to go down the hill with that goddammed rifle . . .

Head down to be out of range, he twisted the key in the ignition.

Swimming on the surface, Tracy heard a car motor start. And realized she'd been swimming in the opposite direction, toward the middle of the lake!

She reversed her body in the water, fast, and struck out, ignoring the splashing sound of her strokes, in the direction of the motor sound, which continued. And which, she hoped, drowned out whatever noise she was making.

When she reached the bank, should she climb out? If she stayed in the water, only her head would be a target. *If you hear a gun up here, Tracy, it'll be mine. His has a silencer on it.*

Did that mean that if Verini was shooting at her, she wouldn't even know it?

One hand touched the ledge and she was reaching with the other when she heard another sound. What?

Nick was scrambling over the console, rifle in hand, when the Volvo, in reverse, smashed into the tree behind it.

He'd heard it backing up while he was lowering the window on the passenger side, realizing that the fucker was *inside* the Volvo now. He was trying to position the rifle out the half-open window when he heard the gears grinding and the headlights came on, all at one time, fast.

He was blinded.

He tried, frantic, furious, to work the awkward rifle into position, but the other car shot forward so fast that, even as he got off the shots—a quick series of putt-putt sounds, a smell of burnt powder—he had to draw the rifle barrel in before the Volvo's nose crashed into the side of the Ferrari with a deafening, crushing impact that caused him to drop the rifle and fall backwards and then to the floor.

At the instant of impact Andrew had been braced for the collision, trying to unbuckle the belt as he turned off the headlights, before he felt a hot stabbing pain in his left arm above the elbow.

His left hand had lost strength, nothing but pain down to the wrist and into the shoulder and into the base of his skull. And he was sick, his body protesting with much more pain as he searched blindly, feeling with his right hand until he located the gun on the floor, then slid his body to the left and dropped to the ground, as planned. But when his left shoulder hit the earth, his mind blanked, and all he could hear was the echo of the harsh crushing sound of metal dying out in the distance.

Tracy lifted her body out of the water. She couldn't bear the cold a second longer.

It was dark again.

She stretched out on the hard ledge, struggling to breathe.

She'd heard both crunching sounds, had seen the light that came on, briefly, between them.

What was going on up there?

All she could think of was trying to force air into her lungs. Would it warm her or only make her colder?

She could not possibly be any colder. Ever, ever . . .

Andy?

Andy, are you all right?

He had no idea how long it had taken him to crawl away from

199

the Volvo in the intense darkness, but now he was trying to stand up, all sense of direction gone, arm dangling, useless, fiery pain zeroing in on the wound itself, the revolver still in his right hand, mind reeling, blood moist and warm down the length of the arm and onto his hand.

A quick sharp flash of lightning.

He saw the red glint of the Ferrari.

No thunder.

No sound.

He managed to stand, unable to crouch now as he staggered in the dark toward the side of the Ferrari. He shoved the revolver into his belt and extended his right arm.

Until it touched metal.

Using his fingers lightly, he felt his way to the rear of the red car.

Until, trying to get his breath, he was at the low bumper.

There was only one way now.

To finish the job.

One bullet.

Only one way. And before Nick Verini could act.

He was going to blow up the goddam car.

And hope the bastard was still inside it.

Nick Verini, having picked himself up from the floor, was finding it hard to think.

The motherfucker had trashed his car.

He still had the rifle. Its barrel was still hot.

Had he wasted the fucker?

He had to know.

He had to get out of the car and find out.

But what if—

How could he get out, not knowing?

If the fucker wasn't dead, he still had one bullet in that gun. Or maybe he was reloading now.

And where was the cunt?

He knew the right door wouldn't open, but if he could get out on the driver's side, not making any noise, get to where that log was . . . where he could see downhill . . . with the scope . . .

No choice now. How do you know you're living if you don't take chances?

Slip out, zip the cunt long-distance, then go hunting for the motherfucker. With the scope—if it took all night!

He looked out both side windows, windshield, rear window: just blackness.

He was goddammed if he was going to sit here on his ass freezing to death!

Andrew was standing ten or twelve feet behind the Ferrari.

He'd backed up four long strides. He had judged that to be a safe distance. But how could he know?

His left arm was hanging. Dripping blood. Limp and cold, with a knot of fire above the elbow.

His right arm was extended, holding the revolver. It was aimed, or at least pointed, at the rear of the car.

Where the gas tank should be located.

Was a Ferrari different?

Would a bullet do the job?

Tracy?

He couldn't call out now.

He was tensed for the next flash of light. With one shot left, he couldn't risk firing in the dark.

But he couldn't see even the shadow of the car now.

He couldn't see anything.

He heard a sound. More thunder. Distant.

But there had been no lightning before the sound. Not so much as a glint or glimmer.

Then he heard another sound.

Close. Very quiet.

As of a car door opening . . .

But he couldn't be sure.

And he couldn't move left. No way to see anyway.

Had Nick Verini climbed out? Or was it a trick to make him think he had?

Her body, regardless of the quivering flesh, had stiffened.

But she was breathing at last. Could she move?

Tracy, please—don't come back up here unless you hear me call you. . . .

She listened.

There was no sound.

None whatever.

Would it be safer to lie here or to try to make it to the woods?

Her body was frozen but her mind was working again. If Verini had a scope that could see in the dark . . .

She forced the flashlight into the pocket of her tight wet jeans, fumbled and found the Thermos, heavy now, and then she stood up, fast, and began to run toward the woods that she could not see.

Before she had gone ten steps, her foot went into a marshy hole and twisted. She felt fern leaves and then wetness around her ankle as it sank more deeply. Pain shot up her calf and she could feel the wetness closing muddily over her bare foot. She was down on one knee.

A jungle caution had taken over Nick Verini's whole body.

Holding the AUG at the ready with one hand, finger on the electronic trigger, body poised to swivel and spray the area at the first sound. With his other hand he was feeling into the darkness, gut hard and cold with anger.

He was convinced he'd offed the fucker—body still bleeding on the seat of the Volvo—but he was taking no chances. Not now, not now that he knew what a tricky wise-ass *crazy* man he was up against!

His knee came against the log. But easy, easy because that's what he'd been counting on. If he tripped over that, he'd go rolling down the hill.

He lifted his right foot to the log and braced the rifle, using the feel of it to place his cheek against the barrel and the scope at his eye.

The cunt . . .

He felt a strange quiet settle over him.

With the scope he could find her. Even from up here.

She'd never know what killed her.

Tracy was crawling along the ground on her hands and knees.

When she'd tried to walk, the pain had been such torture that she'd had to bite her tongue, hard, to keep from crying out. And her whole body, even moving, was shuddering all over. When she'd imagined that she could never be colder than she had been in the water . . .

She'd heard nothing from above, nothing anywhere except

her own breathing and the dry sound of her knees and hands on the weeds and grass. Were those pine needles cutting into her palms? Was she near the edge of the woods?

It was so dark that she could not be sure she was going in the right direction.

She didn't even know where the hill was, or the lake.

Should she risk the flashlight, just once, quickly?

Nick had located the lake's edge and now he was moving his view, dim but distinct, a pale gray loophole with cross hairs, along the water's edge.

If he killed her this way, he'd be cheating himself out of what he'd planned for her once he had the fucker out of the way, but—

A flicker of light, down below, off to his left. He swung the barrel.

Had his eyes played a trick?

No.

There she was.

Kneeling, shoving a flashlight into her pocket.

Cool it, Nick.

He adjusted the knob till he had her clear, fixed.

He worked the focus till her head was in the exact center where the cross hairs met, but she began to move, crawling on her hands and knees like maybe she'd been hurt, so he had to adjust to her moving. Should he spray-shoot back and forth, raking the area? No way to miss then—

There was a sound. An explosion of sound.

Behind him.

His head went haywire.

He turned.

And as he did, he realized what he'd heard. He'd know it anywhere: the Ferrari's engine.

He stood up, fast, knowing, and then he was firing into the darkness, knowing, fast, knowing—

And then he was flooded in light.

The shock caused him to stand staring, still shooting—putt-putt-putt—but helplessly.

What the shit good was it to try to shoot through that windshield?

Andrew was amazed: The single left headlight had come on.

He saw Verini off to his left, heard nothing but the engine but saw the rifle jerking in Verini's hands.

Your turn, you bastard, your turn!

He shifted into reverse with his right, felt the car shoot back, then gunned it, *VROOM, VROOM, VROOM*.

The pain in his left arm, hanging limp and useless, shot up into his neck again. He ignored it.

He threw the stick into low and let the car go forward.

In the single shaft of light the bastard raised the rifle again. Only a tat-tat-tat sound on the glass. Your turn, you bastard. Fire away. It's *your* turn now!

Then he saw Nick Verini's eyes, wide, gleaming and hard, polished glass, as he scrambled to the far side of the barrier, backing away, eyes never leaving the car as its nose approached, inexorable, slow. Till it reached the log. Andrew shifted again, then pushed the fuel feed almost to the floor and braced his body for the resistance of the log.

The rear tires spun angrily in the gravel, and the powerful engine grew steadily louder as the log began, slowly at first, to move, the stanchion at the left end loosening, twisting as it came uprooted, the log itself swinging horizontally from the right end like a heavy gate opening slowly, on hinges.

Andrew felt a spasm of savage satisfaction.

He saw Nick Verini, rifle in hand, looking frantically for a way to escape. Which only stirred a fire in his blood. A barbaric hunger—

To kill. *Kill!*

The opening was sufficient now, so Andrew braked, reversed with his right hand, saw the log drop to the ground and begin to roll at an angle. Then he whipped the wheel with the same arm and pointed the car's low sloping nose toward the glimmer of lake that he could see below the headlight glare over the edge of the drop-off. Leaning his chest against the wheel to hold it, he jammed the shift into low, and urging the car forward slowly, he reached across his body to open the door. Then, bracing his mind and trying to relax his body, he let go of the controls and rolled out onto his wounded arm as the nose of the car tilted down, still moving, and then, as he hit the ground, his mind blanked with the pain again.

Nick Verini was trying not to fall as he ran down the steep slope.

He kept trying to look back over his shoulder, where there was light, but downhill was dim, almost dark; low bushes kept trying to trip him, tackle him; he couldn't hold his body back, it kept plunging faster and faster. . . .

But he still had the rifle, and the Beretta in his pocket, and the girl was down here, but—

He heard a rumbling behind, a bumping. Without glancing he knew, because the light was on him now: his car, his beautiful car, its one monstrous eye flooding him with light. He was trying to slow down and go faster at the same time; he glanced over his shoulder, the light close, sound closer, so he hurled his body to one side and then he was rolling, thrashing, struggling to scramble to his feet, hearing the wheels pass, the light going away. . . .

Because of the headlight Tracy saw the Ferrari rumble across the narrow ledge and, tilting forward, plunge into the lake.

A shiver of satisfaction went through her.

Darkness again.

She was stretched out, only a few yards from the edge of the woods.

Now she heard water gurgling in the silence.

And then a voice: "Get the hell into the woods, Tracy!"

Andy. Andy's voice. From above.

But where was Nick Verini?

Did she dare move?

She thought of what Andy had told her: *Todd's blaming himself because he told the girl to run.*

The quivering in her body had subsided into thin cold shivers. Her jaws were clenched against the compulsive chattering of her teeth.

The silence was broken—by the sound of a car's engine. At the crest of the hill. It had to be the Volvo.

Suddenly, light flooded the area.

What she saw caused a reeling in her head.

Nick Verini.

Not twenty yards away.

Standing on the ledge on the bank of the lake. Staring down at the water.

She followed his gaze. In time to see the red roof of the Ferrari disappearing, very slowly.

Andrew was again tempted to get out of the car and plunge down the hill, as he'd almost done after rolling out of the moving Ferrari, his mind blacking out with pain.

But he broke the impulse now, as he'd done then, when in the dark he'd staggered to the Volvo instead.

The car was between the two posts, its nose precariously close to the drop-off. One headlight had come on—for a split-second of panic he'd been certain they'd both been smashed in the collision—and now he could see the scene below clearly for the first time. He could even see the near bank of the lake at the foot of the hill.

Where Nick Verini was standing, his back motionless.

Like a statue, lifeless.

Holding the rifle upright in one hand.

Andrew got out of the Volvo, taking the revolver from his belt.

One bullet. Make it count.

Tracy was still down there.

He leaned against the side of the car, weak and spent, and extended the gun in his right hand. Which was unsteady, trembling. Would the shot carry that far?

He had to try.

Before he blacked out again.

Then his eye caught a movement off to the left.

Tracy was running, from the direction of the woods. Limping. But running fast. Toward Nick Verini.

Andrew tried to fix his aim again.

But if he fired and missed, the bastard'd be sure to turn— No, Tracy, no! He still has the rifle!

But he was helpless.

If he shouted and caused Verini to turn . . .

All he could do, mind protesting, was watch.

As her flying figure came closer, it bent low, and when she was within two or three yards of his back, Verini turned.

Had he heard? Sensed? Seen a shadow?

Before he could do more than lift the rifle, her shoulder plunged into his midsection. Then she rolled aside, down and into the undergrowth. His body doubling forward, Nick Verini took a few stuttering steps back before he straightened, arms outflung, and fell backward, spread-eagled, into the water.

There were two splashes which Andrew saw but could not hear: the body and, farther away from shore, the rifle.

ELEVEN

Nothing, nothing, nothing. She had nothing left.

The man behind the counter in the little bus station had been so kind. Calling her by name—imagine. *Montreal, Mrs. Durand? Well, there's one comes through at four-fifteen A.M. but it just kinda slows unless you're out on the sidewalk. Almost five hours—that's a long time to wait.* She had waited, though. Her mind was set now. She had just enough money to get to her sister's house. A few dollars to see her through. Till she could get a job. Any kind of job. It injured her pride, though. She'd always told Monique she'd never leave Pierre, no matter what.

When the nice man had closed the shutter over the window at the counter, he'd left the waiting room unlocked. *Gonna rain,* he said. *Gonna pour, then turn bitter.* And about an hour ago, the sky'd opened up. How long had it been since she'd eaten anything?

What bothered her most was not being able to say goodbye to Lynnette. But Lynnette was gone too. What Dr. Nichols had asked her to look at—another nice, gentle man—was really not her daughter. Such a lively, happy child from the day she was born, until, until . . .

Every time she heard a car on the street, her heart had twisted and the breath wouldn't come. Pierre'd be in such a state once he came back to Mrs. Wharton's Guest Home and discovered she was gone.

No telling what he might do. Hate, hate, *hate*. He still had his deer rifle, too. Just before she'd left the room, she'd fiddled with it, trying to figure out how it came apart. And scared every second, scared it would go off in her hands or he'd walk in and find her doing it. But she'd had to give up. All she'd done was hide it, or try to.

Evil. Oh, God, if You love us, why did You put so much evil in the world?

It was, she knew, sinful to think such thoughts and sinful to hate Pierre the way she did. She couldn't help herself. He'd tried to say that what had happened was *her* fault—but what could she have done? Or what was it she had *not* done? You knew what was going on and you did nothing. You stood by, Thérèse. Yes, yes, that was the thought that would haunt her all the rest of her life.

But she'd been so filled with fear. Fear that she might someday find herself just where she now was: in a strange town, without money, and alone. And soon to be dependent on Monique, who had a family of her own.

If God is all-good and all-knowing and if He really does *will* everything . . .

You dare not quarrel with God's ways. Yes, Father, yes. I understand. I accept. His mysterious ways. He is not cruel and He always has a reason and if the evil are not punished in this world, then in the next. I know now. God, please forgive.

Then, through the drumming rain she heard another sound— heavy, not more thunder, a motor, wheels on the wet pavement. She stood up in panic, glancing at the big clock over the counter—4:20. Picking up the carpetbag, she rushed to the door.

Under the shelter of the marquee, in the yellow light, she stood waiting as the two big white lights approached. She could go now, knowing. Accepting. Admitting her own worst sin of all: She should have taken Lynnette and left Baileyville and Pierre years ago. Once she confessed that and received absolution, she could then face all those years. Because some day she'd be with Lynnette again. In heaven. And Lynnette happy again, the way she used to be when she was little. Thank you, Lord, for opening my eyes.

As she stepped onto the bus, she realized that the rain had turned to a fine cold sleet that seemed to cling to her face. But the dim inside of the bus was warm, nice and warm.

*   *   *

209

"If this individual—whoever he is—if he couldn't swim, you probably killed him, Miss Larkin."

Sipping the hot chocolate that the nurse on duty in the emergency room kept bringing her, Tracy could hear sleet beating against the window. And Sheriff Wheeler's voice: "If he's dead, there'll have to be a full investigation. I've sent for the State's Attorney. Now. The rifle—was he aiming it in your direction when you committed this act?"

It was a small white-walled room and she was sitting on the examining table, huddled in a blanket, no longer shivering but not yet warm. "Not at that moment. But he'd already shot Andy. I told you that. I've told you all this over and over, Sheriff. You know that's a bullet wound Dr. Levy's treating in the next room. I heard him tell you."

Seated in the corner by a glass-doored medicine cabinet, Chief Radford said, "We realize you were in danger, Tracy."

"I've also dispatched a car to the lake," Wheeler said. "We probably won't know much till daylight. Except what you're telling us. Where'd Mr. Horgan get the revolver?"

"I gave it to him," she snapped.

"Where'd *you* get it?"

Radford said, "I gave it to her." And then, when the tall heavy man turned slowly about, to tower over him: "She'd been threatened earlier in the evening."

"Threatened? With what?"

"Look at my neck!" She was stiff now, the anger warming her. "He threatened to cut off my head!" She had not yet begun to feel the guilt that she knew had to come sooner or later. "He also threatened, not so incidentally, to rape me."

But she was speaking to the officer's back. He had not turned from Radford. "Why wasn't I told of this?" he demanded.

"Because," Kyle Radford said, rising to his feet, "because you didn't believe Nick Verini existed."

Now Sheriff Wheeler turned on her again. "You said you never saw his face."

"I haven't seen his face *yet*. But he warned me he'd kill me and he did try to kill Andy."

"I'll get to Mr. Horgan, don't worry. Warned you, you said. Warned you not to do what?"

"He warned me to stay out of this, just the way *you* did."

Her eyes were locked on his. "Whose side are you on, Sheriff?"

"I'm on the side of law and order, and that does not include civilians shooting, or trying to shoot, other civilians with weapons they got no permit to be carrying. I don't give a damn *where* they got them." He whirled to look down on Radford again. "You, Chief, could lose your goddam badge."

"I," Kyle Radford said, "could also lose my goddam temper."

"That gun saved our lives," Tracy said. "Thank you, Kyle."

Wheeler faced her again. "I still don't understand what you two were doing up there in the woods that time of night."

"I've explained it three times and I don't intend to explain it again unless Blake Arnold asks me."

"I got enough right now to arrest you and your boyfriend in there. If my men pull a body out of that lake, the charge is gonna be suspicion of murder, and Radford's witness to your confession."

"I'd do it again in the same circumstances," Tracy said flatly, and realized, God help her, that it was true.

Dr. Levy appeared in the door. A short, pudgy man, young but balding. Levy had said to the nurse after examining Andy's arm: *Tarkington, it's a bullet wound. Call the police station.* Now he looked less grave. "It pierced the upper left bicep and went through. No bone damage, no nerve severed. What we call a through-and-through gunshot wound. But he's lost a fair amount of blood. I've had to immobilize the arm temporarily. We'll keep him for an hour or so, but I'm not going to admit him. Sorry, Sheriff, no slug, but I'd judge it was from a large-caliber rifle." Then to Tracy: "He'd like to see you."

Before she could move, Sheriff Wheeler said: "Not until I've talked to him."

Tracy did move then, clutching the blanket, reaching the hall before Wheeler, stepping to the next door. She went into the small treatment room, saw Andy's pale face, saw the bandages, the container dripping blood, the tube needled into his arm. Her breath caught, and then she kissed him quickly on the lips. "You fool, oh you beautiful fool—does it hurt awfully?"

"Not anymore." His eyes were blurred, his smile weak. "I'm sort of floating."

She straightened up. "Before you float too far, what's the name of the dean from the college and where's she staying? Can you remember, darling?"

"Merrill. Ann Merrill. Colonial Motel, I think."

She placed her warm cheek against his very cool one and turned. The two uniformed men were in the door, so she said, "Be sure to tell the Sheriff the same lies I told him, Andy." She was moving to the door when she stopped, turned. "And don't ever worry me like that ever again, hear?" And when he gave her another wan smile: "The left bicep is too damned close to the heart."

She went out, the sheriff standing back to allow her to pass and Radford following her along the short corridor leading to the waiting room with the words EMERGENCY ROOM above the double swinging doors.

"Tracy," he said, "I left the gun under the seat of Savage's Volvo outside." And when she frowned, facing him, he shrugged his small shoulders. "It's loaded again. Just in case mobsters learn how to swim in basic training."

Then, without expression, he returned to the room where Wheeler was probably giving Andy a bad time, or, she hoped, vice versa.

On her way to the stairs leading up to the main floor, Tracy remembered the wild drive back to town when it had begun to rain, herself driving with as much speed as caution would allow. Only one headlight functioning, no windshield, and Andy leaning weakly against the door, eyes closed. *I keep thinking we should go back,* she had said, and Andy, in a tone of voice she had not heard before, had answered, *If the bastard's dead, the world's better off.* She'd been shocked then, but now, conscience clear, she had come to agree.

She passed a closed door marked PATHOLOGY LAB and wondered whether Lynnette Durand's body was in there somewhere and whether Dr. Nichols had made his report. She should have asked Chief Radford.

She climbed the stairs, a pain in her ankle with each step, but not sharp, no longer shooting up her leg now that Dr. Levy had bandaged it. But damn it all, she was still barefooted.

On the main floor she found Janis Tarkington at the otherwise deserted nurses' station. "You wouldn't have a Geiger counter lying around loose, would you?"

Janis—a short, competent-looking girl, very young, brownish hair and eyes—looked startled. "No. And there's none at the high school, either."

By now Tracy was grateful to anyone who didn't ask questions. "I was afraid of that. How about an old pair of shoes? Any size will do, thank you."

In the nurses' room, while Janis rummaged through her locker, Tracy asked, "You know every young stud in town, don't you?"

Janis produced a heavy turtleneck sweater, white, and tossed it to the bench. "I know every eligible stud in Eden County." She tossed a pair of gray flannel slacks to the bench. "Why?"

"You wouldn't know one who's still in high school and stutters, would you?"

"Stutters?" She was kneeling now to slide a gray jogging shoe onto Tracy's right foot, below the tight bandaging. "Only one I can think of. Track star. My kid sister used to have a crush on him." She closed the Velcro strap, firmly but with delicate care. "Bruce Southworth. His mother's librarian. Shepperton Public." She straightened. "That the one?"

"Let's hope," Tracy said, sliding her foot into the other shoe. "Where does he live?"

"Oh, maybe a mile out on the road to Sheldon Falls. I wouldn't walk on that any more than you have to." She was moving to the door. "I have to get back to the floor, Trace. So I'm not going to ask you why you were swimming on a night like this, but I hope Dr. Levy warned you about the danger of pneumonia."

"He used a needle to make his point."

Janis nodded. "There's a car coat in there, or anything else. Luck."

"Thanks, Jan!"

Tracy changed swiftly and returned to the floor below, but by elevator this time. Was she thinking straight? Why had she climbed the stairs? She went into a booth in the emergency waiting room to phone the Colonial Motel, hoping.

The switchboard answered promptly and Ann Merrill came on the line so quickly that she wondered whether everybody in town was sitting up sleepless tonight.

When she introduced herself, Ann Merrill said, "I know who you are. What can I do?"

After she told her, the older woman's deep, composed voice said, "The Physics Department has several. I'll drive the sample to Haddam and we'll get a complete analysis. But you are making an assumption, aren't you?"

"That the drums have been in there long enough for some to have rusted through? I'm full of assumptions, Miss Merrill."

"So am I. Where are you?"

"At the moment I'm on my way to the Colonial Motel."

"So that's the way it is, is it? Well, I'll be dressed. And let's hope we can prove you're right."

After replacing the phone, Tracy discovered that she felt renewed, a fresh energy through her, the excitement returning—and the urgency.

Going out through the doors with the single word AMBULANCE above them, she came face to face with Blake Arnold. He looked half awake and seemed to be in a hurry, but stopped when he recognized her in the pale light under the porte cochere. "The ubiquitous Tracy Larkin," he said. "Tracy, is that Steve Savage's Volvo parked over there? What happened to the windshield?"

"It got riddled with bullets and disintegrated." She was moving off, limping only slightly. "I'm fantasizing—ask the sheriff."

Blake's voice stopped her: "Tracy, those photographs you brought to the house—"

"I'll come see you before the hearing. Try to catch my six-thirty newscast, will you?"

The sleet was coming down, very thin, very cold. There were only three or four cars in the parking lot, including Blake Arnold's ancient Mercedes. What the devil are you looking for, Tracy—a red Ferrari? When she climbed into the Volvo with the smashed front end that Blake had not noticed, she took the revolver from under the seat and placed it beside her. Within reach. Again. By now it had almost come to seem the thing one does when one gets into a car. She glanced at the Thermos on the floor. Assumptions or not, she had seen the drums herself. Regardless of which, the sheriff had said: *Drums? That's Fish and Wildlife Department. And if there's a body, it'll come up when it's ready. We learned that yesterday, didn't we?*

214

Although she could feel it on her face, fortunately the sleet was not freezing on the pavement. Yet. She drove the Volvo around the edge of town—only a few lights in windows here and there behind the thin crystal sheets—and north on route 57.

And then she glanced into the rearview mirror.

He's dead, Tracy. You killed him.

Blake Arnold had waited until they'd come up to the main floor from the emergency room and were in the hospital administrator's office, just the two of them, before he confronted Andrew Horgan with this: "You're trying to mix oranges and apples, Mr. Horgan. What you say's in the lake, and the Durand murder—they don't connect."

"They connect, whether you or Sheriff Wheeler want to think so or not."

Blake began to pace up and down, as he often did in front of a jury box. He was a man who, since college, had rarely overindulged. But the booze plus the tension plus Valerie's strange mood—his head was throbbing with pain by now. And with confusion. "Why don't you sit down, sir? I understand you've lost a fair amount of blood."

Andrew Horgan apparently didn't hear him. "You've seen all the photographs. The truck. The license plate. The two drivers. You know how they were killed." He stepped across the office, shoulders squared, eyes red-rimmed and narrowed. "You don't think I shot *myself* tonight, do you? You think I'm carrying my arm in a sling just to get attention?"

"Oh, I'm not doubting you've been shot, or that you did a little shooting yourself. But I am suggesting that the various incidents might be unrelated—except in your mind." Then he added, "And Tracy's, of course." He stopped pacing. "Sheriff Wheeler suggested several times that you have the right to file charges. So does Tracy. Identify your assailant and I'll issue an arrest warrant myself."

Horgan turned away and sat down on the couch. "We didn't see his face."

Blake knew that was not the reason—which was why he'd felt safe in making the offer. "You don't want Verini in jail while your son's there—isn't that it, Mr. Horgan?"

"You know his name, don't you? Then you must know his connections. How many other people has he killed?"

Blake decided to let that pass. Since Tracy had dropped off the photographs, he'd learned more about Nick Verini than he really wanted to know, or admit. He shook his head. "They don't connect, Mr. Horgan. I have no proof whatever of Nick Verini's involvement in your son's case."

Now Andrew Horgan stood up. "They connect," he said, eyes grim and furious. "And so does the truck."

"Not just because your son identified Kull and Arneson. I'd identify anybody if I was in his spot, wouldn't you?"

"He described them *before* I took the pictures." His voice was a growl. "How the hell would I have known whose pictures to take? He described them on the tape that you listened to yourself!"

But Blake, troubled for a moment, decided to ignore that, too. Hazardous waste, organized crime—now Horgan and Tracy had taken up Valerie's tune. He shook his head and then recalled his conversation with Dr. Nat on the phone during the night. "It just don't wash, Mr. Horgan. Honestly, I hate to tell you this. The coroner's report states that Lynnette Durand died of manual strangulation. And she was not raped, as your son claims." He felt reluctance, genuine and hurtful, tugging at his mind. Nevertheless, he said, "She was pregnant, Mr. Horgan." Then added in a whisper: "Which gives your son a motive, as well."

"Neat. A neat package." He didn't turn away. He didn't even frown. "That's bullshit."

Instantly Blake remembered Valerie standing on the stairs in the dimness. But she had said *horseshit*. "How can you be so sure? You don't know your son that well, do you?"

"I'm sure, that's all."

"Well," Blake said, "it's enough to convince any judge to bind him over to the grand jury."

Blake had begun to admire this Andrew Horgan, but the man was like so many people today: He had to subscribe to a conspiracy theory to explain violence. Like Valerie.

Blake glanced at his watch. "We'll all be in court in a very few hours." He went to the door to make sure it was shut and that no one had come into the outer office. Had he laid the groundwork for what he'd really come up here to do? He faced Horgan across the room. "There *is* a solution." He strolled toward the stiff, waiting figure. "What if I could assure you that your son could be out of jail in about five hours?"

"If he's bound over, I suppose his attorney will ask that bond be set."

"Judge Patton is not inclined to set bail in capital cases." He moved to stand closer. "What I'm going to suggest, Mr. Horgan, is done quite frequently in criminal cases of all kinds—"

"In Nick Verini's circles it's called copping a plea, isn't it?"

"In other more respectable circles it's referred to as plea-bargaining. I didn't want to enter into this area with your son's attorney or Judge Patton till I spoke to you." Even though this was a shading of the truth, since Gerald Usher Lewis had phoned him during the night, it was not an outright lie because no final terms had been reached. "If you could convince Todd to agree to a plea of involuntary manslaughter— which would imply that he was in, say, a fit of rage and temporarily out of his senses—well, it might be possible to arrange a very light sentence."

"Such as?"

"Such as two years. Three at the most. Possibly not in prison but in the county jail. A hefty fine and five years' probation. This is not an offer, or a promise, understand."

"I understand." Andrew said. "I'm beginning to understand too damned well."

"If you mean that I'm suggesting this because the state has a weak case, you're leaping to a false conclusion."

"Am I?"

"I'm thinking of everyone concerned," Blake said, "as well as my duty to my office. We could all save ourselves a great deal of emotional stress and strain, not to mention expense to the state and you. If you don't mind my saying so, you look like hell."

Andrew turned away and went to the door. "Todd might be tempted."

"But you wouldn't—"

"Not if I knew I hadn't done it, hell no."

"Your son will have to consider the alternative. The state would have to press for first-degree homicide. That carries a life-term sentence in this state. Mandatory."

Opening the door, Andrew said, "It's up to Todd. I'm not the defendant, Mr. Arnold." He started out but stopped when Blake spoke.

"Not in *this* case," he said and waited.

"Is that a threat, Mr. Arnold?"

"Not at all. A statement of fact. If Nick Verini's body is fished out of Echo Lake today, his body or any other, and if Tracy sticks to her story, you'll be charged as an accessory."

"And she'll be charged with murder?"

"Manslaughter at least. She's admitted she pushed *someone* into the water."

"I see. But if I could persuade Todd to confess to a crime he *didn't* commit—"

"You really don't know that—"

"You've made it all very clear, Mr. Arnold. What's not clear is *your* stake in this. See you in court, you bastard!" He slammed the door so hard that Blake waited a second to see whether the glass in the upper half would shatter.

Blake stood there then, recalling Clifford Hyatt's phone call last night, fighting doubts. Was it possible that there actually was some larger, more malign conspiracy which he was ignoring, or refusing to recognize? Head swelling, the ache coming and going in waves, he went out of the administrator's office and down the corridor to Grace Hubbard's.

For as long as Blake could remember, Grace Hubbard had been head nurse and general supervisor of Shepperton Hospital. And she always came in before six. When Blake inquired whether the medical examiner's report on the autopsy of Lynnette Durand had gone over to his office, the woman shook her crown of almost-white hair and said in a puzzled tone: "Dr. Nichols did turn in his report late last night. Nurse Tremont saw it on my desk. But then the doctor came back several hours later—he often comes in in the middle of the night—and took the report, went up to visit with his wife, and left the building again, only about an hour ago. I saw him driving away as I came in." Her eyes clouded with compassion. "The man has so much on his mind. Shall I telephone him at home? I don't know when the poor man sleeps."

"No, Miss Hubbard," Blake said. "I spoke with him. I know the gist of it. If Judge Patton wants it in hand, I'll phone Dr. Nichols myself. But it may not be necessary now. Thank you."

"Good luck, Mr. Arnold."

Luck. Luck was with him today.

He went outside to his gray ten-year-old Mercedes, Andrew Horgan's question still quivering in his mind. His stake was high, very high. And he was going to protect it—for Valerie's sake. And in spite of Valerie, too.

The sleet was no longer coming down. But it was cold and the interior of the car was so chilled that he turned on the heater even before he switched on the headlights. Cold and dark. Winter had arrived.

He'd made his own coffee without waking her, but Valerie had come into the kitchen in her robe, so he'd told her about the pregnancy. And she'd said: *Two years in prison and a criminal record, all his rights taken away, never able to vote, maybe not even get a job. Her being pregnant doesn't mean he's guilty.*

And you can't assume he's innocent—

Why not? Don't they make you read the Constitution in law school?

Oh, Val, he's guilty as hell!

Then why let him get away with only two years, for murder? Is that justice?

I'm only doing my job.

Can you say it in German?

For the first time in ten years, Blake had gone to work without kissing her goodbye. He'd been miserable all the way to the hospital.

What he had carefully refrained from telling her was that he'd received a telephone call from Gerald Usher Lewis during the night.

To what do I owe the honor, Mr. Lewis?

Curious about the medical examiner's verdict, that's all.

It's all on my side.

If so, I'm willing to talk. Are you in any condition to do so?

Voluntary manslaughter, first degree. Five years, no parole—

I'd be willing to talk to my client on the basis of involuntary, second degree, two years maximum.

Judge Patton would never go for that.

I've just spoken with Judge Patton. He's amenable.

I'll think about it, Mr. Lewis. We'll talk in the morning. You see, I don't want a public outcry. Rich college boy, actress mother, famous defense attorney, all outsiders. I live here, Mr. Lewis. You don't.

Thank God! Well, let's get it sewed up before the hearing

so I'll know how my client should plead. And so I can get the hell out of here.

The green was quiet as usual, but as Blake drove toward the courthouse, he became aware of a few people gathered on the steps, waiting at six to make sure they had seats for the hearing at ten. Murder—why does it have such a universal, morbid fascination? Even Valerie had become personally involved, as she never had before. *This time you're playing your legal games when it's human life at stake. All we really have is time, and if you take any of that away from a human being, any part of it, you damn well better know what you're doing. And that you're right!*

He parked behind the courthouse in one of the RESERVED slots and went inside, tempted, for some reason he didn't want to explain, to stop in the jail to talk with Todd Horgan. Instead, he went into the rotunda, which was dim and deserted and cavernous, and up the marble steps, his footsteps echoing eerily in the emptiness. Approaching the door of his office, which was at the front of the building overlooking the green, he heard a phone shrilling, so he let himself into the outer office, turned on the light, and answered the phone on his secretary's desk.

"Blake? Jared Patton."

"Yes, Judge? I just came in."

"Your wife said you'd be there. Thought maybe I'd hear from you by now . . ." He didn't finish; it was the judge's way of asking a question.

Picturing Jared Patton in his home in Montpelier—sixty-two or -three, with bull-like shoulders, thick-fleshed ruddy face, eyes that could cajole mildly or flame with judicious wrath, voice that could purr, as now, or boom with authority— Blake said, "I knew you'd be here in time to talk before ten, Judge. You always are."

"Ay-uh, well, I like to mull things over while I drive. What've I got ahead of me up there?"

"Well, sir, the defendant's attorney and I have discussed the possibility of a confession—"

"Always better if things can be settled without a trial. Save taxpayers' money. Saves wear-and-tear on all concerned. Will the defense go along?"

And then, before he answered, Blake remembered: *I've just*

spoken with Judge Patton. He's amenable. "Mr. Lewis will try to convince the defendant," he said, puzzled.

"What about the coroner's findings? Consistent with such a disposal?"

Blake did not hesitate: "I spoke with Dr. Nichols personally."

"I'll approve it if it's reasonable. You and Mr. Lewis put your heads together. Come up with something we can all live with. Civilized people can always reach accord in a civilized society. What's the rest of the docket?"

"Not much. The usual. Todd Horgan's the only one in jail, I think."

"Splendid, splendid. I can be back here in time for lunch. Can't drive fast, this weather. See you in chambers."

Blake replaced the phone and went into his inner office. He did not turn on the light. He sat down in the leather chair behind his desk, surrounded in the dimness by the shelves of books: jurisprudence, theory and case histories, court decisions, precedents. . . .

Why hadn't Judge Patton mentioned that he'd already spoken with Gerald Usher Lewis? And why had he done so?

Of a sudden then, rather than deal with the questions fermenting sourly in his mind, he considered returning home. He was never more wretched than at those times, blessedly few, when there was tension or discord between himself and Valerie. Unable to have children, they had come to value each other all the more.

He took up the phone and dialed his home number. Hearing the buzzing at the other end of the line, he pictured the small, neat, undistinguished house in his mind. And then he thought of houses he'd seen in Washington—the muted elegance of Georgetown, the modern facade of the luxurious Watergate complex, where so many congressmen and senators lived.

"Blake Arnold's residence. Attorney-at-law—"

"Val?" It didn't sound like her voice. "Valerie?"

"Present and accounted for, Mr. Arnold. Hear ye, hear ye, hear ye—"

"Val, what the hell's going on?"

"*You* drank last night, didn't you? Well, your loving and devoted wife is drinking this morning. In celebration of eyes

221

opening, in celebration of the blind seeing, like Lazarus—or *was* that Lazarus?''

"Jesus Christ," he said.

"Don't call for help, Mr. Arnold. God died in the 1960's, remember?"

"Val . . ." He was tempted to say, *Honey, I'm coming home. I need you. Take off your clothes and meet me at the door.* After a few drinks, she was always more relaxed, more passionate. But instead, he said, "I only called to say everything is working out."

"I'm so glad! Mr. Clifford Hyatt will be so glad, too, won't he?"

After a few drinks she could also be impossible. "I told you: I'm doing this for you. And I'm doing what's right, so lay off, *please*!"

"Organized crime," Valerie's voice said.

"What? Oh, Val, don't start that again."

"I told you I'm seeing things clear. I mean clearly." She giggled. "More I think about it, more convinced I am."

"Perhaps," he heard himself say, furious now, "perhaps *you* should have been the lawyer in the family."

"I have too much self-respect," Valerie said.

Click. And he was holding a humming telephone.

It came over him then that, when it comes to the so-called truth, he had spent his entire adult life skating on thin ice.

In his mind he pictured the face in the photographs Tracy Larkin had brought to the house. He was thinking of the printout that Radford had read to him on the phone in the middle of the night.

Dominick (Nick) Verini—*he* was the new element. Dead *or* alive.

If Vincent Verini's son was dead, he'd hate to be in Andrew Horgan's shoes. Or Tracy Larkin's.

But also, if he was dead, he couldn't get in the way of the Todd Horgan case.

Mattie Stoddard heard the knock first. On the front door.

The kitchen was in the rear of the old saltbox house on the edge of the highway, so she had to pass from the warm kitchen through the small chilled parlor to see who was coming to the door this time of morning, not yet six-thirty, and on such a day. She heard Jason's voice from upstairs: "If

that's Jotham Gow, tell him to set and warm up and I'll drive
him into town soon's we have breakfast.''

"Get shaved, Jason," she called up the steep narrow stairs
in the tiny entry. She pulled the flannel robe tighter and was
about to unlock the solid door when she hesitated. She pushed
at her light-brown hair and smoothed it back—not because
Jotham Gow was younger than Jason, younger by more than
thirty years, more her age really, and not because he was a
man, but because she never liked to look all blowsy and
slovenly around the neighbors; they talked enough about Jason and his wife young enough to be his daughter, enough
and plenty.

She turned the key and opened the door a crack. The man
who stood on the tiny stoop, with the water dripping off the
roof behind him, wasn't Jotham Gow after all. At first she
was sorry she'd been so quick to act, but then she saw the
way he was shivering, and how miserable his brown eyes
looked, sort of lost and pleading, so she said, "Yes?"

"Car broke down," the man said. He was young, even
handsome in a kind of dark, foreign way, with a neat black
beard, and he spoke with a city accent: "Could I use your
telephone, please, and get some mechanic to . . ." His small
body was shuddering all over and his jaw was jumping up and
down. Why, he looked like he'd go into a spasm or something, hypothermia maybe, and he was soaking wet, all his
clothes. No hat on his head. Black hair dripping. But, peculiar: It hadn't rained for hours and even the sleet had stopped
rustling on the slanting lean-to kind of roof before she'd
rolled out. "I saw the smoke coming from your chimney, so I
knew you were up. . . ."

She hadn't heard Jason coming down but now his voice
spoke from behind: "Mattie, poor man'll catch his death out
there. Where're your manners?"

She stepped away, returning through the parlor to the
kitchen. Let him handle it, way he always handled everything, not meaning to but making her feel like a child, or a
servant, instead of his wife.

"Come on in, mister. And let's close this door. You look
like you been skinned. Kitchen's warmer. Always is. Phone's
back there, too."

She could see their reflections in the dark window over the
electric range as they came in behind her: about the same

223

size, Jason a tad taller maybe, but his hair was gray and short; the other man's was long—thick and black as a crow's wing and matted wet to his skull. She saw Jason step to the hearth and stir the wood fire. One thing she loved most about this old house: central chimney with fireplaces on two sides and on the back, too, in the kitchen.

"My name's Stoddard. Sit down. And this pretty thing is my wife, Mattie." She didn't turn from the sizzling skillet. Pretty? She knew she wasn't pretty, just plain, all those freckles. But if Jason thought so, that's all that mattered. "I don't think I got your name?"

"Enright," the stranger said. "Excuse me. I'm so cold I can hardly talk. My name's Joshua Enright." He was standing with his back to the fire, shivering so hard she could hear his teeth chatter. She didn't speak, just broke three more eggs and added several strips of bacon to the pan.

"Soon as I can talk, I'd like to use your phone there. Call my old . . . call my father."

His father. He'd said his car had broken down. Joshua Enright: didn't sound like a city name. Maybe his father lived nearby—city people buying up houses everywhere these days.

"Anybody else home?"

Now what kind of question was that? Mind your manners, mister. Mind your own beeswax.

"Just the two of us," Jason said. "We like it that way, don't we, Mattie?"

Well, yes, she liked it. Jason's first wife, Bethany, had never had children, so she'd accommodated herself to the fact that probably she never would, either. But she was content this past year—most content she'd ever been in her whole twenty-nine years. She turned, skillet in hand, and saw a puddle around the man's feet on the old oak floor that Jason had worked so hard restoring. He was wearing cowboy boots, pointed toes and high heels—ay-uh, he was definitely from away. But you had to feel sorry for him. He looked like a long-haired black cat that'd been left out in the rain. "You'll catch pneumonia for sure," she said, sliding the eggs and bacon onto a plate.

"Sure enough," Jason said, standing at the trestle table and pouring coffee. "Here, this'll warm you up. Mattie makes the best coffee in Vermont."

The stranger took a sip and said, "Black piss."

224

At first she was angry, but then a kind of shudder went down her body. She saw Jason frowning, and then heard the man's odd city accent when he asked, "You got a gun in the house?"

"No gun," Jason said, a kind of whisper. And his face had changed, too. "We don't believe in guns."

"Me neither," the man said and took one out of the pocket of his wet blazer.

All she could do, skillet in hand, was stare at it: not a revolver, an automatic, small, blue-black, which he held loose and easy, pointing to the floor. She thought, but only for a split second: What if I threw this grease in his face? But she couldn't move a muscle.

"Soon as I make my call," he said speaking to both of them, not an expression on his face, just his eyes darting from one to the other and his voice low and pleasant: "Soon as I make connections, I'll split. Nobody gets hurt, capeesh?"

It was a word she didn't know. Her mind, working fast, reached for it. She'd had to learn Latin once—could be Italian.

"We understand," she heard Jason say, nodding his head, so she did likewise.

Seeing Jason's face was worst of all, his dear face, lined and lean, so mad, so scared—why, he'd begun to look *old*. She couldn't bear to look at it. She turned away, to place the skillet on the coils again.

"So," the stranger said—whatever his name was, it wasn't Enright—"so, missus, you flip on that little TV on the windowsill. Local news-slut comes on six-thirty. You get the channel. Don't turn on the sound till the redhead comes on."

"Better do it, Matt," Jason said. And while she did, recalling Jason coming home late last evening, saying something about some college girl drowning, body found floating, Jason went on: "I got the weather on the radio upstairs." She'd never heard his voice sound like this before, and when she turned, his eyes looked banked down, fierce. "Snow's predicted."

"Fuck the weather. I want the news." And then: "You're right on target, missus." His voice sounded more alive now, even excited. "I am gonna get pneumonia, stay in these clothes. Old man, haul your ass upstairs and get me some dry ones. And heavy. Boots, too. Me and the missus, we'll sit down here and eat. I'm sick I'm so hungry.''

Jason, silent, was about to go up the rear stair alongside the door to the borning room, her sewing room now, when the man moved, quick as some little animal, across the narrow kitchen to stand beside her. She could smell the wetness, dank, nauseating. ''And don't get no ideas, old man. You climb out the window, try coming down the front stairs, some wise-ass thing, like trying to get away in that Mustang out back—the missus gets a slug right through the back of her neck, comes out her forehead.''

All Jason said, one foot on the bottom step, eyes avoiding hers, was: ''I'm too old to climb out windows.''

''Or come down with a gun, blasting. She gets it first.''

Then Jason did look at her, and what she saw in his face caused her heart to stop dead: a doubt, a different kind of doubt, or fear. ''Go on, Jason, do what he says. If he touches me, I'll make him use that gun. No man's ever gonna touch me but you.''

Jason nodded once, and turned to climb the stair.

Now she was alone with him. He sat down and placed the gun on the table alongside his plate and then he started to eat, ignoring her.

He ate like a pig. He moved like a weasel, or a fox, but he ate like a pig.

And he kept the gun in his hand.

TWELVE

"Good God, Tracy, the way this is written, it implies organized crime's behind Lynnette Durand's death."

Steve Savage looked up from the typescript on his desk, his eyes baffled and accusing. So, trying to keep the irony out of her voice, she said, "I used the word *allegedly. Ad nauseam.*"

He stood up and ran a hand through his thick brown hair. "If Nick Verini's registered at the Alpine Chalet under the name of Joshua Enright, why aren't the police doing something about it?"

"Why aren't the police everywhere doing something about organized crime? That's what I'd like to ask on the air."

"Well, you're not going to." He was shaking his head. He glanced at his watch. "Before this goes on the teleprompter, I'll revise and take out the *if*'s and *maybe*'s." He sat down at the typewriter on its stand alongside his desk. "You knock out your commentary. Chop-chop. I'll want to read that, too, right?"

"You *are* the boss, Mr. Savage," Tracy said, looking at Steve's back. Night before last, she'd slept with him and they'd had sex together. Now he was a stranger, a hateful stranger who had been titillated last night by the thought of her being raped.

Her fury intensified until the thin wire mark around her throat began to throb. "I'll ad-lib the commentary," she heard her voice say—or was it her voice?

"I can't allow that," he said, typing now. "I'm sorry but I can't afford to be sued. Right?"

227

"The mob doesn't sue," she said.

"No, they do worse."

"Tell me about it. Then take a look at my neck."

"I've been looking at you ever since you came in." He turned. "You ought to wear a sweater like that more often. And no bra."

He had been looking, true, but at that part of her that had given *him* satisfaction. He had not even glimpsed her emotional state, or the intensification of it now. So much for that kind of love.

"At least let me say what I have to say in the commentary."

"Not today, Trace. Sorry."

"Todd Horgan's freedom may be at stake. And much more—"

"That's the rub of it, isn't it? *His* son, his son's freedom." He frowned, puzzled. "You only met the guy yesterday."

Twenty-four hours. Yesterday morning seemed a lifetime away and she felt she'd known Andy all her life. "Steve," she said, "I know you're hurt. And angry. I know I walked out on you last night for reasons you don't understand. And I'm sorry about the Volvo—*and* the van. But listen: This is our chance, *your* chance, to use the power of the media to do something real and decent. You can't let something personal between us suppress the news."

"Our job's just to tell it like it is. I can't let you do it, Trace, and that's that." He took the paper out of the typewriter and began to cross out lines with a felt-tip pen. "I've got my reasons."

And then she knew. "What did they threaten, Steve?"

"Threaten? Nobody threatened me."

"They got to you some way!"

"They? Trace, you got an obsession. *They*—that's dangerous thinking."

"Downright paranoid, isn't it? If not threats, what?" She took a step. "If you're not scared, what, Steve?"

His eyes met hers, accepting the challenge. "I'll tell you, Trace. You know what a burden the station's been. Staggering along, nickel-and-dime profit after the salaries. Maybe it's too much for me, I don't know. You know how much I've wanted to unload it."

She'd been wrong. Not threatened—bribed. "How much did they offer?"

"Not *they*. Not what you think. Thurlow MacKenzie—his syndicate owns papers and radio, TV stations all over New England. He's a respectable, politically important entrepreneur—"

"How much?"

Steve's face changed. An incredulous brightness came into his boyish eyes. "You won't believe this, Trace. Two million. A cool two million dollars."

She nodded. "A cool two million to cool it—"

"No, not to cool it!" he said irascibly. "CBS picked up your commentary yesterday. Ran it on the late news last night, and again this morning. Shepperton's big news all over the country. That's what brought the station to their attention. Thurlow MacKenzie himself called me!"

"In the middle of the night," she said. "Strange time for a two-million dollar business conference, isn't it?" And then she was shouting: "Didn't Thurlow MacKenzie give you the terms? He at least suggested you soft-pedal the conspiracy angle. I may be tired, I may be sick inside, but I'm not *stupid*. What was the deal, damn you?"

Steve tilted back in the chair. His face looked both miserable and triumphant. "The deal was that I keep you off the air this morning. He suggested I fire you. I told him I couldn't do that. You see, Trace, I'm not the microbe you think I am, right?"

"You're not a lot of things I imagined you were, that's true. But I never thought of you as a microbe. Till now."

He straightened and his eyes clouded. His hands became two fists on the desk top. "All right, Tracy—you're fired. As of now."

"I'm leaving for Cape Cod after the hearing anyway." Where the words came from, she did not know. Had she spoken them? "I haven't been invited yet," she said, "but I'm going." She moved so close that she could feel the edge of the desk through the slacks Janis had loaned her. "Meanwhile, who's going to do the broadcast? It's too late to get anyone else." She snatched up the typescript from the desk. "I'll read this just as I wrote it. Or maybe *you'd* like to try it."

"You know damned well being in front of a camera scares the shit out of me." And then he warned: "Don't get rough, Tracy."

"I'll get rougher. You and I have a contract. I'm not indisposed except for a very painful ankle and I'm prepared to appear and do my job. When I sue for breach of contract, I'll name Thurlow MacKenzie as co-defendant. He should appreciate that even if you two haven't made a formal deal."

Then, without moving, she waited. Not breathing.

Steve's face curled into a vacant smile. "You're a tough little bitch, aren't you?" He sighed and heaved himself to his feet, towering over her. "All right, but fair warning: If you get too far out of line, I'll cut you off the air and go to the canned commercials. Right?"

"You have that power. Power of the press, they call it. If you own it, you're free to print or broadcast anything you want. So much for freedom of the press, right? Right, you sonofabitch, *right*?"

"Because, for reasons beyond my control, I may not have time to finish my commentary later, the weather forecast, with which I usually sign off, calls for snow. Temperature dipping well below freezing by evening with a blizzard possible tonight. Now a few words from our sponsor . . ."

Judge Jared Patton was watching the screen of the small television set behind the counter while he had breakfast in the roadside restaurant that he favored on the way to Shepperton. He'd finished his second cup of coffee, but now he couldn't leave without hearing what the red-haired girl with the intense blue eyes called her commentary.

She'd already revealed more than he'd anticipated, more than he'd expected to get into, or could get into, in a preliminary hearing. And one helluva lot more than the State's Attorney Blake Arnold had told him on the phone. Puzzling, disturbing in a way. Until now, all he'd been looking forward to was seeing Julia Craven in the flesh. He'd always had a certain lustful admiration for that flesh. . . .

The girl's face filled the screen again: "Since this will be my last telecast for Channel Seven, I'd like to say goodbye to Shepperton in a special way. Now that you know some of what has happened here in your town in the last two nights while you slept and during yesterday while you went about your ordinary business—things that could happen in any town in America today—I want to ask all of you: What are you going to do about it? Every president who's ever elected

promises a war on organized crime—and four years later
nothing has happened. How can we call ourselves a civilized
society, and a model for the world if . . .''

The girl was long on passion and outrage but short on
details and proof. Youthful idealism, unrealistic—like his
daughter Amanda, who finished law school and now was
wasting her life practicing what she called consumer advo-
cacy and environmental law.

" . . . Are you going to go on allowing your government
to spend billions of dollars fighting enemies abroad and terrorism thousands of miles away, instead of using some of that
money at least—it's your money, remember—fighting the
terrorism of organized crime at home?"

Where had he heard that litany before? More than idealistic—
dangerous! Judge Patton drained his cup and dug a five-dollar
bill out of his pocket.

" . . . If your government is not fighting crime, isn't it
then condoning it?"

Take it easy, little lady. No one *condones* crime.

" . . . Now, in the time I have left, J'accuse, as Emile Zola
said. I accuse myself—and you, all of you—of being too
selfish and too blind, too self-satisfied and complacent to see,
to see and care!"

The judge placed the bill on the counter and stepped to the
door, but paused there before opening it. Young fools irked
him: they had no idea what the real world—

" . . . I accuse business, which places profits and greed
above decency. And I accuse the legal profession for collusion with crime and with criminals . . .''

Little lady, you're going too far, too damned far now.

" . . . I accuse my government of talking pious talk and
doing less than nothing, tacitly approving this collusion between the underworld and—''

The screen went blank. And after a brief second:

TECHNICAL DIFFICULTIES
PLEASE STAND BY

Judge Patton went out and lifted his tall, heavy body into
his car. Almost light now. No color in the east, but a pale-
gray glow. The sky overhead was dark, and very low. Well,
the girl was right in one respect: her weather prediction.

He started the motor. Why did they let children like that have a TV screen and a microphone? Subversive nonsense. Driving, he felt his anger take over. He'd heard enough of that radical foolishness when Amanda had moved to Washington, D.C. *Sorry, Daddy, but someone has to represent the people who can't afford two hundred dollars an hour. I'll never get rich, will I? Pro bono publico—that means for the public good. Is that un-American, too?*

As he turned on the heat, he recalled Gerald Usher Lewis's phone call last night. Most unusual. But then the man had a reputation for doing the unorthodox. He'd gone along with the defense lawyer's suggestion that he consider a plea bargain. All he could assume was that the attorney had learned his client was guilty—or at least that he stood a fair chance of being convicted. No man like Gerald Usher Lewis wants to lose a case, especially one on which national attention has already been focused. And when he'd told Mr. Lewis on the phone—and, later, the prosecuting attorney—that he'd entertain the idea of such a deal if the facts seemed to warrant, he'd been thinking of it as just another college murder. Fit of rage, sexual jealousy, maybe adolescent passion. *Crime passionel.* Well, he'd never comprehended such crimes—couldn't even imagine such an intensity of emotion—but there were times when society was better served by compromise. Young hotbloods like that girl on TV—and Amanda—couldn't comprehend that, but it was the way society functioned.

But . . . but perhaps there *was* more going on than he'd suspected. Not that he gave any credence to the nonsense that the red-headed girl was spouting. Attempted rape, attempted murder, gunfire up in the mountains, underworld figures taking over a town, reign of terror—hysterical bullshit. He wanted to keep an open mind, that was his judicial duty, but that girl hadn't done Todd Horgan's case one iota of good by her sensational prattle!

When Tracy left the station, Andy was not waiting. What had she expected? And it was beginning to snow.

She was damned if she was going to go back inside!

Tracy, do we have to break up on a bitter note? You did what you thought was right and I did what I thought was right, right?

She hadn't said *right* then. She'd said: *Steve, I hope you'll be the happiest millionaire alive.*

So now she placed the carton with the odds and ends of personal possessions she'd gathered from her desk on the front seat and then climbed into Steve's Volvo and drove down the hill. The gravel road and the distant hills had begun to whiten, faintly, and the soft light snow continued to drift down.

The anger was still in her, hot and hard. Had she said anything on the air to stir anyone, enrage anyone, shake one person out of the lethargy of habit and comfort and indifference? Probably not. As Chief Radford had said, the truth had been revealed thousands of times before. In the movies, books, on TV . . .

She drove into town and directly to the Cottages on the Green. Her green MG was nowhere in sight. She parked anyway and went into the motel office.

Mrs. Stillwell, who somehow managed to keep a mental logbook on every guest, said: "He didn't leave a message, Tracy, but he come right after your broadcast and drove off in your little car."

"How'd he look?"

"Well, I couldn't say as to that. Must be in terrible pain, though. Imagine—right here in Franklin Forest. You didn't get much sleep yourself, did you?"

Not a word about the questions she'd asked in her commentary. Not a word.

Back in the car, driving toward the courthouse, Tracy glanced into the rearview mirror. No car was following along the green. Perish the thought. Nothing like that ever happens in sleepy little old Shepperton. Or environs. This is a *nice* town. Ask anyone.

She touched the pocket of Janis's waterproof but thin car coat—the gun within reach.

She parked behind the building and went in the rear door and through the rotunda to the jail area. She had promised to come to Blake Arnold's office, but she hadn't yet talked with someone named Bruce Southworth—still time for that before he left for school—and it was too early to have a report from Ann Merrill in Haddam.

"Mr. Horgan?" Holly Ray said. "No, he didn't come in,

233

Tracy, but he phoned. Wanted to see his son again. Against regulations. Anything else?"

"The medical examiner's report on Lynnette Durand?"

"It hasn't come over from the hospital yet."

"Anything from Echo Lake?"

Holly Ray's head turned to both sides before she lowered her voice: "Sheriff Wheeler phoned in to ask for a wrecker. Seems they found a car in the lake. Red. How could that be?"

"Accidents happen," Tracy said. "They didn't find a body, did they?"

"Another one? Not that I know of."

"Well," Tracy said, "you can't have everything."

She then drove to the hospital, which had come to life since she'd left it less than two hours ago.

She went directly to Grace Hubbard's office and inquired: "Why hasn't the Lynnette Durand report gone to the police station?"

"That's easy," Grace Hubbard said from behind her desk—no smile this morning, no pleasant reassuring manner. "We don't have it yet. Mr. Arnold's office has been asking, too. And Mr. Horgan—"

"When?"

"Only a few minutes ago. He just left." And then she frowned. "Tracy, your face. You look absolutely shocked."

"That's not shock, Miss Hubbard." Her voice sounded oddly strangled in her ear and she realized that, just for a second, she may have stopped breathing. "Don't you recognize relief when you see it?"

"This morning, I swear I wouldn't recognize a tropical hurricane if it went right through the whole state of Vermont."

"Did Mr. Horgan seem to be in pain?"

"He did and why not? I told him not to forget to take the analgesic. Those injections Dr. Levy ordered wear off." She was shuffling papers when she went on: "Mr. Horgan asked directions to Dr. Nichols' home. I gave them to him before I was thinking straight. I shouldn't have done it. But I warned him that Dr. Nichols should not be disturbed for any reason whatsoever."

"Mr. Horgan's thinking of his son, Miss Hubbard."

"And Dr. Nat's thinking of his wife." Her tone had sharpened. "If the poor man wants to be alone with his grief, he has that right.'' Grace Hubbard saw the inquiring look on Tracy's face and her tone softened. "Mrs. Nichols expired early this morning. God's mercy if ever I saw it.'' And then, sitting back in her chair, one hand reaching to fix her white cap more securely on her white hair: "One human life. One in so many millions. Yet . . . even knowing it was coming and all, whole hospital's in a state of mourning. We see death all the time, but one human life demands so much respect. Remarkable, isn't it?''

"Yes'' was all Tracy managed to say, turning away. Remarkable, yes. And as she ran, limping, to the car through the lightly falling snow: Most of us respect it, but there are those few, those savage few, who can take a human life as easily as they take a deep breath.

The town now seemed fully awake, cars moving and yellow school buses leaving black tracks in the thin cover of snow. She was fighting a cold persistent fear: for herself, for Andy, for the town, possibly for the world. . . .

No one was following, though. Not yet anyway.

On the old Brookfield Road to Steve's house, she remembered traveling here last evening in the van, the voice in her ear: *Don't slow down. Don't touch the horn. Try to turn your head, it comes off in your lap, capeesh?*

By the time she pulled into the circular driveway, she was shivering, but not from cold. Steve's house—it had always been Steve's house. But there was no regret in her, none, as she went up the steps onto the gray veranda and let herself in. It was, she knew, the end of something. But possibly—although not necessarily—it was also the beginning of something else.

In the spacious center hall, which was warm, she looked into the parlor. She'd take only as many of her books and records as one suitcase would carry; then she'd go upstairs and pack her clothes. But quickly, because she still had to drive out the road toward Sheldon Falls to Bruce Southworth's house.

The telephone shrilled.

She was about to grab it up from the hall table when she hesitated. What if, what if. . . .

But it *could* be Andy. So she lifted it and whispered a cautious "Hello?''

"Miss Larkin?'' A woman's voice, low, incisive. "Miss Larkin, it's Ann Merrill. In Haddam.''

"Yes, Miss Merrill. Yes, this is Tracy Larkin."

"I'm dreadfully afraid I have bad news for you—"

"Yes? Yes?"

"The water sample's not radioactive. Or otherwise contaminated. Not enough time for the drums to rust through, probably. Or . . . that one load was dumped in there when it was intended for someplace else. But probably somewhere in the area. With all the asbestos mines and abandoned quarries around there, why would they take a chance on a lake in the state forest? My theory is that they were in there for some other reason. . . ."

"Maybe," Tracy heard her empty voice say, "maybe those two decided to go hunting out of season. . . ."

"Whatever. But I have three angry young scientists here, with diving gear, who are more than willing to bring up a drum. If you say so?"

"I say so." Her voice was not empty. "The sooner the better!"

During the long sleepless night on the couch in the living room, Harry Lucas had not been thinking of Bruce. Or even of himself, although he knew his whole life had changed overnight.

He'd been thinking of his daughter, Cindy, who was now playing on the rear lawn in the falling snow. Dressed in the gray sweat suit that he wore most of the time at school, and waiting for the coffee to come to a boil, Harry was watching Cindy through the kitchen window, and his mind was aching with a pain so terrible that it had become almost physical, almost unendurable.

What had she heard during the night, how *much* had she heard, and what had her five-year-old mind made of it?

Get out of my bed! Lesley had screeched. *Get away from me, you lying pervert!*

And then, when he'd gone to the living room, she'd followed. *Look at you—forty-one years old, strong as an ox, macho, macho, macho, and you can't get it up!* He'd never heard Lesley use a phrase like that; locker-room garbage, she'd always called it. She was wearing a long flowered robe, and in the half-light from outside, she looked wild and disheveled. *When I think of how I've felt sorry for you, tried to help. Lies, lies, lies! I know the truth now, I know, damn you, goddam you, I know the truth!* A woman transformed, not his chirping little tight-lipped wife at all. A fury out of some awful Greek play he'd seen once in college. *I thought it was my fault, that I didn't know the right things to do!* She had prowled around the room like a caged wild animal. *If you knew the times I've ached to pick up some man, any man. I thought you didn't want me. I blamed myself!* Then she'd swiped her hand along the mantel, his trophies and cups clattering to the floor. *Macho, macho, macho—shit!* When he'd tried to calm her, she'd screamed: *I know now. I know it all! I was testing you tonight. That's why I tried to seduce you!* Her voice was shrill and unreal: *Look at me, Lucas.* She turned on a lamp. *Look at my body!* And she'd thrown off the robe, hurling it to the sofa, standing frail and naked in the light. *You don't want me, do you? You never wanted me!* Which was not true, but before he could protest, she came close, rushing, and her thin arms locked around his neck, her mouth clamped on his, and then her small sharp teeth bit his lip, digging in. He tasted blood and then she was beating his chest with her fists, face contorted and ugly and close, and then she was hitting him on the face, with her fists, swinging wide, first one side, then the other. He hadn't moved, the blows continuing, harder and faster, until she'd spent herself, head going down, pale hair falling. *I'm going to tell my father.* Voice low then, suddenly forlorn and hopeless. *He'll know what to do.*

Then she had gone, leaving the robe, and in a few minutes he'd heard water running into the tub.

Her father. Roger English—First Selectman, banker, leading citizen, chairman of the school board. Harry was looking out the window again: Cindy was running in circles now, head tilted back, trying to catch the falling snow in her mouth. Yes, Roger English would not only know what to do, he'd do it. With pleasure.

He heard a step in the hall, and in a moment, Lesley appeared in the kitchen door. By now, this many hours later, Harry was so filled with pity and tenderness—and yes, love—that he could only stare at her. She wore a gray flannel skirt and frilly blouse now, and when he saw her face—thin and pale and fixed, eyes cold—he knew there was nothing, nothing in the world, that he could say.

"Sit down, Lucas." Her tone was cool, controlled—no sharpness, no hostility. "Sit down so we can talk." Then she corrected herself as she took the chair at the other end of the kitchen table: "So *I* can talk. I want to tell you the way it's going to be." It was as if she had been transformed again—no hysteria, no emotion whatever. "You will go on with your job. When you travel with the teams, I'll go along. When we stay overnight, the team will stay in one motel; we'll stay in another. A room with twin beds." She allowed thirty seconds to pass. "Every day, when practice is over after school, you'll come straight home. No beers or Cokes at Colby's with the students. And when we go out socially, no wandering out to the kitchen with the men. You will stay by my side." She paused again. Her eyes were on his now; they appeared cold and empty. "I'll never tell a soul, and neither will you."

When she waited then, he said, "I'm your prisoner—is that it, Lesley?" And when her delicate shoulders shrugged: "You're going to punish me for the rest of my life—"

"If you don't think that's what you deserve, I feel even more sorry for you."

"Suppose I can't accept what you've just said?"

"Then I shall get a divorce, publicly telling the absolute truth as to why. You will never see Cindy again, and if you apply for coaching or teaching anywhere else, wherever it is, you will not get the job."

"My God," he heard himself say under his breath.

And then the telephone rang. Before he could stand, Lesley had moved to the hall and he could hear her voice: "This is the Lesley Lucas residence. . . . No, I can't hear you. Please don't whisper. . . . Yes, *Brucie*, he's here but he can't come to the phone. . . . No, we haven't heard the news on television this morning, but I'll tell him. And I have a message for you. You will never call this number again. You will resign from the track team for reasons of ill health. And you will forget what you told me about what happened on route 57. You will never again mention it to anyone on earth . . . Brucie—may I call you Brucie, too?—if you do feel obliged to tell anyone, anyone at all, you will be expelled from school on grounds of moral turpitude, and your mother as well as everyone in town will know exactly and precisely why. You will not receive a scholarship because you will not graduate. Don't phone here, ever again. I don't want perverts calling my home."

In the few seconds it took her to return, Harry Lucas made

up his mind. He was standing when she resumed her seat, a tiny smile along her lips.

"Lesley," Harry said, "I know I've behaved terribly. You see, at first I couldn't admit the truth to myself and then I couldn't admit it to you. And I'm miserable as hell because I failed to spare you what you're going through now. None of this is your fault. But I didn't choose to be the way I am, whether you understand that or not. I'm going upstairs to pack now and then I'm going to say goodbye to Cindy." He felt tears scalding in his eyes and he had to struggle to control the havoc inside. "I don't know where I'm going, Lesley, but I'll let you know."

"Wherever you go, you're going to be sorry."

"All my life, Lesley. But I'm not going to be punished forever."

In the early hours of the morning, this same man, whose picture you have just seen, shot and wounded Andrew Horgan at Echo Lake in the Franklin State Forest. Mr. Horgan is the father of Todd Horgan, who is being held in the Shepperton Jail as a suspect in the death of Lynnette Durand.

Recalling Tracy's face on the television screen while he had showered and changed clothes in Cottage Five, Andrew was driving Tracy's little MG with one hand, thankful that he could stay in one gear now and that he was out of town on Longmeadow Road, eyes alert for the turnoff Miss Hubbard had described. The pain in his left arm, wrist to shoulder, had turned into agony in the cold. Especially when he had to work the gearshift with his right. Any movement of his body sent a jolt straight to the core of the wound. He had pills in his pocket but there was no way to swallow one and no place to stop on the narrow, tree-lined country road. Perhaps when he reached Dr. Nichols's house . . .

What were Mr. Horgan and this reporter doing at Echo Lake in the middle of the night? We were there to obtain a sample of the water because we have reason to believe it might be toxic, even possibly radioactive.

Had Tracy reached Ann Merrill? Had she had a report yet? The tiny wipers were clearing the windshield, and the woods were already white and lovely as the little car moved along over the unmarked whiteness, the edges of the pavement obscured and treacherous.

If Echo Lake is polluted, how many others? And what will this do, in time, to the water we, you and I, must drink?

He remembered seeing, through the blur of pain, the shock on Tracy's face when she was driving him back to town last night and he'd said the world would be better off without the Nick Verinis in it. Yet, he had sensed that it had relieved her sense of guilt. What was she thinking now? He hadn't even left a message at the motel. Living alone for five years, a man comes to neglect the small civilized niceties. His mind begins to take the easy, selfish way. Well, not with Tracy, never again.

Sighting the sign—INDIAN HILL ROAD—he turned, wondering whether Chief Radford had allowed Tracy to keep the gun. Had it been reloaded? Because Nick Verini *might* still be alive. If he was, maybe the water he'd swallowed would poison him. The weird irony of this possibility came to him. Justice? Well, he'd sure as hell hate to count on it.

The gravel road curved between the trees and now he was on the old covered bridge that Nurse Hubbard had described. The planks rumbled under the wheels in the wooden tunnel, and when he emerged, he could see the outline of the house, set back from the road only a few yards: high, white, with open black shutters framing every window.

If you care—about your own lives and those of your children and grandchildren—if you cherish human life, you are the only ones who can change what they are doing to us. Tracy's face, aflame on the screen—so beautiful that he had stared in wonder. *Don't you want to live? I do. I do! Don't you?*

Yes. After five empty years, he sure as hell wanted to live!

He stopped the car alongside the road, turned off the engine, and then, as he stepped out into the softly falling snow, he heard music. A piano. Perhaps Dr. Nat, as everyone at the hospital called him, had come home from the hospital, the report absentmindedly left in his lab or shoved into a pocket, slept an hour or so, and now he was playing the piano before returning to visit his wife again. But . . . but Andrew had tried to phone him, even before he'd asked Nurse Hubbard for his address. He'd received a busy signal three times.

He went along the five or six rough thick flagstones and stepped up onto the small stoop, facing a wide door, white framed in black, with fluted Ionic pilasters supporting the pediment over the entrance. He was raising his right arm, feeling the pain, about to lift the bronze knocker, when he saw the sheet of paper protruding from the crack between the door and frame. He slid it out and saw bold hand-lettering done with a black marker-pen below the named engraved at the top: *Nathaniel Nichols, M.D.*

He read: DO NOT ENTER. And below those words: CALL POLICE.

His mind darted to Nick Verini. But he could still hear the piano. Mozart? He couldn't be sure.

He was about to return to the car—he was, he realized, too bewildered and stunned to act swiftly—when he decided to step down into the snow and look through the window nearest the entrance.

The room he saw was dim. And large. But there was no one in it. He saw a grand piano. Its lid was closed. No one occupied the bench. Still, the music continued. Definitely Mozart. One of the concertos.

He stepped onto the stoop again and placed the sheet of stationery under the heavy knocker. Then, about to return to the MG, he changed his mind and stepped instead to a window on the other side of the stoop.

He was looking into a book-framed alcove. An electric floor lamp glowed faintly over a large wing chair. In the chair, slouched low as if resting, his long legs outstretched on a footstool, was the tall thin body of a man whom he took to be Dr. Nathaniel Nichols. The eyes were closed. The lined face was composed. The distinguished-looking white moustache did not stir with breath. Nothing moved.

At once Andrew returned to the stoop and began hammering on the door, first with his fist, to hell with the pain, and then with the heavy-thumping knocker.

Then he stopped. He knew. Dr. Nat was not asleep. His face had in it the waxen pallor, the terrible serenity, of death.

The music from the piano, oddly enough, continued in the winter stillness.

THIRTEEN

In his office Chief Radford listened to the voice on the telephone and then asked, "What the hell was you doing out there anyway?"

But before Andrew could answer, Radford felt a vast sense of relief move through him. Relief and sorrow—he'd known Nat Nichols since grade school.

"I was there because I have to know the contents of the official autopsy report."

"And do you?"

"I did just what the note said. I didn't go in. Do you have the report?"

"Not yet, damn it. I'm not even certain now there *is* one." He didn't ask, although it was the logical question, whether Horgan was certain that Nat was dead. Kyle knew. It all came together in his mind. "It's out of my jurisdiction," he said. "You go back to the house and stay there till the state police get there. I'm bringing them in now whether the sheriff likes it or not."

"Time's running out, Chief. I've still got things to do. Sorry."

Hearing the click and the hum, Radford replaced the phone. He sat back in his chair. There was no urgency now. He wasn't surprised: It was the sort of thing a man like Nat Nichols would do.

And now there was no reason to drive out there himself to ask the official questions that he already knew the answers to.

And no reason to arrest Nat Nichols for the murder of his wife, as the law required.

Mariah Thompkins—he remembered her, too. Prettiest girl in high school. And the liveliest. He didn't know what he'd have done in Nat's shoes. Maybe he'd have pulled the plug long before this.

He sighed, thinking of his own wife—Rachel and Mariah had been in the same high school graduating class—and took up the phone. Sheriff Wheeler was out there in the state forest so he wouldn't have to deal with him for a while, thank God.

Phone in hand, he allowed another thought to intrude into his mind: Would Judge Patton postpone Todd Horgan's hearing if there was no autopsy report available? What the hell could have happened to it in the midst of all this? Could there be any connection between poor Nat's natural grief and sorrow—or guilt for what he'd done—and the missing report?

Hardly likely. He dismissed the idea and dialed the number of the state police barracks. He directed the trooper who answered to dispatch their mobile investigation unit to the residence of Dr. Nathaniel Nichols on Indian Hill Road. "Report of a suicide," he said. "Out of my jurisdiction, but I want the body searched. Also the house and the deceased's car. In about two hours there's going to be a judicial hearing here, on another matter, but we're particularly interested in an autopsy report that seems to have disappeared. Keep me informed. And of anything else unusual anywhere, hear?" Unusual. Hell, the whole night had been unusual and the day wasn't exactly off to a routine start.

Eight o'clock. But since Brucie had not come down from his room, Annabelle Southworth went on reading.

She'd vowed in her teens, when she'd discovered the universes contained in novels—not worlds, whole universes—she'd vowed to herself then to read every classic of literature before she died. While Bruce was growing up and before his father had died ten years ago, her promise to herself had got lost; but once she'd taken the job at the library, out of necessity, she'd found that the late nights and early mornings were the only times she really had for what she loved to do most. From Hardy and the Brontës through Tolstoi, from *Jean Christophe* to *Madame Bovary*, without pattern but with delight she'd devoured them all.

The pity was that she'd never been able to open the door to literature for Bruce. The sadness of that. Such a smart boy, straight A's most of the time, but he lived in a world of rock and country-western music, electronic games, sports, and . . . what else? Not girls—she'd noticed that. But it takes some boys longer to become men. She had not lost hope that, before she was too old, she'd have the kind of family that she and Howard had both hoped for. Grandchildren someday, playing on the old rope swing that was still hanging on the apple tree out back.

When she heard the sound of a car's motor, she did not even take off her glasses; it had to be someone going by out on the road. But when headlights appeared outside the window, she stood up, conscious of her weight, as always, and stepped heavily to the window, *Sons and Lovers* in hand. The headlights did not go out but the motor was cut off and then she saw a slight shadow running through the snow toward the small front porch.

It didn't occur to her to be afraid—or to call Bruce, whom she'd heard whispering on the telephone a short time ago—when she heard the knocking. Then a voice, a feminine voice, called Bruce's name.

When she opened the door, she recognized the girl at once. Not only from television but from the library. Tracy Larkin was a reader.

"You'll freeze out there. Come in, Miss Larkin. Are you having car trouble? Bruce isn't down yet but I'll . . . Here, take off that wet coat and I'll turn up the heat."

"I'm sorry to bother you at this hour, Mrs. Southworth, but it's business. May I speak to Bruce?"

"Of course, child. Here, sit down in my chair. I'll call him. It's turning brutal out there, isn't it?"

She called Brucie without going up the stairs in the tiny hall. He answered at once, as if he'd also heard the car.

"May I get you some coffee, Miss Larkin? I haven't started to make breakfast yet, but it won't take long." And then she got a closer look. "What you need, child, is hot food!"

"I'll settle for coffee," Tracy said, half-smiling.

Going through the small dining room to the big farmhouse kitchen, she heard Brucie coming down the stairs. Turning on the heat under the pot on the range, she made no pretense, even to herself, that she was not listening.

"Hi."

"Hi, Bruce. I guess you know why I'm here."

"N-n-no, I really don't. You're Miss Larkin, aren't you? Channel Seven Newswatch?"

"I want to ask you a question, Bruce. A favor, really."

"M-m-me?"

"Would you come to the courthouse with me and talk to Mr. Blake Arnold?"

"About . . . about what?"

"About what happened last night—well, the night before last now. About what happened on route 57—"

"I d-d-don't . . . I'm sorry, miss, I don't know what you're t-t-t-talking about."

"I'm talking about a white truck that ran you off the road. Massachusetts license 779 OKR."

A silence.

Route 57. Wasn't that the road that ran north on the east side of the state forest? She was talking about the girl who was dead. What on earth could Bruce know about—

"Bruce, you did phone Andrew Horgan and give him that number, didn't you?"

"I don't even know any M-M-Mr. Horgan."

"That was a very decent thing to do, Bruce."

"How d-d-d-did you find out it was me?"

"Never mind that. Will you do what I'm asking?"

But Bruce couldn't have been on that road—not if he was coming home from that hockey game in Montreal with Coach Lucas and the other boys. . . .

"I c-can't."

"Why not? You were honorable enough to tell Mr. Horgan—so he'd believe his son about what really happened at Echo Lake. There *was* such a truck—we know that now. And the two men who were in it are the ones who killed, raped and killed Lynnette Durand. The police still refuse to believe there was such a truck in that area."

A long silence. *Honorable*—it was a word Howard had often used. Annabelle Southworth had not heard it spoken in years. Her body growing very still, she waited out the silence.

"It won't take long, Bruce. All you have to do is tell the truth."

"No." Then louder: "No, no, no, no."

Another silence. The truth. Bruce had always told the truth. She remained at the stove, scarcely breathing, straining to hear.

"It won't take long, Bruce—"

"Why don't you ask them, the ones in the t-t-truck?"

"Because"—Tracy's voice was strained and shaky—"because they're dead."

Death. The girl, now two others. She'd buried her husband ten years ago and she knew what death was: not what it seemed on television, not a casual thing at all but profound, final.

When Bruce did not answer now, she heard Tracy go on: "They were shot dead by someone who was hired to kill them. And do you know why, Bruce?"

"I h-h-heard your broadcast," Brucie said, in a changed tone.

Annabelle had not, but the blood seemed to have drained out of her. *Killed. Shot dead.* What was happening? In her own house—

Then Bruce shouted: "I wasn't there! I d-d-d-didn't see anything! I was not there!"

She moved then. She went into the living room. Tracy's face was pale, her eyes bleak with defeat. Bruce's eyes were on fire, and she had never seen her son look so miserable, not since his father's funeral, when Bruce was only seven. "Bruce," she asked, but knowing the answer, "are you telling the truth?"

"I am, Mama. I swear. I don't know what she's t-t-talking about! I *swear!*"

"You said you heard my broadcast," Tracy said. "Aren't you into ecology at all? That truck was being used to transport hazardous waste. Wherever they dump it, ultimately it'll reach people who'll be poisoned by it."

"I told you, I t-t-told you, I've done all I can do!" His eyes went to his mother. "Mom, I swear, I don't know what she's talking about!"

"I'm talking about someone named Todd Horgan, only a couple of years older than you, who's facing prison. Doesn't that mean anything to you?"

"No," Bruce said. "Yes, it does, but . . ." He stepped toward Tracy. "I'm not in this. It's n-n-n-not my business. I did all I'm g-g-g-going to do, so bug off, lady, bug off!"

He twisted around and ran into the hall and up the stairs.

Tracy's blue eyes moved slowly to Annabelle's. "So much for honor," she said.

"Miss Larkin," she heard herself say. "I think my son has answered your questions—"

"So much for truth," Tracy said, moving to the hall.

A wintry blast entered as Tracy opened and closed the door. Annabelle Southworth did not go up the stairs. *Decency, truth, honor*—those were Howard's words. And Bruce was Howard's son. For the last several years, he had not been one to ask her opinion or advice. Until he did . . .

"Truth. Listen, kid, we're not talking about truth. We're talking about getting you off the hook so you won't spend the rest of your life in a rathole like this."

"Only three years of it," Todd said.

Gerald Usher Lewis was tired. He was also disgusted— with himself, with Julia. If he played his cards right now, he'd be able to get the hell out of this picture-postcard dead end and back to Boston in a few hours. "Listen, kid," he said, "I broke my ass to get this deal. Don't turn me down now."

He watched Todd Horgan get up from the long table. "Nolo contendere—that's the same as guilty, isn't it?"

"Technically there's a difference." But Lewis was damned if he was going to explain it. Christ, how he hated jails. The smell was even in the visitors' room. And he also hated spoiled little rich-kid punks who thought they held the key to the universe. "When the judge asks you, you plead nolo contendere to all the minor charges—you'll probably get a fine for those. Don't worry, your mother will cover it. And when he gets to manslaughter in the second degree, ditto."

"And for that I'll get a three-year sentence."

"I'll try for one year. Maybe we can settle for two. And I'll try to get Judge Patton to let you serve the time here."

"In *this* rathole you're getting me out of—"

"Todd, listen—I got out of bed to come here this early, so for God's sake—"

"How's Julia?"

"Julia's delighted. It can all be wrapped up this morning."

"What does five years' probation mean?"

"It means you report once a week, maybe once a month, in Vermont. God, I haven't got all the details yet. It means you keep your nose clean: no drugs, no reckless driving, no drunk driving, *nothing!*"

The kid's eyes were on him, very quiet, almost flat. "Yesterday you said it was irrelevant whether I actually killed her or not.'"

"Legally, it is."

"You also said *you* thought I was innocent."

"You are innocent—legally—till you're convicted in a court of law."

"Or I confess . . ."

"It's the foundation of the whole judicial system!"

Todd nodded, not otherwise moving. "Magna Carta, trial by jury and habeas corpus, Runnymede, 1215."

Smartass kid. Just like his own son Seymour—all knowing, all smirk. He should have anticipated something like this. "Didn't Julia tell you to do whatever I advised you?"

Another nod. "She said not to use *my* mind, use yours; you'll get me off."

"That's what I'm trying to do, isn't it?"

"Get me off if I plead guilty to a crime I didn't commit— that's the Nixon amendment to the Constitution, isn't it?"

That did it. Lewis felt the restraint give way inside. He might as well be trying to talk to Seymour. "Look, don't try to con me, kid." He stood up. "You know as well as I do you did it!"

"And if I did and won't confess, you'll defend me anyway?"

"I've won some of my best cases in those circumstances!"

"In the name of justice—"

"Now you listen to me, you little prick: the D.A. told me the autopsy report's all on his side."

"*How* did I do it?"

"I'll know that when I see the report. Unless you want to tell me?"

"I stabbed her with an icicle!"

"You had a gun in the car. That's one of the minor charges—"

"Then why the hell did I use an icicle?"

"If it weren't for Julia," Lewis said through gritted teeth, "I'd tell you to go screw yourself."

"Will the autopsy report reveal *why* I killed a girl I was—I still am—in love with?"

"I *know* why. I've done some reconnoitering. Talked with her roommate, Donna Lehrman. You did it in a fit of jealous frenzy. Or maybe you were so strung out on pot or coke or hash you didn't know what you were doing." He paused. "You may have premeditated—because of all the other punks she'd been sleeping with. It's an old familar tune—"

He saw the boy move then, saw it just in time to step aside, going into a crouch. The fist plunged past his ear before he grabbed, pinning the slight body between his two hands and slamming Todd back against the wall. Their faces close together, he growled: "You killed her in a spasm of uncontrollable rage—just the way you beat the shit out of the guy in Haddam who made a pass at her cunt."

He saw hate in the bloodshot eyes. "You've been reconnoitering with Norman Shatsky, too, haven't you?"

Then he felt the fight go out of the boy's body, which squirmed between his two hands. Lewis let go, without backing away. "I was doing it in *your* interest, you stupid prick. That's what the prosecution would throw at us if we went to trial. Psychiatric care, history of emotional problems. Depressions. Two DWI's, three reckless driving, that assault and battery. You think Blake Arnold won't use everything he's got? You think the jury won't hold it against you?" He turned away. He thought of Seymour again. "You're too stupid for your own good."

As he moved away, wondering whether the snow was still coming down outside, he heard Todd Horgan's voice behind him: "It's all out of my hands, isn't it? Julia said you had a bagful of tricks." And then: "Get out of here, asshole."

Asshole. He could see the hate in Seymour's face when he'd shouted it. "You can fire me," Lewis said. "If you want to stay here two or three more days, nights." He faced Todd Horgan across the room. He was beginning to shudder with anger. "I wouldn't be here if it wasn't for your mother anyway. I've had what I wanted from her and I'll be paid anyway. Plenty. So if you don't want to take the only deal that'll save you from the state pen, don't take it. They love

249

getting fresh young meat like you in there. If you go up for first-degree, it means life—that's twenty-five years minimum. You'll be middle-aged, and *if* you come out at all, you won't even be the same person.''

Todd sank to a chair and lowered his bearded face to his hands, elbows propped on the table. ''It can't be any worse in there than it is outside. . . . .'' His voice was desolate with defeat, and Lewis savored the moment. ''It's just like the rest of the world. A crock. What the hell difference does it make?''

''You decide, kid. My plane's gassed and ready.''

The boy's head lifted. ''What about the two bastards I saw? What about the truck?''

''It was a good try, kid. Clever. But I'm not the only one who doesn't believe that fairy tale.'' He moved to stand over the boy, their eyes meeting again. ''I got to admire what you tried. But if I let you go to trial—''

''I identified the photographs—''

''Nobody else did. And nobody else saw the mythical truck. Look, I admit it: The world's a crock.'' He heard his tone, which was almost gentle now. He himself wasn't sure whether he was sincere or whether he was intent only on having his way, but he was speaking the truth: ''I learned it was all a crock long before I was your age. But I taught myself to swim in it. It doesn't even stink anymore, once you're used to it. What's six months or a year to a kid your age? Survival. You've got to think of Number One. Nobody else. Number One.'' He heaved a sigh. ''So what do you say?''

''I'll think about it.''

''Well, think hard, kid. Clock's running. Think very hard and shave off that damn beard. Some judges still think only hippies and commies have beards.''

Once again Tracy was climbing the courthouse steps. Another exercise in futility?

The crowd was larger. And noisier.

She'd driven by the cottages—again. Her MG was not there—again.

Where the sweet hell could Andy be?

She'd also stopped by Colby's just now—Andy nowhere in

sight—and she'd ordered ham-scrambled eggs and told Mr. Colby she'd be right back.

What you need, child, is hot food. Had she realized how hungry she was until Mrs. Southworth had said it? What Tracy Larkin needs, Mrs. Southworth, is for your son to screw up the courage to tell the truth, no matter what that truth is.

Instead of going into the jail area now, she went into the rotunda, also crowded, and climbed the marble stairway to Blake Arnold's office.

"He can't see you now, Tracy," said Susie Pritchard, Blake Arnold's pert blond secretary. "And he told me not to discuss it with the press."

"I'm no longer press, Susie. Discuss what?"

"You don't know?"

"What, Susie?"

"Dr. Nichols is dead. That's all I can say. Please, Trace, I'm busy."

Mrs. Mariah Nichols . . . now Doctor Nat. Had he learned that his wife was dead and then . . . ?

Her flesh was quivering again as she went outside. While packing at Steve's house, she should have changed into her own clothes. And she should have listened to her own weather forecast.

But walking through the snow along Hancock Street, she knew that the cold was not only in her flesh. It went deeper.

In Colby's—even more crowded, even more noisy—Mr. Colby had saved her a stool at the counter. Gray-haired, with a scowl so familiar that it was almost pleasant, he placed the hot plate and the coffee mug before her.

She asked. "You haven't seen Mr. Horgan this morning, have you?"

"Ay-uh. He was here. Didn't eat, though. Just asked if he could buy a fifth of bourbon. Not allowed, I said, so I sent him around the corner to the state liquor store. Say, he looked beat. How'd he hurt his arm?"

Stunned, her mind refusing to accept what she'd just heard, she drained the mug down to its bitter dregs. "Hoisting bourbons," she said then, and slid off the stool.

Her stomach seemed to shrink. Her appetite was gone.

And other things were gone, too. Many, many other things . . .

Why hadn't she thought of that? Why hadn't she guessed? Known?

When she went out into the street, the snow had stopped falling.

"Snow's stopped," George Bone said from the cell window. "Just like that."

Acid rain, acid sleet, acid snow—poison, poison everywhere and what the hell difference did it make?

"Remember what I asked you last night?" The big blond bastard was facing him, legs spread apart. "Remember, Todd?"

"You asked me how about having a little sex to pass the time. Because you couldn't sleep. Remember what I said, Georgie? I said I'm straight. Well, I still am."

And George Bone had grunted a laugh last night and said: *I was too, till my first slide in the slammer. Now, man, I'm a swinging door. Got some advice, kid. Soon's you can, when you're inside, grab on to the biggest toughest queen in your section. Black if possible. And then hang in there an' let the mother take care of you. Ass'll get sore for a while but it's softer than gang rape.*

Fighting the revulsion, even more sickening now than during the night, Todd rolled over on the bunk, his face to the wall. "I'm still straight, George. Sorry."

"Negative. Not that."

"You said it was always easier to cop a plea."

"Not that, neither." His shoes sounded on the bare floor. "About that old dude down in Springfield—what he done."

"George, I haven't seriously thought of doing anything like that since my thirteenth birthday." Standing on the subway platform in New York, ready to throw himself in front of the next train. "My own lawyer told me: The world's a crock, George, but it's all we got."

"Change your mind, kid, I could lend a hand, like they say." Another step, but whispering now, chewing gum while he talked: "Seen one dude drowned hisself in the toilet bowl. God's truth. They couldn't figure out how he done it."

Todd's body, without moving, had gone stiff. Something ugly and quivering came to life in his stomach. Swiftly he remembered how quickly George Bone had sobered up once he was in the cell. He rolled over, sitting up.

"Y' listening to me, pal?"

No, he was listening to another voice in his mind: *No, not pray. But not stop hoping, or trying.* Where the hell was Andrew now? Maybe he'd bowed out, too.

Eyes on George Bone, he realized that his breathing had become shallow. He could feel the blood throbbing in his neck, at his temples.

He could yell but would Kopit hear? Would he come?

"I just hope," George Bone said, "just hope when you did it to her, you knew how. That certain spot on the throat—carotid artery—y'find that, hold it, that one little spot, just long enough, it don't even leave a mark." He took another step. "Want me to show you where it is?"

"Mr. Kopit!" Todd heard himself shouting. "Mr. Kopit!"

George Bone was grinning.

The old man appeared, limping and frowning, in the passage between the two rows of cells. "Stop yelling. You want me?"

"Mr. Kopit, I'd like to be moved to another cell," Todd said, shaking. Knowing. Certain.

"Another cell?" the old man growled. "Two cells, two prisoners, more work. This ain't no hotel, college boy. You only got an hour and a half to wait. You set in there and you pray God's forgiveness before you face the judge."

After old man Kopit disappeared, George Bone, still grinning, asked: "Y'think I'm gonna hurt you, turkey? I got nothin' against you. Why'd I want to zip you and hang your body up like you done it yourself?"

Todd had no answer.

But he had an hour and a half to go and he was damned if he was going to take his eyes off this George Bone, if that was his name—not for a second. Or turn his face to the wall again . . .

He was still wearing his heavy hiking boots, even if they didn't have laces in them.

And he remembered what he'd done to that bastard in Haddam. By now he was scared enough and angry enough to do it again if he had to. Or worse.

Oh, God, what did we do to deserve this?

That was the thought that Mattie Stoddard kept returning to

over and over. Why? Why us? What had she and Jason done to have this horror visited on them?

From the sofa she was staring out the front window at the grass and plants and pine trees across the road, all covered white with snow.

Soon as I get the call, I'll split, Dominic Verini had said when he drew up the straight chair to sit by the front parlor window, but out of view of the cars that had been passing. Police cars, some of them. She knew his name now. *The photograph you see on your screen is a picture of Dominic Verini, age thirty-one, son of Vincent Verini, reputed mob leader. Reputed, reputed, reputed. If he is still alive, Nick Verini is in the area, and last evening he threatened to rape this reporter on Longmeadow Road. He is allegedly armed and should be considered dangerous. Not allegedly—really. Really dangerous.*

She couldn't look at him sitting there, gun in hand, eyes darting from the road to them and back again. She couldn't bear to see his ugly face; but looking at Jason, who was sitting next to her on the sofa, was worse. He was like a statue, as if his eyes weren't even seeing the other man, or her. But his lean hard hand holding hers was pressuring it every so often, like he wanted to reassure her that soon, soon this incredible horrible dream would be over, had to be over, soon. . . .

It wasn't so much the ugly black gun in the man's hand as it was the waiting. Waiting for the phone to ring out back in the kitchen, that's what frayed her nerves. The waiting and the knowing. Knowing somewhere, not in her mind but somewhere deeper inside, what Dominic Verini was going to do—to them, to both of them—had to do, after he got the phone call.

Then that other thought came back again, like an echo: Nothing good ever happened to me in my life, ever, nothing good ever did come but what something bad always came along to take it away.

Don't let him do it, God. Jason and me, we hardly had time to live together yet. Only a year, God, please . . .

She could hear the plane returning now. There'd been all kinds of police cars up and down in the last two hours—which seemed like forever, or longer—and the one plane, like it was circling, searching the forest. It droned away again.

She did glance at Dominic Verini now. He no longer

looked like the half-drowned man who'd come to the door, or like the picture on the TV screen. In the kitchen, after Jason had come down with the dry clothes, he'd made her and Jason watch while he peeled off his wet ones till he was naked and she'd had to look away. *Not for you, missus,* he said, not grinning. *Savin' that big dong for somebody else. Somebody that's got it coming.* And now, because of what she'd heard him say on the phone later, she knew who he meant. If only there was some way to warn that girl, who seemed so tired and so angry on television . . .

After he was wearing one of Jason's plaid flannel shirts and a pair of work denims, he'd made her cut off his hair, which had been long and oily even when wet. Then, while he kept the gun on her, he'd made Jason shave his whole head with his electric razor. And his short beard, too. Then, when he looked at himself in the kitchen mirror, he scowled, like he really hated what he saw, but when he put on Jason's old hunting hat, with the ear flaps, a kind of grin came over his face. And then he'd even laughed—only no real gladness in it, no joy, a funny sort of sound, hollow, that made her shiver. If he came to the front door now, that look in his eye, she'd think he was some loony escaped from the state hospital over to Estherville.

That was when they'd heard the first siren. And that's when he said: *Any fucker comes to that door, they're gonna find you two in a pool of blood, capeesh?*

Mattie's whole body had gone faint and sick and she couldn't find her voice. Jason was holding her hand so hard she thought the bones in it would crush.

Then she heard another sound outside. And above. Approaching. A motor and a clacking . . .

The man returned to the window, fast, crouching down. But he kept the gun pointed in their direction.

By now she had recognized the sound: a helicopter, flying low.

But it clacked away and in a few moments she could hear it only faintly in the distance.

In the quiet, Dominic Verini stayed on the floor by the window.

But Jason's hand relaxed and she heard him take a deep, shuddering breath.

Joseph Hayes

"Please," she heard herself whisper, "please, Jason, just do what he says, just humor him—"

But Jason said, aloud: "Next thing, it'll be a cruiser stopping in the driveway. Oh, you can kill us then, like it was our fault, but there's four hundred acres of woods and hills out back. How're you gonna get to that lodge in Ontario then?"

No answer. The man didn't move.

He'd dialed a long-distance number after they'd listened to the news, and instead of getting his father, he'd spoken with someone named Angelo. *What the fuck're you doing on Poppa's private line?* And then: *You don't give me orders, Angelo.* His hand had been white-knuckled on the gun and his voice sort of throttled with rage: *You tell Poppa to call me at this number. I want someone to do a snatch and take her to the lodge in Ontario.* Then shouting: *None of your goddam business who! Just take this number down. I ain't moving till I talk to Poppa.*

After giving the number, he'd banged the phone onto the wall, and that's when she'd seen that look on his face that told her he was going to kill her and Jason no matter what: that hate, that simmering anger in those brown-black eyes, like he might explode and destroy everyone and everything.

Knowing what he planned later—that's what had sealed their doom, no matter what else happened, or who came to the door, or whether the phone *ever* rang or not.

But Jason was talking again: "You asked about that new Mustang out there." It was as if he hadn't spoken. "It's my wife's car—new." A birthday gift, her gift—because Jason wanted her to have a sporty car, because Jason wanted her to feel young. "No one would pay any attention to it if I'm in it with you."

Slowly, Dominic Verini, still on the floor, turned his head. His face looked tiny and pinched and blank and his bare skull was pale and ugly.

"If you tie up my wife, and don't harm her in any way, I can get you to the Canadian border." Oh Jason, no, no, I won't let you. "I know every back road in this whole area."

Then Jason waited.

Very slowly, Dominic Verini stood up. He pointed the gun at her. Not at Jason, but at her. "I give the orders," his voice said.

"I'm offering you a way out," Jason said. "If you pull that trigger, I'll make you kill me, too."

"Beretta holds ten rounds, Pop. I ain't fired one yet."

She spoke then, staring at him over the gun. "It won't shoot anyway," she cried, fighting hysteria, fighting the hate burning in her blood. "It won't shoot after being in the lake!"

It had come to her all of a sudden. And she was certain. And she didn't care now. She wanted to rush at him, herself, to claw his ugly face, tear out his eyes.

She saw doubt come into those eyes. A thrill of satisfaction swept through her.

And then there was another sound. Outside the house. On the highway. The crunching of heavy tires on snow.

She saw the man duck down, twisting his body, keeping it low to look out the window.

She felt her own impulse to act pass through Jason, too, although he did not move.

Over the man's bald head she saw a truck pass by on the road. A wrecker. With two yellow lights blinking on the top of the cab.

Behind it, hoisted at an angle, she saw a small, sleek red sports car, its nose and side a mangled mass of metal.

Then she heard a sound she'd never heard before—part scream, part moan, loud and inhuman and unearthly.

She saw the man stand up and turn to face the two of them.

His face, twisting in agony, was a terrible thing to see. He looked like an animal in a trap. Or gone mad, ready to froth . . .

She edged toward Jason. She felt him place an arm around her.

The man's eyes were glistening with tears, and sort of stunned and furious at the same time. They looked like black fire.

Then he stepped forward till he was close, very close.

She was too weak to move.

She saw the arm coming up, the one with the gun, slow, coming up to Jason's forehead. She felt Jason's arm stiffen on her back.

She heard a laugh and a tangled kind of whisper. "Le's *see* if it'll fire, old man."

The whole room seemed to explode. The whole house—

The arm on her back jerked, then let go. She turned. She saw Jason's face, going down, and a black hole in his forehead, it began to fill with blood, then the blood gushing, something crumbled inside, she saw the man's face staring at the hole, he was backing away, she heard Jason's body falling on the floor, and she rushed, no fear, not caring, rushed toward the man and the gun and then she had her hands up, claws bared, her mind reeling with one idea: kill, kill, kill, kill—

There was a red-hot poker stab, quick and sharp, below her breast, and that was all.

FOURTEEN

Tracy was again trying not to think of Andy. Where he was, what he was doing.

And she was still trying, foolishly, to fight the doubts, to deny the certainty. *Didn't eat though. Just asked if he could buy a fifth of bourbon.* Thank you, Mr. Colby. So much for willpower, good intentions—delusions.

When she'd left Colby's to get into the car, she'd never felt so alone, so lonely and at sea. Three suitcases, two duffel bags, flight bag, a carton of records, her portable ten-inch TV—everything she owned—in the back seat of a car that didn't belong to her and no place to go, no one to go to.

Her MG had not been parked at Cottage Five but she'd pulled in anyway—there were no empty spaces along the snow-covered green—and had gone to the door, which was unlocked. Typical. Typical of any boozer. As she let herself in, she had half-expected that he might be sprawled out, *passed* out on the bed, sleeping the innocent sleep of the unknowing, uncaring drunk. Then, seeing the bed, realizing how spent and exhausted she was in every fiber, she'd locked the door and collapsed onto the bed.

Now she was stretched out on her back, tense and stiff, unable to shut her eyes, the turbulence inside beyond her control. The windows were curtained and locked, the door double-bolted, the black revolver on the bed only inches from her hand. Too much. There was too much happening. She'd been drawn into an appalling and incredible nightmare that

259

was not her own. And it went on and on and now she could not even *think*!

Say, he looked beat. Looked beat, felt worse, she knew; she knew: Charlie Larkin's pattern. Feeling great, let's have one! Feeling low, Tracy, feeling low—so have several, Pop, get smashed, disappear, no message, no word, no care!

She leaped up from the bed.

It was over. It was all over now! Love or no love. I loved Pop, too, but now I'm not a child. I won't go through that again. Will not, cannot, will not! So get lost, Andy Horgan, get lost

The telephone rang.

She rushed to pick it up and realized that her hand was shaking, so she brought up the other one and pressed the mouthpiece rigidly to her face with all the strength she still had.

But she did not speak. What if . . . ?

What if Nick Verini was still alive? What if he was dead and they, *they*, those people, his people, what if they had learned who . . . ?

Then she heard: "Mr. Horgan?" A woman's voice, dimly familiar. "Mr. Horgan, are you there?"

"It's me," Tracy said, her tone strangled. "It's Tracy Larkin, Miss Merrill."

"Oh, Miss Larkin, thank God. And I hope you're sitting down. These blessed ecology freaks of mine, whom I love, brought one drum back here to the lab sooner than I could believe. They've just tested the sample. Please sit down if you aren't. Your assumptions hold water. Isn't that a terrible pun?" Ann Merrill laughed on a nervous, excited note. "The chemical is Dioxin. Tracy, we were right! . . . Tracy, are you there?"

"I think so." Tracy felt tears in her eyes, heard them in her voice. "Thank you, Miss Merrill. Thank you so very damned much!"

"My *very* great pleasure, my dear. One of the professors here will phone the EPA in Washington as soon as they open, and I'm coming back there with an official typed report. See you."

Tracy lowered the phone and, as she snatched the gun from the bed and went to unlock the door, all of a sudden she was not tired, not in the least.

But when she stepped outside into the cold, her bag over her shoulder, she held the gun in her right hand, its muzzle pointed to the ground, inconspicuous, she hoped, as she made up her mind to drive instead of walk those two short city blocks along the green to the courthouse. Safer? Who knows? She moved to the car, eyes warily scanning the area.

Julia was not prowling the visitors' room this morning. Seated at his elbow at the end of the long table, she reminded him more of a jungle animal that had been tamed, or broken.

She spoke very softly: "Only one year, Todd. Maybe less. Not more than two. You're so young, darling. You've got your whole life in front of you." And then, even more softly: "I'm only thinking of you."

"Isn't everyone?"

"You know how fast time goes." She was wearing makeup today, her face and eyes more vivid, and a wide-brimmed felt hat, and a trim suit under the leather trenchcoat—Julia Craven, spotlight shining down today, newsreel cameras whirring away. "And if they let you stay here, Merle and I will visit you every chance we get. And then after it's all over, you can come home."

Home? Had he ever had a home? He stood up from the long table and moved away. "Suppose the judge or the prosecutor, after I confess, asks me *how* I killed Lynne." Her name still tasted sweet on his tongue and he had to choke down the bitter emptiness that pushed up into his chest. Then he said, "Here's a headline for you, Julia: Defendant confesses crime but cannot recall method."

"We can face that when Lewis gets the report from the pathologist—"

"You mean I can make my lie conform to the autopsy report?"

"Oh, Todd, why must you always look at things the way you do? It's not so bad here, is it, really? You always did like to be alone."

"Chance to get a lot of reading done—Kafka, Dostoevski, *The Gulag Archipelago*."

"What's the fucking alternative?" Julia suddenly snarled, standing up. "They could put you in prison for the rest of your goddammed life!"

"Is that what that asshole Gerald Usher Lewis told you to say?"

Julia bore down on him, moving closer. "No one sent me here. I'm your mother. I had to see you before the hearing, didn't I?" And then she began to move, lithe and graceful, and again he became conscious of the tensions threatening to erupt.

Quietly he said, "I loved Lynne, Julia. How can I say I . . . ?" He turned away.

"She's dead."

"I've accepted that." And he had. Finally.

"What difference can it make to *her*? She'll never know."

"I'll know!" He heard his voice rising, so he returned to sit at the table. "What if there *is* a trial?" he asked in a controlled whisper. "They can't prove I killed her if I didn't."

"Oh, you poor boy, you innocent, naïve child. Don't you know the prisons are full of people who—"

"I believe *that*," he said. "I sure as hell believe that now."

"What about me, Todd? Do you know what you're putting me through? Just to have to go upstairs and into that courtroom . . ." And then she was almost screaming: "You can't do this to me! Today's bad enough. I can't face a fucking trial!" And then she was circling the table—long strides, chin jutting—and talking in her own voice, not the throaty whisper that her fans loved: "I spoke with Merle. Do you know how they're talking in New York? Sniggering! Do you know the fucking *pleasure* they're taking over this at Sardi's bar? The gossip columnists, *Hollywood Reporter, New York Post, Daily News*—there was even a short piece in the *Times* this morning. And while I'm here, Merle's prancing all over New York with his playmate of the month! And Andrew—what a shit he's turned into!" She was breathing hard now as she stopped at the other end of the long table. Her tone flattened: "I honestly don't know how much more I can take." Her eyes were on him, miserable and pleading. "How could you do this to me, Todd?" And when he didn't—because he couldn't—answer: "You really hate me, too, don't you?"

So then he was sitting there gazing at her, really seeing her again: He might go to prison for life, but she was looking through a single lens, the only one she had, and seeing only herself reflected. For some reason, the old familiar and expected anger did not ignite. Nothing new. He, as a separate and distinct human being, did not exist in her mind.

Yet he had difficulty speaking. "Julia," he said, "I'm scared. I don't want to go to prison."

She rushed down the table then, to take his face between her palms. Now she *was* speaking in that hurried, throaty whisper: "Darling, you don't have to. Isn't that what I've been saying?" And then: "If there's no trial and you stay here in this nice little jail, it'll soon be all over and forgotten."

Their faces were close now, closer than they had been for years except when she kissed him hello or goodbye. Hers suddenly seemed old, pathetic. In that moment he wondered whether she, not he, could get through this.

When he could not bear the silence, or her closeness, any longer, he said: "You mentioned my father. Is he coming here before I go to court?" That did it. She released his face, her blue-green eyes changing. Is this what he had intended?

She stepped away. "No one knows what Andy will do! I *never* knew!" She moved to sit. "He was always such a cruel, uncaring man." Todd did not believe this now. "And the way he drank. He's probably getting smashed somewhere right now."

"I don't think so," Todd said. "He's over that."

Julia was shaking her head. "That's right. He walked out on you, but you always had to romanticize him, didn't you? Idealize him? It's so goddam fucking unfair!"

"What isn't?" he heard himself ask.

"Has Andy been poisoning your mind against me?" She stood up so fast that the chair tumbled over behind her. "It's just like him." She was moving again, in short agitated steps, directionless. "You should never have brought him into this. What right has he now to . . ." Then, again at the far end of the table, she whirled to face him, eyes blazing, boring into his. "Todd, I didn't want to tell you this. I've never told you, but you keep talking about the goddam truth, so here goes: Andrew Horgan is *not* your father."

"I know you," Pierre Durand said, peering into the sitting room. "You're his old man. Got nothin' t' say to you, mister."

Andrew had stood up when the huge man had finally come in through the front door, and now he watched, undecided, as

Pierre Durand shambled across the center hall and climbed the stairway. Less than an hour and a half before the hearing now. Had he wasted time sitting here, waiting? What the hell did he hope to accomplish anyway?

He'd knocked on the door of Mrs. Wharton's Guest Home and then, when she'd appeared—a tall, spare, white-haired lady with lace at her throat and an aristocratic but troubled voice—he had not had to introduce himself. *I'm so sorry about what's happened, Mr. Horgan. No, he's not in. And Mrs. Durand left around midnight. When he came home, he must've gone wild. Their room's a shambles. I really ought to inform the police but I don't want to add to their woes. Would you care to wait?*

Well, he hadn't waited only to give up now. He went up the gently curving stairway, passing the portraits of Mrs. Wharton's ancestors, faces stern and stoic. The second door to the right stood open and Pierre Durand's heavy tall figure filled the frame.

"Get out," he said, his accent turning *out* into *oot*, but what Andrew heard was the word *keel, keel, keel;* the huge man plunging furiously down the courthouse steps yesterday morning while Andrew was stretched out on the concrete, tasting blood, the pain beginning. "Got nothin' t' say to that bastard's father."

"You're going to listen to me, Mr. Durand, because if you don't I'm going to file charges for assault and battery and have you arrested. Several thousand witnesses saw what you did to me on television and there's a tape. I don't want *you* to say *anything.* I want you to *listen.*"

Pierre Durand lifted his hand to his shaggy black moustache, but the hand was trembling, so he rubbed his unshaven face instead. The shakes. Andrew recognized the symptoms: The man was suffering the hell of withdrawal and he felt a gnawing pity, the universal comprehension of one alcoholic for another's misery. He reached into the sling under his flight jacket, which was hanging loose over his left shoulder, and produced the fifth of bourbon he'd bought at the store around the corner from Colby's. "How about a snort?"

He saw something like relief, more like elation, rise into the red-streaked eyes as they opened wider. Deliverance. Hope. He remembered the sensation.

Pierre Durand turned about and went into the room, leaving the door open.

When Andrew entered, he realized what Mrs. Wharton had meant: a table upended, two legs snapped off, a floor lamp smashed, drawers gaping, one upside-down on the bed, and on top of the bureau several empty bottles, others on their sides on the carpet.

Before Pierre Durand caught sight of him in the bureau mirror, he saw the rifle. In plain view. On the bed. And then he knew, taking a deep breath that sent a stab of pain along his arm, that he had made the right decision. He set the bottle upright on top of the bureau.

Pierre Durand shoved out a hairy paw and picked it up, face intent, still scowling. He twisted off the top, that familiar slight metallic *squeash,* and then he tipped it back and gulped, the bottle shaking between his two hands.

Afterward he heaved his massive shoulders, his face twisted, and he uttered a huge gratified sigh, blowing air. He shoved the bottle toward Andrew.

"It's for you," Andrew said, stepping away. "I don't drink, thanks."

The bluish beard-shadowed face changed again. "You too good to drink with Pierre?"

Andrew, again realizing how tired he was, went to the only chair and let himself down into its softness. "I don't drink with anyone," he said. "I don't drink. Period."

"Then take bottle. Go. I buy my own *alcool.*" He came forward, bearlike, slow, extending the bottle. "Stuff it."

Andrew considered, swiftly: One drink, a single drink could trigger that thing inside, whatever it was; one was too many and then a gallon would not be enough. His curse. The demon he'd subdued but which was always there.

He made the decision: This was the only way he could get what he came for. But he was aware of the cunning in the mind of any alcoholic—had he found an excuse? Yet he had no desire. "May I have a glass?"

Pierre Durand laughed then. He'd never heard the man laugh before—a raucous explosion of sound, at once triumph and scorn. Then, mockingly: *"Mais oui, m'sieur!"* He took a quick swig, the bottle in one hand, *not* shaking now, as he turned away. His other hand picked up a short, squat glass from the top of the bureau. *"Voilà!"*

Andrew, stiff with apprehension now, watched Pierre Durand fill it to the brim. Christ, what was he letting himself in for? Was it worth the risk? He took the glass, aware of the dark eyes on him, and lifted it to his lips, sipped carefully. The whiskey tasted raw, and it was chokingly hot going down his throat. Maybe he could fake it—not actually swallow enough to trigger the craving that, he knew, could leave him without willpower, helpless. . . .

"I don't talk with no one who don't drink with me." Durand's voice already sounded hearty. He lifted the bottle, as if in a toast. "What you say—cheer? *Santé!*" Over the bottle, as he drank again, his gaze was watchful and ugly and cruelly triumphant.

"You drink now, I listen."

Andrew brought the glass to his mouth again and drank, not a sip but a swallow. He felt the familiar, unforgotten sensation in his stomach, the warmth spreading and bracing, a calm settling through his whole being. Not enough to turn into the need for more, the craving, just enough to placate Durand into listening . . .

"Never trusted no man that didn't drink," Durand said, setting the bottle on the bureau and beginning to unbutton his plaid flannel shirt. "I go to court soon. Now—we talk. *Que voulez-vous?*"

"First, I want to tell you, Mr. Durand, just what I tried to tell you yesterday: My son did *not* kill your daughter."

Durand was staring into the mirror, eyes on Andrew. He uttered one word: "*Merde.*"

"If you use that gun there to kill Todd, you'll spend the rest of your life in prison."

"*Merde.*" Without a shirt, his torso looked even more massive, black hair matted at the unbuttoned neck of his soiled, yellowish flannel underwear. "They never catch Pierre," he said, taking another shirt out of a drawer. "Pierre too— what you say?—too *habile.* Too smart. He live in woods. Nobody ever find him." With the wool shirt on now, he took another long gurgling drink. "Best shot in Maine. Deer, moose, bear."

"What about your wife?"

"Thérèse? She gone." Another quick swig. "She leave me. Took clothes. Took money. Gone." Then he shouted, "Bitch." And, after another swallow, buttoning the shirt: "Pierre all alone. *Bon, très bon.* Ugly bitch.'' Then he turned, the neck of the bottle in his hand. ''Not like Lynnette . . .'' His eyes had taken on a faraway look.

''Have you been watching TV, Mr. Durand?''

''Yesterday.'' His mind was elsewhere. ''Not today—''

''Then you don't know.''

''Know *what*?'' He moved slowly, heavily to the bed. ''Don't care . . .''

''I have a picture here of the man who murdered your daughter.''

Durand did not seem to hear. ''You ain't drinking,'' he said.

Andrew downed a swallow and reached into the pocket of his flight jacket, took out the envelope with the 4 × 6 photographs. ''His name's Jesse Kull. Don't you want to see his picture?''

''You're lying, ain't you?'' There was a faint knowing grin under the moustache. He shook his head. ''You come here to lie to me?''

''I came here to show you this.'' And then, after Durand had taken the print and was staring at it, Andrew went on, knowing the risk but taking it: ''He raped her and then he killed her.''

''Rape?''

''Rape.'' The word seemed to have the effect he'd hoped for, so he repeated it: ''Rape.'' Then, very consciously, he risked the lie: ''The State's Attorney has told me the autopsy report reveals your daughter was raped, Mr. Durand.'' And he added, ''Brutally.''

''Then''—Durand stood up suddenly—''then your goddammed son did it!''

''Why? Why would he rape her?''

''Because''—he was not shouting; his voice was a low snarl—''because my Lynnette was a good girl, because she'd never let . . .'' He took a long step. ''You say she not good, mister? You say her and your goddam son . . . ?''

Had he said the wrong thing? His mind might not be clear. . . .

''Answer me, mister!''

''No, no, no, Mr. Durand. You're right. Todd told me: She refused him—''

''She refuse, so *he* rape her!''

"No."

Andrew saw the man's hand, black with hair on the back, holding the bottle by the neck.

"He told me he loved her." Seated, he felt helpless. But if he tried to stand up now . . .

Then it came to him. He saw the photograph in Durand's other hand: Jesse Kull's monstrous skull and the beard. So, sure of this now too, he said, "That man weighed more than three hundred pounds. He crushed her to death."

He knew this now—had the booze sharpened his mind? He *knew*. "That's what the official report says." But did it? How could he be sure?

Durand turned the bottle around in his hand and tipped back his head to gulp down more whiskey. Christ, the man could go wild again. Then what? Or perhaps he had enough reason left to believe that if an official document . . .

He saw Durand staring down at the photograph again.

So he said, "I saw the man. Three hundred pounds, at least."

"Wha' your son weigh?"

"Not more than one fifty."

The black eyes were slits again. "You not lie to me?"

Andrew managed what he hoped was a convincing shrug. "Go down to the courthouse and ask to see the medical examiner's report. You must have met Dr. Nichols when you identified your daughter. Why should a man like Dr. Nichols lie?"

A long moment passed.

Then Durand asked, "Where's this *bâtard*?"

"He's dead." Andrew handed over the photograph. "This man was with him. His name's Rolf Arneson. They both had their heads blown off yesterday. If you don't believe me, go out and buy a newspaper." And then he added, himself amazed at the fact for the first time: "They've already been punished."

Durand turned away. He went to sink down onto the bed in a sitting position, head down, shoulders hunched forward. He began to sob.

Had Andrew won? Had he emptied Durand's rifle of the bullets intended for Todd?

Durand was weeping openly, without shame or restraint.

And then—because his mind, with the booze driving it, had become alert or wily, or because he saw in that instant a way to make sure that Nick Verini, if he was still alive, might also be punished—he said, "I have another picture here, Mr. Durand." Could he do this? Had he any right? "This man is named Nick Verini."

Durand, his face streaked with tears, his great shoulders shuddering now, blinked at him and, like a robot, took the photograph. "Nick Verini?" His tone was vague.

"He's the man who hired Jesse Kull and Rolf Arneson." Andrew stood up. "He's still alive, and if there's anyone who caused your daughter's death, it's Nick Verini."

Standing, he realized that he was drunk. Or almost drunk. After ten years, it wouldn't take much. He looked around for a place to put the glass—and realized, with a shock, that it was empty.

He took a step and set the glass on the bureau. "I'm sorry," he heard himself say.

All Pierre Durand, still staring at the photograph, seemed able to say was: "He's got a beard, too."

Andrew glanced at the rifle on the bed. "The bastard tried to kill *me* last night." Was he pushing his luck? Should he grab the rifle and make a run for it? "Why do you think I'm wearing this sling on my arm?"

Instead of going for the rifle—his mind wasn't too clear now—Andrew went to the door and turned. Durand was slumped, unseeing, his face blank.

Going out and down the stairs, Andrew realized that he was waiting for that sense of buoyancy and confidence to set in. But it didn't. Instead, he began to wonder whether he'd accomplished anything here. Had Durand even heard him? And if he had, would he believe what Andrew had told him once he finished the bottle?

Well, he'd shot his wad. He was doing all he could. And more to come . . .

His step was slightly unsteady. The cold seemed colder, the snow whiter.

He went down the steps of the high white-columned house. The air seemed to penetrate the jacket and the bandages, to pierce the exact spot where the bullet had torn through the flesh.

Maybe if he had another drink. Anesthetize the pain . . .

He was walking along the side of the green toward the courthouse. No carnival atmosphere now, no music . . .

In this state, or mood, or condition—he warned himself—a man does not behave rationally, or think rationally. He'd learned that, hadn't he? Learned it with pain, with guilt, with shame. He thought he'd put all that, this agony, behind him.

All he wanted—no, needed; the craving was in him, all through him—all he really had to have, *honestly*, was one . . . well, one or two short ones, just enough to brace him for whatever was coming. Any excuse, Andy, any excuse in a snowstorm. Or a rainstorm. Or a lovely summer's day. Any excuse, anywhere, once the addiction had been awakened, stirred . . .

Then if you know what's happened, why the hell can't you control it?

No answer to that. Doctors had no answer. Only: *The trick is not to take the first one. One ounce of alcohol equals one ounce of cyanide. Because you are an alcoholic. Because that is your nature.*

But you do have a choice. Insanity, prison, death—or recovery.

Death. Tracy's father.

He killed himself and he killed my mother in a car accident on an icy street in Boston when I was very young.

Tracy . . .

They'd told Andrew in the hospital: *You can't recover for the sake of anyone else. Only for yourself.* But that had not been true. He had recovered for Cassie's sake.

He had recovered because he wanted Cassie to be happy.

Not for himself, then?

Yes, for himself, too, because he could never be happy if Cassie was not.

He had said: *I love this woman, I want this woman, only her, and I want to live with her and see her happy.*

Then, five short years later, Cassie had died. . . .

Everyone dies.

It's the time *before* that matters.

Without being aware of it, he had turned the corner and was approaching Colby's.

It was then that he realized he had said goodbye to Cassie. Her lovely face, beach and sky and blue water beyond, faded in his mind.

And in its place—Tracy's face. Vivid, alive, brimming with intensity and promise.

He turned into Colby's.

Your choice, Horgan. Steak and coffee at the counter in the front room or cyanide with soda at the bar in the rear. Your choice.

"Has Mr. Horgan been here, Susie?"

"Hi, Tracy. No, he hasn't. Tracy! What's happened to you?"

"I've got to see Mr. Arnold," Tracy said.

"No way, no way. Chief Radford's with him. This place is an insane asylum this—"

The telephone rang.

"Sorry," Susie said, smiling apology, and took up the phone. "State's Attorney's office." And then she was frowning, listening to a booming male voice, so loud that Tracy could also hear the words.

"This is Judge Patton and I'm waiting in chambers. Mr. Lewis is here but Mr. Arnold is *not*. It's now exactly one hour till court is scheduled to convene and I *always* convene on time. Convey this message to Mr. Arnold, please."

"I'll tell him at once, sir," Susie was saying when Tracy heard a click, and then the humming on the wire.

"Whew," Susie said, and turned to the intercom and pressed down a key, waited for Blake Arnold's voice, and then said: "Mr. Arnold, Judge Patton—"

Blake's voice, charged with excitement, cut off her words: "Never mind. Susie, is there a machine in the building that will play a cassette tape?"

"Well, sir, I—"

Tracy Larkin did move then. She took two steps and leaned low over the desk to say, loudly and distinctly: "Mr. Arnold, this is Tracy Larkin. We've had the contents of those drums analyzed. They contain Dioxin. A written report is on its way from Haddam. So much for conjecture and paranoia."

As she turned to go, Tracy caught the expression on Susie's face and thought she heard Blake Arnold's voice on the intercom. It sounded as if he said, "Jesus Christ."

She decided not to leave. She had to know. "Susie, what's going on?"

"Nothing. Everything! A suicide and now a murder. A double murder. Trace, I can't take time now to—"

"Murder?" She was not breathing.

"Some couple out in the country—"

"Suicide?" She began to breathe again.

"Dr. Nichols." Susie reached for the phone again. "Trace, I'm not free to talk about any of this. Honest. This place is coming apart at the seams."

Tracy was on her way. She was almost running down the corridor to a public phone, which was not in a booth but was not in use.

Dialing, she heard a siren somewhere outside.

Steve himself answered. "Tracy, where are you? I need you."

"Who was murdered, Steve? And where?"

"Tracy, Larry's at the courthouse with the camera. For God's sake—"

"Who, Steve, *who*?"

"Jason Stoddard. I don't have the particulars yet. Jason Stoddard and his wife, Mathilda. He owns the hardware."

Picturing Jason Stoddard's pleasant face behind the counter, trying to remember his wife's, Tracy was ashamed of the relief that had been streaming through her since she'd learned from Susie that it was not Andy who was dead.

"Not Andrew Horgan," Steve said into the silence. "But I did hear from him, right? He phoned here and asked for you. Not more than fifteen minutes ago. If you ask me, he was looped."

Earlier, driving down the green from the cottages to the courthouse, she had allowed her mood, after some resistance, to change from fury (how could he, at a time like this?) to acceptance and pity (you'll destroy yourself, Andy), and then a harrowing sense of loss had settled through her. So much for love . . .

"Trace, are you there? Mr. Horgan said he was having breakfast at Colby's. He's probably still there."

Now, fighting an overwhelming urge to replace the phone, to go running down the stairs, she asked, "Where . . . where do . . . did the Stoddards live, Steve?"

"Out on route 57. North." And then he added: "Less than a quarter mile from the entrance to the state forest."

She could hear the commotion from the rotunda below. It

was a wonder she couldn't hear her own heart. It was pounding, fast and furious and hard.

Again Steve seemed to know. "So, Tracy . . . so you didn't really kill anyone, right?"

"Right," she whispered into the phone. "Oh, Steve, thank you."

"Both cameras are at the courthouse. If you could——"

"Sorry, Steve. Priorities."

And then she was moving, fast, down the corridor, between half-glassed office doors, to the marble stairway. Pain shot up from her ankle but she was no longer limping.

The rotunda was more crowded than before, the line at the double doors of Courtroom Three was longer, uniformed officers trying to keep order, no news cameras in sight, and then she was outside.

The green—more people now and more cars everywhere—had begun to lose its pristine whiteness, streaked with the dark crisscrossing of boots and galoshes. Only the surrounding lawns glittered with sheets of unsullied snow. Going down the steps, she was again trying not to think of Charlie Larkin, dead and buried and long gone, alive only in her memory. *I forgive you, Pop. I forgive you because Andy taught me how, and I forgive him, too, if he's taken the same tragic downward path. But I can't go through all that again. Never, never. I won't, I won't, I won't!*

And now was the time to tell him. Now, early, not waiting till she was in deeper, and helpless . . .

Turning off the green, she saw Colby's entrance down Hancock Street and, past the vacant lot between, the sign and glass facade of STODDARD HARDWARE. Several people had gathered at the door: friends, silent, mourning already. And then Mattie Stoddard's face drifted into her mind. She remembered her now: her plain, young, freckled face, oddly sweet and trusting.

Two more good decent people dead.

Because of him.

Because he had not drowned.

Because she had *not* killed him!

If the bastard's dead, the world's better off. How shocked she'd been when Andy had said that. She understood now, and agreed. Human life was precious, yes—but not *all* human life.

She went into Colby's. It was also crowded, also noisy.

Andy was not at the counter.

He was not at a table. Or in a booth.

The back room then. Never too early for booze if you're a boozer . . .

Mr. Colby was not there and there was no one behind the bar.

She went out the side door onto Liberty Street.

Colder every minute. Damn him! If he could start drinking again at a time like this, damn him, *damn* him!

Arriving again at the snow-covered green, she turned toward the courthouse. To get Steve's Volvo, which was parked behind. Which was also filled with all that she owned. All packed up and nowhere to go.

So much for love.

The fury inside Nick Verini had turned from hot to cold by the time he reached town. He'd been wild, steamed to the gills, sizzling, when he turned into the Alpine Chalet on the way to fix the fucker's plane. But now, after circling around on the back streets—little piss-hole houses where the suckers lived—he was driving the shitty little Mustang in the traffic along the green toward the courthouse. Where the jail was. Taking chances. You don't take chances, how you know you're alive?

Even if the hick fuzz was looking, even if his picture'd been on TV again this morning—he'd seen it himself— nobody'd recognize him now. Not in this cornball getup, hunting cap, no beard. He knew how he looked, he looked like shit, but not even his own brother'd know him now, even if he was not in the car but walking on the street, nobody'd recognize him.

And if anyone did, he still had the Beretta he'd used on the Stoddards. Ten rounds, he'd only used two. Plenty, more than enough—

Then he saw her. The cunt herself. Red hair, bright even in this light, no hat. On the walk going around to the rear of the courthouse. Her back to him, but he'd know her anywhere, anytime. If he'd done what he'd threatened in the van last night, instead of letting her go like some *idiota*—she didn't scare easy, dumb bitch—if he'd done it then instead of *talking*. When he had her naked, scared, shaking all over. That body,

Christ on calvary, that slender girlish body, white, he could've had it under him, pushing his thing in, over and over and *over,* her begging, crying, helpless, and then at the end, his hands on her throat, just as he was about to come, waiting and plunging till the last second, then closing all the way, like a last gasp, same second him coming inside her, her dying, both at the same second like a goddam *explosion.* One thing he'd always wanted to do and never had. Way he thought of doing it when he was a kid, jacking off. Fuck and kill, fuck and kill—same thing anyway.

But if he'd done it then, he wouldn't have it ahead of him now. Soon. She'd get hers and he'd get his. Soon as he got her up there to the lodge in Canada, in the woods, alone, nobody for miles, take his time, just the two of them, her tied up, helpless, begging, naked . . .

Her slim figure had disappeared behind the stone building. Should he grab her now, while he had the chance? What the fuck did he care what happened at the goddam hearing? He was off the job now. Poppa'd said so on the phone.

Angelo was probably in town by now, his own plane. Let him take over. He always took over anyway. Poppa always—

Oh, sweet mother of Christ, his cock had stiffened. It was throbbing.

Not yet. Plenty of time. Anytime before she gets on that plane with that fucker. If he waited till then, she'd get hers anyway, but not the way he had in mind, not *his* way.

And he was doing things *his* way now. He had it all mapped. First, Georgie wastes the kid in the slammer, then the fucker gets his in the plane, then the slut gets hers, he gives it to her up in Canada. Clean sweep.

And look at that crowd! Like Christmas. Snow everywhere, people everywhere. Waiting for the show inside to start. Well, Nick Verini had a surprise for all of them. A big one. That old familiar bolt of pleasure shot through him. Nick Verini had the power.

Now if only dumb Georgie-boy was awake in there . . .

Double bull's-eye this way. Everything they'd tried, the fucker and the cunt, it'd been to save the kid.

At the end of the green he drove straight on, slow, passing along the side of the courthouse—barred windows on the ground floor beyond the snow-covered lawn. Then he touched the horn: two longs, three shorts, like he'd said.

But all he got was little beep-sounds.

The woman driver of the Volks in front twisted her head. Fuck you, lady.

He jammed the heel of his hand, hard, on the horn. And he heard the same sounds. And at the same time remembered: *Listen, Georgie, Ferrari horn don't sound like no other.*

Oh Christ, had he fucked up again?

Kill him, Georgie. Kill him and hang him up. Kill, do your job, what I told you, *kill the sonofabitch*!

FIFTEEN

Annabelle Southworth was shocked to the depth of her soul. How blind can a mother be? Or had she been too lost in her books and library duties and routine to recognize the truth of her own life?

Bruce drove the old Dodge Dart slowly, silently now, on the road toward town, snow-covered but soon to be cleared by the plows. He had insisted on driving; a lot of kids were cutting classes this morning, he'd said.

She was not a woman given to expressing her emotions—a way of living that was both a blessing and a curse. At times such as this a blessing, because it prevented the gnashing of teeth or unrestrained weeping that part of her longed to give in to. But she had accepted herself, and her own nature, long ago. Could she accept her only son's true nature?

Finally Bruce said, "I've wanted to tell you, lots of t-t-times. Then Mrs. Lucas c-c-called me a pervert on the phone. And . . . and when Tracy Larkin came, talking about truth and honor and that k-kid my age in jail. And . . . and on the TV, all that about toxic wastes killing us and how we m-must be insane, all of us, to *let* it happen. She's right, too—the cost of one spaceship or warship p-p-probably *could* clear up the waste and put the criminals out of business at the same time, once and for all." He shook his head as if to clear it. "It all got m-m-m-mixed together some way, so I had to t-talk to you."

"We don't talk often," she said. "*Honor* was one of your

277

father's favorite words. And now? What are you going to do now, Bruce?''

His eyes were on the road again. "I think if I had any g-g-guts, I'd drop you off at the library and drive to the courthouse. B-b-b-but—''

"You had the courage''—she'd always despised the word *guts*—''to tell me the truth about yourself.'' And that truth was a burden she could feel becoming a terrible weight inside. Thank God, oh thank God, Howard is not alive!

"Mrs. Lucas said if I told anyone, she'd make sure I d-d-don't graduate.''

"You're seventeen years old, Bruce. An adult now, really.'' She was remembering his words, earlier: *I can't help the way I am, Mom.*

"What about you? If p-p-people knew, what about *you*?''

He was thinking of her. Imagine. He'd never seemed to think of her before. She felt the sudden impulse to place a gloved hand over his on the wheel, to whisper: *It doesn't matter. I don't count now.* But she couldn't. Because that wouldn't be the truth. How could she face all those people coming into the library, their faces knowing, their whispers?

"Please tell me, Mom! What should I do?''

He had turned the car into the parking area alongside the library, a very old, very white building with a steeple, which years ago had been the Congregational church before they decided to build the new one on the green. He did not turn off the motor.

"Do my feelings really matter?'' she asked.

"T-t-t-to me, they do, yes.''

"Well, if that's true,'' she said, "I'd be mightily relieved if you went straight on to school and put the whole thing behind you. But if you did, you'd have to live with that the rest of your life. If you do go to the courthouse, you'll have to live with whatever comes of that, too. It's your decision, Bruce. Not mine.''

Then she leaned toward him and kissed him on the cheek—a most unusual gesture for Annabelle Southworth, especially in broad daylight, in a public place. "We shouldn't be ashamed of what we are, dear. It's what we *do* or *don't* do, that we have to be ashamed of. Or proud of.''

"Mr. Horgan's still waiting, Mr. Arnold.''

"Waiting?" Blake Arnold barked into the intercom. "Susie, I thought I told you to tell him I don't have time."

"I'll tell him again, sir."

Blake Arnold knew that he should be downstairs in Judge Patton's chambers by now, but everything seemed to be happening so fast. The CBS reporter wanted an on-camera interview and a stringer for *The New York Times* had called— but there was always the risk of saying something that might jeopardize his case. Still, the public exposure would be smart politics. *I'm so glad. Mr. Clifford Hyatt will be glad, too, won't he?* And then there was Valerie, the new Valerie—it'd be just like her, in this mood, to show up at the hearing plastered. Christ, what a morning! Two respectable, law-abiding citizens dead of gunshot wounds, bodies discovered by a neighbor who couldn't rouse them on the phone; no clues except a new Ford Mustang stolen; too early for fingerprints. And Dr. Foster Martin phoning to demand that, sad as the circumstances admittedly were and regardless of motive, Dr. Nat Nichols should be placed under arrest for the murder of his wife. Followed by an angry sermon on the sanctity of human life and the will of God—until Blake had interrupted to say, *I can't have Dr. Nat arrested, Foster, because he's dead. He killed himself.* And Dr. Martin had said, *Well, that's an admission that he did wrong, isn't it?* As if that somehow settled the entire matter to *his* satisfaction.

And then there was the fact, the frustrating fact, that he couldn't face Judge Patton until he could make some sense out of the incredible news that Dr. Nat had filled out two different autopsy reports on Lynnette Durand.

"Excuse me," Andrew Horgan said as he entered, slamming the door behind him. "I won't take a minute, Mr. Arnold. I've got a right to have certain information before the hearing." Andrew Horgan, arm in sling, body stiff, looked even worse than he had looked at the hospital—and more determined. "Dr. Nichols is dead, isn't he?"

Blake nodded. "But there's no suicide note. You didn't go inside, did you?"

"I decided Dr. Nichols was in no condition to tell me what I'd gone out there to find out."

Then, if he hadn't gone inside, he had not seen the two printed forms, folded and attached to the cassette tape with a rubber band. "We don't have the official cause-of-death report yet," Blake said. Damned if he was going to say he had two conflicting ones under the legal pad on his desk. Also, Horgan's eyes suggested he'd been drinking. "I'm a busy man."

"You don't suspect any connection whatever between Dr. Nichols' death and my son's case?"

Blake heaved a sigh. "More wild conjecture! No, goddammit, you can't tie in everything that happens in and around this town with your son."

"What about what happens at Echo Lake?" Andrew demanded, his tired, bloodshot eyes scowling. "They find a body?"

"Would you care if they did?"

"I'd care because Tracy'd probably be charged and I'd have to testify that she'd pushed the bastard in, in self-defense."

Blake decided to smile. He hoped it was convincing. "Well, fortunately, we won't come to that. The State Police divers found no body." What had been preying on his mind, though, was that they *had* found metal drums, or canisters of some sort, on the bottom, and that Tracy Larkin somehow had had the contents analyzed. Two facts that he hadn't had time to assimilate yet. "Relax, Horgan. They did find a red Ferrari. So your story stands up in that respect. Satisfied?"

"They'll find it was registered in the name of Dominic Verini."

"We already have. But that's a far cry from proving that he had anything whatever to do with Lynnette Durand's death."

"Is there a police search on for the bastard?"

"In town, yes. Sheriff Wheeler doesn't buy your story."

"Meaning the bastard can do anything he wants to do outside the town limits!"

Then the intercom clicked on and Susie's brisk secretarial voice asked, "Will you accept a call from Sheriff Wheeler, Mr. Arnold?"

"Put him on," he said. Picking up the phone, he looked up at Andrew, who had stopped with the doorknob in hand. "This is business, Horgan."

"I know," Andrew said, and did not move.

Blake spoke his own name into the phone, glaring, and

then he heard the sheriff's heavy, gruff voice: "Mr. Arnold, I'm out here at the Stoddard residence. We're still waiting for the medical examiner to come in from Wyndam. State Police unit's taking prints here but the phone was tore out from the wall, so *those* prints are already in the works. Anything new there on Dr. Nichols' death?"

"Not official, of course, but no one doubts it's a suicide. You'd better send the Wyndam coroner to the Nichols house when he's finished with the bodies there. Thanks for calling, Sheriff, and I suggest you get back here right away. Your testimony may be needed at the Horgan hearing."

He set down the phone—and discovered Andrew Horgan's haunted and demanding eyes on him.

"Bodies?" Andrew asked, and waited.

"Coincidence, Mr. Horgan. Couple named Stoddard. Somebody shot them both and took their car. We don't know what else is missing."

"Where?"

"North on fifty-seven."

"Outside the town limits?" And then he snarled, "When you get fingerprints, make sure they're matched up with Verini's. I'm sure *his* are on file." And then, fear in his eyes now: "Have you seen Tracy Larkin?"

"Fortunately not. But she *was* in. My secretary spoke to her only a few minutes ago."

"Thank God." Andrew stepped to the desk. "How many double murders has this town had in the last century? How many suicides?" Then, as if struggling for control, he leaned over the desk. "Now listen to me, Mr. Arnold. You're going to see that an all-points order goes out on Nick Verini. You have his photograph. You know his history and his connections. You're going to give me the description of that car. And then you're going to call the jail and tell whoever is in charge that Andrew Horgan is going to visit his son *before* the hearing—"

"What the hell makes you think—"

"Shut up and listen! If you don't, I'm going down to see Judge Jared Patton personally. I'm going to tell him that my son will plead *not* guilty to *all* charges and all he can do is bind him over to the grand jury—"

"You're risking—"

"Shut up or you'll force me to use my right arm to break

your jaw.'' He rushed on, each word distinct: ''That means the case will drag on for weeks, maybe months, and *that* means you'll have to *prove* a charge that you know by now is false, and I'll have a public trial in which to expose the conspiracy that you also know by now is not a paranoid delusion.'' He paused. ''I still don't know what your stake is in this, but that'll give me time to find out. You decide.''

While Andrew waited, Blake remembered Clifford Hyatt's second phone call, the one he'd received less than an hour ago. *You do understand, don't you, Blake? I don't care how you do it, or, for that matter, what it costs. Close the case. Today!*

He didn't even try to smile now. ''The car is last year's model Ford Mustang, two-door, metallic color. Registered in the name of Mrs. Mathilda Stoddard.'' He was relieved that his voice sounded reasonably normal. ''No one's trying to keep you from your son, Mr. Horgan.'' He snapped down the lever on the intercom. ''Susie, get me whoever's on duty at reception in the jail, and after I hang up, get me state police barracks. I want to issue an all-points bulletin. Thank you.'' Then, squinting up at the very still, very stolid man before him, he asked, ''What makes you think I want to get your son's case over with?''

''You want to get the case *closed*, not over with.''

''How do you know that?''

''Because if you wanted to get it over with, you'd drop the charges. That wouldn't close the case. And the investigation would have to go on.''

''Are those accusations, Mr. Horgan?''

''Not yet. No.''

This time Andrew Horgan did not slam the door. The silence was worse.

Valerie Arnold, sitting in the waiting room, jumped when the door to her husband's office opened and closed.

Then she saw Andrew Horgan—whom she'd seen before only on that first television newscast yesterday morning—charge past Susie's desk and out. As Valerie rose to her feet, the intercom popped on again and she heard Blake's voice: ''Susie, did Chief Radford send up that cassette player?''

''I have it right here, sir. And I gave Holly Ray the

message about Mr. Horgan, and the state police will ring back—"

"Call down to Courtroom Three right away and inform Judge Patton that I'm requesting a fifteen-minute postponement. Got that?"

"Right away, sir."

But Susie Pritchard was clearly in a dither, so Valerie stood, picked up the small black machine on the desk, winked, and then opened the door into her husband's inner sanctum. Sanctum sanctorum. Why did all the courthouse offices have to look so dreary?

"Val! What the devil are you doing here?"

It was a good question. But she had the answer—another question: "Blake, I just heard about poor Mr. Stoddard and his wife. Is there any connection between that and the hearing?"

"Val, listen—everything's coming down this morning. Judge Patton's waiting and—" He broke off and stared up at her from behind his desk. "Are you still tight?"

"I? Not tight at all. Loose." She placed the tape player on his desk. "Loose, counselor. Did you know you married a loose woman? Judge, Your Honor, please instruct the witness to answer my question directly."

"No connection, no. Why do people always attempt to tie everything up in a neat bundle?" He stood up. Not tall, but dignified, impressive, in his striped gray three-piece Brooks Brothers uniform. "The police are doing all they can do!"

"And you?"

Blake snapped a lever down and leaned over to say: "Susie, call down and make sure Mrs. Arnold has a seat in the reserved section. She's going down right away."

She took out a cigarette and sat on the edge of his desk, crossing her long legs when a tiny yellow light began to flicker on the intercom.

He flicked the lever again, eyes on her. "Yes, Susie?"

"Chief Radford telephoned from Dr. Nichols' house. He only wanted to report they've found no note. They did a thorough search of the whole house, he said. I told him you'd received the tape recording that he sent in. And the two autopsy reports."

"Thanks, Susie."

Valerie knew that her eyes were asking, but she said it

anyway: "Two reports?" She lit her cigarette. "On the Durand girl?"

"It's a legal matter, Val. One postdates the other—that's the one we have to regard as official."

"Postdates?" She stood up, feeling just a trifle wobbly. Her mouth was very dry. "Would that mean that one was written before midnight and the second one after?"

"Maybe for some reason Dr. Nat went back and did a more thorough job." Blake came around the desk. "The last one written is legally valid. That's the end of it."

"Not for me." For some reason her heart seemed to be aching, and somehow she didn't seem able to control herself this morning. "Let me guess: The last one written is the one that incriminates Todd Horgan and makes your case—"

"Val, I've had about as much as I can take." He took her by the arm and, his hand tight, led her toward the door. "I'm not on trial here."

"When you spoke to Dr. Nichols last night on the phone—"

"I'm warning you, Val—"

She wrenched her arm free. "The second time, when you were so worried that I suggested you find out for sure. But what'd he tell you the *first* time that bothered you so much?"

"Valerie, I've had it! Now you get the hell out of here and stay! I'm telling you, I've *had* it!"

And so, she realized, had she. She reached for the doorknob. "Tell me, what's the legal penalty for suppressing evidence, Blake?"

She heard his teeth gritting. "Nobody's suppressing evidence! How the hell can I explain legalities to someone who's not trained in them?"

"You never, never could." She opened the door. "Well, when Mr. Clifford Hyatt calls, please give him my coldest regards. And tell him, please, that your wife has decided she would *hate* living in Washington, D.C."

She strolled out. Perfectly casual, not tight in the least now, just a reasonably attractive thirty-five-year-old woman, wearing a tweed suit, medium heels, and an expression, she trusted, of detached good humor, no sadness, please, outrage out of vogue this season.

She nodded to Susie, who was again on the phone, and went into the corridor and along it toward the marble stairway. No hurry, no rush. You shall know the truth and the truth shall make you free.

And the truth was—*her* truth was—that no matter what was between them, what had been between them, nothing would ever be quite the same again for the rest of their lives.

Descending the stairs, she was stopped by a boy who looked like a high school kid—rather handsome, brown crew cut, athletic—who inquired whether the State's Attorney's Office was on the second floor. The boy looked very pale, very determined, and miserable. And he spoke with difficulty, with a noticeable stutter.

"God, you look tired."

It was all Todd could think of to say to this man Andrew Horgan—who might or might not actually be his father.

The man closed the door behind him and moved, slowly, to pull out the chair at the far end of the long table. All he said was: "I *am* tired." Then he peered down the narrow table. "How are you making it, Todd?"

"What happened to your arm?"

Andrew shrugged; then he winced, but only briefly. "I got in the way of a bullet. Luckily, it was dark at the time."

"A bullet?"

"It's too long a story to go into now. Time's running out. I asked you: How are you making it?"

"I'm not sure I'm making it at all. And I'm not sure I give a damn."

"What are you going to do at ten o'clock, damn it?"

"Julia thinks I should confess—"

"To what?"

"Ask Julia."

"To hell with Julia."

"My erstwhile attorney, Gerald Asshole Lewis, he thinks that if I do, he can fix it for me to get two or three years' free board in this Château d'If."

Andrew made an impatient gesture, the palm of his hand coming down flat on the table. "Manslaughter, fit of jealous rage, temporary insanity—I talked to Blake Arnold. Not once but twice. Speaking of assholes."

Todd felt a spasm of warmth in his midsection. He was tempted to smile. "You came here to give me the same advice?"

"I'm not much on advice—not having had any children till about thirty hours ago."

Todd decided to stand up. "Maybe you shouldn't bother. Did Julia give you the good news?"

"Julia's always brimming with good news, isn't she?"

"If you're doing everything you're doing—like getting shot—maybe you should know: Julia says you're not my father after all."

Andrew said nothing for a long moment. Then his face twisted into a smile, his eyes finding Todd's. "Well, Julia should know. . . ."

How can I remember who was balling me at the time? Julia had snapped, after she'd delivered the blow.

"That's it," Todd said. "She *doesn't* know. Can't be sure. So I could be anybody's little bastard."

"So . . . so we'll never know, will we? Either one of us." Shaking his head, Andrew pushed back the chair on the concrete floor, stood up. "I had to practically *bribe* my way in here, blackmail anyway, and I did it to find out what you plan to do." He came down the length of the table. "And I'm goddammed if I'm going to ask you again, so spit it out."

"What do *you* think I should do?"

"I don't count. If you haven't made up your mind yet, say it."

They were close now and Todd's bewilderment and depression caused him to back away, his body turning. "I've just about decided to go along, get the phony game over with. . . ." Then he swung about. "What do I care? I can't go back to Haddam. My life's shot." He felt his throat closing. "And . . . Lynnette's dead."

A moment passed.

Then Andrew said, "I've been through that one, too, you know."

"I didn't."

"What're you going to do, lie down and give up? I did, for five years."

"No, I didn't know—"

"And if you go along with their idea, it won't be two years, or three, or five. Your life *is* finished. Now."

"And if I don't, *what?* Life in prison?"

"If you're convicted"—Andrew stepped toward him—"which I damned well doubt now."

"But you're not sure."

"There's nothing *sure* about anything. Haven't you learned that?"

"Especially Justice, with a big J."

"Yes, *especially*. But you know you didn't kill Lynnette because you couldn't. And I know it too."

"If you do, we're the only two." Puzzled, Todd stood frowning into the man's bright brown eyes. "*Why* do you believe me?"

"Because I think I've come to know you. At least a little. And because now I know who did kill her, and why, and possibly how."

"Those two, the pictures you showed me?"

"One or both. It doesn't matter now that they're dead."

"Then how can we prove . . . ?"

"Maybe we can't. But that's not what Nick Verini and his people—if you can call them people—that's not what they're scared of anyway. It's more than that now. I know what they're up to, and if you go up those stairs out there and *lie*, say *Yes, Judge, sir, I killed her and I'm sorry*—that closes out the investigation and that's all they give a damn about!"

Beginning to tremble all over, Todd stepped back and away to look across the narrow table. "You've found out all this in twenty-four hours?"

"Nothing I can prove—yet. But enough so that the authorities can't back away—unless *you* give them the excuse. Unless *you* allow them to close the case now, this morning."

"And if I plead not guilty?"

"You'll automatically be bound over to the grand jury, I guess, and that'd give Tracy and me time to put the rest of the facts together."

"Time I'll be spending here on my ass staring at the X's I've carved on the wall . . ."

Andrew Horgan's eyes took on another expression, one that Todd had not seen before, and his voice sharpened: "A few minutes ago you were willing to settle for a year or two. I'm talking weeks, months. Why, you spoiled, self-centered bastard, when are you going to stop demanding guarantees? Damn you, you're not even grateful! When the hell are you going to grow up?"

In the silence Andrew, who no longer seemed so tired,

strode down the room and rested his back against the wall, glaring at him.

It was then that Todd recalled: *I was in a hospital once . . . twenty-eight days. Long enough to learn . . . to really live, the best way is absolute honesty.*

He said, "All you're asking me to do is to tell the truth—is that it?"

"I'm not asking you to do *anything*." The fury was still there, the voice lower. "You're nineteen years old. It's your life. You may be my son; you may not be. That fact doesn't matter now, either. Your job's to decide *who* you are, *what* you are, and then who you *want* to be and how can you become *that*."

"Existential bullshit."

But Andrew ignored this. "You got only ten minutes to do it, so I'm going to get the hell out of here." He moved to the door. "Because I don't want you to do anything or say anything just to please me or defy me." At the door he turned. "Or to get even with your mother—or to punish her. You're on your own now, kid. Whatever you decide, it's your responsibility. To the world and to yourself." He opened the door. "And there's no way to separate the two."

"Andy—" astonished, he spoke before he knew what he was going to say—"Andy, nobody ever talked to me this way before."

"Well, they should have." But his father said that softly, a lot of regret in it, regret and maybe even a kind of love.

"Thanks." It was the best he could do. "You seem different this morning, too, you know."

"Do I? Well, maybe it's because I had a long, long drink and my whole damn body's crying for more."

"Is that what you're going to do in the next ten minutes?"

His father shook his head. "That's what I'm *not* going to do." Then his tone changed: "You see, I've just rejoined the human race and I'm damned if I'm going to lose what *that* feels like."

He went out then. The door swung shut slowly, and clicked.

Todd stood staring at it until the lame old man came in to escort him back to his cell. Todd had begun to smile a little. Andy was right: Whether they were father and son by blood— that fact *didn't* matter now.

In the cell, George Bone was still at the barred window, still looking out at the cars passing in the street.

"Spotted any Ferraris, George?" Todd asked.

He had heard the madman on the street a half hour or so ago, the horn bleeping over and over, two longs, three shorts. And the blond gum-chewing Neanderthal had asked, *That sound like a Ferrari to you?* At the time Todd had been struggling, after Julia's visit, to hold on to the state of melancholy—or despair—that he'd hoped might carry him through the hearing. So he'd asked, *What the hell would a Ferrari be doing in this town?* And George Bone had growled, *I got a buddy's got one, that's why.*

Now, sitting on his bunk again, Todd was also remembering his terror earlier in the morning when George Bone had offered to show him exactly where the carotid artery was located on the neck. And the several times he'd mentioned the old man in Springfield who'd been found hanging in his cell . . .

Todd felt the cool dread return. Stronger now, more definite. Where was Mr. Kopit? He'd said something on the stairs about the shift of guards changing at ten. . . .

Why hadn't he thought of this before? All along, the dim-witted giant with the strange cruel grin had been waiting for a signal. A signal to do what?

He knew now.

Finally.

Too late?

How soon would the old man, or someone, come to take him up to the courtroom?

If he yelled . . .

If he yelled, it could all be over before Kopit could get the cell door open.

Todd stretched out on his back, placing his two palms under his head. "George, I lied to you last night. I just wasn't in the mood for sex then."

"Too late now, kid."

"I was having another one of those sick spells. They're always worse at night. And the goddam pain's enough to drive you bananas. When you got what I got—"

George Bone came closer. "You don't look sick to me."

"That's the reason I don't give a damn whether I go to

289

prison or not. They'll just put me in the infirmary. I'm going to die anyway.''

"Die?"

"And once they find out what I have, they won't let any other inmates near me.''

"Don't shit me.''

"That's why I asked for a separate cell, George. That's why I wouldn't have sex with you. It was for *your* sake, not mine.'' He sat up. "You ever hear of Acquired Immune Deficiency Syndrome?''

"Talk English,'' George Bone snarled.

"AIDS. Everybody's heard of that.'' And when George Bone's eyes narrowed, his jaw going slack, Todd rose to his feet. "I would've warned you if you'd started to sit down on the toilet.''

It took George Bone a long moment for the doubt in his mind to turn into panic. But it happened. He whirled around to return to the window. Todd could not be certain but he thought he heard George Bone say, "Up yours, Nick.'' Then he turned again and stepped around Todd in a wide semicircle and strode to the door of the cell, "Kopit!'' he called, hands gripping the bars. "Hey! Hack! Jailer! Get your ass down here!'' And then he was shouting: "I want another cell, I know my rights! Get me the fuck outa here!''

With Mr. Kopit in the door of the cell, Todd stretched out again, and said: "Didn't sound like a Ferrari horn to me, George.''

Figliuolo mio, you are dead to me.

Those were the words, Poppa's words, echoing back in his head now, over and over. No matter how hard he'd tried to explain, holding the phone hard against his ear, him in the kitchen, two bodies in the front room, and no time to piss away—anybody come to the door, he'd have to waste a third one.

You blew it, Nickie. I have only one son now. Angelo's already on his way there.

He'd been whining then, that sound he hated, and crying even, his face wet, after he'd whacked the two nobodies and then called Poppa's private number again and this time got Vincent Verini himself, not that shit brother of his. All he'd wanted was for Angelo to tell him how to make the fucker's plane crash after it was up five, ten thousand feet, some trick like stuffing a vent—he'd heard of that—but hell no, it was Poppa he got: *Network news, front page Boston Globe, Daily News—you call that keeping the lid on, Nick?*

Didn't matter how much he pleaded, tears blinding his eyes, like a little boy, begging—Poppa had said the one thing he thought he'd never, ever hear.

But he was goddammed if he was going home. If he was not the son of Vincent Verini, he did not take orders from Vincent Verini. He wished he'd said *Fuck you, Poppa.* Someday he'd get up the guts to say it. But he was going to finish the job. Which was why he was here now, standing in the back of the courtroom. He'd slipped a damp bill, a C-note, to some hick clown to get his place in line, and now here he was leaning against the wooden wall, jabber-jabber all sides, like a buzzing in his skull. . . .

"Attention, please. Attention." Some old turkey up front, polite, bailiff—he knew bailiffs. "Attention. Judge Patton has asked me to tell you there will be a postponement of approximately ten minutes before court will be commenced."

A little flutter of a groan, and whispers and voices. Oh Christ, could he last another ten minutes?

Sure he could. Shit yes, he was Nick Verini. He could do anything he had to do.

"Attention, please." The same asshole. Old man, old suit, old voice. "Judge Patton would like to see Miss Tracy Larkin and Mr. Andrew Horgan in his chambers. Come this way, please."

Them two. Both of them. He saw the fucker stand up from a table inside the rail up front and turn to look out over the crowd. Arm in a sling. Tough shit, tough. Sorry I missed. Won't miss next time. Wait till you get up there in that plane, fucker. Wait till that dirt and sand in the tank gets up to the engine. Splutter, splutter and down, down, down—total you *and* the plane, way you totaled my Ferrari.

Tracy Larkin was going down the aisle. He watched her go through the low swinging gate in the railing and then she passed right by where the one-armed fucker was waiting, not so much as a goddam nod, and through the door the bailiff had gone to, where he was standing alongside the steps going up to the bench.

The laugh was on them. The big laugh. His. He knew what

the goddam judge had to tell them: *Your son, Mr. Horgan, was found hanging in his cell. . . .*

If only he could be in there to see their faces, them two; they were the reason Poppa had said, *Figliuolo mio, you are dead to me. I have only one son now.* They were the reason, but when he got home and told Poppa how he'd handled it: *Suicide's good as a confession, capeesh? My idea. You wanted the case closed—well, your son Nickie did it. Completo. His way.*

You'll see, Poppa. Whole world'll see who Nickie Verini is, *what* Nickie Verini is, what kind of real man he is.

SIXTEEN

Ten minutes? Ten minutes, shit!

If everybody'd just clam up, stop talking! Jibber-jabber, gibble-gabble, chitter-chatter—Jesus, it had to be a half-hour by now. Longer. Seemed like years. And Tracy Larkin—why hadn't she come back to the courtroom?

He'd rather die than face Poppa's contempt. If he didn't do what he had to do, he'd bring dishonor to his father's name. And his own.

First thing, soon as he was sure, he'd phone Poppa again. Case closed. College kid dead, Poppa. Like that time in Springfield. Only this time *he* gave the order. *Nick*—nobody else.

Then . . . then he'd get up there to the lodge . . . with the cunt . . . do what he had to do to her . . . then find a priest, any priest, go to confession, beg God's forgiveness, his mercy, and his soul would be purified and it would go to heaven, everlasting happiness. . . .

Shut up, shut up, oh, Christ, make them shut up!

Heads were turning. The turkey next to him was staring.

Cool it, Nick. *The college can say unstable, Francesca*—Poppa's voice in his mind again, years ago—*what scares me is: What if someday he goes off like a firecracker on the Fourth of July?*

Not me, Poppa. Not Nickie.

He looked over the heads. Nobodies. All the good respectable citizens. Shit. Like he'd heard Poppa say once, in one of his good relaxed moods: *They're all law-abiding till they need*

*us. World War Two, FDR needed Luciano. JFK needed us,
Bay of Pigs. And what about those movie stars singing and
dining at the White House—Nixon's pals, Kennedy's, Reagan's
buddies from Nevada?*

Vincent Verini knew. And his son—he knew, too. Knew
what he'd almost lost. The mansion in the country, the one on
Beacon Hill, the lodge, suite in the Carlyle, island in the
Bahamas, Momma's pearls, diamonds, emeralds—oh Christ,
did the Verinis know how to live!

And who was paying for it? Not just the druggies on
smack, or the high rollers on coke, but these people, here,
these little shit-nobodies. Chumps. Dirt. Worse than shit.
Like those two Stoddards: two pieces of meat on the floor.
That's all, meat. He'd as soon waste a couple of them as take
a crap.

A kind of hush began to fall on the room. Like in church,
waiting for mass to begin. Solemn. No more hubbub.

The door to the left of the judge's bench was open now.
Old bailiff standing to one side. And then there she was, the
cunt, with the fucker standing alongside. Over the heads he
could see both faces—serious, sad. That electric shock of
power shot through him again. The fucker'd got his. Good
old Georgie Bone, he'd done his job. Now, Poppa, who
needs a confession? Case dismissed, defendant *morto*.

Now Poppa'd be sorry for what he'd said.

The lawyers came out behind them. The big hot-shot mouthpiece with the face he'd seen in the newspapers walking in
like a big baboon, across in front of the bench and out
through another door. The little one—most likely the DA,
gray pinstripe, tight lips—he went to sit down at the table on
the right and began to shuffle papers.

Then he saw Tracy Larkin come out through the gate and
stand at the front row looking out over the room. I'm here.
Take a good once-over, I'm here. Nick Verini never gives up.

Her gawk passed right by him. Not even a blink.

You'll see me later, baby. You'll really see me.

She turned, like she was satisfied, and sat down in the front
row.

But no judge. Where was the goddam judge? Let's go,
man, let's *go!*

The door to the right of the bench opened then and the
baboon came back in, and another hick cop, and then . . .

He couldn't believe what he was staring at.

The kid.

It was Todd Horgan, just the way he'd looked in that picture on TV, beard and all.

Jesus.

Georgie, Georgie, you are in deep shit now. I'll do the job myself. I'll blow your goddam blond curly head off!

"All rise."

When they did, he couldn't see over their heads.

If Georgie was in deep shit, he was in deeper.

Judge Patton had expected a crowd, but nothing like this.

Black robe swishing, he mounted the steps leading to the bench and stood frowning behind his chair. He always enjoyed the respectful hush that fell as he swept into a courtroom, especially a packed one. In his twenty-one years on the bench, had he ever conducted a hearing in one as crowded as this? Celebrities, television, lurid crime—bread and circuses. Tall and straight and imposing, he stood staring out stonily until the room quieted.

Then he began, in his very soft, very resonant voice: "Ladies and gentlemen, the Court apologizes for the delay. But since admission is not charged, I know you'll forgive us." A small titter—well, it was a start. "In normal circumstances, if this were a trial, the Court would not permit standees in the rear. I'm going to make an exception today but I must insist that the aisles be left clear at all times." Then he added, with just a hint of a smile: "The Court has no desire to send anyone out into that Indian summer blizzard." More tittering, a few giggles—nothing like a reference to the weather to touch the universal. "I should like to explain to all of you: This is a judicial hearing. You will note that the jury box contains, instead of jurors, members of the press. Whom I must warn: positively no photographs of any kind in the courtroom."

He looked down on the prosecutor's table, where Blake Arnold sat alone, and at the defense table, where the famous, or infamous, attorney Gerald Usher Lewis sat next to the defendant. The boy's father, whom he'd just met in chambers, looked drawn, and very tired. If only the young realized what they put their parents through. "I would caution the prosecution and defense counsel that I shall allow broad leeway, but they are not to turn this proceeding into a trial.''

Someone in the rear began to cough. Judge Patton cleared his throat and the coughing stopped. ''This proceeding is for the purpose of the Court's deciding whether an accused citizen should or should not be bound over for trial—that is, whether there is sufficient evidence to indict.'' He smiled then—it was time for another smile—and lifted his voice: ''In short, ladies and gentlemen, our purpose is to cut through the red tape and save you taxpayers your hard-earned money.'' They laughed then, a general laugh, the ice broken. Weather and taxes, he chided himself—motherhood and flag to follow. He pulled out the high-backed swivel chair and sat down. ''You may call the first case.''

''State of Vermont versus Todd Horgan.''

That did it—no preventing the rustle-bustle, the straightening to attention, the craning of necks and sibilant whispers. No need to try to prevent it. The curtain was going up.

Todd Horgan stood, facing the bench, but did not come forward. Small kid, face not quite obscured by a short sandy-colored beard. Personally, he despised beards. Always had. Reminded him of his daughter Amanda's friends. Well, chalk up a strike against the accused.

''Your Honor,'' Todd Horgan said, ''may I approach the bench?''

Startled, the judge said, with what he hoped was a wry smile: ''You may. Mr. Horgan, where did you learn that phrase?'' Might as well get established who's in charge here.

''I go to the movies, Your Honor.''

Jared Patton scowled. The boy had managed to defy and to accede at the same time, in one sentence. Fresh. Chalk up another strike.

''I've decided to represent myself,'' Todd Horgan said.

''That's your legal privilege. And when you address the Court, you will remember to do it properly. May I ask *why* you have reached this decision?''

''Yes. Because I'm not guilty.'' And then he added: ''Your Honor.''

Jared Patton was tempted to quote that old but valid saw about a lawyer representing himself having a fool for a client, but decided against it: this kid might twist it somehow to his advantage. ''Mr. Lewis?'' he prompted.

Gerald Usher Lewis rose to his feet. "I've advised my client what to do, and why. If he chooses to go against that advice, I'll be *delighted* to withdraw."

"He advised me," Todd Horgan said, "to plead guilty to something I did not do . . . Your Honor."

"The Court grants you permission to withdraw, Mr. Lewis. But please resume your seat. I have other matters to take up with you very soon now."

Gerald Usher Lewis's broad, homely face was mottled red with anger and frustration as he sat down. Judge Patton nodded to Todd Horgan, who returned to the defense table. Then he riffled through the probable-cause affidavits before him—he'd already absorbed the details thoroughly—and said: "Putting aside for the moment the primary issue at hand"—he took a deep breath—"Mr. Horgan, you are charged with illegal possession of a controlled narcotic substance in a misdemeanor amount—namely cannabis." And then, for the sake of the audience, confidentially: "Vulgarly known as marijuana, grass, or *pot*." Sure enough, sniggers and snickers, two or three outright grunts of laughter here and there from the college kids. He thought of Amanda again: *Oh, Daddy, you are such a sweet ham on the bench.*

"Guilty, Your Honor," Todd Horgan said.

Jared Patton leaned foward. "I haven't asked you yet." Everyone enjoyed this. "You seem to be in a hurry to go back to jail, Mr. Horgan. Is it the food you like? Or the view?"

In the laughter, Todd Horgan's face did not change. Nor did the boy's eyes leave his. Nor did any expression of either contrition or defiance enter them.

"Illegal possession of a firearm unregistered in the state of Vermont—namely, a .357 Magnum Smith and Wesson revolver." The courtroom was very quiet. "Guilty or not guilty?"

"Guilty, Your Honor."

"Before I pronounce sentence on these charges, you may sit down, Mr. Horgan."

As the boy joined his father and Mr. Lewis at the table, the judge shuffled through the documents again. He had the audience in the palm of his hand now. "I also have before me," he said, "your record of previous offenses and arrests, Mr. Horgan. Traffic charges, drunken driving, reckless endangerment, etcetera, etcetera . . ."

In the silence he again heard Amanda's voice in his mind: *You won't understand this, Daddy, but I've decided that the courts themselves are often guilty of turning people into criminals.* Damned right I don't understand, Amanda. I haven't understood you or your friends for years.

He was squinting down on Todd Horgan at the table. "Also," he said, holding a paper so that it could be seen, "also assault and battery, bodily harm. A conviction and fine. Do you recall the incident, Mr. Horgan?"

The boy nodded, saying nothing, and Jared Patton was about to demand that he speak up when he realized that the blue-green eyes were moist with tears. Then he recalled reading what Todd Horgan's defense had been in that case— something about the victim's having made a lewd pass at the girl Lynnette Durand in some student hangout in the town of Haddam.

Another idea occurred to him, one he hadn't considered earlier. "Mr. Horgan, Senior," he said, "before sentencing, the Court sometimes likes to hear from the parents of a defendant this age. Is there anything you'd like to add? Limiting yourself, for now, to the charges at hand, no others."

He watched Andrew Horgan rise. Slowly. He understood now that the father and son had not even met until yesterday, but he was curious. Not that anything the man could say would influence the sentence he had in mind . . .

When Andrew Horgan said, "Your Honor," the low rustling of voices in the crowded room trailed off into an expectant silence. "I'm not sure that, within that limitation, I can say what I've been thinking. You see, I have to remind the Court that my son has already suffered a great deal for a crime he did not commit. If he's to be punished now for what he did do but which would not have come to the attention of this court if he had not reported a far greater crime, then I think justice itself demands that you consider this: He has lost a girl whom he loved. Since I've known such a loss myself, I'd like to suggest that the Court take into consideration what he has already suffered, and will suffer because of that. He's young, Your Honor, very young, and love, real honest-to-God love, doesn't come often to any of us, does it? Whatever he did, it was not done in malice. And I damned well know now what malice is. I've learned it since I came here. That's all, Your Honor. Thank you."

Judge Patton's face remained impassive but he heard an odd note come into his voice: "I know your profession, Mr. Horgan, but maybe you missed your calling. Thank you."

No, love doesn't come often: He granted that. To some, such as himself, not at all. He and Amanda's mother had lived in the same house like polite but hostile strangers for thirty years.

He didn't miss the looks that passed between Andrew Horgan and his son, and especially between Andrew Horgan and Tracy Larkin, as the man turned to sit down. When he rested his wounded arm on the table, a flash of pain crossed his features. Sitting in the front row beyond the railing, Tracy Larkin appeared to be on the verge of tears and angry at the same time. Recalling her face on the television screen, he also remembered that she was one of those young radicals of whom Amanda was so fond.

He tapped the gavel once, restoring order quickly, and then let his gaze roam toward Julia Craven, sitting across the aisle from Tracy Larkin in the front row. He kept the gavel in hand; he'd probably need it now.

"Miss Craven," he said, and the silence was complete. "Miss Craven, we have time for your input." He had been saving her for last, but he apologized: "Perhaps I should have asked you to speak first. Would you care to add whatever you feel?"

Julia Craven stood up, and he allowed the whispered drone of recognition, followed by murmurs and exclamations as she moved, slowly, through the gate. The crowd may as well get its money's worth. She looked somewhat older than she'd appeared on the screen, but she was still one hell of a sexy woman, with a belted leather trench coat hanging from her shoulders down to her high boots.

When she was standing before him, her eyes on his as if waiting for a cue, he tapped again, twice this time, and nodded to her. "Miss Craven?"

"Judge," Julia Craven said, "it's not Todd's fault. It's mine." He hadn't quite expected this. "I take full responsibility for anything he's done wrong." But he *should* have expected the tears he saw welling into the woman's beautiful eyes. "I only wish I could live my own life all over again. I've failed Todd. I've failed myself. I've failed everyone." She was speaking in that throaty emotional rush that he remembered from her films. "It's true, Your Honor. I haven't been a good mother." She glanced over her shoulder. "Have I, Todd?" And then Jared Patton, seeing her tear-filled eyes on her son, realized: She was playing a scene. As if she were on a stage, or as if there were cameras on her. And playing it *damned* well. The audience was hushed, expectant, eager for the next word. Her eyes were on him again. "So, Judge Patton, if there is anyone to be punished, it should be me. I thought I wanted fame, wealth . . ." He heard an audible sniffle from somewhere behind her. "I was wrong, Your Honor. I'm the one who should be on trial here." She said it with such utter simplicity, sincerity, that he even nodded in sympathy, almost amused. Yes, Amanda, it takes one to know one. Damn, he liked this woman! If only there were some way to get her into bed. Her womanly shoulders shrugged, with sadness, helplessness. "That . . . I guess that's all I have to say, Your Honor. I don't have any words for how I feel." A long pause, beautifully eloquent. "The one that comes to mind, the only word I can think of, is . . . mercy." If he had her under him in bed, he'd give her mercy, and more! "For both of us," she said, her voice drifting away.

He heard someone start to clap, and in the rear of the room a nose was blown, very audibly. He did not rap for order but watched her make a slight curtsy to him, as if to a king on a throne, her face sober, suggesting pain inside, and then she turned to face the crowd, producing a handkerchief from nowhere.

There was a smattering of applause that began to crescendo, and when he did not use the gavel, she lifted one hand in a wave and made another little bow—a modest curtain-call—before returning to sink into her seat, head down. He allowed the applause to die somewhat before he rapped, sharply, and realized that she had told him more than he might have guessed. She had, in fact, and in her own way, caused him to reduce the length of the sentence in his mind. Even minor offenses, especially when admitted so that there is no doubt of guilt, should be punished. The public demands it. It makes them feel that law prevails and reassures them that they are themselves safer in society.

But imagine having spent a childhood with such a woman. He still thought she'd be one hell of a lay, but as a mother . . .

"Mr. Horgan," he said, "you may rise, please." And when the boy was standing, "Is there anything you have to say first?"

"No, Your Honor. I'm guilty of what I'm guilty of, and nothing else."

"We'll come to that, sir." The silence was total now. "The Court sentences you to eighteen months' imprisonment—nine months on each of two counts, sentences to be served consecutively—and two years' probation. Time to be served in the county jail in Shepperton, Vermont."

He saw Todd Horgan's eyes close, saw Gerald Usher Lewis shrug and shake his head as if to say he could have predicted or prevented this. Had the man ever been publicly dismissed by a client before? Judge Patton saw Andrew Horgan reach with his uninjured arm and place his hand over his son's on the table. As for Julia Craven, she appeared to be weeping. And Tracy Larkin, damn her defiant blue eyes, was glaring at him.

He tapped for order and waited. Then: "Now we shall move on, if you please. Mr. Arnold, I do not find among these papers the information that I understood was to be filed on a charge of homicide."

Blake Arnold stood up. "No, Your Honor."

"Or any information on the reduced charge of involuntary manslaughter."

He heard the sound he expected now: Some, perhaps most, of the good solid citizens had begun to feel cheated. But he didn't rap, only leaned over and said, "Mr. Arnold, as State's Attorney, are you prepared to explain to these good people the absence of these papers?"

He waited. Knowing. Because this had been discussed in chambers. But he had his own reasons for playing the game this way.

"Your Honor," the young prosecutor said, his face expressionless, "the State has seen fit to withdraw those charges on the basis of insufficient evidence."

There was some applause, and here and there a voice raised in protest. The judge allowed it to go on, savoring the expression on Blake Arnold's face.

When the sounds died a natural death, he lowered his voice to a whisper: "Perhaps for the sake of these citizens, and the media, the State had better explain."

"Your Honor, we do not have grounds to believe that Todd Horgan had anything whatever to do with the violent death of Miss Lynnette Durand."

The quiet was heavy. Judge Patton pushed back his chair and stood up. He was aware that every eye was on him now. "In case any of you were wondering what the attorneys and I do in that room back there behind the . . . uh, scenery"—a ripple of nervous laughter—"in what we call the judge's chambers, I am now going to tell you. In that meeting a while ago I was handed several puzzling documents which we shall now explore together, shall we? One was an autopsy report on the cause of death of Lynnette Durand. It is dated the twenty-ninth of October—which I believe was yesterday—and sparing you the medical jargon, it established that poor little Lynnette had been forcibly raped and that she had died because two broken ribs penetrated her left lung. Since there were numerous other bone fractures, this caused Dr. Nichols, the coroner, to conclude that her small, helpless body had been crushed—crushed almost certainly by the body of the assailant during the act of criminal sexual assault." He paused. "And then, ladies and gentlemen, I was given another curious document." He displayed an official form. "Lo and behold, we have here a *second* autopsy form, filled in and signed by the same Dr. Nathaniel Nichols. How did Lynnette Durand meet her death? Asphyxiation by manual strangulation. In brief, she was choked to death."

A long sigh went through the courtroom—the exact effect he was playing for.

"This second report postdates the first. Being dated October thirtieth—which means, if my intelligence is not playing senile tricks, that we may safely assume it was fllled out by Dr. Nichols some time *after* midnight last night. Legally then, this report would obtain here. Asphyxiation by a human hand. Which, of course, could be that of the erstwhile accused, Todd Horgan."

He sat down and looked at Blake Arnold, who was still standing. "Mr. Arnold, since you delivered both of these documents to me, perhaps you would like to explain why it is not possible to call Dr. Nichols in here and ask him why or whether he made a mistake on his first diagnosis."

"Dr. Nichols is dead," the State's Attorney said, in a small voice. "He . . . he took his own life during the night."

THE WAYS OF DARKNESS

"Precisely. Leaving no suicide note. It is also safe to assume, I think, that before committing this act, he removed the life-support system keeping his wife alive."

Now there was a sound: a long drawn-out sigh that turned into a low, protesting moan, which faded slowly away.

"What makes this tragedy all the more horrendous is the *reason* Dr. Nichols committed these acts. I have just heard played"—it was difficult for him to know now whether he was still acting or whether his own emotions were hardening his tone—"I have just heard a most remarkable tape recording. On it a strange voice not only suggested *what* the contents of that second report should be but also threatened—in the most sinister and horrible way—each and every member of Dr. Nichols' family. Living in various parts of the country. His children, their mates, his grandchildren . . ."

Spellbound, the audience strained to hear every syllable.

"Whoever's voice that is, that individual is the murderer of Dr. and Mrs. Nathaniel Nichols."

Something close to a low communal growl passed through the crowded room.

"Dr. Nichols, having complied with this monster's instructions, must then have had second thoughts. Possibly even as he signed the document. What would a man think at this terrible hour in his life? That if he himself were dead, there would be no reason for those threats to be carried out against those he loved—that is indeed what must have gone through his mind. And this, then, was the reason that, instead of writing a suicide note, he attached both official forms with a rubber band to the cassette tape that explains the discrepancy, *and* his desperate motives. In order for us to understand what he had done. And why. How could he possibly, in his condition, have explained in a note?"

A long silence. Jared Patton sighed. "Nat Nichols did his job well and his duty even better: He has named his murderer."

The excitement in the room was palpable now, electric. He saw Blake Arnold back toward his chair and sit down, lowering his head. He remembered the photographs he had been shown, photographs that had been in the possession of the police and the State's Attorney since some time yesterday afternoon.

"I'm not boring you, am I, Mr. Arnold?" Judge Patton asked in a silken tone.

303

"No, Your Honor," Arnold said, without lifting his head.

"I realize that some of these facts are not fresh for you, but bear with me, sir, for just a few more minutes."

Had he intended that as a threat? Possibly, possibly—he had not yet decided. Nor had he decided yet what action, if any, he intended vis-a-vis Gerald Usher Lewis, whose scowl had turned into an expression of superior forbearance. As if he were not involved. If not, why had he been so eager to close out the case?

"A voice print," Judge Patton continued, "is similar to a fingerprint with the sophisticated facilities available to law-enforcement agencies today. And Miss Tracy Larkin and Mr. Andrew Horgan, a few minutes ago in chambers, identified the voice on the tape. Once that man is in custody, we shall know more. And believe me, he will be in custody soon. Meanwhile, those of you who had the good fortune to hear and see Miss Larkin's telecast this morning know that all of this is only, as they say, the tip of the iceberg. There is every reason now to believe that hazardous waste is being dumped into our lakes and that if this is allowed to continue, it will inevitably infect our drinking-water supply. The toxicity of the chemical in Echo Lake has been scientifically confirmed, thanks to Miss Larkin and Mr. Horgan, and I am turning my copy of that report over to a young woman I know in Washington. Today. The substance is Dioxin. We all know about Love Canal. The Dioxin is contained in drums at the bottom of Echo Lake in the Franklin state forest. Where, if it is not removed, some of your children would be poisoned by it when they swim there, come summer. We owe a debt of gratitude, I think, to Miss Tracy Larkin—whom I see sitting in the front row—for publicly exposing these various crimes and the threat to our quality of life. Perhaps to the survival of some of us. An example of our free press at work, ladies and gentlemen."

Daddy, if only you'd look hard instead of accepting any old cliché that comes down the pike.

And then he recalled, for the first time, how Tracy Larkin's newscast had ended this morning:

TECHNICAL DIFFICULTIES

PLEASE STAND BY

He tapped with the gavel, although there had not been a sound. Then he allowed his voice to boom: "Since we know that a murder has been committed and since we know that Todd Horgan is not guilty, this case is *not* closed."

He stood again, towering. "For reasons that must be explored—that *will* be explored!—the Court has come to suspect that there have been undue and illegal pressures brought to bear to terminate this case as speedily, not to say as precipitately, as possible." He paused and allowed this idea to sink in. "I want to assure the people of this state—including the State's Attorney, who was elected to represent the people, *all* the people, *and* the esteemed defense attorney, whose job was to represent the best interests of his client"—his voice was thundering now—"if there has been any malfeasance, misfeasance, or suppression of evidence or attempt at the obstruction of justice in my Court, it will be dealt with severely!"

He paused for the full effect, then fixed his eyes on Todd Horgan and lowered his voice until it was almost casual. "Mr. Horgan, please rise."

Looking bewildered, the boy did as he was told.

"You have been sentenced to eighteen months on two separate misdemeanors. In view of what I have just said—and in view of your father's eloquent words—that sentence is suspended."

He rapped quickly. "Mr. Arnold, Mr. Lewis, I should like to see you both in chambers in exactly five minutes." Another tap. "Court is recessed until one o'clock."

At which time, he thought as he turned and went down the steps, His Honor will deal with the vagrants, drunken drivers, ski bums, and other riffraff cluttering up the courts. He'd probably be criticized for being too lenient. If he'd gone the other way, he'd have been criticized for being too harsh. A judge is the one person in court who can never win.

He went into the office and sat behind the desk to dial Amanda's office number in Washington.

He'd been moved and impressed by the father's simple sincerity, but it had been Julia Craven who'd tipped the scales of justice today: beautiful physical specimen but imagine having to spend a childhood as her son!

He spoke his daughter's name into the phone—"It's her father, Judge Patton, calling long distance"—and then he

waited. This was just the sort of situation the girl loved to dig
into. Not that her digging ever really accomplished much, but
once he'd put her onto it, he'd done his part. Oh, he'd enjoy
throwing a scare into Blake Arnold and he looked forward to
browbeating the great Gerald Usher Lewis but once he'd
talked with Amanda now, that was really the end of it for
Jared Patton. He'd been elected to adjudicate specific cases of
law, not to monitor the workings of business and the underworld. Or to protect the environment. It wasn't his job to
change the world. Only immature, angry fools like Amanda
even imagined it was worth doing. Nevertheless, he couldn't
wait to hear the astonishment in her voice when he used the
words *toxic wastes.* He decided he'd better act as if he really
gave a damn. She'd like that.

"Daddy! What a pleasant surprise! How are you, you
sweet old phony?"

The pomps and vanity of this wicked world . . .

Imagine Tracy Larkin remembering her catechism at this
late date. Behind her now, a rumbling sea of voices, the
shuffling of a thousand departing feet, a receding wave of
sound. She remained seated in the front row. Andy's speech
had reached her, shaken her. Making it all the harder now for
her to make him understand. Or . . . or did he understand
already? Was that the reason he hadn't come to her at once?
Or had he started toward her when Julia Craven stepped
through the gate, going to him instead of to her son?

Seeing Andy and Julia Craven standing at the table beyond
the railing, that dazzling smile she remembered from shad-
owed screen, brilliant stage, Tracy felt a quick stab of jealousy. And sudden hate: Had the woman no idea what she'd
done to him?

Now that famous throaty whisper: "That was beautiful,
darling—what you said about losing someone you loved. Oh,
I *did* hurt you, didn't I? I had no idea how much."

"Julia," Andy said, "I was not referring to you, or *us.*"
His face was coolly composed, brown eyes filled with compassion, tone gentle: "And I can't fly you to New York
because Tracy and I are going direct to Provincetown."

Julia Craven was shocked. Incredulous. But no more so
than Tracy Larkin: Provincetown? Cape Cod! He really *didn't*
know; he really didn't realize it was over.

She saw Julia take a backward step. Her lovely face tightened. "I could never count on you, could I?" Her voice became a hissing sound: "You always let me down, *always*! Even last night!" And when Andy didn't answer, Julia Craven whirled away dramatically and went toward Todd, who was surrounded at the bench by five or six students, Donna Lehrman and Norman Shatsky among them, all faces exultant. They fell back at Julia Craven's approach, and when she kissed her son on the cheek, they moved off.

Tracy saw Andrew step to the railing, eyes on her, and her body stiffened.

He came through the gate, then hesitated, studying her face. Their eyes met. "Where've you been all morning?" he asked.

"I might ask the same question. Except that I know."

"Do you?"

She was about to stand, to say *please don't bother explaining*, when she heard Todd's voice: "I'd call it a four-star performance, Julia. Worthy of an Oscar. Or another Tony award."

Tracy made no pretense that she could not hear, or see. Julia Craven's face was furious, but also thunderstruck, staring at her son with a look of shocked disbelief. "You haven't changed a bit, have you? You'd rather go back to that college than come home where you can recover from—"

Todd was shaking his head. "I've never had a home, Mother." But then he reached for her and kissed her on the cheek. In that moment Tracy saw on his face an intensified reflection of Andy's cool, knowing compassion. "You have a performance tonight, don't you?"

"I'll never be able to go out on that stage after this, never!"

Todd was smiling, rather sadly then. "Oh, I'm sure Merle can get a plane here in time. Just think what a keyed-up audience you'll have tonight. After all this . . ."

Very softly then, but loud enough for Tracy to hear, Julia Craven said, "You're just another fucking bastard like your father, aren't you?"

"Well, a bastard maybe. We'll never know, will we?"

Julia pulled her coat around her body and whirled away, pushing through the students and brushing by Ann Merrill, who was about to join them. She strode directly to where Blake Arnold and Gerald Usher Lewis stood talking together at the jury box, which was empty now. "Lewis," she cried, "oh, darling, how long before we can get out of here?"

At Tracy's shoulder, Andy did not move. Were his eyes on her, still baffled, or was he also watching Julia?

Gerald Usher Lewis glanced at his wristwatch. "*I'm* getting out, Julia, as soon as Judge Patton reads me the routine riot act. I have a dinner engagement in Chicago."

Julia Craven took an audible breath, not quite a gasp. "Chicago?" Then her eyes flamed. "You . . . you *promised*!"

"I agreed to get you here, Julia. You're here." He stepped around her. "Excuse me. I have to attend a lecture on the ethics of law."

As he moved toward the door alongside the bench, Julia called after him: "Well, fuck you, you phony shitheel! And don't send me any bills. I'll send them back rolled up for your convenience!"

But Gerald Usher Lewis had disappeared. Blake, his face troubled and apprehensive, followed.

Julia glanced around. The huge room was quiet, almost empty. Her blue-green eyes, shimmering with contempt, went to Andy, then fixed on Tracy. She came slowly, catlike, down through the gate.

Tracy felt her body stiffen again. And she waited.

In the aisle Julia stood gazing down on her till Tracy looked up to meet her eyes. Then Julia said, sweetly, almost a whisper: "Are you sure you shouldn't be romancing Todd? You're scarcely old enough to pass as his mother, darling."

Tracy, amazed at herself, was not even tempted to an angry retort. There was something in the woman's eyes, something lost and miserable, and her face seemed no longer young. So Tracy said, "There's a private service in Lebanon. That's in New Hampshire. They can have a plane here in less than an hour, Miss Craven."

For an instant the woman looked as if she'd been struck across the face. Then she muttered, "Don't do me any favors, kid."

Julia Craven went up the aisle. And Tracy gave in to her pity. Had anything said or done here really reached Julia Craven? *Could* anything? Or, somewhere inside, had the insulation begun to unravel?

Ann Merrill came through the gate, brushed her hand over

Tracy's shoulder—"Let's stay in touch"—and, nodding to Andy, went up the aisle.

Todd came down to the railing. His eyes were on Andy. "Well," he said, "now that you don't have to go on acting like a father, maybe we can be friends."

"I rather enjoyed acting like a father," Andy said, "and I thought we *were* friends."

Both faces and voices, totally dissimilar in every other way, had an easygoing, self-mocking amusement in them—which somewhat startled her.

"I was thinking something like that myself."

"I've always thought genes and bloodlines were really important only in racehorses."

"Terrific. I may be a bastard, Andy, but I'm not really an ungrateful one." He shoved out his hand and Andy took it across the railing, shook it firmly, then took a step forward and clasped the boy in an awkward one-armed embrace.

Tracy did not look away. Except for them, the courtroom was empty now.

After a moment Todd stepped back, smiling, and turned to her. "I promise never to call you mother. How about Tracy?" His smile was shy. "May I?"

Certain to be alone with Andy soon, and dreading it, Tracy ignored what Todd was trying to say. "I'm teribly sorry about Lynnette."

The smile faded and he frowned. "You're the only person besides Andy who's mentioned her today," he said.

He turned away and, striding, disappeared through the door to the right of the bench.

Now it was Andy who was staring down at her. And the moment had finally come.

She rose to her feet—and realized that her legs were unsteady. "Well, Mr. Horgan," she heard herself ask, "what'll we do to celebrate?" She hadn't meant to say that. "Shall we go to Colby's and join the merrymakers?" God, Tracy, what are you *doing*? This is *not* the way! "One for the road—or two, or three, or four." The look of bewilderment on Andy's face drove her on: She remembered that expression of startled innocence just before the lie. "Or," she continued, "or, Mr. Horgan, has a fifth since breakfast been enough? How long will it hold you?"

"Hey now," Andy said, as he came closer, "hey there, Tracy—"

But it was over, so why not get it done with! She moved to stand close, then lifted herself on her toes and kissed him on the lips, careful not to touch his bandaged arm, just a quick goodbye kiss. "Figure it out, Andy. I'm sure you will. If you haven't already. Goodbye."

She pivoted and then she was almost running, carrying the car coat, trotting up the aisle to the closed double doors leading to the rotunda, hoping he would not follow, hoping he would. . . .

The rotunda was not crowded now. She saw Larry with his camera on his shoulder and Steve beside him, saw Valerie Arnold in conversation with Bruce Southworth, who would not have to testify after all, saw Sheriff Wheeler with a state trooper, a few other familiar faces—hey, Tracy, slow down, what's the rush, where do you think you're going, where the sweet hell *is* there to go?

And then she became conscious of someone at her side. A man had fallen into step beside her—farmer type, clean-shaven face, hunting cap—but she continued toward the double doors at the far side of the huge circular lobby.

And missed a step when she heard a voice at her ear, a familiar voice: "We got a date, cunt." She felt something hard, very hard, jabbing into her ribs. And heard: "We got business to finish, so just keep walkin' toward them doors, capeesh?"

SEVENTEEN

Once he'd heard the TV announcer in the courthouse lobby say the hearing was over, case dismissed for lack of evidence, Pierre Durand had lost interest in what was on the screen up there behind the bar in Colby's back room.

If the kid's old man hadn't told him who really did it, he'd have thought the same as he thought when he got here: They'd find some way to get a rich kid off. But *c'est la guerre*. If the ones who'd done the harm to his Lynnette were dead now, out of reach—well, he just had to accept. The way he'd have to accept, someday, that Lynnette was really gone. And Thérèse, too. He didn't have anyone left, not a goddam soul in this world.

So why not have another, Pierre? No place to go anyway. Truck packed, the thirty-ought-six in its sling, rent paid, too much, too goddam much, white-haired old bitch! "*Merci*, Claude!" Tasted weak—drinks always got weaker. Snowing again outside, hairy drive back to Baileyville. Only he wasn't going to Baileyville—not enough gas, not enough *argent*, almost broke, she took it, Thérèse, no *argent* to buy gas—

"Now what?" he heard the bartender ask, reaching to turn up the volume. "What's going on over there?"

The redhead reporter—the one he'd seen on the courthouse steps yesterday morning when he'd knocked the kid's father down—she was trying to get through the courthouse lobby, and the announcer, the tall brown-haired guy, was shoving a microphone at her and asking for just one comment, please. And she was saying, "For God's sake, Steve," and then

311

glancing at the ferret-faced guy alongside her, little dark-skinned guy in a hunting cap. Then a kind of steely glint came into her blue eyes and she reached out and took the microphone in her own hand and said, "I'd like to introduce you to Dominic Verini, known as Nick Verini—"

Then the little guy in the hunting cap growled something and he grabbed her, hooking one arm around her neck, shifting to stand behind her, the mike falling and a clatter and crackling on the TV, and then he brought up his other hand, with a gun in it, little automatic—

"Jesus," someone down the bar whispered, because the ferret-faced guy was putting the muzzle of the gun at the girl's ear, not touching. Someone else down the bar said, "Oh my *God*!"

Pierre Durand wasn't sure he was seeing what was on the screen. For a second he thought maybe the bartender had changed channels, tuned in on some movie. Or maybe he was drunker than he thought he was—

The little guy was yelling, "Anybody takes a step, one goddam step, redhead's brains spill out her other ear, capeesh?"

Somebody at the bar growled, "That's right in the court-house, God's sake. Where's the police? Where the hell—"

But the voice broke off, because from the TV there came a terrible scream, a woman's voice, but not the girl's; her eyes were bulging and her face all twisted up, too scared to scream, even if she could, with that arm crooked around her neck like that.

Nick Verini? He sure as hell didn't look like his picture.

Alone in the empty courtroom, stunned by the finality of Tracy's tone and her goodbye kiss, Andrew had sat down in the seat she'd occupied. In the few moments that had passed, he could not, tired as he was in every nerve anyway, handle the shock. Did she really think he'd killed a fifth of booze? Would she believe him if he told her he hadn't had an ounce to drink since leaving Pierre Durand?

But that shock was as nothing compared to the electric jolt that shot through him now, hearing the scream from the lobby. It brought him sharply upright and then to his feet. Tracy's voice?

He broke into a run up the aisle, hearing other voices now, but no more screams.

*   *   *

Valerie Arnold still could not believe she had let out that terrible shriek when she heard Tracy Larkin's words, the man's name, and had seen the gun come out of nowhere. Had that sound really come from her?

She had turned and started to run, away from the scene, away from the man, and up the marble stairs, in panic, her heart exploding. Reaching the head of the stairs, she plunged down the corridor to her husband's office. The police didn't even know what was happening!

It took a long moment for Andrew, stopping dead in the frame of the courtroom doors, to take in the scene.

A wide semicircle of spectators, some aghast and wide-eyed, some cowering but sullen, no more screams, a whimper here and there, a masculine growl. All eyes were riveted on the two people against the curving wall of the rotunda.

Tracy. His heart faltered. No mistaking that hair, but her face, Christ, her face was a contorted mask—mouth wide open, eyes glazed. Had she been the one who screamed?

As he took a step forward, he saw the gun. Automatic pistol. Black. Barrel held level, pointing into Tracy's ear. One arm locked around her neck, the man stood partly hidden behind her body—a man he'd never seen before. Plaid wool jacket, cap with earflaps turned up, dungarees. He forced down the quick black rage that threatened to take over. Except for the whirring of a camera off to one side, the room was hushed now.

At his ear a harsh voice whispered, "Who the hell's this nut?" Without removing his gaze from Tracy's anguished face, Andrew realized: The tall hulk of Sheriff Wheeler stood beside him.

"Just keep the camera rollin'," the stranger said.

The sheriff groaned. "I knew it—some creep wants his picture on TV."

But Andrew knew otherwise. He had heard that voice. No mistaking it. And his flesh began to quiver. His mind froze.

"Keep it spinnin', man."

Andrew felt his body take an involuntary step forward.

And heard: "One more, fucker!" The dark-brown eyes were on him. "One more step, she gets it, then you, bang bang."

313

Then he heard Tracy's voice, saw her mouth writhing, her eyes pleading. "No, Andy, no!" Breathless, strangled, not Tracy's voice at all.

"One more step, motherfucker."

Andrew heard a gasp somewhere—at the word. This killer was threatening to kill again and someone was shocked at his *language!* But Verini's voice was not quite the one he'd heard before: Shrill and high-pitched now, it was the voice of a kid, uncertain, shaky, desperate to sound confident and menacing. Realizing this, Andrew felt his own terror grow colder still. Whatever was driving the bastard now, wasn't he more dangerous if he was on the edge of losing control?

"When I'm finished with her, man, you won't even want her, capeesh?"

In his own office Chief Radford was thanking Mrs. Arnold for telling him and instructing her to stay in her husband's office upstairs. Then he was putting down the phone with one hand while his right was unsnapping the holster that held his .38 and picking up his walkie-talkie radio.

He was moving fast, right leg aching as usual, through the waiting room toward the main courthouse area when he changed his mind, halted at the counter to bark: "Mrs. Arnold has just reported that some farmer kid is holding Tracy Larkin at gunpoint in the rotunda. Get every available man to cover all exits. But tell them the girl's life comes first, goddammit!"

He retraced his steps, putting Holly Ray's astonished face out of his mind, and went down the stairs to the jail on the ground floor. Had to be three or four officers in the courtroom area—*someone* had to be outside on the front steps in case the assailant tried to come out this way. And to keep anyone else from going in.

He went out the side door and circled the building. It was snowing harder. He took out his revolver. Tracy Larkin—did she still have the one he'd made her keep this morning? Hadn't the child been through enough?

And that's when it came to him: Could the so-called farmer be one of Verini's gunmen?

Would she hear the shot that killed her?

Faint with fright, helpless, Tracy felt herself being drawn, step by slow step, along the curved edge of wall toward the solid double doors, which were closed. Verini's face was out of sight behind her, the gun once more stabbing into her ribs, his arm still gripping her neck, but she was breathing again. She could see only the crowd facing her: Steve and Larry with the camera, following cautiously, Andy shoulder to shoulder with Sheriff Wheeler, two or three police uniforms, no one moving, the shocked intensity of eyes on her—and the terrible, terrible silence.

Her mind, numbed at first, vague with shock, had cleared somewhat. It was on the gun in her bag. Which she had somehow clung to. The revolver that Chief Radford had given her. *Six bullets, Tracy. Keep that in mind if you ever have to use it. God forbid.* If the gun probing her ribs also held six . . . and if it had taken two to kill the Stoddards . . . and if it was the same gun . . . four left. More than enough. Three more than enough.

She stiffened her legs and body, felt the arm tighten around her throat as he yanked, tugged, hissing, "No tricks now, bitch," gouging with the gun. Then shouting: "We're goin' out them doors and down them steps." Some of the shrill uncertainty had gone from his tone. "Any cop goes for his piece, any sucker gets brave, redhead gets hers first, then he gets his!" He'd regained some of his arrogant confidence—a note of exhilaration in his voice. And then she heard another voice. "Nickie, when are you going to wise up?"

She felt Verini's body go rigid.

The man, who had been hidden behind Sheriff Wheeler's wide frame, now stepped forward: very tall, very dark, about her own age, wearing a business suit and a silk tie. FBI? Lawyer? Who? *Nickie,* he'd said—Verini's lawyer?

His voice was low and controlled. He had stopped to face them, legs apart, a small smile along his wide thin lips. "Give me the gun and I'll get you out of this, Nickie."

Silence.

She felt the hard end of the gun leave her bruised ribs but the arm around her neck was choking her now, and then, before she realized what had happened, she saw the gun, saw the arm outstretched and heard the explosion. Close. Deafening. The whole building seemed to shudder. A muffled scream somewhere . . .

The detonation in his ears, Andrew saw the tall man's body

stiffen, saw his hand reaching inside his jacket, heard another shot, saw Verini's hand jerk with the second shot, then watched as the stranger began to fall, his legs crumpling under him, his body twisting to sprawl facedown on the stone floor.

There was blood on the floor now, and for an intense moment no one moved.

Then Verini, instead of placing the automatic on her, dragged Tracy forward, almost lifting her off the floor, her feet sliding, and stopped to stare down at the motionless body. Verini straightened his arm, pointing the automatic directly at the base of the fallen man's skull, his own face white and pinched, and then he fired again.

A dagger of ice seemed to plunge through Andrew's own body but the dead man on the floor did not move. Blood began to bubble out of the hole in the back of the man's head, soaking his black hair and spreading red across the white marble floor.

Then Verini was shouting again, his voice mingling with the echo of the last shot: "Anybody else?" It was a savage bellow—excitement, triumph. "Anybody else want to die?"

No one moved. Tracy had stopped struggling. Her eyes were closed.

Verini began to laugh. "Get that camera over here! Closer." And as the cameraman took another step, Verini raised the gun and placed the muzzle of it against Tracy's cheek and brought her closer to the camera. He leaned to whisper something into her ear. Andrew could not hear. Then Verini was staring into the camera. "Hey, Poppa—you watchin'? You seen what your son can do? It's me, Poppa!" The hand that held the gun lifted and ripped off the cap. His skull was bald, totally bald, obscenely white and grotesque, and now he was grinning. "Recognize me now, Poppa? I'm your son!" His eyes were glittering with a strange and eerie joy. "Your only son. You see me do it, Poppa?" Then he looked to the side of the camera, into the operator's face. "Show Poppa what I did."

The camera on the young man's shoulder was trembling but he swung it slightly and then leaned down to focus on the corpse on the floor. Verini's dark eyes were moist, glittering. He laughed. And the sound, wild and hollow, echoed through the high rotunda.

* * *

What Verini had whispered into Tracy's ear was: *I ain't gonna kill you here, cunt. We got better plans.* Glee in his voice, insane glee.

Tracy, eyes tightly shut, hearing but not seeing anything after watching the man fall, had moved into a dreamlike state.

Her mind was refusing to function. Everything was blurred and unreal and at a distance and happening to someone else, somewhere else; she was not a part of it, but the one word came through the haze: *here.* He was not going to kill her *here,* but he was going to kill her later, somewhere. She was going to die.

All she heard now was a whirring sound. Like a camera.

Andrew saw something happen to Tracy—to her body. She was standing now, on her own, eyes closed, as if she were only waiting for whatever was to come.

Was she even aware of what was happening?

The cameraman had straightened and was again focused on Verini, who was releasing Tracy without taking the gun from her head. As if he knew the gun was enough now. He spoke into the camera.

"Poppa, *you* listen now. I'm doing it *my* way. And I'm gonna win yet! So . . . so fuck you, Vincent Verini. *FUCK YOU!*"

Tracy felt herself moving, being guided, being led. As if she had no mind of her own, as if it didn't matter . . .

When Verini and Tracy reached the doors, Andrew felt, rather than saw, a movement at his side. Sheriff Wheeler was dropping to one knee and drawing his revolver, extending two arms straight out, taking aim—

Tracy heard a shot. Another shot. How many had she heard before? Something . . . something about a gun holding only six . . .

It was Verini, not Sheriff Wheeler, who had fired.

Andrew watched the huge body take the bullet, he heard the thud, or perhaps imagined it, and then he saw Wheeler toppling, falling to the floor, his gun, which he had not fired, clattering to the stone. When he looked up, Tracy and Verini were going out the door.

Chief Radford, hunkered down with his head above the stone balustrade rising up one side of the high bank of steps, had heard the shots—two close together, then another after a few seconds . . . and now a fourth one. He had not moved.

Earlier, he had hastily positioned a man across the steps from him, also fairly well protected behind the stone, with orders not to shoot, and he had dispatched cars to await instructions at the main roads leading out of town. More state police vehicles were on the way. One state cruiser and one Sheriff's Department car were double-parked along the curb, and a town patrol car, dark-blue, along the side of the green. Now, with his old Ruger .38-caliber service revolver, which he had not used in many years, gripped in one hand and a walkie-talkie in the other, he was watching through the leaf-less bushes and the steadily falling snow.

He saw one of the two wide, heavy doors open slowly.

Tracy Larkin appeared. She seemed to move like a sleep-walker. Shock, probably. At the back of her head, a hand held an automatic pistol. Slowly then, very slowly, the man emerged. A short, slight man with a bald head, but Radford did not have to ask himself who it was.

Now, laying down the walkie-talkie and taking the .38 in both hands, bracing it on top of the balustrade, he had to choke down an impulse to take careful aim and blast away.

The two figures did not move. A voice called out: "We're goin' for a joyride in the snow, the slut and me. We're headin' for that Mustang parked across the street there. So fuck off." Then he lifted his voice: "Hear me? You shoot me, you kill her. Capeesh?"

Chief Radford was wondering whether, even if he could get a shot off fast enough, Verini's finger would squeeze the trigger—a reflex action to taking a bullet in whatever part of the man's body he could hit at this distance, in this weather. He knew he couldn't take the risk. But he also knew that, goddammit, he could not allow an abduction from the court-house itself!

Andrew edged one of the two doors open a few inches.

In the eruption of voices that had followed Verini's going

318

out the door, he had bawled *Get an ambulance!* as he picked up the fallen sheriff's revolver from the floor and charged to the door. Now, the heavy gun in his good hand, he shouted through the aperture: "Chief Radford, are you out there?" No answer. Maybe he was hiding, waiting. Maybe he didn't even know what was happening. Nevertheless, Andrew called again: "Don't let anyone get trigger-happy out there!"

But Verini was at her side. The gun was at her ear again. He was not holding her. All he had to do was pull the trigger—Tracy would fall tumbling down the long flight of steps.

Would his finger pull that trigger automatically if someone, anyone, shot *him*? Andrew could not be sure. And could not take the chance.

The bastard was winning. Again.

They had begun to move slowly down the snow-covered steps.

Instead of lifting the revolver, he called out, "Verini! I meant what I said on the phone. If anything happens to Tracy, I'll find you and I'll kill you if it takes the rest of my life!"

His words sounded hollow in his ears.

He turned and ran through the crowd, his arm jolting pain, looking for an EXIT sign, hoping to find a side door.

Tracy was wondering whether she had lost her mind.

She could feel the snow on her face. She could see it hanging on the lilac bushes alongside the steps and, far off, on the tops of cars, and farther off on the shrubs and trees on the green. She knew, but only vaguely, that she should be wearing the car coat. Had she dropped it somewhere? And her bag—she was no longer carrying her bag. Which had something in it, something important. Her breathing was shallow. But it was as if this were happening to someone else, some stranger, not to her. . . .

She had heard Andy's voice, but it had reached her from a great empty distance, and the words came to her only now, the same words she'd heard in the cottage, some time, some long time ago—when was that? how long ago?—she'd heard him . . . say the . . . same thing . . . the very same words. . . .

*　　*　　*

Through the thin white curtain of falling snow Blake Arnold was looking down from the window of his office.

Where he'd found Valerie after he'd heard the shooting and had rushed out of the judge's chambers and up the back stairs. *I can't bear to watch,* she'd said, clinging to him when he came in.

Now she asked, "What's happening?"

He did not turn. She was sitting behind his desk, head down.

"They're going down toward the sidewalk," he said. "Tracy and the guy with the gun."

"Why doesn't someone *do* something?"

"Two patrol cars parked out there. May be cops inside. And another car along the side of the green—"

"Why don't they kill him, *kill* him?"

"I think I see somebody hiding in the bushes at the foot of the steps—"

"Why, if they've got guns, *why*?"

"Tracy's on the sidewalk now. The bald-headed guy's right alongside—"

"Bald-headed guy. You know who the bald-headed guy is, don't you?"

"They're off the curb, starting across the street—"

"He *wants* you to know. It's Nick Verini."

He heard her words. Had he known all along? Even when he heard the shots, climbed the stairs, had he known and refused to let himself believe it?

A savage impulse streaked through him. "If I had my rifle, I could pick him off myself." If he had it, would he try? "He could probably kill her even if someone did shoot him," he said. *"That's* why they can't use their guns, Val."

Then he saw the car. The two were standing beside it. It was covered with snow. Tracy opened the door on the passenger side. When the snow fell off, he saw the color: metallic silver. "He's making her move over to the driver's seat," he said. A Mustang. The one described in the report. Jason Stoddard's car. "He's getting in alongside her," he said.

"Who?" Val asked. "Who's getting in? What's his *name*, Blake?"

"You just told me, Val."

"Say it!" she snarled.

But he didn't turn. He saw the headlights of the Mustang

come on. "Nick Verini," he said. But not to please her. To punish himself.

"That's the scum you've been trying to protect," she said softly.

The Mustang was pulling away from the curb across the street. He could see the pale bald head at the open window, mouth working. He was shouting something that Blake could not hear.

Then he saw a figure appear from around the side of the courthouse, running to the street. Running a bit awkwardly because his flight jacket was dangling from his right shoulder and his other arm was in a sling. He had a revolver in his good hand.

As the red taillights of the Mustang disappeared, turning north off the green along the side of the courthouse, a second figure materialized, standing up from the bushes by the balustrade. Chief Radford was speaking into the walkie-talkie in one hand, while his other rammed his gun into its holster. He must have been there all the time.

A tan-colored sheriff's car, double-parked, suddenly showed life: engine revving, headlights coming on, red dome light revolving, a single warning wail of a siren.

"I want a divorce," Valerie seemed to say behind him, but those couldn't have been the words, and, seeing Chief Radford running into the street to plant himself in the path of the patrol car, his arms outstretched and waving up and down, Blake turned from the window.

He stared at Valerie.

Who met his eyes. "I mean it, Blake. If anything happens to that girl, I'm going to get a divorce."

Chief Radford was already furious.

The stolen-car alert on the silver-colored Mustang had been out for three hours and the vehicle had been parked in a no-parking space in plain view and across the street from the courthouse and police headquarters!

Now, having heard his radioed order not to fire, here was this young moustached kid in a sheriff deputy's uniform climbing out of his cruiser, his face one big question mark. "You didn't say no pursuit, Chief."

"I did say wait for orders, goddammit!"

"You're not going to let them get away, are you?"

"Didn't you hear him, deputy? Didn't you hear what he yelled out the window?"

What Verini had bellowed out the window, while Chief Radford, kneeling, had been tempted to take his one desperate single shot at the bald head, was: *Anybody follows, I'll blow her away!*

While the young officer stood frowning at him, someone at his shoulder growled, "Have you got a rifle, Chief?"

"What the hell good's a—" But it was Andrew Horgan standing there, so he didn't finish the sentence. The man looked as if he'd aged twenty years. Maybe he had. But his eyes were glinting and his jaw was throbbing visibly. "Forget it, Mr. Horgan," he said.

"I've got one in my cruiser," the young deputy said.

"Let's go," Andrew Horgan snapped, and headed toward the patrol car.

Following, the kid said, "I can't let you have it without Sheriff Wheeler's say-so."

At the door of the car, Andrew Horgan stopped. "Sheriff Wheeler's been wounded. Maybe killed." Then to Chief Radford as he approached: "Chief, I've got a plane at the Alpine Chalet landing strip."

It didn't take Radford more than a second to make up his mind, hearing a siren's approach in the distance—sounded like the hospital ambulance. "I haven't gone hunting in years." Then to the deputy: "You drive. No flasher, no siren, but fast as you can on this pavement."

Then another patrol car was roaring along the edge of the green, past the side of the courthouse. One of his own. It disappeared, following the path that the Mustang had traveled.

Almost wearily, in a rage now, Chief Radford picked up the mike and began to speak into it. Didn't anyone follow orders today, *anyone*?

EIGHTEEN

It was not so much hopelessness as resignation that had taken over.

Driving, Tracy had been aware, distantly, of passing the Colonial Motel, the stone posts at the entrance of the Alpine Chalet, everything obscured by snow. She also knew that she was driving north, and also knew where they had to be going: the Canadian border. How far ahead? Forty miles? Less?

There was a quiet inside her, an emptiness—a calm which she knew somehow, very hazily, was unreasonable, irrational. In the circumstances, absurd.

Even the man in the other high-backed bucket seat—who for some reason was kneeling to look over the headrest and out the rear window instead of using the mirror outside his window—even he seemed unreal. Grotesque, weird, a creature out of space, An ugly, malevolent ET. Or a strange animal of some sort . . .

The windshield wipers were swishing. The road ahead showed black tire-marks but the falling snow was covering them.

She glanced in her own rearview mirror on the outside. No one was following. She knew that. No one was coming. It was too late for that.

Then, ahead, she saw two tan-colored state police cruisers. Parked in the driveway on the right. Two other dark official-looking cars along the shoulder of the road. A white saltbox house beyond a strip of lawn. The Stoddard house. Poor Mr. Stoddard—always so pleasant, so mild-mannered and obliging. But no fury came, no horror, no sense of outrage, or even hate.

She saw the bald-headed animal twist to sit down, looking into his mirror now. "Didn't even see us," he said. With more than pleasure in his ugly voice—glee. And contempt. "Dumb mothers. Know who I am. Know who they're dealin' with now."

The Stoddard car passing the Stoddard house, where it had been stolen—strange, strange.

He was looking at the road map again. The Stoddards' road map, the one he'd taken from the compartment in the wide console between them. *Curiouser and curiouser . . .*

"Slow down," he said.

She did as she was told. Automatically. Like a robot. Now that she had the hang of it—where the brake was, and the throttle, and how the five-speed shift worked—it was really easy to drive, and smooth, even on the treacherous snow.

"That road through the state forest, comes out at Enoch Falls—you listenin', bitch?"

"I can hear you," she heard herself say.

"Looks like a shortcut on the map."

She pictured the forest in her mind. She expected terror; she even remembered what had happened at Echo Lake last night. But no terror came.

"Answer me, goddam you—is it shorter?"

"If it keeps on snowing, that road . . . it's closed in winter."

"It's stopped snowing," he said.

It was true. The wipers were clacking on a clear windshield.

"So turn the fuckers off," he said. Which she did. "And turn in that goddam road if it ain't blocked. You listenin' to me?"

She did not answer. Her eyes had begun to search for the sign on the left.

"Won't be no heat cruisin' in there. Fool the mothers!" He was laughing. "Other side of the woods, make a right. Can't be more'n twenty miles to the goddam border. Everything chimin', baby! I got my head screwed on right again. Got my shit *all* together, baby. I'm gonna make it!"

It occurred to her then, but from a distance, that once they were in the forest, there was no hope of anyone even knowing

324

where they'd gone. And that ahead, on route 57, there were towns, people, police . . .

What if she ground down on the gas-feed pedal and sped past the entrance—

"Just you and me," the animal said. "Like we was on our honeymoon. An' listen—you don't seem to be *listenin'* to me—that's what we tell 'em at Customs. We're on our honeymoon, you and me, capeesh?"

In her mind she tried to picture the small road north of the village of Enoch Falls: the high falls itself, roadway cut through stone. Was there a Customs station at the border? If so, would it be open?

Nevertheless, when the sign came into view, FRANKLIN STATE FOREST, and when she saw no barricade across the entrance, she turned.

The wind sock on the airstrip had been limp. It was, Andrew decided, the only thing in their favor.

Ceiling not more than a thousand, probably lower, and black as hell, visibility so limited that it looked like dusk with wisps of dark clouds drifting against the windshield unexpectedly, no snow falling. If the wind factor was negligible, by God, nothing else was! Then there'd been that bad moment on takeoff when the engine misfired, not much but enough to make him wonder whether he'd skipped something in the cursory preflight checkup.

But when they were aloft and leveling off, altimeter showing 600 feet, and after he'd turned off the auxiliary fuel pump, the snow had stopped clouding the windshield. Two things in their favor. Out of how many thousand?

And now, unable simply to trim and relax, as he usually did, forced to control the wheel with his bandaged arm whenever he needed to use the throttle or adjust the other controls with his right, he was listening to a female voice on the radio—quiet, businesslike, neither slow nor hurried—reporting to Chief Radford in the other seat: " . . . so they allowed the vehicle, positive identification, to pass the house as if they hadn't seen it. Per your orders, sir. It's headed north on route 57. No pursuit. State police cooperating in every way. Any other orders, Chief?"

"What about the sheriff?"

"He's in surgery, sir. I'll keep you posted."

"I want to know the caliber and *kind* of bullet."

"Roger."

"What about the other victim?"

"Positively identified—Angelo Verini, age thirty-six. Arrest record a mile long, only minor convictions. Son of Vincent Verini—"

"Dead?"

"Very dead, Chief."

Kyle Radford lowered the microphone in his hand and glanced at Andrew before he said, "Small loss."

"Yes, sir," the voice said. "And what are your whereabouts, Chief?"

"Damned if I know. And if I did, it's nobody's business. Over-out."

"I'm following route 57, Chief," Andrew told him, "or trying to." He was flying S-turns above it. "We just passed the entrance to the forest. They can't be too far ahead of us. I ought to be up there another five hundred feet so the bastard won't hear the engine, but up there, we couldn't see a damned thing."

Chief Radford was using Andrew's binoculars. "I can't see worth a *damn* down here. Not many cars on the road when I *can* see it. Mostly pickups and four-wheel drives."

"How far to the border?"

"About forty-five miles, I'd judge. Down there. Maybe less up here as the hawk flies. You heard? That presents me with a problem, Mr. Horgan. By rights I should be alerting U.S. Customs, Canadian Customs, and the Royal Canadian Mounted Police."

"You think they'd listen, any more than Sheriff Wheeler did?"

"Ay-uh, you got a point. Question is: Once we spot 'em—*if* we spot 'em—what you got in mind?"

"I've got in mind killing the bastard once and for all." Andy was remembering: *When I'm fnished with her, you won't even want her, capeesh?* But he said, "If you're asking *how*, I'll let you know if I figure it out."

He was struggling with an old impulse—to overcontrol, to grip the wheel with his left hand, which shot pain like a dagger-stab into the wound, as he eased the throttle in with his right and watched the airspeed needle climb to 110. It was banked down in him now, but stronger and more urgent than ever, that need to kill Nick Verini. A ferocious savage *desire*. To kill him personally!

The visibility had improved. Only slight but enough so that, from above the pines, he could see the road twisting and rolling but hugging the edge of the woods, visible because of the dark wheel-marks in the snow where the black asphalt was exposed.

He, too, was searching, but now the road was deserted, stretching and winding ahead. Empty.

Then it came to him: he had passed over the entrance to the forest. How far back? His stomach began to tighten. He eased the wheel back and worked the left rudder-pedal, and his solar plexus began at once to register the turn as the plane went into a forty-degree bank. "Christ!" was all he said and he wasn't sure he'd said that out loud.

Radford did not ask what he had in mind, so Andrew said, "How much shorter to the border on the road that goes past Echo Lake? The one that cuts northwest at an angle through the forest?"

"Ten miles? Something like that. Shorter, but gravel, and it ought to be closed by now, snow and all."

"We'll soon know. I'm going to go down a bit. Stay on those glasses."

"Never know what a mind like Verini's will do. I'd have said, back there, his was too far gone to think of that."

"If they were still on fifty-seven, we'd have seen them, wouldn't we?"

"Play your hunches," Radford said. "I'm fresh out."

Completing the 180, he was now descending to 300 feet. Could Verini hear the engine at that distance? Then what? Would Tracy hear it?

He could see a narrow dark space winding between the white tops of the pines, so he throttled down, and then he saw the glimmer of what could be water beyond the twisting swath between the treetops. He began to bank right, his heart quickening. And now he was flying above the canyon that ran in a curving path between the trees.

The narrow white base of the canyon, which should have been a solid white ribbon, was marked by double wheel-tracks, dark and distinct.

"Would there be any other vehicles in here?" he asked, hearing the excitement in his tone. "Hunters?"

Radford was peering down through the glasses. "Not likely. Hunting season don't open till tenth of November."

"Rangers?"

"Possible. Not very damn likely. Oh hell, anything is possible."

Leveled off, Andrew still could not see more than a hundred yards of the road because it kept bending, disappearing.

"State police?"

"Search at the lake was called off long ago."

"Then let's pretend. Let's just pretend for a few minutes that those marks were made by a silver-colored Mustang."

He throttled back and nosed down, his eye on the altimeter. He didn't want to get to treetop level: no telling what the bastard would do if he realized he was being followed. In the distance he could see the hulks of mountains, their peaks lost in the low, solid overcast.

"How many shots did Verini fire altogether back there?" he asked.

As if he knew at once what Andrew was thinking, Kyle Radford answered promptly: "I counted four."

"So did I," Andrew said. "And two more if he used the same gun to kill Mr. and Mrs. Stoddard—"

"Six bullets," Chief Radford said.

"Could the bastard be so far gone that he's already emptied the goddam gun?"

"You don't know much about firearms, do you?"

"Not much."

"And Tracy?"

"Less, I think."

"Well, according to his printout, Dominic Verini favors a Beretta Seventy-six handgun. That's why I asked about the bullet they're digging out of our friend Captain Wheeler. If Nick Verini's using a Beretta Seventy-six, the magazine capacity is ten rounds."

"Christ!"

"Let's just hope Tracy didn't count and doesn't jump to any false assumptions."

Before Andrew, his left arm throbbing again, could respond, Radford said, "There's a vehicle moving. Dead ahead." And when, on impulse, Andrew steadied the wheel with his chest and bandaged arm, and was reaching for the throttle with his right: "No rush. It's not the silver Mustang. Looks like dark-blue—'' His tone changed to a growl: "It's a police vehicle. Strip lights on the roof." Then, in a voice Andrew had never heard before: "I honest-to-God don't believe this!"

"Say it, Chief, so we can get back to fifty-seven. Say it!"

"It's blue. It's one of *my* cars."

The ghostly white, underneath and ahead and on all sides, added to the dreamlike stillness as she drove, very slowly. Then there was a sound. Over the low muttering of the car's motor. The drone of an airplane . . .

Had she really heard it?

Had *he* heard it?

"What's the matter, baby? This heap'll go faster'n this. You don't want to get there?"

"I don't want to go off the road." By now Tracy had begun to sense, vaguely, that her trancelike state was all that had carried her through. So far.

When she'd flipped on the headlights again, in the forest, about the time they were passing the Echo Lake sign, he'd snarled: *No lights.* And she'd automatically obeyed. Like any robot. But there was nothing to mark the edge of the narrow road: Both sides were one wide level stretch of white. She knew there were no gravel shoulders along the edges, under the snow. Very few shrubs, very little underbrush between the car and the dark trunks of trees. If she even once let the car slip to either side, if the wheels mired in the soft snow off the pavement, she'd be marooned in the car with *him*.

Which would be worse, far worse, than being shot.

Some of the numbness had faded from her mind. Enough to know that until they reached Enoch Falls, they—she and this animal—were the only two inhabitants of her universe.

"Wouldn't be so tough, off the road, you 'n' me." His voice charged with that manic exhilaration again. "Heater going. I'd have to make you strip down again, way I did last night, remember?" He was still on his high. Which could mean that he was cracking up, as she'd thought in the courthouse. Or it could mean that he had solid reason to believe what he'd said: *I'm gonna make it!* Or, if he could believe that, maybe his mind *had* gone off the deep end. She could feel, but not see, his eyes, bright and sharp, boring into her. "Only I got a new wrinkle now, baby. Something I been wantin' to do ever since I started jerking off . . ."

She did not take her eyes from the road. His voice sickened her; his words, suggesting obscenities beyond her imagination, sickened her. If she looked at him, she would be so sick she'd be unable to drive. Some of the hate came ebbing back, a flush of heat. A sign of life?

This time when she heard the plane, it was closer, lower, louder, not a drone passing over, and now she realized: Andy. It had to be Andy.

She risked a glance at the animal in the other seat. He was looking at the map again. The gun was in his right hand. Her mind cleared: The gun was empty.

She'd realized that in the courthouse lobby when he'd shot Sheriff Wheeler. The fifth and sixth bullets.

Her blood was flowing again. She was no longer sick. Andy was up there. No one else. Andy.

The state of shock had probably protected her, nature's way. But it could have defeated her, too. But hadn't. Had *not*!

No bullets left in the ugly black gun . . .

She could swing the wheel, shoot the car off toward the woods till it mired, then leap out, run into the trees.

Would Andy see her? Was he behind? Ahead? Did he have the car in sight? Or was he still searching?

Or . . . should she hit the accelerator, try to stay on the road, hope there was someone, police, anyone, waiting, blocking the road at the exit from the forest in Enoch Falls?

No. If he blew his cool, tried to shoot while she was driving, discovered the gun empty—he could still use it, fracture her skull, beat her to death, or choke her to death, or worse, whatever he had in mind now, worse.

She flipped on the radio. What would the animal do, if he heard the plane? Was it still there? Had she imagined it?

Music. Country-western rock—whang and whine and thump. *Perfect!*

Then, as casually as possible, she turned on the headlights.

"No music," the animal said. "I'm tryn' to think."

She said nothing.

"Not too far, once we get into Quebec. Not far then to—" He broke off. "I told you, slut—no lights!"

"Who's going to see them in here?"

"*Off*, I said!"

She reached to comply. "If we go off the road, nobody'll

find our bodies for a week." She turned the lights on again, feigning anger: "*You* might want to starve to death. I don't!"

He lifted the gun to point it at her head again.

"Go ahead," she said, tromping on the accelerator, feeling the rear wheels spin and then the car easing forward, the wheels gripping, the sudden jolt throwing her back against the seat.

"Go ahead, pull the trigger. If you've got a bullet left, we're *both* dead!"

The car was gaining speed.

"Goddam women, all alike—"

"We're both *dead*!" she screamed.

And then, gripping the wheel with one hand, she reached with the other to flip the headlights, on and off and on and off, over and over.

"Stubborn bitch!" the animal yelled at her ear. "Do what I say! I'm Nick Verini. Do what I tell you!"

That's when she felt the gun. He lowered it from her head and jammed it into her right breast, a blow so sudden and hard that, with the pain, she went faint and sick all through, stomach hollowing out, pain so intense that she lost the wheel. The car swerved wildly, then slid sideways. She felt the rear end fishtailing. She fought the wheel, bent over it, gasping, blinded, sick, sick, sick. . . .

Then, through the haze of nausea and pain, she heard his shout: "There's a cop car in back of us!"

And then, as the car slowed almost to a stop, she heard his window sliding down, his voice again—"Told you, warned you, you mothers!"—and then she heard the sound of a shot, outside the car, and his voice again: "Move it! Move it, slut, fast, *move* it!"

As she accelerated, head reeling, the pain knotted and hard in her breast, she glanced into the rearview mirror above the windshield. The road behind was clear. But when she looked into the mirror outside her window, she could see farther: There was a dark-colored police car without lights, some distance behind, disappearing as she guided the Mustang around still another bend in the twisting road.

He had fired the gun again. It was not empty.

When he saw lights flashing on and off in the murky distance, at least fifty or sixty yards ahead of the dark patrol car,

Andrew decided that not only was the Mustang on the road but that Tracy had heard the plane.

A few seconds later he had it in view, its silver top blending in with the snow, which may have been why Radford had not spotted it before. No headlights before, traveling at a normal rate of speed. He cut his own speed carefully, aware that the stall signal would begin to beep over his head if he dropped below 68 mph. He didn't need the controls loosening up and the tail buffeting, let alone a full stall. Enough other things on his mind—more than enough.

Such as why the police car was staying back, keeping its distance. And what was on the driver's mind: Was he planning a move as soon as both cars were out of the forest?

I don't know what the hell he's up to, Radford had growled into the mike. *I want his identity, I want him ordered to desist, and I want his badge! Get back to me fast, and I mean fast! Over and out!*

Now the chief was using the binoculars again. "Tracy must've lost control at one point—tracks all over the road." And then: "Can't we get any lower?"

"The bastard may have heard us even at this distance," Andrew said. "And sure as hell if we overtake him."

"You figured out what we're going to do, if and when?"

Angry because he hadn't, and angry at the frustration drawing leechlike at his nerves, Andrew said, "If you've got any ideas, spit 'em out!"

"I'm just about ready to radio Customs and the state police to prevent that Mustang from crossing the border."

"Then what happens to Tracy?"

"What's going to happen to her *this* way?"

Kyle Radford had changed: He was no longer the slight, grizzled, polite, small-town police chief. He was a man itching to use the rifle he'd commandeered from the young deputy at the airstrip. And he was a man suffering the same furious sense of helplessness that was gnawing at Andrew's mind.

When he spoke again, his mood as well as his tone had changed: "My wife Rachel's been nagging me to retire. Florida. Trailer park. Sunshine. When this is over, by God, I think that's what we'll do." His glasses were on the patrol car now. "Especially if that idiot up there fouls up everything."

"Tracy's driving too fast," Andrew said, his own eyes on the Mustang.

Chief Radford's focus moved to the other car. "Only hope is if that sonfabitch has to take a piss. How fast could you get close enough for me to get off a shot? If he got outa the car?"

"Maybe your man's waiting for some damn thing like that, too. It's not going to happen, but you be ready, Chief. All I have to do is slam that throttle all the way in and dive between the goddam trees!"

The radio crackled and the same female voice said: "Shepperton Headquarters to Maule ZWT—"

Radford, cradling the rifle, reached for the mike. "Let's have it, Connie."

"The only vehicle not accounted for is Number Four— Officer Malcolm Cornish. Last seen parked along the green at the time of the shooting. I can't raise him on the radio. Must be out of range, sir. Over."

"If he's out of range, why the hell ain't I? I'm almost on top of him."

"Well, he doesn't respond, Chief. I'm sorry. Over."

"Maule ZWT out." Radford replaced the mike and growled: "Kids playing cops and robbers. Children! Cowboys and Indians. All they want's a uniform, a badge, and a gun. Authority. We scrape the bottom of the barrel and then we wonder why we don't get proper law and order."

Ignoring this, understanding, Andrew asked, "When the road comes out of the woods, what?"

"Enoch Falls. Village. Not much more'n a post office, general store, fifty, sixty houses. This road's curved west by then. Dead-ends right there."

"If he forces Tracy to turn north, how far to the border?"

"Fifteen, twenty miles. Maybe less."

Andrew was wondering then what would happen at Customs even if they hadn't been alerted there. "How many men at the border?"

"One man. Open eight A.M. to eight P.M. And no telling what they'd do if we told them the Prince of Wales of the Verini family was crossing in. Canada's got its own share of such muck."

The frustration in Andrew went deeper. Hardened.

Then he heard the same call as before. And heard Chief Radford answer.

"Chief, the sheriff's going to be okay. And we've got the report from the hospital on the two cartridges. It's a Long Rifle bullet. That doesn't make much sense to me—I thought the shooting was with an automatic pistol—"

"It makes sense to me, Connie. Thanks. And out." He was staring down without the binoculars when he spoke: "The Beretta Seventy-six is chambered for Long Rifle, Andy." His voice was very low. "Unless he's used some since he left town, he's got four left."

Before Andrew could answer, there was another sound. The engine stuttered, then coughed. He felt a shudder pass through the entire fuselage.

Tracy had, almost imperceptibly, reduced speed.

The car behind was no longer visible in either mirror. Had the single shot caused him to give up? Or was he staying back, biding his time, reporting by radio, requesting orders?

Over the radio music, the animal was laughing. That weird manic glee again. "Told you, baby, told you, didn't I? Got it all together—"

"That," she said, "or you're losing it."

What was she doing? Why?

Hoping. That's what she was doing. Still hoping. Ever since he'd held that gun at the back of his brother's skull and pulled the trigger the third time, making sure, he'd been on top of it. As if it had purged his soul. Eerie thought. But she was tempted. . . .

She ignored the pain in her breast—the nausea had subsided slightly—and began to wonder: Would it be possible to freak him out? He was close. Even his elation was spooky, too much, too much. . . .

"You're beginning to see things," she said.

"See things? What I *see* is, I'm almost there!"

"There's no police car in back of us. Why'd you shoot at something that's not there?"

"It was there," he said, confidently. "I saw it."

"*You* saw it. Nobody else did."

"*You* saw it! You know the fucker's back there. Horgan, probably—with the heat."

"I wish," she said. "I wish."

"You didn't think I had a slug left, did you? Got real brave all of a sudden. Well, you heard it, baby, you heard it."

"I heard you waste one. Shooting at nothing. Because you're scared, Verini. You're scared out of your skull."

"Nobody scares me." There was a thin strain of doubt in his tone. "Anyone's scared shitless, it's you, baby."

The word *baby* and the pain in her breast drove her on: "Maybe you're not scared. Maybe you know there's no reason to be scared because you're going to die anyway—"

"Not me. Shut up. I gotta think."

The music on the radio stopped and a disc jockey's voice began its cheerful, empty patter. She strained to listen above it. And couldn't. If she couldn't hear the plane, neither could he.

"We get to this Enoch Falls," the animal said, bent over the map again, "we turn north, capeesh?"

"Left?"

"North!"

"Left or right?"

"You tryin' to bug me? Listen, cunt, I got *plenty* of firepower left." His tone was shrill, uncertain. "One thing Poppa learned me: Always know how much firepower you got left!"

It was as if she couldn't stop herself. As if, now that she'd begun, she had to carry it wherever it was going. "Your firepower," she heard herself say, "is all in your gun."

"What the fuck does that mean?"

"It means, if you were a man, you wouldn't need a gun to prove it."

He reached with the gun and smashed the dial of the radio. The disc jockey's voice went on. He switched off the radio.

"We get where we're goin', I show what kinda man I am!"

"The way you showed me last night?"

Silence.

And, in the silence, she heard the plane. Closer. Louder.

The animal heard it too.

He lowered his window again, fast, and shoved his head and shoulders through the opening, twisting his body. A blast of cold air filled the car.

The plane's engine was louder now. And it had a strange sound. A sort of spluttering sound. Like the motor in a car misfiring, just before it goes dead . . .

Then the animal was upright in his seat again. Driving very

slowly, she turned her head. Beneath the ugly exposed dome of his skull, his face had an expression of delight—sheer joy.

"Hear that?" the animal asked, his tone soft and ecstatic. "Hear it?" Then he faced her, eyes glowing, peace on his face: "I'm gonna get to see it happen."

"I'm sorry, Chief," Andrew said. "Check your harness. We might have to land."

His body and mind were at full alert. He scanned the instruments for some hint of explanation—none. Plenty of fuel, both tanks. In the quick cursory preflight check he'd allowed himself, he'd secured the caps—didn't want the tanks sucked dry by a missing cap, nothing like that now. The engine was running normally once more and the airspeed held. He reached to the floor to change the tank-selector switch, turned on the fuel pump, jammed the throttle forward, and drew back on the wheel; he had to get enough altitude to find a smooth place, a clearing or a flat straight length of road. Climbing, the engine backfired, once, hard, and then it caught with a roar of smooth power. Had there been an impediment in the line, or in the other tank? Then why the hell had it backfired *after* the change of tanks?

At 500 feet again, he leveled off and began to study the terrain. All the clearings were too small; the road offered no strip.

But now the engine sounded normal again: Maybe whatever it was had worked itself through and out. . . .

Radford was on the radio again: "Connie, get this. This is an order. Alert state police and U.S. Customs at East Richmond and all along the border—subject Verini with hostage en route." And then his tone changed: "Armed and damn close to insane." His voice dropped lower: "Spare hostage if possible. Over."

"At once, sir. Are you all right? Over."

"Me?" Radford said. "I'm flying high. Over and out." And then in a different tone: "Sorry I had to do that, Andy."

"You do what you have to do and I'll—"

And that's when it came to him.

Nick Verini.

The bastard or one of his men. If you could call them men. Someone, somehow, had polluted the fuel.

But he had no time for anger. He pulled the canopy open.

A rush of cold air brought in the smell of trees. And the engine sounded normal. He was about to close the canopy when the engine quit. Only momentarily, only two or three seconds, but it was the kind of gulp that could not possibly be mistaken for automatic cough. He pushed the mixture to full-rich, and plunged the throttle to the wall. In response, the engine roared back to full life again; the plane shot forward.

But he knew.

He was positive now.

And he was remembering the crash landing in Iowa—from which, half drunk, he had staggered away. But in Iowa there had been farmland, acres of flat field. Here, there was nothing but the forest itself—mile after mile of pines packed tight together, small lakes surrounded by more trees, and hills, and cliffs. The road out of the forest—he was far beyond the two cars now—rolled and curved to the west. Reaching a small cluster of structures in the distance, where it ended at a T. Enoch Falls: a crisscross pattern of streets surrounded by woods. The few fields he could see behind the houses were more like gardens, hemmed by trees, woods everywhere. If only there were a school, a football field! The only road ran north-south: less snow on the surface than on the forest road, almost as narrow, just as rolling, just as curving, just as impossible.

A light sweat had broken out on his forehead. He eased his foot onto the right rudder, eyes on the propeller now, and then the engine began to pop and spit convulsively while he felt a shivering and quivering under him.

As if ignoring the sounds, Chief Radford said, regret in his tone: "I hope you understand, Andy. I didn't have any choice."

But Andrew had made up his mind, too. "I don't have much of a choice myself, but I'm not going to let them get to the border."

"It's up to you now."

"Let's see if there's any flat space between here and the border station. I see what looks like a waterfall." He also saw more bluffs and crags and trees.

He risked a careful bank to the right.

"They ought to be almost out of the forest by now," Radford said.

*　　*　　*

The animal in the other seat was still in a state of high elation. *Nothin' the fucker can do,* he'd cried earlier. *Nothin' but crash, baby! Hear that? Y' listening now? Crash! Nobody does what he done to Nick Verini gets away with it!*

She'd been certain then. And hearing, off and on, the strange faltering sounds from above, she'd realized, a picture leaping into her mind: the plane plunging down, twisting in the air, crashing, bursting into flames.

Hopeless, hopeless, hopeless, hopeless . . .

Verini had not closed his window since he'd heard the plane, and now, as they passed the sign—ENOCH FALLS—and approached the village, he kept the gun in his hand, ready to fire out the window or to turn it on her. But as she slowed almost to a stop at the dead end, facing a tiny weathered frame post office, its lights burning, all he said was: "North, baby, north." No one appeared on the streets. At midday the dimness was that of a winter's dusk, lights behind a few windows. But, thank God, no police, no guns.

With the window open, she was cold again. Yet she did not want him to raise the window. She had to know the plane was still up there. . . .

She turned right, and as she peered ahead—was that a tunnel far down the road?—she heard the plane again.

From behind. It was flying low and it passed over the car, going in the same direction.

She could hear the engine spluttering.

"Tracy turned north," Chief Radford said, the binoculars at his eyes.

"I saw it," Andrew said.

"My car's closer to them now. Still following. Jesus, will someone please tell me what that kid has in mind?"

Andrew did not answer.

Beyond the village now, he was reluctant to reduce speed: The more fuel he fed, the less likelihood of a stall. Ahead, he saw a glitter: perpendicular, narrow, white-silver. The waterfall. He was above a shallow canyon, the road running between steep stone walls. Between the end of the canyon and the falls, a flat white surface of road. How could he estimate its length? He was passing over it.

A stone fence ran close to the edge of the road on the right and curved sharply left at the base of the waterfall to form a barrier between the road and the pool into which the water was tumbling. Almost a ninety-degree curve, so that the falls, framed in bluffs of stone, stood high and solid at the end of the space—how far from the end of the canyon? And how high were the canyon walls if he could go back and come in over it from the south?

He banked again, turning his head. Maybe he could get a better estimate going over it again—not that he had a choice really. Not the way that damned engine was crackling!

"Poor Tracy," Radford said, looking down. "My God, how much can the girl take?"

That did it: The sound of her name, over the sound of the popping, threatening engine, did it. "I'm going to make a full three-sixty," he heard himself say, applying pressure on the rudder pedal and back pressure on the wheel to gain altitude again, but carefully; he couldn't tip the wing too sharply, not too high an angle of attack because he was in a hurry now, not too steep. "We're going to come back and land on the road in front of the car before it reaches that curve at the waterfall."

Above the only flat space he'd seen, he was studying it more carefully now. He needed five hundred feet. Minimum. There might be that much between the north end of the canyon and the curve. If there wasn't, he'd crash into a low stone fence and into the drink. If the plane went into a skid when the wheels touched down, or if the engine gave out—

To hell with the *ifs*! He'd made up his mind.

It was the only way to force the car to stop.

Recklessly, aware of the risk, he gave it full throttle.

If Verini freaked out when he saw what was happening—

No more *ifs*, goddammit!

No telling what the bastard would do if he got boxed in . . .

But he *knew* what the bastard would do if state troopers appeared with guns at the Customs station.

He saw the two cars approaching the low-walled canyon, slowly, the silver Mustang possibly three hundred yards from the southern end, the blue police car about fifty yards behind it.

Could he make the turn and get back in time to bring the plane down before the Mustang emerged from the canyon?

Through her windshield Tracy had seen the plane make a

half-circle and return, higher and farther away, off to her left. She could no longer hear that stuttering sound in the engine. The plane appeared to be going away. Where was he going? What did he hope to be able to do? What the sweet hell could anyone do?

When she looked into her rearview mirror, she could not see the plane but she could see the dark cruiser again. It had also turned in the village and now it was closer, still following.

Peering ahead, she saw the road entering a ravine between two walls of stone cliffs, very close to the edges of the road on both sides. Through the unroofed tunnellike passage there appeared, farther on, to be a glitter of water falling, and now she remembered the region: There was a parking area at a curve, the road making a sharp bend left where it reached the waterfall and the pool into which the water plunged—

"Bitch," the animal said. "No heat, no cop car, you said! Lying slut—look in your mirror!"

She didn't need to. But she was damned if she was going to give up! So she reached to adjust the rearview mirror and glanced. "I don't see a thing."

"What's that plane doing up there?"

"What plane?"

"Don't start that again!"

She could no longer hear the drone of it.

He was kneeling on the seat, looking out the rear window. "Fucker ought t'be down by now, *down*!"

Then she heard the plane's engine again. Behind her. Or was she imagining it?

The car entered the sheer-walled chasm between two cliffs.

She could not take any more. *Would* not!

She stamped on the accelerator, hard.

The animal fell to the floor, cursing, and then he was crouched, looking up into her face, scowling, the gun pointing at her directly from an angle above.

"Slow down!"

Less snow on the pavement between the walls.

"Go ahead," she said. "Shoot me."

"Slow down, I said!"

It *was* the plane she'd heard. Approaching. Lower. From behind . . .

"Shoot me," she said, "and this car's going to climb the cliff, one side or the other—"

"Slow down, slow down!" His voice was screeching, frantic—

"Suicide pact. We'll die together, just you and me, love. On our goddam honeymoon!"

"I'm not gonna die!" A boy's voice, a scared child's, begging, pleading—music, sheer music!

"You pull that trigger, you slimy little *shit*, we're *both* dead!"

"What the hell is she up to?"

Chief Radford's voice. He no longer needed the binoculars.

Andrew—hearing the coughing engine, thinking of Tracy in the car behind him as he had made the turn over the village, too fast, too steep, too desperate to get back there—could now see the car speeding toward the other end of the canyon. He ignored the airspeed needle; he'd already given more throttle than he dared, or could afford.

It occurred to him that the bastard had panicked—or perhaps had guessed what Andrew intended to do—and was forcing Tracy to try to reach the flat stretch of road beyond the cliffs before the plane could get there.

He was descending over the top of the stone bluffs now, trying to judge the car's speed against the plane's speed and yet not to gain so much that he couldn't bring it down once he was clear.

Dead ahead, he could see the short stretch of white flatness, with the glimmering waterfall beyond. Was it far enough beyond? Had he miscalculated?

He had to put it into glide, clearing the end of the canyon walls, and bring it down—not too fast, not *this* fast!—and then cover the strip of road and come to a stop before the plane reached the curve at the base or the falls. Out of habit he tested the brake pedals. They, at least, were tight and functioning. But the coughing in the engine had become a crazy popping-cracking sound, no matter how he worked the mixture or throttle, and the prop was fluttering and stuttering, the plane shaking all over. If the power went, his control went with it. . . .

"Pray," he shouted.

And the chief shouted back: "What the hell do you think I'm doing, goddammit!"

*   *   *

As the car emerged from the low canyon, the plane was so close that overhead Tracy was deafened by its roar, felt the vibration through the car. Then she heard the sound change and remembered watching Andy land in Lowell: He'd idled the engine going into the end of the glide. . . .

And then she realized that the plane was coming down to land on the road ahead.

She applied the brakes, fast, too fast, and the car fishtailed on the light snow-cover, then began to spin crazily, making at least one full turn as she tried to fight the skid with the steering wheel, forcing herself not to apply the brakes again—

"You did this to me!"

It was all she heard, because then the car was sliding sideways, off the road to the right at an angle, and into the stone fence that seemed to take forever to reach the passenger side of the car—

Breaking the glide with back-pressure on the wheel over the end of the small canyon and holding the nose high after the flare-out, Andrew felt the nose-wheel touch the snow-covered highway—no slippage—and it was then that the engine gave its final convulsive cough and died.

After that he was almost helpless, but not quite. He tried to steer with the rudder, still holding the wheel well back, but he knew better than to ride the brakes at this speed, so he fixed his eyes on the nose, seeing the propeller begin to slow, hoping the nose would not tilt, and then, hoping he'd lost enough speed, he applied the brakes carefully, seeing the curve ahead, seeing the waterfall looming, and knowing now that he was going to crash, he saw Chief Radford in a quick glance—head down, arms locked over it—and he forced his body to go slack and loose in the shoulder harness, and then, not yet shutting his eyes, he made one last effort and put a final pressure onto the brakes, almost standing on the left pedal to ground-loop in that direction and away from the stonefence barrier, and then, with the sickening acceptance of the inevitable, he threw his hands in front of his face to ward off the blow from the instrument panel.

Tracy, out of the car and running, stopped when she saw the plane, on the ground, tilting, swerving left, like some metal animal desperately trying to escape its fate. The crunching crash, filling the cold thin air, stunned her into immobility.

It had taken her only a few seconds, after the car had smashed into the stone wall, to unbuckle her belt, open the door, glancing back, seeing the animal curled up, face down on the floor, unmoving. She hadn't been able to see the gun. He was probably lying on top of it. She didn't need it now, so she'd climbed out, hearing the plane's engine stop, and then she had watched the plane skim over the snow and twist into the stone.

Now, seeing the tail of the plane tilted up in the air, trying to picture Andy inside it, the splintering angry sound of the crash still echoing over the mountains and in her ears, she began to run toward it.

Would it burn?

Explode?

Her sprained ankle, which she'd forgotten, gave way, shooting pain up her leg, and she stumbled, falling, one knee cracking on the asphalt under the slippery snow, then she was on her feet again, limping, knowing that she could not possibly cover the distance before the plane burst into flame. . . .

While the fuselage was still shuddering, Andrew slipped out of the harness, saw Radford's startled, bewildered eyes, knew he was alive, reached to unbuckle his passenger's belt, grabbed the rifle, and leaped down from the plane, calling over his shoulder: "It may burn!"

He'd switched off the power just before the crash but . . .

He saw Tracy running toward him, some distance away, stumbling, running and stumbling again, but alive, alive, alive. . . .

Nick Verini wakened in a sea of pain. His neck felt broken, his nose felt smashed, pain everywhere, nothing but pain, his head bursting with it; there was blood on his face, everywhere. . . .

He managed to claw his way to a sitting position, beginning to remember.

When he moved his neck to look out the windshield, the pain shot down his back and out both shoulders, and his face was dripping, nose spurting blood. . . .

The slut was running, or trying to run, making tracks in the snow. There was an airplane standing on its nose with water coming down on the other side of it.

It came back to him then, so he searched the floor with his two hands. More blood on the floor—oh, God, don't let me die. He had the gun, the Beretta. How many slugs left? Poppa learned me. He was not going to make it—God have mercy on my soul—he was not going to make it, but he was going to take the cunt along.

Still running, or trying to run, Tracy saw Andy coming toward her. He was carrying something.

Behind him, the plane was not burning.

He was not in it anyway. . . .

He had stopped running.

He'd dropped to one knee and he was lifting the thing he carried—it was another gun, a rifle. He was doing something to it, and then he had it against his shoulder and he was yelling her name, he was shouting to her, for God's sake, to fall down. . . .

So she plunged forward, bending low fast and then diving flat out on her stomach. She tasted snow and felt it wet on her face.

Andrew had never fired a rifle except in a carnival shooting gallery, but when he'd seen the bastard getting out of the car behind Tracy's running figure, he'd dropped to his knee, trying to remember how to cock it, trying to work the bolt with one hand, savagery raging through him, the need to kill. So he used his bandaged aching arm to brace the rifle, gritted his teeth against the pain, and pulled back the bolt, shot it forward, and then he was ready to fire and Tracy was on the ground and he had the bastard in the sights, a good target— wide open, standing up and holding the automatic in outstretched hands, white skull and blood-red face behind, both hands steadying the gun to fire at Tracy on the ground. Before Andrew could pull the trigger, a shot rang out.

The radio in the plane was smashed. Climbing down from the cockpit Kyle Radford heard a single shot. It sounded like a rifle.

Before he could leap for cover, his mind struggling to rally from the shock of the landing, he saw Andy Horgan on one knee, rifle in hand. Perhaps thirty yards beyond him, Nick Verini—the slight figure, the naked head—was keeling over, the black automatic falling to the snow, and then there was a second explosion, definitely a rifle discharge, and the body jerked, once, as it fell.

He saw Andy Horgan standing up. Very slowly.

Then, beyond him, alongside the road, something brilliant caught his eye: Tracy Larkin's red hair against the snow. Her head was down and did not lift.

Radford was starting toward him when he saw that Andy Horgan had not moved. He was staring at something beyond the body on the ground and beyond the Mustang smashed up against the stone wall.

Another figure stood on the road. At the fender of car Number Four.

Not Malcolin Cornish, the young officer to whom it was assigned.

A huge man, legs spread, lowering a rifle.

If Kyle was not mistaken—and he knew he wasn't—it was Pierre Durand.

Tracy heard muffled footsteps in the snow. One pair went past where she lay; the other stopped. She did not, could not, lift her head.

She had heard the two shots but, head down, had seen nothing since she fell, too stiff with terror to move. But in that brief time she had realized what Andy had tried to do with the plane, and why. No, not tried; she knew what he had succeeded in doing. But, having seen Andy with a rifle in firing position as she dived, she was puzzled at the direction from which the sounds had come. Had the animal killed Andy?

Above her now she heard a voice speaking her name. Andy's voice . . . She rolled over onto her back and opened her eyes. His face shocked her—lined and tired and grim. She realized that she must have been mistaken about the direction of the shots. He *had* fired, after all.

When she scrambled to her feet and stepped to him, careful not to touch his dangling arm, he released the rifle he was holding and its barrel brushed against the back of her hand as it fell. It was not hot. It had not been fired.

"You all right?" he asked, holding her with one arm, looking past her shoulder.

She became conscious of the pleasant sound of water tumbling into a pool. "Alive," she said. "What about you?"

"Ditto." And then he added, "I think."

"What about *him*?"

"Kyle's taking care of that." As she started to turn her head, his grasp tightened. "Over this way, Tracy." And then he was leading her, in a firm grip, toward the low stone fence. Tempted to look back, she didn't.

But what she saw at the base of the falls caused her to miss a step, appalled. "Your plane," she said. "Your beautiful plane."

"Things," he said, and they stood staring at it.

Kyle Radford had had to decide whether to walk past what he thought was a dead body to Pierre Durand or to stop and examine the sprawled corpse. Since Durand had not moved from alongside the patrol car, he decided to look down on what was left of Nick Verini.

What he saw in no way, in no smallest way, resembled the bearded young man in the photographs he'd seen or even the bald, shouting madman who had come down the courthouse steps with Tracy Larkin. The head was on its side, but at an odd angle, as if it were no longer connected to the body. The eyes were closed. There was no nose, only a bloody mass of tissue where the nose had been. And the entire mask was a crazy pattern of red, blood still seeping from the gaping hole of a mouth.

Along the top of the bare white skull there was a distinct red line: the first bullet, the one that had stopped him. Behind the ear that he could see, there was a dark hole, gushing blood: the second shot, the one that had killed him.

Then he heard a sound, saw the lips move in blood, and he stooped down.

To hear a single word which at first he could not make out. And when he did, he could not believe. Nick Verini was asking for a priest.

But the body was still now.

Very, very still.

Nevertheless, he knelt on one knee and reached down to check the carotid artery. Nothing. His hand came away red.

He stood up and found himself facing Pierre Durand. The big man was staring down on the body, a strange look of peace on his square weathered face.

"I'm going to have to put you under arrest," the chief said, reaching for the rifle. Durand made no objection. Possibly didn't even know he'd surrendered it. The barrel was still warm. Had he even heard what Kyle had said? That same abstracted, almost otherworldly look of contentment, inner calm.

"Come with me, please," Kyle said, and the other man complied at once, meekly, nodding his head.

As the chief turned to accompany his prisoner to the patrol car, he heard a sound. He did not have to look back to see it.

The plane had burst into flame.

"Well," Tracy said, and her voice over the sound of the crackling flames was filled with wonder: "Well, that's everything, isn't it? Plane, cameras, everything."

"Things," Andy said, eyes on the fire.

"Your house. Now this. You don't have anything left, do you?"

"I've got a hell of a lot more than I had when I came," he said.

He heard a siren wailing in the distance and then the plane exploded.

In the rear seat of car Number Four, Shepperton Police, as it passed slowly through Franklin State Forest, Tracy was beginning to feel warm again.

And words were streaming through her mind: *Revenge is a kind of wild justice.* Who said that? She couldn't remember. Or even where she'd read it.

Andy was sitting close beside her, holding her hand under the blanket and staring out at the snow, which was falling again now, heavily. He, too, was silent.

A wind had come up, and even with the heater purring up front and over the crackling of the police radio, she could hear the wind against the windows and whistling though the tall pines.

Pierre Durand, stolidly upright, was next to Chief Radford, who was driving, peering through the windshield and listening to the woman's voice: " . . . reason Officer Cornish

347

didn't report the loss earlier is that he was too ashamed, he says—''

''Where'd this . . . uh, theft of a police vehicle occur? Did Officer Cornish say?''

''On Hancock Street, just off the green. In front of Colby's Restaurant. Officer Cornish is so upset he's resigning.''

''Ay-uh, well, tell him not to be hasty. Sometimes God takes good care of idiots. Over, out.''

Then, amazed, Tracy heard Pierre Durand's heavy voice: ''My truck was outa gas.''

''Most folks,'' Chief Radford said, ''don't steal police cars when they run out of gas, Mr. Durand.''

''I seen him on the TV—and he yelled out who he was.'' He had not turned his head, but he lifted his voice. ''He didn't look like the picture, though, Mr. Horgan.''

''Picture?'' Radford asked. ''What picture?''

''The one Mr. Horgan give me.'' And then he turned to face them. *''Merci,* Mr. Horgan. Did I ever thank you for that whiskey you give me?''

''I think you have, Mr. Durand,'' Andy said. And then added, ''In more ways than one.''

Tracy had it then: She knew where Andy had gone after discovering Dr. Nat's suicide, and she knew why.

''Mr. Durand,'' she heard herself say, ''have I thanked you for saving my life?''

''I didn't even see you back there, miss,'' Pierre Durand said. ''All I seen was *him.* He's the one who killed my little girl. And I ain't sorry. Even if I go to prison, I ain't sorry. He was *merde.''*

And then he was silent again, and remained so even when the chief said, ''You're not under arrest for murder, Mr. Durand. You're under arrest for theft of a police vehicle while under the influence of alcohol. You shot that *merde,* because he was about to kill Tracy Larkin. I'm a witness.''

Still, Pierre Durand said nothing.

Tracy discovered that she was holding Andy's hand with more strength than she thought she had left. ''I want to thank you, too,'' she whispered.

''Love and war,'' Andy said. And then he was facing her, his brown eyes puzzled. ''If you thought I was boozing it up, aren't you afraid?''

She didn't have to consider her answer, Charlie Larkin's

sad face flickering in her mind. "Not much," she said. "Because if you love a person and he has a curse on him, it's your curse too."

Now *his* hand was crushing *hers*.

So she went on in a whisper: "And if you *had* gone back to the bottle, I figured you'd stop. If you loved me. The way you stopped because you loved Cassie."

Out the window, through the snow, she saw the sign with the arrow below the words: ECHO LAKE.

"And it *is* a war, isn't it?" she asked, anger rising in her again. "Or should be. No matter what happened today, *they're* still winning, aren't they?"

"Maybe," he said. "Probably."

About the Author

Joseph Hayes attended Indiana University, which later made him an Honorary Doctor of Humane Letters. He studied for the Catholic priesthood in a Benedictine abbey until he climbed over the wall to explore the world. After editing plays for Samuel French he became a free-lance writer. Four of his novels have been major book-club selections, including *The Desperate Hours*, *Bon Voyage*, *The Third Day*, and *The Long Dark Night*. He has written numerous plays and screenplays, produced and directed on Broadway, and with his wife, Marrijane, he is the co-author of eighteen published plays and many short stories.